BLUE MIST
on the
DANUBE

BLUE MIST
on the
DANUBE

DORIS ELAINE FELL

Fleming H. Revell
A Division of Baker Book House
Grand Rapids, Michigan 49516

Published by Fleming H. Revell
a division of Baker Book House Company
P.O. Box 6287, Grand Rapids, MI 49516-6287

Printed in the United States of America

Library of Congress Cataloging-in-Publication Data

Fell, Doris Elaine.
    Blue mist on the Danube / Doris Elaine Fell.
       p.   cm.
    ISBN 0-8007-5677-0 (paper)
    1. Title.
PS3556.E4716B58   1999
813'.54—dc21   99-22961

For current information about all releases from Baker Book House, visit our web site:
http://www.bakerbooks.com

To

Ryan Matthew, Jesse Michael, and Hannah Marie Judd
from the Great-Aunt who adores you

And to

Grace, my eyes and ears in magical Vienna
Catherine, for the sights and sounds of Everdale
Mary Louise, for her musical heart and musical friends
Wendy, for journeying with me through a computer
blackout

And especially to

Linda, for believing in the *Blue Mist on the Danube*

Prologue

Springtime

Kerina Rudzinski loved Vienna. Vienna was a tangled maze of old and new, of the ancient and contemporary, like a timeworn clock ticking away the centuries. Thrusting her back. Thrusting her forward. She had allowed the city to wrap itself around her. This was her refuge, a place of beauty and suspense, a many-sided city as complex as Kerina herself. Here she could lose herself in the music she loved. Here she was acclaimed as one of the world's most accomplished violinists. It was like a homecoming each time a concert brought her back; no audience received her more warmly than in Vienna.

Wednesday!

The third Wednesday in April, a balmy spring morning.

Kerina awakened with the exhilaration of last evening's applause still filling her mind, her heart. It had been a spontaneous clapping of hands that began in the front row and spread within seconds through the massive music hall, up to the high balcony. The faces of those in the audience were obliterated by the stage lights, yet she remembered the whispering rustle of her blue silk chiffon gown as she stepped forward and blew them a kiss. The Viennese were on their feet at once, cheering her, begging her to play one more waltz. And she had lifted her bow and pleased them.

She stretched languorously now, feeling the smooth silk sheets against her bare skin, as smooth and supple as her bow gliding over the strings of her Stradivarius. As Kerina turned toward the open window, strands of her burnished hair fell softly across the pillows. She felt caught in a moment of timelessness. Slowly, deftly her fingers crept over the sheet to her traveling calendar. She clasped it, her eyes focusing on the large black numbers: 15. Her pounding heart went wild.

April.

April 15.

Another April careened into her thoughts, coloring her memory—a chilly, rainy day, gray-washed with mist that had shattered her life forever. Faces coming into sharp focus as though it were yesterday. Aloud, she quoted,

> April is the cruellest month, breeding
> Lilacs out of the dead land, mixing
> Memory and desire, stirring
> Dull roots with spring rain.

She could not remember any more of the poem—only those haunting words and the melancholy in Bill VanBurien's voice as he whispered them to her. *The Waste Land* had been one of Bill's favorite poems, and T. S. Eliot, Tennyson, and Wordsworth the poets he quoted most frequently.

T. S. Eliot's words. Hers now. *April . . . the cruellest month.* The applause, the joy of last night faded into troubled thoughts, the past that she so carefully guarded filtering into her memories. The wasteland of her lost years plucked like lilacs out of the dead ground, out of the depths of her pain.

April. Twenty-six Aprils breeding dead memories as fragile as lilacs. She—that young concert violinist from Prague. And he—her first love. Lanky and blond and charming her with his promises. On their last good-bye so long ago, he had promised to come back, to find some way to always be with her.

"Oh, Bill, even now after all these years, I cannot despise you for your betrayal; I cannot blame you for the past," she murmured.

Thrusting back the silk sheets, Kerina sat up tremulously and slipped her feet over the edge of the bed. Her thick, dark lashes were still sticky with sleep, but she allowed her gaze to follow the path of the coral sun rays filtering into her suite, highlighting the things she treasured most. Her priceless violin rested in its open case on her dresser. Diamond earrings sparkled on the bedside table beside her. Last evening's soft blue gown lay draped over the chair back, the chiffon neck scarf crumpled on the floor. Again she recalled the swishing, crinkling sound of the flared skirt sweeping across the stage. She tried to recover the sound of the music and the thrill of last night's ovation but heard only the pounding of her own heart. Yesterday was gone. Last evening gone. A season of yesterdays plucked from dead ground.

As she fled barefooted to the luxurious marbled bathroom, a strap of her negligee slipped off her shoulder. It didn't matter. She stepped out of the gown and into the scalding hot shower, and cried for the unfurrowed ground, the dead roots of yesterday.

Swirling the lilac-scented soap over her naked body, she felt a lump in her breast, pressure. She felt again. No, nothing. Her fingers slipped quickly from it. *I'm upset this morning,* she thought. *Imagining things.* As she flicked the brass faucet off, the waterfall slowed to a trickle and then fell like the last drops of a spring rain. Blindly she reached for the Turkish bath towel and buried her swollen face in it.

Enough, she told herself, toweling down. *No need to mix memory and desire. No need to dwell on lost dreams, on the dull, dead roots of long ago. I am alive. I have my music. No one, nothing—not even this cruellest of months—can take my music from me.*

An hour later Kerina picked up her journal and left her hotel suite dressed in a trim, dusty teal sheath with cutaway sleeves, a Shetland sweater around her shoulders, her red-rimmed eyes shaded with dark glasses. She slipped out through the garden cafe past the round intimate tables shielded with red umbrellas.

"*Guten Morgen,* Fräulein Rudzinski," the young waiter said.

"*Guten Morgen,* Jorg."

He ran ahead of her to open the gate. The crisp air cooled her flushed cheeks as she walked beneath the ivy-covered arch and out into the clear spring morning, her whole life mirrorlike with echoes of the past. She felt connected, yet disconnected, a part of her surroundings and yet distant from them.

"Lovely morning," Jorg called after her and, perplexed when she didn't respond, added, "*Auf Wiedersehen,* Fräulein."

Yes, it was lovely, the kind of day when she wanted to touch everything, to reassure herself that she could still feel and enjoy the beauty of nature—the briskness of the air on her skin, the softness of a rose in bloom, the blueness of the sky above. At this moment, she was alive and free, in command of her own destiny. The solitary, pre-breakfast hours were her own. She was accountable to no one. Not to her manager, her publicity agent, her public. She was free to wander through the streets of Vienna and bask in the memories of strolling alone in other cities—those memorable times of brushing past petals in a storm in Paris, picking flowers in the rain in London, or catching the crystal flakes of winter's first-fallen snow in Budapest. Or simply hurrying over the leaf-strewn sidewalks of New York City, her cheeks chafed by the stinging autumn morning.

After ambling down the Karntner Strasse, she circumvented the Ringstrasse once more and made her way toward the park. But memories tripped her up at every corner. *Bill. Music. Bill.* She had not allowed herself to think of William C. VanBurien for months. Now his presence gripped her, like a cord of three strands wrapping itself around her heart and crushing her wounded spirit.

Her steps slowed as she entered Stadtpark through the ornate Jugendstil Portals and paused as she always did beneath the gilded statue of Johann Strauss playing his violin. Everything seemed to have the face of Bill VanBurien this morning. Even the sculpted features of the King of Waltz looked more like Bill's dimpled grin.

Kerina quickened her pace as she crossed the iron bridge to her favorite stone bench in the municipal park. She sank down, savoring the view of the city she loved more than any other in the world. Then she opened her journal, took out the faded snapshot from the zippered fold, and looked down at the smiling face that had once been so dear to her. Bill. His name as American as apple pie and ice cream or a home run at a baseball game. As American as a foot-long hot dog at Disneyland or a donkey ride down into the Grand Canyon. Bill had introduced her to all of these. Kerina had loved them, loved them because she was with Bill, and she thought their love would go on forever.

Gently, she ran her fingers over his features, awakening the pain. Her first love with those large, smoky-blue eyes and hair as fair as the wheat fields of Kansas. One year out of her life. A thousand promises. A lifetime of memories. She thought of Bill backstage in the concert hall in Chicago, picking up her Stradivarius and running the bow across the strings. *He was a tease and at times, deceptive, but he loved music, and no one who loved music could be entirely Machiavellian.*

She tucked the photo back into the zippered pocket, took up her pen, and wrote: "April 15. Today I remembered Bill VanBurien. Remembered what might have been."

Ahead, she saw a seagull swoop low over the distant river, watched its wings spread, felt the strength of the bird in flight. Always when the schedule was tight and the demands of her performances pressed in, she would find comfort in walking along the Danube or retreat to one of the park benches near the lake as she was doing this morning, sometimes groping in her heart for something hidden even from memory.

At the most unexpected moments, the elusive dream haunted her again. And then half awake, half asleep—while she was sitting here, or playing her violin, or resting—the picture of a country house on a hill with the quaint gazebo behind it came vividly to mind. Sometimes the house was drenched in budding spring flowers—sometimes with autumn leaves drifting across the walkway. White pillars framed the porch. Red-leafed dogwood and sumac grew in the woods behind it. Wisteria tumbled over the picket fence, and a pink rosebush grew unchecked by the corner of the house. Sometimes the fragrance of sweet gum trees and honeysuckle bushes replaced the scent of roses. And always—breaking the stillness—the sound of a baby crying.

Kerina could not recall being there. She knew that she had never gone inside the house, and yet it was part of her, that lost something she wanted to find. There was no house so vivid in her memory, none that tantalized her as this simple country home on the hill. Empty. Neglected. Sometimes she remembered the backyard gazebo with its chipped, white paint on the railing and twisted vines growing along the steps. The image sat at the edge of her mind, some truth waiting to be grasped. Each time it came—as it did now—she reached out to unlatch the gate. Rusty hinges creaked as she pushed it back. But she could not enter, could not take the winding, cobbled path up to the house. A tangle of weeds and bracken and gnarled roots scratched at her legs. She pulled back, left with only the facade of the house looming in the distance. The wind blew the frayed curtains in the windows and banged the shutters against the flaking paint.

Above the banging came the call of the whippoorwill and the cry of the baby. As Kerina sat alone in Stadtpark in this undefined state of half dream, half wakefulness, she saw again the mother and child on the wide, wraparound porch. Madonna and child? No, an ordinary mother cradling her infant, soothing its cries. She longed to be the mother, ached to hold the child.

She stirred, then stumbled from the park bench and fled down to the water's edge, slipping and sliding on the pebbles along the embankment. In her mind's eye it was the porch steps that crumbled beneath her; but she was left staring down at the Danube—a deep chasm separating her from the house and the child as the water's blue mist veiled her elusive past.

One

The clippety-clop of a horse-drawn fiacre snatched the picture from Kerina's memory and hurled her back into the heart of the city. She turned, half expecting to find the house, yet knowing it was not here in Vienna. She felt troubled without reason, the place as real as if she had just climbed the hill to its crumbling porch, to someone waiting there for her.

Without measuring her steps or noticing the street signs, she circled back and was even now within walking distance of the Sacher Cafe. As she reached the cafe, she touched her bejeweled watch with her tapered finger. *Oh, Jillian. I almost forgot our appointment.*

Entering the cafe, Kerina gazed around the intimate cozy room at the exquisite oil paintings that graced the red velvet walls. The tall, well-groomed maitre d' hurried forward to greet her.

"Miss Rudzinski, your usual table?"

"A table for two, Karl. Jillian is joining me this morning."

"Fräulein Ingram?" He flushed, pleasure visible in his dark eyes. "This way, Fräulein."

He led Kerina to a corner table beneath a chandelier and handed her a menu. She left it closed and smiled up at him. "Tell my waiter that I'll just have coffee for now."

He flushed again as their eyes met. He was around thirty, much too young for her, but he came faithfully to her concerts. Yesterday, when her publicist was with her, his eyes spoke volumes. Karl was just the right age for Jillian, but Jillian had a mind of her own and no time at all for the young maitre d', no matter how handsome or eligible he was.

Bending down, Karl asked, "The usual, Miss Rudzinski?"

"A *pharisaer* this time. We'll order when Jillian gets here." When her drink arrived, she sipped and found herself drawn to the whispered comments of the young woman at the next table. "Elizabeth, is that Kerina Rudzinski, the concert violinist?"

Her companion gave a quick appraisal, squinting at Kerina from beneath a wide-brimmed lavender hat. She locked her fleshy hands together. "Oh, Raquel, I heard her play at the Musikverein last evening. A marvelous night of Bach and Beethoven."

Raquel's thick glasses sat perched on the tip of her narrow nose. She gave the frames a decided shove. "She is lovely."

Elizabeth's jowls slackened. "My husband and I saw her at the Opera Ball in February, looking elegant as usual. She had such a handsome escort, a distinguished gentleman. Petzold. Franck Petzold. Something like that."

She flashed an appreciative smile toward Kerina, a smile that Kerina returned with equal grace. Abruptly Kerina turned away as a blinding light shot across her right eye, the threat of another tension headache. She sat erect, her palms cupping the demitasse as the waiter refilled her coffee.

Delighted again by the public that adored her, she allowed the steaming liquid to melt the lump in her throat. She blocked out their voices now, embarrassed that she had heard them at all, but she found herself reflecting on what they had said. Franck Petzold was a handsome escort, her constant companion for years. He was always there protecting her, directing her career, waiting patiently for her to return his overtures of love.

But here in the Sacher Cafe, her thoughts went back to Bill VanBurien. *Where is he now?* She prayed that she would one day see Bill again. Her prayer ping-ponged to the ceiling and dropped back to the floor, her words little more than an uncertain plea to a distant God. A God that she wanted to know, but could never quite find—the forgotten link with her childhood faith that these days seemed lost forever.

As she sat fighting her headache—that miserable precursor to every concert—the mysterious dream came back. Vapors of memory rose like fleecy clouds. Through the mist she saw the country house on the hill taking shape in her mind again. Behind the ancient oaks lay the faint outline of the gazebo, the pink buds of the dogwood drifting over its blue conical roof—and out of reach, the shadow of a man walking into the woods, walking with his back to her, his thick, blond hair tousled in the breeze.

She blinked and looked up with relief to see Jillian Ingram entering the cafe and Karl Altridge rushing to greet her. As Kerina caught Jillian's eye, the pink petals of the dogwood drifted away. The image of the gazebo and the man faded. But those images would come back to haunt her again until she found that house and made peace with her dreams.

Kerina brushed back loose strands of hair from her forehead, long shimmering russet locks like the brilliant flecks of a sunset—her crowning glory held back with a black velvet bow. She had untold wealth and the acclaim of music lovers around the world, and yet, in this instant, she wished she could be young again, not forty-five but vibrant like Jillian Ingram with all of life's failures erased from the record. Jillian had the pizzazz and sparkle of a fashion model, an enviable way of stepping lightly across the room, her long, tawny hair bouncing against her narrow shoulders. She looked chic and sophisticated in her new charcoal-gray suit, those black-strapped pumps making her three inches taller. The form-fitting jacket was classic and feminine, and the short skirt only served to emphasize those elegant legs as she came sashaying toward Kerina.

"Thank you, Karl," she said, brushing the maitre d' off.

She dropped her attaché case on the table and slid into the seat, her lively eyes a perceptive delft blue as she met Kerina's gaze. "The reviews were all good. Except one."

"The one who called me too solemn when I played? I no longer worry about my critics, Jillian. They're unpredictable as a sudden storm. They come. They go."

"But even that critic applauds your grace and beauty. So let's celebrate the good reviews with a Sachertorte?" She beckoned to the waiter hovering nearby and gave the order.

The matchmaker song danced in Kerina's head. "Jillian, why are you so demeaning with the maitre d'?"

"Karl Altridge? I don't like the way he gushes over me."

"You should be flattered. He likes you. I find him charming." She hummed, *Matchmaker, matchmaker, make me a match.*

"He's yours then." Amused, Jill hummed back. *Find me a find. Catch me a catch.* "But please, not Karl. I'm not ready to settle down, not after getting burned in Rome by Santos Garibaldi. And before him, Brian in Ireland. I'm such an easy target for a good-looking face, Kerina. Or maybe I'm just unlucky in love."

As I was, Kerina thought. "The right person will come along someday. Don't let Santos or Brian keep you from happiness."

"Once singed, caution prevails." Jillian switched her scowl to a smile. "We'd better talk business. There are several things on the docket. Franck Petzold for one."

"And what does Franck want?" Kerina asked softly.

"He wants you to have dinner with him after the concert and then take in a private showing at the art museum."

"Not tonight. Just tell him we'll have coffee and one of our evening chats in my hotel suite. He'll like that."

"Will you?"

"We're good friends, Jillian. Nothing more."

"That's good news. I don't trust Franck's romantic maneuvers any more than I trusted Santos."

Kerina gave a chuckle. "What else do you have for me?"

Jillian ticked them off with a snap of her fingers: "A hair appointment at the hotel salon today at three, your Tuesday morning fitting with your dress designer; and don't forget your luncheon with Nicole McClaren. I set that one up for next Thursday."

"I did forget."

"Nicole won't. I've marked it on your calendar. And don't worry, I'll remind you." She grinned. "Nicole loves being with the right person at the right time; she will turn your luncheon into a newsworthy event on the social page."

"She doesn't need me for that."

Jillian considered. "I think it's more this time. The McClarens are loaning another collection to the Academy of Fine Arts. Nicole wants you to attend the exhibit with her."

"Not this time." Franck would go, but she was staying as far away as she could from another art exhibit.

"Should I tell Mrs. McClaren or will you?"

"She's persistent. She'll call me."

"Kerina, you're close to Nicole. You should warn her against risking their collection like that. It's like putting a billion-dollar investment into the hands of the general public. You'd think they'd be more cautious after that last robbery." She inspected a chipped fingernail. "That Rubens painting alone would go for millions at a Sotheby auction."

"The McClarens are heavily insured, Jillian."

"What good is insurance if you lose a treasure like that?"

"My dear, I didn't know you knew so much about art."

"Perhaps your interest has rubbed off on me."

"I think not. Franck is right. You know more about the value of paintings than you let on. Even Nicole insists she read your name in a magazine from the Art Theft Registry."

Jillian took on a lighter tone. "Oh, there can't be two Jillian Ingrams on the continent. I trust that the one Nicole read about did not steal art?"

"Quite to the contrary. Nicole said she wrote knowledgeably about the Italian Renaissance paintings stolen in recent years."

Jill's answer came slowly as a faint color rose in her cheeks. "You know I lived in Italy and studied in Rome. Even took courses on the Renaissance, but I don't call myself an authority. Why does Franck insist on linking me with the art world?"

"He said it was your lifestyle. Your father with the American consulate—living abroad, going to the best schools in Europe. He feels you were exposed to art and music."

"And so I was—but I was more interested in languages and skiing. The more languages I knew, the more friends I made at the ski resorts, and the more invitations I had to party around."

She disliked Jillian's flippant response and frowned. Outside of the intimate music world that they shared, what did she really know about Jillian Ingram? "Parties," she repeated. "Is that why you came to work for me? So you could travel free and attend the best social events in Europe?"

A blush of innocence touched Jillian's cheeks, giving her the sweetness of the girl next door appearance. She was beguiling and yet like two people in one—a resourceful, keen-witted publicity agent one minute—a shy, warm-hearted friend the next. And now this third front—this pained expression at Kerina's accusations. To cover her own embarrassment Kerina asked, "Is there anything else on that list of yours for me to consider?"

The flush in Jillian's cheeks receded. She tapped her briefcase. "Your fall tour in America."

Kerina moved her arm as the waiter returned. Her torte glistened with apricot jam and a thick, smooth chocolate coating as he set it in front of her. As he walked away, Kerina lifted her fork and said, "That schedule was finalized months ago."

"But I'm getting more requests and you have some dates available. Chicago has written three times. Faxed. Called."

"No, Jillian, not Chicago."

"Why not? That's where you made your American debut."

"Then there is no need to go back."

The crushing headache sharpened at her temples. Chicago was Bill's stomping grounds, the place where he wanted his name in gold on executive row. But he was an avid concertgoer. She jabbed at the torte and dangled another gooey bite on the tip of her fork. *What if he comes to my concert with another woman on his arm?*

"What is it with you and Chicago, Kerina?"

"I hate their blizzards."

"You survived the Prague winters."

"But not the bitter cold in Chicago." *Nor the loneliness.*

The searing pain behind her eyes intensified. Even as she stared across at Jillian, the white house on the hill came back with the autumn leaves falling this time, the nip of winter on its heels. She frowned, uncertain. *No, the house does not belong to Chicago. But memories of Bill do.*

Jillian flipped open her briefcase and ran her finger down a memo. "You play two concerts in Detroit and two in New York. Then five days free. Can't we squeeze Chicago in?"

"Darling Jillian, not this time." *Not ever,* she thought.

"I hate it when you call me that, Kerina."

"But you are a darling sometimes. So, please, wire Chicago with a definite no. I am taking those extra days for myself."

"Are we going on holiday?"

"I am going alone—a side trip a long way from Chicago."

"It sounds special."

Kerina touched her fingers to her lips. "It is."

Everdale, the town that Bill had called a dot on the map. She had never planned to go back. Now she longed to go there once more. Bill's hometown, his roots. Perhaps by

21

some miracle he would be there on vacation, strolling through the center of town, and they would meet again.

Jillian watched her intently. "Anyone I know?"

"He was long before your time."

"I'm not to ask questions? Don't you even have a picture?"

"One. A snapshot."

"Am I to see it?"

"Someday, perhaps."

Jillian pursed her lips. "What was he like?"

"I don't remember."

Yet as Kerina spooned her empty cup, she still pictured Bill as attractive, well-styled in his casual way, as rangy and straight-backed as the young waiter crossing the room to their table. With a quick smile, the waiter refilled her coffee cup and left her with her thoughts of Bill.

Jillian demanded her attention, saying, "Kerina, I'd show you a picture of Santos if I hadn't thrown them all away. Oh, well, you'll need a break by the time we reach America. No matter how cold it gets there, nothing can match that three-week tour in Moscow. The hotel and concert halls were stone cold."

"But the Muscovites received me warmly."

Kerina's skin prickled with the glad remembrance of the encores in the Tchaikovsky Concert Hall and the Palace of Congresses. She still slept with the music of Tchaikovsky running through her dreams. Yet she dreaded the trips to Moscow, convinced that communism still lingered in the hearts of many politicians.

"I'm always uneasy on those trips to Russia," she said. "They remind me of my childhood under communism."

"So why do you go?"

"To please Franck. He was born there, you know. Most of his art collection is in his home on the Black Sea." Across the table she met Jillian's gaze and flashed a disarming smile. "You worry too much about me, Jillian."

"That's my job, isn't it?"

"You just worry about having everything ready for my concerts at the State Opera House in four weeks."

Jillian's eyes darkened and gleamed like sapphires. "That's Franck's baby. I won't cross him. But he really came through arranging your solo appearance with an all-male orchestra. No ballet. No opera! Not even Wagner's *The Flying Dutchman*. How will the Viennese opera lovers like that?"

"They welcomed a female guest harpist. Why not a guest violinist?" She ran her fingers over the rim of her water goblet. "We'll know in four weeks. Whatever happens, try to get along with Franck for my sake. It took him two years to arrange this engagement."

"And all of Vienna will turn out to hear your music. It will be my first time there." A smile tweaked. "I did buy tickets for *The Cavalier Rose* once, but I went to a polo match instead."

"With a handsome escort, I trust?"

"Would you believe—with Santos."

Kerina's laugh rippled. "And you fuss at me about Franck."

As the women at the next table glanced their way, Kerina's words softened to a whisper. "I will give the audience at the Opera House a star performance, one they will never forget. I won't cancel out—and no one cancels out on Kerina Rudzinski."

Jillian clicked her tongue. "I'm sorry, Kerina. I'm going to be a first. I hate to remind you, but in six more months, I'm out of here. The publicity gig is over."

"You still plan to leave? I thought we got on well."

"We do. I even tolerate your moods when you're practicing." She took the last swallow of her torte and licked her lips. "But remember, Kerina, that's what I told you when I hired on. One year as your agent and that was it. So . . . with Chicago on your black list, what about this request from the Czech Republic?"

23

Kerina kept despair from her voice. "I'll go there for a visit after the tour in America."

"Won't you get homesick before that?"

"Vienna is home now. My father says I am saving Prague for my grand finale, my final performance. But Franck thinks I'll never retire."

"If you quit, he couldn't afford all those trips to Moscow."

"Careful," Kerina warned. "Franck has been my friend for years. Far longer than you and I have known each other."

"But I don't trust his friends in Moscow, especially that man we met on the steps of the Moscow Conservatory of Music."

A regrettable encounter, Kerina thought, her skin prickling again. "Jokhar Gukganov? He is an art collector like Franck."

"He's Russian Mafia, if you ask me," Jillian muttered.

Kerina poked mindlessly at her Sachertorte, her fork tines leaving streaks of chocolate on the plate as she thought of the dark-haired Russian with the sallow face. "I don't choose Franck's friends, Jillian, and I rarely go outside of Moscow to meet any of them. I'm too anxious to get back to Vienna."

"So why do you allow him to schedule so many trips there?"

"It keeps him happy. If it weren't for the Petzolds, my family would have starved to death in Prague. If it weren't for Franck, I would never be a violinist. We're old friends."

"Childhood sweethearts? He should have given up long ago."

Not childhood sweethearts, she wanted to say. *But part of the communist takeover of my country—an acquaintance that never quite went away.* "Jillian, you are such a romantic. Franck and I, we are nothing but friends and business partners."

Jillian hummed the matchmaker song again. "That may be how you see it, but not Petzold. He'd take you to the altar in a second, given the chance."

"I won't give him the chance."

24

"Nor any suitor. You worry about finding me a beau, what about you? You never leave time for love yourself."

"There is always time for love, Jillian."

Kerina's words flowed like tiny ripples across the table that separated them. "I must get back to my room and rest before this evening's concert." Kerina gave an imperceptible nod to the women at the next table. "Would you arrange for Elizabeth and Raquel to have tickets for my opening night at the Opera House?"

"You know them?"

"No, but they know me."

"Fans? I wish more people knew about your generosity."

"What I do in private is my own business."

Jillian shoved her cup aside. "What's wrong with your public knowing that you give generously to charities and children's hospitals in Prague and the Balkans? And even this—guest tickets for total strangers. Don't you see, Kerina? It would make the violinist that the world so admires more approachable, more ordinary in the eyes of the media."

Kerina touched Jillian's hand in a rare gesture of friendship. "But I am not ordinary, Jillian. And what I do with my money and my heart are private matters." *And no matter what I give away, nothing will ever erase that April so long ago.* She picked up her purse.

"Wait. There's this request from Chandler Reynolds—a music critic who wants to interview you at the Opera House."

Kerina's frown pinched her skin. "Chandler Reynolds? I don't recognize the name. Does he work for the *Standard* or *European?*"

"He works for the American army. Part of the last of the I-For forces still in Bosnia."

"A soldier! You know I'm selective with my interviews. I have a reputation to live up to. Why have you come to me with this one when you know time is precious to me?"

"Oh, Kerina, don't be a snob. It's not like you." Her well-shaped lips curled into a grin. "The truth is I did throw his request into the reject pile, but I kept taking it out. I tell you I have a soft spot for a good-looking man in a uniform."

"The maitre d' wears a uniform," Kerina reminded her.

"A tuxedo," Jillian corrected.

"Did Santos wear a uniform?"

"His standard was a white polo shirt and shorts with a tennis racket in his hand."

Kerina stared down at the stains the torte had left on her platter. "Jillian, you never called me a snob before."

"I never thought about it before. But why don't you do this one for me?" The glint in Jillian's eyes brightened. "I've been checking the lieutenant out. He's in his twenties and single. I had the fax machine churning out memos on him right and left."

Jillian yanked a folder from her briefcase and slapped it on the table, jarring the water goblet and adding rivulets of ice water to the chocolate stains. "See for yourself. He actually has quite an impressive resumé. Violin. Piano. Trombone."

"He plays them all?"

"Plays at them probably." She flipped the pages. "Private lessons at Juilliard. Maybe he washed out like I did at finishing school in Switzerland and saved face by joining the army."

Kerina gripped her fork again, twisting it idly. *Reynolds.* His name played games with her. A musician named Reynolds? A violinist? A fan? No, something different. But it stayed elusive like another dream. "Jillian, I suppose you have a picture of him in that briefcase of yours?"

"Couldn't get one, but I tracked down this old copy of *Time.*" She shoved the magazine across the table, spinning it around so the young man's picture faced Kerina.

What Kerina saw looked like the face of Bill VanBurien. She felt color drain from her cheeks; the fork tumbled from her hand. She reached for her goblet, but her hand was unsteady. What was wrong with this miserable day? Everything reminded her of Bill.

"Good-looking, don't you think? If you don't want the interview, I do . . . Kerina, are you all right?"

Kerina traced the outline of the soldier's face, but in her mind she was tracing her mental image of Bill. The young man's jaw was thrust forward by the chin strap. The camouflage helmet covered his forehead, hooding the pensive eyes that looked so much like Bill's. Wide eyes. Long lashes. Bill had long lashes and that same straight, narrow nose and Grecian cheekbones. They looked like Bill's striking features, except for the finely chiseled mouth, giving the young man a sensitivity in that otherwise manly, military face. It was like seeing Bill's handsome face on the cover of *Time*, bridging the years from Montgomery Airport to now, unleashing the memories and the pain.

"Kerina, are you ill?"

"It's just the sweet torte on an empty stomach."

Her headache was excruciating. She wrapped her hand around the goblet and swallowed thirstily. Her gaze fixed on her white-knuckled hands, her bright, manicured nails.

In that instant she remembered Everdale—saw again her knuckled grip on the side rails of her hospital bed so many years ago, felt her polished nails digging into her palms.

There were two beds in the small hospital room, the one by the door empty; her own by the window looked out toward a row of weeping willows. A clean, dust-free room with the floors polished to a high gloss; a yellow curtain hanging between the beds, blocking her view of the corridor. It was a plain room with the walls crushing in on her and the windows too high to see much more than the trees. Her fingers slipped from the rail, and she picked at the coarse nap of the dull yellow spread. Clutching, releasing. Clutching, releasing.

The night nurse had tiptoed across her room. "Kerry, we have to remove your polish," she said as she lifted Kerina's hand and ran the cotton wads over the nails, washing away the scarlet red and leaving Kerina's fingers colorless.

Two

Even here in the Sacher Cafe in Vienna, Kerina remembered the pungent fragrance of the polish remover. Nausea swept over her. She struggled to recall the nurse's name. She had known it back then, but like much of her past, the name had slipped away.

Shaken, she asked, "William *VanBurien?*"

"No. His name is Chandler Reynolds. The lieutenant will be in Vienna next month, by the fourteenth of May."

"The first day of my performance at the Staatsoper?"

"Yes. What should I tell Lieutenant Reynolds, Kerina?"

She took a drink, then dabbed at her lips. "No interview."

"Do I wire the soldier and tell him to stay in Bosnia?"

"No, he needs a break from the rubble of war-torn cities."

"It's not like they're still at a full-blown war. Reynolds is there protecting the peace. He may be with the reserves. He didn't say, but he's coming to Vienna on a medical leave."

"A medical leave? Was he injured?"

"My guess would be he just tripped over his big boot."

"Don't be flippant, Jillian. An accident there could be serious. What about the land mines hidden there waiting for a soldier to step on them? The lieutenant will be safer coming to Vienna—but let him interview someone else."

In the silence that followed, memories of Bill paved the way for the American soldier. Bill had wanted success and found it in the lucrative business world. Yet in the back of his mind he had yearned for a place in the media as a music critic. Instead he had joined the navy. After that, it had been college. The music dream faded. No one gave him the opportunity to pick it up again.

Kerina glanced at the soldier's face one more time, her thoughts on Bill VanBurien. She ran her finger over the strap on his helmet, as though by touching it, she could relieve the pressure. The soldier still dreamed of a music world. For Bill's sake then, Kerina recanted.

I will give the lieutenant an interview, she decided. *What he does with the article is up to him. I won't block his chance to find his way in a music career.* Her pounding headache was unrelenting as she shoved the magazine back into Jillian's hand. "You win. Tell your lieutenant I will see him for ten minutes after the concert."

"*My* lieutenant? Don't I wish; but couldn't you be a little more generous with your time?"

"Ten minutes is ample for any unknown music critic."

Jillian snapped her attaché case closed and glanced at her watch. "Kerina, something's upsetting you. What's wrong?"

Kerina gripped the edge of the table to steady herself against the onslaught of so many yesterdays. "It's one of my miserable headaches. It will be gone once I reach the stage this evening." She smiled to reassure Jillian. "But we need to write that letter to Sarajevo today. I want to visit that hospital and see how the new children's wing is progressing."

"The one they're naming for you?"

"Yes. That was so kind of them."

"Not half as generous as your half million."

Kerina shied away from the credit. "I'm just investing in the lives of children who have been scarred by war and land mines." She shook off her sudden depression. "They've promised to pattern the children's wing after the one in Prague."

"They should have named that one for you too."

"In a way they did, Jillian. I asked them to name it the Kerry Kovac Center because of a little child I knew once."

"Maybe the soldier from Bosnia can put in a good word for us and get us quick passage there before the next winter sets in." Her eyes twinkled. "You could do a concert for the soldiers—especially if I like the lieutenant. Luciano Pavarotti has been to Mostar with his music. If you'd like, I'll contact him."

"No, let me call Luciano and talk to him." Kerina stood and dropped some money on the table. "Take care of the bill for me—and the tickets for those two women for my performance at the Staatsoper. . . . No, don't get up. I will find my own way."

Jillian's words followed Kerina as she fled between the tables. "Perhaps you have done that for far too long already."

Kerina heard a baby crying as she stepped from the cafe into the late morning sunshine. As a woman pushed a perambulator down the street, Kerina donned her dark glasses and hurried in the opposite direction, blindly crossing against the lights and stepping off the curb unmindful of traffic.

April 15. The cruellest of months. The cruellest of days. With deep pain, she allowed her thoughts to slip beyond Bill VanBurien to encircle the memory of Bill's child. Her child. He had for years been a child without a face, a nameless little boy lost in the sea of faces she passed each day. A grown young man now with unfamiliar features, a stranger she would not recognize. At twenty-six, did he look like Bill or have his dimpled grin and charm? Was he hungry for power and leadership as Bill had been?

Or in that mysterious way of human nature did he inherit some of my shyness and talent, my love of music? she wondered.

She hesitated by the Giants' Doorway at the Stephansdom, not certain what one would say to the clergy inside. It was Monday, not Wednesday. But there was no rule about entering on certain days. Nothing to prevent her from going inside and taking her Wednesday pew far to the front. Still she hesitated. How could she tell the priest that without warning—without provocation—she was being torn apart by longing and memory? By rejection and guilt. By the nameless child she had left behind in Everdale.

In her pain, she wandered the narrow back streets of the city, through the parks, past the museums and coffeehouses. Seeing, yet not seeing the passing pedestrians. Aware of the street musicians, yet not hearing them. Hours later, with her energy spent, she found herself circling the Ringstrasse once more. She was back to something familiar. Her mind cleared, her headache easing in the fresh air.

As dusk settled in, she caught a taxi to Bosendorferstrasse. A long queue of concertgoers stood in front of the theater, dressed in their evening finery, waiting to go inside to hear her music. Waiting with anticipation as she had all these years for the sound of her child, for the joy of his fingers around hers.

Even as she left the taxi, the long-ago memory of Everdale persisted—the nurse unfolding the receiving blanket, the baby's pink toes curling, his legs kicking. She felt the grasp of those tiny fingers on her own. Gurgling, cooing sounds had filled the hospital nursery as the nurse said, "It's not too late to change your mind."

She had hardly breathed when the nurse put him into her arms and left them alone, alone so she could cradle him for the last time. When the nurse took him from her she knew then—as she knew now—that some of the warmth of him would stay with her forever.

It was all that she had. All that she would ever have.

Whenever Kerina stayed in Vienna, she took one of the three spacious suites on the top floor of the Wandlsek Hotel, all of them overlooking the Danube. Her favorite was the corner suite, the one she was in now with its unobstructed view of the city from three sides. She kept her curtains drawn back, allowing her to see the star-studded sky with the moon rising above St. Stephansdom as she lay on her bed or to view familiar landmarks from the soft, winged chair in the corner of her sitting room as she was doing now. Franck's dozen red roses filled the vase beside her. She ran her finger over the velvet petals, wondering whether she could ever add up the number of roses he had given her over the years.

Moments ago she had incensed him by mentioning Bill's name. Angered, Franck had stepped out on her enclosed patio to cool down. He was there now watching the riverboats meandering along the Danube Canal, cruising beneath the bridges with their metal parapets. The banks of the Danube were buttressed with stone, the boat traffic heading toward Hungary. He turned at last, came back into the room, and, easing into the chair across from her, refused the steaming cup of black coffee that she held out to him.

He stretched his lanky legs and plucked a thread of lint from his gray flannel trousers. He was a serious man of more than medium height, his jet-black hair parted on the right, his beard well-trimmed. She thought him handsome, but he had an unsmiling mouth, his expression one of infinite sadness whenever he was with her. Tonight he was quiet. Usually in their moments together he talked passionately about art and music, of the latest painting he had acquired, or the one he coveted. He was most animated when he spoke of Cezanne and Monet, Pissarro and van Gogh. He read voraciously and often quoted from articles on art thefts and museums the world around. Yet he was a good listener, sympathetic to Kerina, patient with her. Sometimes they would sit listening to music or talk at great length about artists and musicians who had touched their lives—Franck expounding on van Gogh or Picasso, Kerina on Isaac Stern or Niccolò Paganini.

"What are you thinking about, Franck?"

"How beautiful you are. How much I still love you."

Ever since Prague, she thought.

His life was like a reversible fabric—protective and devoted toward her, yet distant to others and outright antagonistic toward Jillian. Kerina felt indebted to him for helping her escape the Czech borders with her precious violin in her hands and was endlessly grateful to him for opening the concert halls of the world to her. She treasured his friendship, but try as she did, she could not return his love. They shared music and art and the love of Vienna, but they were at odds politically, and niggling in the back of Kerina's mind were those thirteen years that separated them. They mattered to her, not to him.

Franck smiled now, relaxing in her presence, untroubled by her silence, the evening's concert safely behind them. "As always, my dear, you played beautifully this evening."

"Do you never grow tired of complimenting me?"

"I never grow tired of being with you, Kerina."

"We've known each other a long time, Franck."

"Since you were fifteen. And I've loved you all that time." His dark eyes smiled. "Well, maybe not that first year. Not that time you hung over the fence and told me to go away."

"That was the second time you saw me, Franck. The first time I was playing my violin."

"Oh, yes, and I tried to take it away from you. What a good scrapper you were."

"It seems we've known each other forever, Franck."

"A long time. You hated me in the beginning."

"I hated you being in my country. You represented everything my family had suffered. Everything they feared after the Nazis left—after the Russians came." Softly she said, "Until your family took over our farmhouse, I thought my papa owned the farm. But you told me the communists were in control."

"My father's politics, not mine."

"But I grew up under your father's politics."

His solemn dark eyes held hers. "None of it was my doing."

Deny it, she thought. *Czechoslovakia! My country, the land of my birth. And you were a foreigner, an enemy on my soil.*

Czechoslovakia was a landlocked country lying miles from the sea, its countryside filled with rugged mountains and rolling hills. Ten years after the war, when she was born, trout bubbled in the streams for the taking, but many farm-lands lay barren and uncultivated, ravaged by the last days of battle and deprivation. Some of the lower mountain slopes were wasted where the trees had been stripped down for fuel during the war years and seedlings had not yet been planted. She knew nothing about the Nazi rule except for her parents' bitter recollections. She had grown up during the communist domination under the watchful eye of men like Franck's father. Always she dreamed about escaping. Escaping from Franck's father, the cruel head of the secret police, his iron rule as hard as the granite of the White Carpathians to the west.

Franck toyed with his tie. "I did not like your country until I met you, Kerina."

When she met Franck, the Prague spring warmed the country and the Velvet Revolution was two decades away. The Petzolds took over the Rudzinskis' isolated farmhouse outside of Prague, forcing Kerina's family to move into the thatched building that had once housed the work hands. Even now she was proud of her father. Karol Rudzinski had defiantly farmed his own land when most farmers to the north and east were consigned to collective farms, run like everything else by the people in power.

Franck drew her attention again, saying, "Kerina, marry me. I know I could make you happy."

"It would still displease my parents for me to marry you." She lowered her voice. "Besides, I don't want to marry anyone."

His fingers locked in an iron grip. "You did once."

"Just once."

"Is there someone else, Kerina?"

She laughed. "Who would know that better than you?"

"We're not always together. You fly to Prague without me. You choose to vacation at that villa of yours alone."

"You have never wanted to go the Riviera with me. There is plenty of room, you know. But you always tell me you need that time away from me to work on your art collection." She imagined that Franck had a mistress somewhere. "Surely there is someone else, Franck. In Moscow? You go there often enough. Or back in Prague?"

"No one that I want to spend my life with."

He had never married, but surely he had many paramours in his life. Kerina could not picture him as celibate. Under that comely, serious face and that cultured and dignified manner, he was too passionate a man to not need the love of a woman.

Morosely, he said, "You always have an admirer backstage wanting to take you to dinner. That Count from Spain always writing. The Frenchman who calls."

"Just fans, Franck."

She dared not mention the soldier from Bosnia and the scheduled interview with him at the close of the concert in May. Franck had an aversion to Americans. If he considered it the remotest possibility that the soldier had reminded her of Bill VanBurien, he would block the interview. Taking the last swallow of her coffee, she steered the conversation to the present-day art theft in Italy and to the pilfering of art treasures from the Jewish people during the German occupation.

"Franck, doesn't it bother you building your own collection from those unclaimed works of art, one piece at a time?"

"The Swiss would claim them. Why shouldn't I?"

"You never put them on display."

"And lose my collection? My grandfather lost his back during the war. I won't take that risk. I told Elias McClaren that you think him foolish for exhibiting his art treasures again."

"It is Jillian who feels that way. She says he almost lost a Rubens in the last robbery. You never told me that, Franck. But I'd rather Elias have his display at the museum under

35

Plexiglas than hide his collection in the basement of his home."

"As you think I do?"

"Don't you? Nicole says half of their collection remains in storage. What is the value of art if you hide it away?"

"Resale value." He twirled a piece of lint in his fingers. "Keep it off the market long enough and the price goes higher."

"Hoard it? Haven't I made you a wealthy enough man?"

"Collecting art is my passion, Kerina."

"I thought *I* was. But you keep your collection hidden away from everyone. Nicole and I agree. Art was meant to be shared with the public, not grabbed up by a few wealthy collectors."

His beard twitched. "What does Nicole McClaren know of great paintings? She would still be modeling clothes in Paris if Elias hadn't married her."

"And without you, Franck, I would still be living on my parents' farm—still dreaming of the concert halls?"

"Every painting I've acquired was for you. They all hang in my home on the Black Sea. Marry me and you will see how lovely I have made it for you. Masterpieces in every room."

She would never live there with him. When she retired—years from now—she would go back to Prague, back to her family. "Franck, please don't get involved with McClaren this time. The last time you did, something was stolen."

He laughed. "And you think I took it?"

"Of course not, but someone did."

His laugh turned bitter. "I know about the concert thefts, but I was with you at the concert hall that evening."

"And this evening?"

"I was standing in the alcove as I always do, waiting with a dozen red roses when the concert ended."

She touched the rose petal nearest to her, then rearranged the flower. *You were there when the concert ended,* she thought, *but you weren't there the whole time.*

"Tomorrow on the front page of the newspaper, there will be mention of another stolen art piece. It always seems to happen when I am in concert. Please do not get involved, Franck."

His brooding eyes sought hers. "Elias McClaren is determined to buy another Josef VanStryker."

"VanStryker? He's not even that well known."

"There's renewed interest in his paintings now. He was just coming to his own at the turn of the twentieth century. He did numerous landscapes. Mountains and forests, mostly. His life and work were cut short after Hitler came to power."

"Because he was Jewish?"

He nodded, his eyes darkening. "His great-grandmother was. Enough to have Josef imprisoned. He died in Ravensbruck."

"Then his work was probably stolen or destroyed in the war."

"Five of his canvases were reportedly smuggled out of Germany in thirty-nine. Since then a couple of authentic pieces have come on the market. Elias found one at Sotheby's a year ago. I have traced another one of them. Elias is willing to go seven digits to buy the one in Moscow."

"And you will take a hefty commission?" Her stomach muscles tightened. *What if the sale he is negotiating between Gukganov and Elias fails? What if this becomes a financial disaster for the McClarens? We can't risk the loss of their friendship.* "Franck, Elias already has a VanStryker. Stay out of it. What if this one is a fake? Let Elias deal directly with Jokhar."

"Jokhar assures me that the painting is genuine."

"How will Elias ever get it out of Russia?"

"I will arrange for shipment. You don't trust me, do you?"

"Not lately, Franck. Not when you work with Jokhar." *Not with Jillian always pointing out your shortcomings and the risks you are taking. But I have no right to question your friendships.*

For a moment Kerina resented Jillian for planting suspicion in her mind. No, it wasn't Jillian who had caused her to discredit Franck. Jillian had simply awakened her own fears.

Franck's sad, brooding expression drew sympathy like a magnet from most women, but not from Jillian. She found Franck annoying, someone who needed women, needed their approval. But Jillian had discovered in Franck the harshness that few others saw. It came out in its full blast of fury against her. What existed between those two Kerina could not imagine, but she kept them apart, and, when they were forced together socially, she placed them at opposite ends of the table or at different tasks in the room.

Franck began tapping the air with the tip of his black Italian shoe. To calm him, she asked, "What about the Degas masterpiece you mentioned the last time we were here in Vienna? The one plundered by Russia at the close of World War II? Surely you would want that one for yourself?"

"Why the sudden interest, Kerina?"

Because I am frightened for you. Jokhar Gukganov cannot be trusted. Niggling doubts crept in. Franck? She shrank back from the idea. She shoved the fears from her mind, ashamed to even think it, to question the man she had known for so long. But she must persuade him to stop associating with Jokhar Gukganov.

"Jillian wonders why you don't look for the Degas painting. It's been listed as missing or destroyed for fifty years."

A scowl burrowed between Franck's brows. "That would be a find." He twirled his signet ring. "And what does Jillian say of Josef VanStryker's work?"

"She never mentioned VanStryker. What will you do with the Degas if you find it before Jokhar does? Sell it to him?"

"I would hide it in my own museum."

Doubts crept in again. Anguish for Franck. She owed him her loyalty for all he had done for her. She could not allow her doubts to linger, not against Franck. Franck had been her friend, her best friend since she was fifteen.

Franck ran his hand over the books on the end table, stopping as he touched Kerina's journal.

Kerina cringed as she thought of the photographs within its pages—photographs of Bill and of her newborn son.

His hand reached out instead for a small volume of poetry, the T. S. Eliot volume she had been reading when he arrived. He took it up, examined the cover, opened the book. His eyes darkened as he scanned the inscription from Bill. His face went rigid. *"The Waste Land,"* he said, turning to the first poem.

"T. S. Eliot. I often read him."

"But not recently?" *April is the cruellest month!* he read, and then he read the words again. "Oh, Kerina. You only make yourself sad thinking back to Everdale."

"That was a significant part of my life."

"No, part of your past. Leave it there."

Snapping the book shut, he stood up wearily and crossed the room to her. He leaned down and kissed the top of her head. "Good night, my dear."

Even as the door closed behind Franck, *the bolted chamber of her heart creaked open, drawing slowly back on its time-aged hinge, unveiling a small town and the forty-four-bed hospital with its brick facade outside and the smell of antiseptic within. From out of the past she heard a sharp-tongued nurse saying in a Southern drawl, "Why on earth do you think that girl came all the way to Everdale?"*

The nurse was right. Kerina had come to the unknown, weaving dark threads into the fabric of her life in a town that could have been called Nowhere, so unfamiliar were the surroundings.

Kerina felt the color drain from her face. She pressed her temple, *trying to shut out that April so long ago, trying to block out the grating rattle of the train traveling at breakneck speed through the middle of Everdale, its whistle blaring. Bill's car squealing into the hospital parking lot. Muted voices at the nurses' station. The cry of the infant in the nursery.*

Her son. No, another woman's child now.

Three

Spring came slowly to Bosnia, the ground thawing at last, the bitter cold of winter finally gone. Lieutenant Chandler Reynolds leaned on his crutches and welcomed spring, convinced that the melted snows would expose any of the land mines still hidden in the fields. Chandler's work with intelligence confined him to a crescent hunk of land east of the British sector and north of Sarajevo and the French zone. He was housed near Tuzla, locked away at a top security command post, but locating concealed mines had become a *cause celebre* for him. Whatever it took, he would do everything in his power to prevent another explosion from destroying innocent lives. He'd just spent the last five weeks in a hospital, injured in the same blast that had killed his best friend.

A sickening chill cut Chandler between the shoulder blades. He already regretted discarding his wool sweater and cold-weather gloves. Spring or not, it was a damp, foggy morning, a north wind sweeping across the field, sapping his strength as he waited for the armored Humvee to arrive. The mists above the mountains kept the sun at bay. Or maybe the sun didn't shine on Bosnia. He would prefer being on the Adriatic Sea, on one of those sand and pebble beaches in sunny Dubrovnik where tourists once flocked on holiday, but the American zone was far from there.

His impatience mounted as he scanned the road in both directions. "Come on, come on, before my leg gives out."

No matter which direction he turned, there was bleakness, blackness, devastation. Too much restructuring still to be done. Too little started. And ethnic discord erupting to the south. As far as he was concerned, the terms of the Dayton Peace Accord seemed more paperwork than cooperation.

What have we accomplished? Politics control the rebuilding of the land, he thought. *Too many indicted war criminals still run free. The nation is still divided ethnically. Is that what Randy Williams died for?*

Chandler saw Randy now in his mind's eye as clearly as if he were standing there, blessing the driver for being late. Randy, with his shock of flaming red hair and the freckled face that went with it, always popping peanuts as though they were candy—a big guy with a quick grin and bullying shoulders that could push their way through a crowd of defiant civilians or through government red tape. He was passionate about villagers. Yet he was hot-tempered and strong-willed with a tongue that spewed expletives, a language of his own that had never been nurtured on the front pew of a church. Still, he had been a good friend and Chan missed him.

Their friendship went back a long way. They'd met at the university, but with little in common, there was no real tie-in until their senior year when they were thrown together in a tennis match. Randy had cussed Chandler's blunders on the court. Chandler had fought back with an inner rage that forced Randy to sweat and stretch and race to whack the ball back over the net.

Their handgrip at the end of the game was anything but cordial. In the dressing room, after they had showered and changed and looked halfway presentable, Randy had asked, "Why don't we have a beer together and talk about teaming up for the doubles?"

"Don't drink," Chandler had told him sourly.

"But you do play a good game of tennis. We'd do better playing on the same side of the net." Randy eased off. "How about a Pepsi instead?"

"You're on."

Randy had almost chucked their friendship when he discovered that Chandler came from a pastor's family. "Don't pull any of that religious stuff on me," he warned. "About the best I can offer you is my loyalty and a good game of tennis."

They had gone on to win the tournament in their senior year and afterwards competed in a stateside tennis match. Randy was like the brother that Chandler had always wanted and still wanted even as a grown man. They hit it off after that first encounter with long chats into the wee hours about politics and religion. They roughhoused like a couple of teenagers, mountain climbed on the weekends, and put their noses under the hood of Randy's '76 jalopy trying to make it run a little bit longer. Their paths parted after graduation without Chandler ever taking that visit back to Ohio to Randy's hometown.

Chandler shifted on his crutches again and nodded at an old Bosnian plodding by. He didn't get a flicker in return. *Okay, so you want NATO out of here. At least give us credit for trying to help you,* he complained silently. *At least give my buddy credit for dying for you.*

For almost a year after graduation, Randy and Chandler kept in touch with periodic phone calls. One of them had reached Chandler at Juilliard when Randy called from an Irish pub in New York City. "Hey, man, I'm in walking distance from your slave factory. But I couldn't walk a straight line to you right now. I'm thinking about giving the army three years of my life. Why not trash that music world of yours and join me?"

"Thought you were joining the reserves, Randy."

"I want to go for the big thing. I'm signing on the dotted line in ten days with a fair chance at officer's training."

Randy's spur-of-the-moment decision appealed to Chandler. For weeks he had known he wasn't cutting it at Juilliard. He faced the daily pressure of preparing for a music career that had no end in sight and no guarantee of personal success. He had given it his best, had practiced until his arms ached. He had learned a great deal about music—about himself. Randy offered him another option, a way out, a chance to quit with a purpose. Ten days later he left Juilliard, met Randy outside a recruitment station, and signed on. After all, they were like brothers, weren't they? And brothers did things together.

They struggled through the humiliation of basic training, slithering in mud up to their ears with live bullets zooming over their heads, and locked horns on the wrestling mat. Preparation, they were told, for the possibility of another Gulf War.

But they came out looking proud and took the next eight weeks of advance training before parting ways again. Chandler was off to specialty training that would take him into intelligence work with lieutenant bars on his shoulder, and Randy was steering clear of any job that kept him behind locked doors.

Running into each other again in the officer's club in Germany was a back-pounding reunion. An hour at the bar followed with Chandler drinking water as Randy downed three beers to celebrate meeting up again. They'd caught a good duty, close to the mountains, and were soon back into hiking in the Bavarian Alps on weekend getaways that put them in top condition.

You were the picture of health, old buddy, Chandler thought. *Invincible. Strong enough to make it to a ripe old age.*

Chandler ground a deep hole in the dirt with his crutch. "Oh, God, why did you let Randy die? I don't understand!"

At the end of one of those weekends in the Alps, they had finally been reassigned to the American headquarters in Tuzla, part of the second influx of I-For troops heading for

Bosnia. Randy flew in weeks ahead of Chandler, landing when the visibility was almost down to zero.

Now, two rotations later, Chandler had been asked to finish out his enlistment in Bosnia, to reenlist if necessary, with the promise that it would earn him a fast promotion and get him out of the computer lab and directly into intelligence fieldwork for which he was trained. Scuttlebutt ran wild among the officers. Only single men were being tapped for a special mission—an intelligence team that would infiltrate the Serbian line. Men who might never go home again.

Randy had been tapped two weeks before his death and flat out refused, giving an inappropriate thumb swipe to his nose to confirm his refusal. Chandler's interest sparked, anything to remove himself from analyzing intelligence reports at the command post. He latched on to the promise of action with strict orders from Colonel Bladstone that from now on nothing they discussed would go beyond his office. That was easy. The place was like a cement vault, and Bladstone was powerful enough to silence most men.

It hadn't silenced Randy. "Bladstone isn't recruiting for the army," Randy had warned. "It's something bigger."

"Then I'm in."

"Then the CIA has a stranglehold on you."

Chandler laughed. "The CIA? Bladstone asked us to reenlist. That means three more years with the army."

"Your interpretation. Don't go in blindfolded, Chan. The Langley boys are already grabbing you by the shoulder."

They had little more than three weeks to argue about it—and then Randy was blown to bits before Chandler could reach him. Reenlist? He felt torn asunder, right at the gut line, debating with himself even more since Randy's death. Somebody had to stay on as part of the team willing to put down every uprising and unearth every land mine to make Bosnia safe for its people. He knew why he wanted to stay in Bosnia. Could put a name on it. Could even hear the shrink at the makeshift hospital advising him to forget Captain Williams: "Your leg is healing. It's the guilt that is killing you."

Guilt? Chandler had had nothing to do with Randy blowing up in a land mine. If he volunteered to stay on, he might face another bitter Christmas in Bosnia as part of an advisory team or a token army held on to quell the guerrilla activity to the South. Chandler had missed that first Christmas when the troops were deployed to Bosnia while the ink was still wet on the Dayton Peace Accord. That wasn't his choice. His training was geared toward setting up the computer systems at Tuzla, but at the last minute his unit had been kept in Bavaria in a state-of-the-art physics lab as streamlined as any in the Pentagon.

There he sat, an action man glued to his seat in a secure communications room crowded with human think tanks and physics majors—he was one himself—visualizing Bosnia from a safe distance. Massive computer-controlled maps covered what should have been windows. He spent his time at a conference table with other men and women staring down at the dregs of their empty coffee cups or at the multi-colored computer screens in front of them, screens that graphically portrayed the arrival of troops in Bosnia, bound by the old adage that knowledge is military power. That's what he got for going magna cum laude at the university, a desk assignment trained to identify threats or to provide the military logistics for moving the 60,000 troops of I-For rapidly into Bosnia. Granted, it was a complex system capable of distinguishing the multinational NATO soldiers from the Serbian army holding out in the foothills. It could differentiate between a sniper and a charred telephone pole and within split seconds send a warning to peacekeepers with their boots already on Bosnian soil.

Chandler scanned the desolate road again in both directions, growing more uneasy as he waited for the armored vehicle. His leg was giving him fits, his temper rising. He saw the Humvee at last, rumbling over the rutted, muddied roadway toward him and squealing to a stop inches from the tip of his left crutch. Randy Williams's old driver was at the wheel, his face a mask, his emotions still as shattered as Chandler's had been.

As Chandler struggled for a comfortable position in the front seat, he turned for a hasty appraisal of the men behind him. Colonel Bladstone, his own unit commander, sat behind the driver, another unidentified colonel beside him.

Like the rest of them, the man was wearing his protective vest and camouflage pants, the khaki-green poly-knit shirt visible at the open neck of his parka. He was holding a British walking stick in his hands, not an M-16 rifle. The man's eyes were hard, disciplined, bluer than the cloudy sky, his face rugged and freshly shaven. His I.D. badge was pinned to his parka, but Chandler's appraisal had been too fleeting to catch the name.

As Chandler faced forward, the driver took a familiar route out of Tuzla. *Randy's road to no return,* he thought. Behind him, above the roar of the vehicle, he heard the steady beat of the walking stick in the stranger's palm. "Slow down," Chandler warned.

"I know these roads, lieutenant."

"At this speed, you'll miss the hairpin turns."

"I can handle them."

Like the Bradley Fighting Vehicle last month? Chandler thought. *And the Abrams tank before that?* Both of them went off the road. Both of them blown with anti-tank mines.

"I only have two more weeks in Bosnia," the driver boasted.

"I thought you had three months to go, like I do."

"Somebody messed up. But who's complaining?" He swerved, then gained control again. "Ever since Captain Williams caught his, all I want to do is get out of this man's army and go home to the Puget Sound. What about you, lieutenant?"

"I have a thirty-day medical leave coming up."

"The leg, eh? I can't wait to get out of this place. I hate the cold and the sun not shining. I hated losing the captain."

Chandler fell silent, but he understood. How old was the kid? Nineteen? Twenty? The best part of his youth wearing camouflage uniforms. At the first deployment of troops to Bosnia, *Newsweek* had called the assignment "Hell in a Cold Place."

Good description, Chandler thought. The desolation of his surroundings reminded him of those old hellfire-and-brimstone sermons of his boyhood. His father's sermons held a lighter, positive note these days, although Chandler still felt the heat of his message. But even when it came across with the polish of an orator, you couldn't miss his dad's message of hope.

Bavaria had been like a winter holiday, Bosnia like walking into Hades itself. Chandler found the Bosnian winters deplorable. Randy took them in stride, roaming around in defiance of caution and taking on the plight of the kids of Tuzla. He particularly liked a boy named Rasim Hovic with an attractive, older girl in the family. In their spare time, limited as it was, Chandler and Randy did push-ups, played pool or Ping-Pong in the officer's room, and taught Rasim how to build a snowman, Ohio style.

When the Humvee reached the Hovics' village, the driver eased to the side of the road. Here on the outskirts of town, the rubbled ruins left the farmland unproductive with nothing but scrub brush, charred gray trees, and sparse patches of new growth visible. Off to their right, a de-mining team scoured the barren fields—two eight-man teams stabbing every inch of the ground with long ice picks and Schiebel detecting sets.

"They've detonated two more land mines since Captain Williams's death," the driver said.

"And the people?" *The Hovic family,* he thought.

"Evacuated the day after the captain was killed."

They left the driver by the Humvee and moved off the road, Colonel Bladstone and his guest slowing their steps to Chandler's pace. Chandler could see the name on the visiting colonel's parka clearly now. *P. Daniels. Paul,* he guessed.

"Do you recognize the place?" Colonel Daniels asked.

You know I do, he wanted to say but said instead, "It looks like the spot, sir."

"Let me assure you, Reynolds, it is the exact location." He stretched his arm and pointed. "About thirty or forty yards from here. Tell us about it, lieutenant. What happened that day?"

"I've given that report at least a dozen times."

"Then oblige me. Make it a baker's dozen."

The muscles in Chandler's throat tightened. On March 25, three weeks before his twenty-sixth birthday, he had ridden along on Randy's patrol. Now he stared between the damaged houses, his thoughts marking the path that Randy had taken. The sniper's fire had come from the hills behind the village. No, that was too far away. The sniper had been closer in, hiding out in one of the homes and, afterwards, taking off for the safety of the hills.

"Captain Williams knew better than to race over those fields," Daniels said. "He knew the risks."

The picture came back—Randy sprinting over the field. "There was a small boy in the line of fire," Chandler said.

"So Williams took off after him?"

"We were on an inspection patrol, Colonel Daniels. Just heading back toward Tuzla when the sniper attacked."

"Bladstone here tells me that's not your usual command."

"I know, sir, but we were old friends. Randy—Captain Williams invited me to go along for the ride. I'm usually confined to an intelligence desk at the command post."

"You've ridden with Captain Williams before?"

"Three or four times. I always welcomed the chance to get away from staring at intelligence reports all day long. Even the seat of my britches is worn thin."

An amused smile touched Daniels's blue eyes, veiling his harshness. "So you rode with him without incident before?"

Chandler nodded, his gaze fixed forty yards in front of him. "We had three armored vehicles just ahead of us. They'd just passed the village checkpoint when the sniper fired."

"And your job was to get out of there, not to return fire," Bladstone reminded him.

He swallowed. "That's what Williams said. And then he saw the boy darting between the houses. The kid was terrified."

"And Captain Williams went berserk?" Daniels asked.

"He was as clearheaded as you are today, sir. But he saw something that needed doing, and he was out of the vehicle before the driver could come to a complete stop."

And running with the speed of a jackal, his protective vest taking one of the sniper's bullets. Chandler could only hope that the driver had given the same account of the incident.

"Did you follow him, Reynolds?"

Colonel Daniels wore an army uniform. The right insignia. The right bearing. But was he really army? The colonel was trying to put words in Chandler's mouth, to blow the accident out of proportion. To trap him in lies. But why? Other men had died in accidents since reaching Bosnia. Why the particular interest in Randy's death? Was this leading to a posthumous court-martial for Randy? Or to his own for being there? But something was up, bigger than a land mine exploding. He had to hang cool, in spite of how much just standing here was tearing at his gut.

Volunteer nothing. Remember Randy's honor. His sacrifice.

"I started to follow Williams, but he ordered me to stay near the vehicle. He scooped up the kid and turned him back toward our truck." Sweat poured down Chandler's back, his knuckles white as he gripped the crutches. Standing here was bringing it all back. "I think Randy swatted his bottom and headed the boy towards me."

Colonel Daniels said abruptly, "The child's name is Rasim Hovic. Captain Williams knew the boy, didn't he?"

We both did, Chandler thought. "Did he?"

"We believe the captain was in this village on a number of occasions to see Rasim's sister, Zineta Hovic."

It was too soon to say that the Hovic family had taken Zineta in when her own family was wiped out during one of the Serbian attacks. They had found her wandering dazed in the war-torn streets of Tuzla, foraging for food in the empty stalls of the outdoor market. As Randy had described her, she was sixteen then, her dress tattered, her arms and feet bare, her sad face strangely appealing and her dark, soulful eyes unforgettable.

"We don't encourage mixing with the people," grumbled Daniels. "And courting a Bosnian woman is definitely out, lieutenant. But from what I gather, Captain Williams rather handled things in his own way."

"They were just friends, sir. She wasn't his steady girlfriend or anything like that. Randy helped repair the Hovics' roof just before winter set in. That's how he met her."

"He was that kind of guy?" Colonel Daniels asked.

"He had his own definition of keeping peace, sir."

"It got him killed."

"The captain and Miss Hovic were just friends," he repeated.

"Really, Reynolds? Just friends? The girl is pregnant."

Chandler's gut cramped. He bent at the sudden pain. *What a mess you got yourself into, Randy!* But he thought about Zineta too. How would the people in Tuzla accept a young woman impregnated by an American army officer?

"What will become of the girl?" he asked.

Bladstone cleared his throat. "We will have to transfer her to another zone. British. French. Whichever one will take her."

"Away from the security of the Hovic family?"

"Do you have a better plan, lieutenant?"

Chandler's thoughts churned pell-mell. Finally, he suggested, "Send her to America where she has a chance for survival and the baby has a chance to grow up in peace."

"Her reputation is against her." Daniels glared at him. "She has no relatives in America. She's penniless. Someone would have to sponsor her. Who wants to assume responsibility for an unwed mother and her newborn?"

"Or maybe someone could marry her," said Bladstone snidely. "Are you up to the job, lieutenant?"

Chandler emitted a throaty chuckle. "Sure, why not?" he quipped. "My mom's just waiting for me to tie the knot one of these days." The words were no sooner out of his mouth when he remembered Randy's final request: "If anything happens to me, Chan, will you make sure that Zineta gets to the States?"

He had given his word. Of course, the oath wasn't signed in blood. Or was it? How far would he go to keep a promise to a friend? Randy had died for him—had fallen on a land mine to save Chandler's life. Didn't that make the girl his responsibility? The wheels in his mind kept spinning. It would be a marriage of convenience. He didn't love the girl, barely knew her, but he liked her, and they were already friends. And what did he have going on in his own life these days? He was footloose. Who was to say he couldn't marry the girl and give Randy's child a name? Marrying her was the quickest way he could think of to cut through military red tape.

Chandler felt a dry, humorless laugh rise in his throat. His dad would have fits over a marriage of convenience, but he would only be lending Zineta his name, gaining her a quick passage to America. You could get these things annulled, couldn't you?

"Colonel Bladstone—" he started to say.

"Don't hang yourself, Reynolds," Bladstone cautioned. "Don't ruin your career just to be noble. A dead friend isn't worth it."

"Let me be the judge of that one, colonel." *I have to help the girl get to America. I owe that much to Randy and his child,* Chandler thought.

"Colonel Bladstone tells me you are scheduled to go on a thirty-day leave," Daniels said. "We'll want your stateside address in case we have to get in touch with you."

"I'll be in Vienna, sir."

"Vienna?" The word exploded like a land mine going off.

Chandler tapped the ground with his crutch. "I lucked out. The music in Vienna will be part of my recovery phase. But, sir, I want some time with Zineta Hovic before I fly there."

"Let's arrange that when you get back, Reynolds."

"By then you will have found her a safe place in the British sector or in Serbia. The army won't want any reminder that Captain Williams had an unborn child."

"You're right. We must avoid a clash with the Muslim faction in Tuzla at all costs. And the Hovics are Muslims."

"Zineta is Croatian." *But would that make a difference when she lived with a Muslim family?* he wondered. He rubbed his eyes, perplexed by his own concern. The void, the darkness felt like his own. "Does Miss Hovic know about Captain Williams's death?"

"We have no reason to inform her."

"Colonel Daniels, the baby should be reason enough."

The colonel slapped his stick against his thigh. "Williams's parents stirred up public opinion against us when they descended on Washington, demanding an immediate withdrawal of all U.S. troops. Now the public is challenging our mission in Bosnia insisting that we withdraw before our latest deadline. But our military presence is vital to our national security interests. And absolutely essential to the people of Bosnia."

Chandler despised the colonel's arrogance. "You want peace?" he asked. "My dad would say it's man's heart that has to change."

"And what would you suggest, Reynolds?"

Prayer popped into his head, his father's old standby. But he said, "I'm still working that one out, sir. But until these people patch up their differences, not even another Olympics would change the situation."

Bladstone looked sullen. "You sound like Captain Williams."

"We shared a lot of ideas."

"But did you share intelligence secrets?" Daniels asked.

You sleazeball. Accusing me of a lie. Robbing Randy of any honor in dying.

"The White House wants everything we can get on your friend's time in Bosnia. If the girl is pregnant—and we have no reason to doubt it—we'll force his parents to back off. The senator from the Williams's district is flying over here in ten days. He and his committee want answers."

"And you want them to think Randy was killed off-duty and off-limits from the base, under suspicious circumstances?"

"You catch on quickly, lieutenant."

Gruffly the colonel said, "When our troops were first deployed here, the president knew there would be casualties. Every peacekeeping mission has them. Having another unexpected death like this one and the public bites into it, especially when the young woman may have been a Serbian courier during the war."

"A courier? That's crazy, sir."

Daniels scowled. "We know for certain that she served as a courier during the war, and since then, she may have carried messages to the Serb forces in Kosovo."

"She's not Serbian, sir."

"Her sympathies might be. Did you ever discuss your work with her, lieutenant? Or with your friend Williams?"

"I told you. Never. I don't discuss classified data."

So that was it. That's why they had interrogated him at the hospital and brought him back to the Hovics' village. "Randy and I never discussed the work I did. Spy satellites and intelligence reports would have bored him."

Chandler's mind ran in fast forward. *If you suspected me, I would not be going on a medical leave. You want me out of Bosnia while the senator is here, and you're willing to risk letting me go for a month. But you will follow my every move in Vienna. So much for the pretty girls in Austria. What I need is someone with me to deflect suspicion.*

"Tired, Reynolds?" Daniels asked.

Yes, tired of the trap you're setting for me. Mad clean through at what you're doing to Randy's memory. "I'm okay, sir."

"Good." His harsh eyes glinted. "I want to know all about Captain Williams's relationship with the Hovic family right on up to the day he died."

Chandler boiled inside, but he licked his lips and began to whistle the clear notes of a Christmas carol, concentrating on the words: *It came upon a midnight clear, that glorious song of old . . . O rest beside the weary road and hear the angels sing.*

"Feeling festive, lieutenant?" Daniels roared.

"I'm following your orders, sir. I'm just going back to where it all began." Chandler adjusted the crutches under his armpits and swung awkwardly over the uneven ground. "This way, colonel."

He led them toward a small house off the beaten path, a house still pocked with bullet holes and crumbling cement steps. "It all began here. Just before dusk on Christmas."

"You're certain this is the Hovic house?"

"Yes. I saw it the first time on Christmas Day and the last time on the day Captain Williams died."

The music of that first visit with the hope of Christmas in a war-torn village faded from his memory, and the sound of a land mine exploding deafened him. Refusing to be less than a man, he fought down the lump in his throat and blinked back the tears that had never flowed for Randy.

As he leaned on his crutches and stared vacantly at the Hovics' battered front door, he no longer sensed the presence of the two commanding officers. He had stepped back in time before Randy's death to Christmas Day. He spoke haltingly, his pain welling up from the depths of his despair, his words coming slowly like spring; and with their slowness, he felt the first touch of healing as he told them what happened.

"It was Christmas," Reynolds said, his eyes no longer on Bladstone or Daniels. "My second miserable Christmas in Bosnia."

Four

On Christmas Day four months before, the town lay smothered in snow, the ground frozen solid, a new winter storm swirling in above the mountains. Lieutenant Chandler Reynolds rolled out of the sack at dawn just in time for the chaplain's service and went away homesick for his dad's cathedral, the one he had often viewed with contempt.

As he crunched over the packed snow, the sound of carols came from the tents, the music only intensifying his isolation. At noon, he walked into the mess hall with "O Come, All Ye Faithful" blaring over a loudspeaker rigged up in one corner. A life-size Santa Claus in dyed-red long johns dangled from the ceiling, its cotton beard off center. Reynolds gave no thought to backslapping or offering a hail-fellow-well-met salute to any of his fellow officers. He didn't even look up when Randy Williams plopped his tray on the table and dropped down beside him.

"Merry Christmas to you too," Randy said. "Came in here thinking we could go caroling, but with a sour face like that, you'd sing off-key."

Chandler felt a slow grin coming on. "Cheers and all that to you too. But no caroling."

Minutes later, he went back to chowing down the army's version of turkey and stuffing and chewing the cranberries and dry, overcooked turkey as though it were beef jerky—the mess hall so cold that he blew steam with every bite.

"Hey, buddy." Randy's voice again. "You didn't hear a word I said. I just asked you to ride patrol with me today."

"You got the duty?"

"Someone has to do it. Are you tied up in the computer lab?"

"I'm free until six in the morning."

"Then you're on?"

As they made their way out of the mess hall, Randy asked, "What did you think of the president's visit yesterday?"

"Got to shake hands with him. Seems a nice enough fellow. He came into security while I was on duty. And you?"

"Missed him. I was out in the village."

"That's going to get you in a heap of trouble, Randy."

"Can't let my friends freeze to death. The Hovics took a lot of war damage, so Kemal and I climbed up on the roof and did a makeshift repair with some old timber."

"Was that your only reason?"

"Just checking up on Zineta. I should have sent her home to my parents for Christmas."

Chan frowned. "You can't solve everybody's problems, Randy."

"I'd like to solve hers. The president should have gone out and taken a look at her battle-scarred village."

"The army considers anything outside of Tuzla or Sarajevo unsafe for him."

"They stick us with six- and eight-month tours. Double that for us. And he pulls out after three and a half hours."

Chan tugged on his gloves as they got into the Humvee. "Randy, you know foul weather cut his trip short."

"Just an excuse for a whirlwind holiday. I'd think more of him if he stayed on and had canteen turkey with us today."

"Something tells me you didn't vote his party," Chandler said as the driver crossed beyond the city limits.

"I don't vote any party. I vote for the man, and right now, Chan, I'd vote for anyone who got me out of this country."

"That's not what the president has in mind."

"Yeah, he rides around in a motorcade. We've got 8,000 Americans here hoofing it over frozen ground. Freezing to death. Homesick. And he wants us to stay indefinitely."

"Admit it. We don't want the peace to fail either."

"I don't call that skirmish in the South peaceful." Randy blew on his gloved hands. "I should have asked him if he had any room on board Air Force One so I could get out of here too."

"Hey, what happened to the cheerful patriot? Take some antacid, Randy. You've got political indigestion."

"It's the bloody war. Zineta lost everything. Her home and family. Her mother killed right in front of her. If the Hovics hadn't taken her in and treated her like a daughter, she would have ended up as a beggar—or worse."

For the next three hours they skidded over the narrow, snow-crusted roads. Randy's driver took too many risks. To keep from worrying about spinning off the road into a land mine, Chandler's thoughts drifted back to his last Christmas at home. He could almost smell his mother's cooking even now, as though he were wandering into her kitchen and snatching up a turkey leg or one of her freshly baked cookies before she topped it with sprinkles or slapped his hand.

That day Chandler had balanced on top of the ladder, capping the pine tree with a star. "Mom, why don't we use something different this year?" he had grumbled.

She looked up at him, biting her lower lip, that fragile smile mellowed with her soft words. "Not this year, Chandler. The star was my brother's. It must go on the tree."

He argued with her often, but not on her holiday traditions. Especially this one. An age-old star that her twin brother had made in school, a hand-me-down. Not much to treasure of a brother who died before his time.

He let the top branch swing back with only an inch to spare to the high ceiling, then scrambled down the ladder and headed for the door. "I vote for an angel next year."

"Where are you going, Chandler?"

"To watch the ball game with Dad."

"Don't forget—your grandmother will be here soon."

His grandmother—the worst part of every holiday! He liked her all right, but not in the same house with his mom. Grandmother Reynolds would swoop into the parsonage, a stylish woman with silver-gray hair, ready to take charge in the kitchen. He wondered why the two women were constantly at each other and why his dad, so sensitive to the needs of his parishioners, was unaware of their feuding.

After dinner, Chandler had knelt at the brick fireplace, feeding more logs on the fire and listening to the crackling and hissing as the flames wrapped around the scented logs. As they splintered, charred fragments dropped through the grate, the ashes forming burned out ruins on the floor of the fireplace. They looked like dark, desolate holes, black and empty, the way he felt inside, as if a piece of himself were charred or missing.

Across the room his grandmother smiled at him. "Come play the piano for us, Chan."

He tossed another log on the fire and went over and sat on the piano bench with her, his fingers moving skillfully over the keys. One familiar carol after the other. "Away in a Manger" . . . "The First Noel" . . . "Silent Night, Holy Night."

Yes, it had been a night to remember. But as touch-and-go as Christmas could be at the parsonage, it was more miserable here in Bosnia. Chandler turned to Randy in the armored vehicle beside him. "I wonder if we'll ever be home for the holidays again?"

Randy shot him a side glance, an amiable grin spreading across his freckled face, his bad mood on a ninety-degree turnaround. "Trust me, they may replace us with more troops if they can bluff their way through Congress, but *we'll* get out of here."

"Then what happens to the peace accord?"

"It's not up to us, Chan. We're just a stopgap, not a solution. Peace here is up to the Croats and Serbs and Muslims."

"But once we pack away our M-16s and move out, men like Radovan Karadzic would be in position to shell Sarajevo before our ships steamed out of the Adriatic or the C-130s had time to level out above Tuzla."

"What's the matter? No letters from home? No gifts?"

"Another tin of cookies express mail from my grandmother that took nine days to reach me. After one bite, I trashed them. I get letters but rarely send them. Since quitting Juilliard, I can't think of anything to nullify Dad's reaction to that one."

"Your dad should blame me. I'm the one who talked you into the army. What did he want—a ballet dancer?"

Chandler's deep chuckle sent his breath rising in puffy vapors. "No, he was trying to grow a concert violinist."

"No joke! Come on, Chandler. You're no Isaac Stern."

He rubbed his unshaved bristles. "Tell that to my folks. They put a violin in my hands when I was four. By the time they admitted I was no Menuhin, my voice was changing, and my face was a maze of pimples. That's when Dad let me switch to piano."

"Sounds more your style."

"It was. More my thing. I already played by ear. The lessons helped. But I still enjoy a violin concert. And I can hit the notes on a trombone when I'm in a room alone."

"So you need music to cheer you up! I know just the place."

"I don't drink, Randy. You know that."

"No bars. No carousing. I'm not out to muddy the life of a preacher's kid. But I still say you're missing part of life."

"The question is, which one of us is on the missing side?"

Randy lifted an imaginary beer tankard and said, "Cheers." His wide grin rearranged the freckles on his face in a pleasant, cocky way. "How did we ever get to be friends? It's like coming from the opposite side of the tracks."

"We're good for each other."

As the Humvee rumbled over a rut in the road, Randy flicked a peanut into his mouth. "Back home in Ohio, we have towns with broad, paved roads. No bombed-out conditions like we have here." He popped more peanuts. "I've given this volunteer army a good slice of my life already. Once I kiss the military good-bye, I'm going to buy me a farm along the Ohio River. My grandfather worked the old sandstone quarries and Dad was into manufacturing steel. But I want the simple life in the country." Randy tapped his temple. "Can I confide in you, Chan?"

"Why not? I've got all day."

He scratched his freckled cheek, grinning. "I've found the girl for me, Chan. If I can work through the red tape, I'm going to marry Zineta and get her out of this mess. We'll have six kids and stay so isolated we won't even know where the NATO peacekeeping missions are headed."

"You're going bonkers. Must be the turkey we had for lunch."

"Life is short. You grab at happiness when you can get it."

"Then I'll be your best man."

Randy reached over and clamped Chandler's shoulder. "I'm going to hold you to that. I'll do the same for you."

He was silent for a moment. "If anything happens to me, will you make sure Zineta gets to the States? Make sure she's okay—ready to handle life on her own."

"You're not even married yet."

"I will be. What about it, Chan? Will you watch after her?"

"Sure. No problem. But me—I'm going to spend some time in Vienna and Salzburg. And catch some concerts."

"You're really into that stuff."

"I considered going professional once. But about all I qualify for is writing music reviews. Nothing more."

"You do need some music to cheer you." Randy leaned forward and tapped his driver's shoulder. "Make a stop just ahead. You know the place." The Humvee slowed. "The Hovics live here. The old man's been traumatized by war, but he can still make music."

It was almost dusk when they pulled to a stop and parked. In another half hour, it would be black as midnight. As Chandler followed Randy to the house, he heard the distinct sounds of a cello playing a carol. *It came upon a midnight clear, that glorious song of old.*

They followed the music to the gutted home of the Hovic family and knocked. The door creaked open. At the sight of Randy a buxom woman in a long apron and black shawl swung the door back and gave him a shy welcome. "Captain Williams."

Her smiling eyes grew wary as Chandler stepped inside.

"He's a friend," Randy said. He glanced at the man sitting on the bed. "Keep playing, Kemal. My friend is a musician."

As music filled the little house again, Randy gave a piece of candy to each child, tousled Rasim's hair, and then turned uninvited to sit at the table beside a young woman. She was nineteen perhaps, and pretty in a sad sort of way.

Randy took her hand. "Zineta."

As he stared into the girl's eyes and she stared back at Randy, Chandler had the uneasy feeling that Randy had indeed found his girl. Their eyes held like magnets. Randy touched her cheek, then ran his finger down her chin to loosen the head scarf. He pushed it away from her face.

Take it easy, Randy, Chandler thought. *This is a Muslim family.* As if reading his concerns, Randy said, "I told you, she's Croatian. The Hovics took her in during the war."

Randy's eyes never left the girl's face. The scarf had slipped from her shoulders now, her wan face visible in the dwindling light. Her dark hair was cut raggedly, cropped above her ears. Her eyes were dark saucers as she looked up at Randy.

"I brought you something for Christmas, Zineta."

For a moment Chandler's attention was drawn back to the haunting sounds of the cello. He patted the old man's shoulder. "Beautiful, Kemal. How did you learn to play the carols?"

"Before the war the Croats and Serbs and Muslims lived and worked together, intermarried. We learned one another's ways and music. My family even sang the carols at Christmastime."

Chandler turned again to Randy and the girl. He was slipping his college ring on her finger. *This will never work. I've got to get him out of here,* he thought. Chandler strode to the table. "This village is off-limits, Randy. Let's go. It's getting dark."

He shrugged off Chandler's grip. "My friend doesn't like the darkness," he told the girl. "But you can trust him. Chandler here is a good man."

"Chan-leer," she repeated.

Chandler drew a circle with his crutch and for a moment focused on Colonel Daniels, as though surprised to see him. "That's about it, sir. Now the village is like a ghost town."

Daniels pointed to the de-mining teams. "Once it's safe, the people can move back. But why would anyone want to live here with its constant reminders of war?"

"Where else would they go?" Bladstone asked. "This is home."

"Are the Hovics coming back, sir?"

"I would think so, Reynolds."

But will Zineta be with them? Chandler wondered. Or had the army already transferred her to the British sector? Or the French zone? It had been more than five weeks since the accident. A lot could happen in that time.

"Was Christmas the last time you saw Miss Hovic?"

No, Colonel Daniels, Chandler thought. *I saw her in March—saw her peering through the plastic window covering the day Randy was blown away.* He remembered the horror on her face.

"The last time Randy—Captain Williams and I were here in the village was late in March."

"The day Williams died? Tell us about it, lieutenant. Are you certain that Williams didn't go inside—that he made no contact with the girl at all that day?" His lip curled. "Is there a chance he came face-to-face with the sniper? Spoke to him even? Let him escape for the girl's sake?"

"I don't think so." He had watched Randy's every move, except for those few seconds when he disappeared behind the Hovic house and reappeared. The gunfire had ceased in that moment. Had it been long enough to talk to Zineta or to confront the sniper?

Three weeks before Chandler's twenty-sixth birthday, when they rode into the Hovic village en route back to headquarters, the sniper had fired at them.

"Get out of here," Randy told the driver, then canceled the order, shouting, "Stop! That's Rasim Hovic in the line of fire!"

Not even three minutes all told. Randy was out of the truck before it came to a stop—that lean body sprinting across the field toward the boy. Another sniper shot. Chandler expected Randy to fall, but he kept at his marathon, scooping the child into his arms. Turning him around. Swatting his bottom. Sending him back toward the safety of Chandler and the Humvee.

Randy had halted for a second to glance up at the Hovic house. He lifted his hand, perhaps to wave. And then he was racing in another zigzag relay back toward the Humvee.

From thirty or forty yards out, he tossed Chandler a cocky, triumphant grin. Then Chandler saw the split-second change in his friend's expression—the surprise and gritty resolution frozen on his face. As though he knew. One foot was off the ground, Randy's balance gone. Then he plunged forward deliberately, his arms outstretched as he took the full blast of the PMA-3 anti-personnel land mine.

A loud, deafening boom. A blinding, white flash.

Metal fragments exploded toward Chandler and the child as Randy's body catapulted upward and tumbled back, his legs and torso slamming back to earth in separate pieces. Chandler took up the cry where Randy left off, but he knew his friend was dead. He jerked forward in an effort to reach him, stumbling as his leg buckled, not even realizing that he had been wounded himself. He staggered a step or two more, but Randy's driver held him back.

"There may be other mines buried out there, sir."

Lieutenant Reynolds faced Colonel Daniels again. "I couldn't help the captain, sir." The wind swallowed his words as he turned and hobbled back toward the Humvee.

"Let him go," Bladstone called. "The lieutenant has told you everything he knows, Paul. Don't hound him another second."

Later, back in Bladstone's cramped office, Paul Daniels flipped through the files on Captain Williams and Lieutenant Reynolds. He opened them. Closed them. Opened and scanned them again, drumming his fingers on his briefcase.

"Looks like Captain Williams was a poor choice for our special operation. And even our investigation on Lieutenant Reynolds has pock holes." He slapped the folders back on Bladstone's desk. "One of the boys at Langley swears that Reynolds's birth certificate is an amended document. If it is, that leaves us with some question marks on his background."

"Trust me. Reynolds's reputation is flawless, Paul."

"Trust goes both ways, Joe. Why doesn't his army record indicate that he's adopted? If he was."

"Adopted? Maybe the lieutenant doesn't know it."

"Come off it, Joe. He's twenty-six. Been out of diapers for almost as many years. Time for him to know the truth."

"What difference does adoption make? You said you wanted to tap some of my best men for a mission before NATO pulls out of Bosnia. That's why I recommended him."

"You recommended Williams too."

"My mistake."

"Reynolds may be another mistake. We've sent for his vital statistics. Adoption puts a new twist to our investigation. We have to know if there are any mental problems in his background. Any family history that would make us look like fools."

"Like arrests? Like a drug dealer for a father? Or some fraudulent lawyer-father who cheated on his tax form?"

"Don't judge us so harshly, Joe. Langley has to know the man's background, weed out any inferior candidates now. We're training an elite group."

"An expendable group."

"That's always a risk. But as long as we can maintain a measure of peace in Bosnia, we keep Washington happy."

"You haven't changed since Vietnam days," Bladstone said morosely. "You'd still sacrifice the cream of the crop."

"We need the best. As far as I'm concerned the old intelligence officer in the flesh is worth his weight in gold. We don't have to bring him down from some spy satellite." He thumped Chandler's file again. "I have to agree with you on one thing, Joe. Reynolds is a brilliant young man. A degree in physics. Close to a year at the Juilliard School of Music."

He tapped his fingers. "Quitting there so unexpectedly is another blot on his record; we have to check it out. But so far, everything considered, his qualifications look good as long as his background checks out. . . . As long as we find he didn't pass intelligence information to Captain Williams."

"His records in Bosnia have been excellent."

"Really? Until today we didn't know he was in contact with the Hovic girl. What if he let something of importance slip?"

"He's smarter than that."

"I trust so."

Bladstone shrugged. "I have other men to choose from."

"Until now I thought Reynolds was our best choice. A university grad. Good experience here in Bosnia. Single. No children. No family commitments."

"What if he takes Zineta Hovic seriously?"

"We can't let that happen, Joe."

"I wish I had never given you his file. You would waste him if it met your goals. I want you to keep him alive."

"No promises," Daniels said. "We have a few months' grace. Thanks to the president. No thanks to those in Congress who oppose him. But we need several months to train these men. And with this messy business with Williams's death, Reynolds worries me. He's had access to top security."

"So far we've found no cause for alarm."

I wish, Bladstone thought, *that you would pack up and head back to Washington. Back to Langley.* But Daniels was staying on at least until the senator from Ohio made his appearance.

Daniels drew him back with a question. "Do we have contacts in Vienna? I'd like to put Reynolds under surveillance. I want to know where he stays. What he does. Who he sees." The bushy brows knit together. "Every man has his Achilles' heel. I want to know the lieutenant's. If it isn't his birth certificate, it will be something else. If he causes us any trouble on his return to Bosnia, I intend to ruin his career."

"I'm missing something, Paul."

"We're trying to defend our military position in this country. Death by a land mine is a political disaster." Daniels's rugged face flushed with displeasure. "I don't like it any more than you do, Joe, but I'm only twenty-four months from retirement with Langley. Just enough time to get that elite team ready for action. I can't let Reynolds spoil that. Next thing we know, he'll want to put up a monument in his friend's memory."

Daniels ran his broad hand over his chin. "You understand, don't you, Joe? There are bigger things at stake than the death of one soldier. If we pull out of Bosnia, other NATO countries will follow. It's too soon for that. We have to stay on in one residual form or another just long enough to train a nucleus of intelligence operatives for this country."

"A little army of your own?"

"Like the president said, there's no way we can go down to zero troops. Williams's death swept the issue of land mines back into the headlines. That means public sympathy. My orders are to keep Congress from putting Bosnia on the front burner again, but I'm afraid Lieutenant Reynolds may not see it that way."

"He's lost a good friend, Paul."

"We've all lost friends. War is always costly."

"This isn't war. It's a peacekeeping mission."

"It's not just the young man's death, Joe. It's the girl. The CIA insists that Zineta Hovic was a courier between the Serbian army and Radovan Karadzic during the civil war. And there is strong evidence that she has been running messages between the Serbs in the hills and Kosovo even recently."

Bladstone whistled. "Does the Hovic family know that?"

"What is important is whether Williams knew. Whether Reynolds knows. But if that girl is working for the opposition—we'll sacrifice Captain Williams's reputation. We'll leak word that he was working with the girl—especially if she's still a courier for Karadzic supporters or the guerrillas."

"Then pick her up."

"That was the plan, but pregnancy complicates matters. She's carrying the child of an American officer. How could we sweep that one away?" He rubbed his jaw vigorously. "We have no way of knowing whether Williams shared more with her than a bed. Military secrets or Washington diplomacy, for instance."

"The captain served under my command. I respected him. But that won't matter." With remorse he said, "The captain was an open target long before he stepped on that land mine, wasn't he?"

Paul Daniels swung around and confronted Bladstone head-on. "If he was going to die, he should have done so before he met the girl. And if Lieutenant Reynolds's use to us at Langley falls through, he might as well have been blown away with his friend."

Joe Bladstone's expression grew grave. "You've changed since our army days together, Paul. You're not the man I once served under."

"And you have turned soft. What's best for our country is what matters. We both know it costs lives now and then."

"That *was* a Serbian sniper that took Captain Williams down, wasn't it, Paul? Not one of your operatives?"

Daniels stared back at his old friend. "The records say a Serbian. Let's keep it that way, Joe."

"Do you really think the captain worked with the girl?"

"We can't take a chance. We'd have to abort the whole mission." He stood. "There's one other thing. Lieutenant Reynolds must not contact the Hovic girl again. Make arrangements to have her shipped to the French or British zone."

Bladstone frowned. He had promised Reynolds that he could see the girl again before he flew to Vienna, but he looked at Daniels and nodded. "The French agreed to take her."

Five

It was only May but already hot as a summer day in Southern California. Ashley Reynolds sat slouched in the lawn chair, a trowel in her hand, her polished nails caked with soil as she surveyed her corner of the world. Above her it looked as though someone had brushed strokes of lilac across the heavens and added the fleecy clouds skittering through that lake-blue sky. A pair of mourning doves had taken up residence on the tree limb above her. She reached over and turned up the treble on her CD player, drowning out their cooing with Schubert's *Unfinished Symphony.*

Music comforted her, but no more than her yard. Her yard, freckled with spring flowers, dazzled her senses with sweet fragrance and splashes of color. The showy pink azaleas and stalks of blue larkspur. Salmon and coral impatiens in planters by the back of the house and creeping red phlox by the water wheel. The air alternately filled with the scent of sweet peas or gardenias. Velvety pansies still hugged the concrete walkway. She shaded her eyes with the trowel, her gaze lingering on the rosebush by her bedroom window, already blooming with tiny yellow buds. Her backyard was her refuge. Here she never felt totally alone.

Her yard was the one place where David seldom came; it was as though they had drawn a silent truce to give each other space. She stayed out of his pompous world, and David was too busy to admire her handiwork in the garden. They no longer danced stocking-footed in the living room, not since their son went away. And these days they rarely took time to drive up to Lake Arrowhead for a candlelit dinner at the *Seasons.*

She ached for one of those evenings there with David, sitting at a table for two overlooking the crystal blue lake, knowing that when the evening ended they would be together, alone in one of the honeymoon suites at the hotel—David's busy schedule left behind at the foot of the mountain. If only they could go back there, back to where they had gone so many times. Then it would be as it had always been, special, intimate.

But lately David was flying in every direction—too preoccupied in being the senior pastor at the magnificent Grace Cathedral across town. Too immersed in writing his theology books and his latest series on Living in Grace and Gracefully. Ashley could no longer define the topic, had no interest in it, had no warmth toward its message.

In their frequent, self-imposed silences, David sought his study and the comfort of his books. In relaxed moments, he took one of his favorite chairs on the sun porch, backed against the expanse of windows that overlooked Ashley's garden, but he rarely took notice of her flowers. Ashley found solace in the garden or at the piano—or on the cushioned divan, her long legs stretched out, her feet bare, a good book in her hands, the CD console playing softly in the background.

Sometimes she simply closed her eyes, trying to lose herself in the music of Bach or Mozart or Rachmaninoff. She'd remain there alone, trying to block out her greatest rival—her husband's schedule. David was too involved in being a guest speaker up and down the West Coast. Too absorbed two days a week as a university professor expounding his love of archeology. Too busy to know she was hurting.

They stayed together in their lovely, well-polished house, divorce or separation totally alien to David and totally unacceptable in the lofty position that was his. She no longer suggested it. If they could talk about Bill—if they could talk openly about their son Chandler—perhaps they would be happy again. Ashley wanted that. She longed for David to hold her in his arms, to make love to her again. Yet it was more than Bill and Chandler that kept them distant from each other. She had deliberately shut David out, not willing to trust him with the truth. The awful truth. Her own failures lay hidden in the coves and inlets of her heart. Now and then they resurfaced, and she'd tie a rock to them and watch them sink back into the abyss.

Ashley wiped her brow with the back of her hand, tufts of her short, honey-blond hair catching in her watchband. She tugged them free and absently examined the strands that broke off in her fingers. Dreaded streaks of gray were defiantly marching in on her fifty-four years. She dropped the hairs on the lawn and trowled them into the ground, hating even the thought of growing older.

She fought the fifties with facial creams and hormone therapy and with three days a week at the health club. And just last month she celebrated retirement and spent her last paycheck on a wild shopping spree that put a wine chenille tweed suit in her closet, her first outfit with a St. John label. She didn't dare show up in it at church though; that would set the tongues wagging. No matter what she did, except for her garden, Ashley's world kept falling apart.

Above the high notes of the symphony, she heard the persistent ring of the phone. She struggled out of the lawn chair and ran, stumbling at the kitchen doorstep as she grabbed the receiver seconds before the answering machine kicked in. "Reynolds residence," she said breathlessly.

"Mom. Mom, it's Chandler."

She grew faint, confused. It was Bill's deep voice. No, Bill was dead. It was Chandler's, their voices so much alike now. For a moment it was like an eclipse, like the moon obscuring the sun, leaving her in darkness; just as suddenly the shadows passed and her kitchen turned brilliant with sunlight again. Still she couldn't speak. Couldn't think. Months of silence. So much like Bill. Months of pain and now, as though nothing had ever put a distance between them, Chandler was calling. His voice sounded so close that he could be calling from next door or from his dorm room near the Juilliard School of Music. Eons ago.

"Mom, it's Chandler," he said again. "Are you all right?"

"I'm fine. I'm just surprised . . . pleased. But, darling, where are you? You sound so near."

"In Tuzla."

So he wasn't in the next room or in New York City, but halfway around the world, still part of the multination peacekeeping force in Bosnia. "Oh, why haven't you written or called?"

"I am calling. And I never know what to say in letters. But I get yours—and Dad's. You got my Christmas card, didn't you?"

And that was all, she thought. *Six cards in one year.* Bill's old trick. Bill's way. "Darling, we wanted to phone you on your birthday, but there was no way to patch a call through."

"Birthdays aren't a big thing out here—unless you count it as a day closer to being a civilian." She reveled in the sound of his deep voice, the remembered picture of the young boy becoming a tall, muscular man. Remembered his clean-cut manliness, that sharp mind, the lighthearted chuckle.

He was chuckling now. "What were you doing? I thought you'd never answer the phone."

She looked at the trowel in her hand. "I was in my garden." She whacked the trowel against her shorts, knocking away a clump of dirt. "The garden is full of spring flowers with a few summer buds breaking the ground already."

"It's that California sunshine."

She heard the sudden shiver in his voice, the wistfulness for something familiar. "So it's still cold there?" she asked.

"Bleak. It's always like winter, but the snow's gone, and I packed away my long johns."

73

"I am lucky—the weather here lets me spend hours in my garden. I still have the lawn to mow before your dad gets home."

"Then I'll let you go."

"No, Chandler!" She fairly shouted the words, belted them out as though he were still a child—scolding him like she did when he spilled jam or broke a dish or tore his Sunday suit playing football. "Please, don't hang up."

"Okay. Okay. I'm still here."

Don't you dare let me go. Don't hang up. She tried to picture his manly face. Tried to visualize him three years older. Cold and tired in a bleak country. "The lawn can wait."

"That's one good thing about army life. No lawn to mow in Bosnia. No lawns period. Mom, did you know I always hated mowing your lawn or picking up those slimy worms for you?"

And now you're picking through fields of land mines. Her voice tight with worry, she said, "I suspected as much, so it's a good thing I'm the family gardener, isn't it?"

"What happened to your nursing career, Mom?"

"I packed it all in a month ago—I told you that in one of my letters, didn't I? Just hung up my stethoscope and put my uniforms out in the thrift box for immediate pickup."

"No regrets?"

"None!" Did he notice the uncertainty in her voice?

"Hey, did you see that copy of *Time* magazine with my picture on the cover?"

"Yes. We loved it. It's framed and hanging on the wall in your father's study."

And we wept over it, she thought. Chandler's handsome, unsmiling face on the front of the magazine for all of America to see, for all the world to see. Just one of the army troopers in Bosnia, his auburn hair hidden beneath an olive green helmet, the chin strap tight against his jaw. She remembered thinking how boyish he looked with those pensive eyes looking straight ahead.

His father's gaze.

She had cried when she bought the magazine. Or had she wept over the clerk's words? "I don't agree with the White House," the man had said. "They should get our boys out of there, not send more troops in. A covering force? What will they call it next?"

"My son calls it a peacekeeping force," she had mumbled.

"Call it what you will, lady, but do you really think Bosnia is worth dying for?"

No, she didn't. But Chandler did.

"Chan, isn't your time up in Bosnia?"

"Long gone, but I-For isn't ready to pack it all in yet."

"Darling, don't take any risks with those land mines."

"Me?" he asked with an odd click in his voice. "Most of the time I'm stuck in a computer lab—a nice secure place. Don't fret. With any luck I'll make it out of here all in one piece."

"You're all right?"

"Fine."

"Your dad and I miss you. You're being discharged soon, aren't you? David will want to know."

He teased. "Tell him in three months unless I sign over."

"I thought they were going to rotate you home long ago."

She heard him suck in his breath, heard the distinct click of his tongue against the roof of his mouth. "That was plan A. I volunteered to stay over and finish my army days in Bosnia."

Her fingers went white around the phone. "Why, Chandler?"

"I'm still needed here."

"You're not reenlisting?"

"Nothing definite yet."

"Please don't."

"Why not? Bosnia is far from peaceful. If we all pull out—"

"It's not your responsibility."

"Whose then?" he shot back.

She felt the old floodgates opening and envisioned Chandler stubbornly piling sandbags between them. Next he would tell her not to meddle or coldly remind her that David's family pulled strings to keep him out of Vietnam. To keep David safe, alive.

"Mom, you haven't walked through these ghost towns or watched these people trying to put their lives back together again. I've seen kids without legs, without eyes. People without hope. Girls without husbands. Friends dying for no reason at all . . . and the rebuilding here moving at a snail's pace."

"Don't, Chandler."

"Don't what, Mom?" he asked huskily. "Don't think about it? Don't make friends here? Don't get involved? Don't fall in love?"

She tugged at another gray hair. "I can't imagine what it's like to live under siege."

"I can't either. But they burned their furniture for firewood. Scrounged around for a slice of bread. Saw their families marched off to concentration camps. Turned their parks into cemeteries. I've met some of these families who are trying to put their lives back together. I'd like to make a difference. I'd stay on if I thought I could do that."

"Is that why you're offering them three more years of your life? More if I know you. And if you don't reenlist, Chandler?"

"I'll stay on in Europe for a while. Maybe get married."

"You're not—you're not falling in love?"

There was a decided pause, long enough to make her heart race. *He's old enough,* she thought. *But not there. Not so far away from us.* "Is there someone special, Chandler?"

"A girl? Here in Bosnia?" He hesitated for a second time and then blurted out, "Yes, I suppose there is. A young Croatian."

"Is it serious?"

"It could be; she's pregnant."

Ashley's world spun. *The sins of the father visited on the son.*

"Will you marry her?"

"If I can cut through the red tape."

"Chandler . . . are you in love with her? A marriage of obligation—you mustn't do that."

Don't ruin your life, son. But the baby—the girl is carrying my grandchild.

"I'd like you to meet her, but it's impossible. No papers. And she has a name, Mother. Zineta."

"Zineta." She wrapped her lips around the word like a prayer. She sympathized with the girl, ached for her son, feared what would happen when David heard.

The officer's uniform had set Chandler apart, making him even more attractive to the girls at university and in the church choir. But three more years in uniform. She dreaded David's controlled fury when he heard his son's plans, feared even more what David would say when he learned about the girl in Bosnia.

"Mom, whatever I do, I'm staying on in Europe."

He was talking like Bill, demanding space of his own, willingly staying away from his family. But she couldn't scold him long distance, not when Chandler was paying the bill. Not when she and David were playing the same game.

"Why do that when we miss you so?"

He kept his voice light. "Yeah, I miss you guys too. But I've been checking into the conservatories in Bern and Vienna."

Her throat tightened. "You're going back to your music?"

"I'm considering it. If I chuck the army, I'll try my music again. Just a refresher course. I can never go professional. But maybe I can write music reviews. I'm good at that, Mom."

"A music critic?" He was sounding like Bill again. Bill when he was young and still at the university majoring in business and economics. Bill before power and profit took over. And now she sounded like Bill, saying, "That won't be very lucrative, Chan."

His tone rebuked her. "I wasn't considering the money. I just want to be happy. I just want to find myself."

"Reviewing operas and symphonies? You can do that at home."

The operator interrupted. "Reverse the charges," Ashley told her. And then she said, "Chandler, it will break your father's heart if you stay in Europe. Come home first."

"We'll talk about that later. Right now, thanks to my commanding officer, I've chalked up a thirty-day leave." She heard excitement building in his voice, excitement that hadn't been there when he spoke of the girl called Zineta.

"Mom, I'm flying to Vienna on the thirteenth—if I can get a military flight out of here."

"But that's just six days from now. And Vienna! You can't afford a month in Vienna on your army pay."

"I figured my budget would cover a pension. And I could flirt with a pretty girl who would take me home for dinner."

Ashley twisted the phone cord. *Flirt with a pretty girl? Had this Zineta already slipped from his mind?*

"But I called Grams and hit her up for a big loan instead."

"You should have called us, Chandler."

"And have you insist on my coming home? Grams was at least reasonable. You know I'd do anything for her and she'd do anything for me. Besides, she's too old to spend it all in her lifetime. Mom, she did better than a loan—staked me to a whole month at her favorite hotel in Vienna. I'm going first-class."

"The Empress Isle? You should have asked us."

"That's what I'm about to do. I want you and Dad to join me. Grams offered to pay your hotel bill as an anniversary present."

"And obligate me to her? I won't hear of it."

"You'll hear about it if you turn down her gift."

"You're too old to be taking her money."

"She takes pleasure in showering me with gifts. Always tells me—whatever I need, just call her." She heard him grind his teeth. "Come on, Mom. Money is no big deal for Grams. She's loaded. All you have to do is cover your airfare. Surely Dad will kick through for that. You do have passports, don't you, Mom?"

"Yes," she said pensively. "And the truth is, I'd love seeing Vienna again. But I could never talk your father into going abroad, not right now."

"Even to see me?"

"Oh, Chandler—"

"So he's still angry about me joining the army? He's had three years to cool down."

"It was your not talking to him about it first."

"So he could change my mind? Just tell that old stick-in-the-mud to forget his busy schedule. They have plenty of cathedrals in Vienna. He can have his pick of them. You and I can do the museums and take in a special performance at the Opera House."

She gasped. "That magnificent State Opera House?"

"I've ordered tickets for a violin concert. Way up in the high balcony. But wait until you hear who's playing."

Ashley dropped the trowel and stretched the phone cord to the limit as she sank into the chair, praying to the silent house that it would not be Kerina Rudzinski.

"Kerina Rudzinski is the guest violinist, Mom."

The room spun, ceiling to floor, forcing the door of Ashley's memory back to the hospital and the beautiful young woman with a Stradivarius violin beside her.

Ashley's voice didn't sound like her own as she asked, "But why Miss Rudzinski? There are so many other performers."

"I've wanted to hear her again ever since she performed at Juilliard three years ago. You remember. I told you about her. Mom—" Urgency filled Chandler's voice. "Are you all right?"

"Just surprised . . . shocked . . . pleased at the thought of seeing you again." Her stomach knotted. "But, Chandler, it's too expensive spending money for a month in Vienna and tickets for a Rudzinski concert. Dad won't want to go to that expense."

"Tell Dad I'll pay for the extras. It won't come out of the collection plate."

"Oh, honey, you can't afford the concert."

"I've saved up. You want to hear Rudzinski, don't you?"

She prayed that her words wouldn't betray her. "Of course, Chandler. You bragged about her music often enough in the past."

"I did? Must have been right after she came to Juilliard. She whipped out right after her performance before I could talk to her, but I never forgot her." He added, "She did her stateside debut with the Chicago Symphony. Back in the dark ages."

I know. Another eclipse passed between Ashley's eyes and the sun, blackening the kitchen once more. Her grip on the phone tightened. *Twenty-seven years ago.* It was the concert where Bill heard her play, that moment in time that had ruined all of their lives.

"I've scheduled an interview with her. Backstage after the concert." The phone wires crackled now, his voice growing distant once more. "There's a lineup behind me, Mom. Like a bunch of storm troopers. They're going to start tossing their canteens at me if I don't get off this phone."

"I don't want to let you go—"

"That sounds familiar. Gotta go, but, Mom, Vienna on the thirteenth. Okay? We're already booked at Empress Isle Hotel. Just come. I love you. And bring my birth certificate and university transcripts. I may need them while I'm in Europe."

He was gone, the telephone line disengaged, Chandler's voice replaced by the steady hum of the dial tone.

80

The phone fell from Ashley's hand, the receiver dangling over the end of the table. Her son was alive, well, in touch with them again. The thirteenth. The Empress Isle Hotel. He wanted them both to come. She must call David, but her momentary joy was suddenly snatched away. Chandler wanted his birth certificate. *His original birth certificate?* she wondered.

She pressed her face against the oak tabletop and wept. Give him that—unveil the secrets that she had hidden for so long—and she would lose Chandler. She would lose her son forever.

Ashley was back in her garden when David came home on time, surprising them both. He had loosened his tie and was carrying his suit coat in one hand, her garden trowel in the other.

"I didn't expect you this early, David."

He tossed his suit coat over the back of the lawn chair and snapped off the CD player. "I'm ravenous."

Flustered she said, "I haven't started dinner."

"We can go out. Maybe drive up to the—"

"You should have called me."

His eyes twinkled. "The line was busy."

"Oh, I'm sorry, David. I never put it back on the hook."

"I did. Just now."

"I forgot. I came out to pick some flowers for the table."

"You usually do that when you have good news."

He was smiling down at her, looking like his old self, the crinkle lines around his blue-gray eyes relaxing. His thick, wavy hair had turned a silver gray, making him look distinguished, gentlemanly. And she thought as she looked up at him—as she always thought when he stood behind his pulpit in those velvet clerical robes—that he was a handsome man, a kind man.

He leaned down and kissed her on the cheek, a perfunctory kiss that chilled her. "What's wrong, David? Did something happen at the office today?"

"Something special. Chandler called me."

"He called you too?" She pulled a bruised petal from one of the rosebuds in her hand. "Then you know about Vienna?"

He cleared his throat as he set the trowel in the flower bed beside her. "I won't be able to go," he said.

No, it was not the old David who had come into the house. It was the David who had rehearsed his excuses on the way home, ten miles worth of excuses. The smile was to keep her at bay.

"Another pastoral conference?" she asked acidly.

"It's a busy time of year for me. Lectures at the university and an article on archeology due for the September issue. And, Ashley, I can't miss that appointment with my editor. We're working out a new idea for the grace series."

"You're always busy. Doesn't *Living in Grace and Gracefully* include your own son?"

"That's not fair, Ashley."

In spite of the warm evening, she shivered. "Chandler wants both of us to come."

"He told me."

And did he tell you about the girl? she wondered. No, he would not do that long distance. "David, we haven't seen Chandler for so long. Are you still angry at him?"

"About leaving Juilliard? No—just disappointed when I allow myself to think about it. He qualified for a school like that and quit. Quit before the year was over."

She stared down at a clump of pansies crushed beneath David's foot. "It was the practice rooms. Chandler hated practicing alone in those windowless, airless rooms."

"What he didn't like were the long hours. But don't worry, my dear. I am not a brooding man. I try never to let the sun go down on my wrath."

And when that fails, you let your silence beat the sun down.
This wasn't the old David, not the David she had loved. This was the pulpit man again, the perfect public image that she had come to despise. The gifted orator, elegant as crystal, and lately cold as ice. The stranger she couldn't remember marrying.

"David, I find it hard to believe that you are never angry about Juilliard."

He met her gaze over the bouquet of flowers and shrugged. "We invested a lot of time and money in his music."

"It was something you wanted him to do, David."

"We both wanted it, Ashley. I don't believe in quitting once you start something. All he seems to do is mess things up."

"Don't say that. He graduated with honors from your alma mater."

"And threw it all away for the army. I didn't want that for my son. Chandler could have had honors at Juilliard too."

Inflexible. Unbending. David had dreamed so many big dreams for Chandler. But what about Chandler's dreams? His choices? *No,* she thought, *it was that miserable promise that we made to Kerina Rudzinski that we would expose Chandler to music. Music was Kerina Rudzinski's choice.*

"Juilliard was never Chandler's choice, David."

His broad shoulders stiffened. "Then wasn't it up to us to make it for him? With his background—we both saw his talent, his potential—" David bit off the words. "But as Chandler reminded me on the phone, a man has to find his own way."

"You didn't have it out with him again?"

"No, we had a good conversation. And I told him I couldn't make Vienna. He understands."

"Don't blame him, David. He wanted to go to work after the university. We're the ones who wanted him to go to Juilliard before he took a job. Our son went there to please us."

"Our son?" His voice sounded ragged. "The boy doesn't even know who he really is. We've lied to him long enough."

"We didn't lie to him."

"No, we simply buried the truth."

"We kept our promise to Kerina Rudzinski. A closed adoption. Chandler was never to know."

His lips turned as ash gray as his hair. "And I have had to live with that every time I stand behind the pulpit. But, Ashley, you made that promise. I didn't. You'll have to go to Vienna alone. This is between you and Chandler. And please," he cried, "tell him the truth even if you have to tell him about Bill." He touched her cheek, gently, his eyes suddenly misty. "Work it out between you so we can be a family again."

The barrier between them crumbled enough for her to see the painful candor in his eyes. She longed to fling herself against those strong shoulders and feel his comforting embrace. "There's nothing to work out, David. Chan and I are the best of friends."

"Is that why he writes so often?" David's face was a mask, his words restrained. "You're so foolish, Ashley. So foolish. Chandler has an appointment to meet with Kerina Rudzinski—an interview following the concert. Yes, I can see by your expression, you already know that. How long do you think you can keep the truth from him then?"

He toed the trowel with his shiny black shoe. "You must have been gardening when Chandler called. I found that in the kitchen."

"Yes, I was. Does it matter?"

"I hoped you might ask what I was doing when he called me."

She couldn't bear the pain in David's eyes. "Tell me."

"I had just looked up the number to the Lake Arrowhead Resort—to make a dinner reservation for tonight."

She stared at him. "At the *Seasons?* That's a long drive."

A sardonic smile tugged at the corner of his mouth. "You know the food is worth it." The smile had reached his eyes now. "And they have our old room. They're holding a reservation for us. I thought—I thought the two of us—"

"You should have asked me first, David." She felt a mixture of anger and irritation. He wasn't willing to go to Vienna with her, but he expected her to rubber stamp his plans.

His smile faded. "The phone was off the hook, remember? And I just couldn't ask you over the phone. I was afraid you'd turn me down."

"Oh, David, you know I wouldn't say no. Not usually. But now I have to start packing, making arrangements. I have a trip to plan, a plane to catch."

"Another time," he murmured, turning his back to her.

"David, it's not too late to change your mind. We could still go to Vienna together."

He didn't answer. He didn't look back but just kept walking, shoulders rigid as if deflecting her rejection. Then he disappeared into the library, his sanctuary that kept her out.

Six

Kerina stood on the port side of the *Swiss Jade,* her arms resting on the railing as the elegant river vessel slipped from its Passau moorings and began the journey back toward Vienna and Budapest. She had played here in the beginning of her career and was often lured back by the city's quaint beauty. It was here she had stowed on board an old fishing vessel for her first journey down the Danube to Vienna. Passau lay on the western branch of the Danube on the border between Austria and Germany, a university town where three rivers enclosed the city. She had come back to play her Stradivarius on the open campus as part of the town's multicultural celebration.

She waved at Jillian and Franck on the dock below and watched them part ways and walk away. Jillian paused by the Italianate fountain, and Franck strolled back over the cobbled streets with the ancient fortress and cathedral towering above him. Kerina felt the vibration of the engine beneath her feet, the gentle movements of the vessel as it glided on the Danube, heard its waters lapping gently against the hull.

A river had always been part of her life—the Vltava in her childhood, the Danube throughout her career. She had grown up near the crossroads of Europe watching the Vltava winding around the bends and dividing the city into parks and gardens on the left bank and a thriving commercial center on the right. Kerina had longed to follow the river to another world, to freedom.

She leaned over the railing of the river vessel and allowed the fine mist to touch her cheeks, much as she had done along the banks of the river in her childhood. Stone embankments and dams and canals held back the flood waters, and castles and old ruins dominated the shore as they did here along the Danube. Kerina wished she could lean all the way down and put her outstretched hand into the depths of the Danube, letting the water course through her fingers like tiny tributaries, making her fingers tingle from the cold. Once when she did this in her childhood, she had tumbled into the Vltava, slipped beneath its icy, wintry surface and came up with her skin so blue her parents thought she was dying. Her father had rescued her from certain disaster yet she had come up sputtering and laughing because she had been part of the flow.

Standing on the deck of the *Swiss Jade,* she was reminded of springtime in Prague with the gardens bursting with color, the river meandering by them to places unknown, many of them known to her now. She had not lost that childhood love of the river, nor the spirit of celebration when spring came. Her homesickness became acute; she longed to visit her parents on their farm outside of Prague. It would be months before she could go back, but she promised herself that when she did, she would spend time on the banks of the tributary that ran below the farm where she had often run along the banks chasing the flow of the river.

Even when she had escaped into the night and fled across the Czech border into Germany, thoughts of happiness along the river went with her. The Danube was her first memory of Vienna, the river that had carried her into the city and from there to the concert halls of the world. The breeze on the river caught her laughter. She was gloriously happy in this moment. *Strauss's Blue Danube. And mine as well.* The river that waltzed its way straight into the heart of the people. Vienna! The Danube! Linked as one.

She braced herself against the railing of the *Swiss Jade,* thinking back to the water lapping against the hull of the fishing vessel so long ago. She had been a frightened sixteen-year-old, huddled by the coiled rope and seasick on that first voyage on the Danube. Sick from the smell of fish and sick with fear. And lonely for her parents who were no doubt wondering where in God's world their child could be. On that journey her violin lay safely beneath the smelly canvas, protected from the mist that swirled above the river. Thus she was when one of the mates came sauntering over to her—his beard straggly and his eyes twinkling as he held out a mug of tea, insisting that she drink it. And then she was violently ill again.

By morning she had grown accustomed to the steady swell of the water, to the uneven chugging of the ancient boat. She had slept and awakened in the same place to find herself draped in the yellow oilskin of the mate and less fearful by the unexpected security of the cracked fabric against her skin.

"You will be all right," the man had said, kneeling beside her with another cup of tea. "Drink this, and then you can go below and wash up. I've set you out a pair of dungarees and a sweater to warm you. The mates won't touch you. I'll see to that. But if you be running away, then go home."

"I am going to Vienna to play my violin."

She slept again after that on a berth in the pilot house, her hand resting over her violin. She slept remembering home and those last few hours on the farm outside of Prague. Even as she slept, she knew that she must prove to herself that she was born to music. She would at all costs make her parents proud. No matter how many times he probed, she did not tell the seaman about leaving home or even mention the muffled voices of her parents and Franck talking into the small hours of the morning.

Prague—late 1969

In the cramped quarters of her tiny bedroom, Kerina heard her mother weeping. Her father's voice rose in despair. "Hush, woman. Hear Mr. Petzold out." His voice lowered to a grumble. "Speak your piece, Petzold; then leave."

"I won't go without Kerina," Franck said stoutly. "She can never play in concert if she stays in Czechoslovakia. Not without teachers or opportunities. I can give her both."

"She is only a child."

"Old enough to be put in work camps. Let her go while she has the strength to leave you. These days, writers and musicians are grouped with dissidents. Do you want that for Kerina?"

"Your father's doing."

"I don't follow the politics of my father."

"Do you approve the Soviet occupation? Where were you when Jan Palach burned to death protesting the Soviet occupation?"

"Your daughter is outspoken. It is unsafe for her to remain in this country. Leave her here and she will surely follow those who are trying to crush the Soviets."

"What side are you on, Franck Petzold?"

"I declare no politics."

"Then your father will have you burned at the stake."

"That is why I wish to leave and take Kerina with me. I have money. Power. Contacts in Vienna. I promise you she will play her violin before thousands."

Kerina sank beneath her eiderdown as Franck's voice hardened. "This is not a time for creative people in your country, Karol. Playwrights are being sent to prison. Actors and musicians banned from the theater. I will take her across the German border and on to Vienna."

"And we will never see her again." Even the eiderdown tight against her ears could not shut out her mother's weeping. "I can't let my daughter go. You will corrupt her. Defile her."

"I promise you, I will not lay a hand on her unless she permits it. I will always take care of Kerina."

"She's only a child," her mother sobbed.

"She is a musician. She could be a great violinist."

During a lull in the kitchen, Kerina drifted to sleep, only to be awakened at midnight with her father's work-worn hand gripping her shoulder, calling her to wakefulness.

"Get dressed. You must go with Franck. No. No. Take nothing with you but your violin." His voice caught. "It will be all you need."

He hugged her extra hard as he said good-bye.

She felt small, crunched into the front seat beside Franck, her violin on her lap, her bare legs numb in the cold, unheated car. Franck drove over the back roads, his jaw clamped tight, dots of perspiration beading his high brow. They rode with only one headlight casting eerie shadows on the narrow road. She dozed and awakened, huddling deeper into her worn sweater. Her fingers were raw from the chilled air. Still she clutched the violin case, her arms wrapped tightly around it.

"You will cross the German border as my wife. Say nothing."

"Your wife? I will not marry you."

"No," he said sadly, "but someday perhaps. You will play your first concert in Passau. And this time next week you will be in your beloved Vienna. I have arranged for lessons there."

She gave him a haughty twist of her head, a movement felt by him but not visible. "I already play well, Mr. Petzold."

"Mr. Petzold, is it now? But no harm." He reached out and knuckled her cheek in the darkness. "You are so sure of yourself, but we must polish your genius."

"What is wrong with my playing?"

"It is you," he said. "You must be groomed for the work that lies ahead. For the social world in which you will live."

"Do my parents know where I am going?"

"They have guessed. They will not oppose me."

"Will I see them again?" she whispered.

He braked so suddenly they skidded on the gravel. His fingers drummed on the steering wheel, his eyes blazing in the semi-darkness. "I have risked my safety for you. So choose well, Kerina. You begged me for the opportunity to play in the concert halls of the world. I have the power to do this for you. But if my father learns that I took you across the border—"

She feigned bravery. "Then do not cross it with me."

The moon peeked through the clouds and disappeared again, leaving misty-gray clouds whirling above them. "If there is trouble at the border, you must not be afraid."

"I will pretend that my father is with me."

"In a way, he will always be with you, Kerina. He loved you enough to let you go. He fears what I might do to you— but I have given him my word that I will always take care of you."

"Why would he be afraid of you?"

Sadly he said, "Because he says that I have a way with women. He does not know how deeply I care for you, Kerina."

When they neared the German-Czech checkpoint, he pulled to the side of the road again, edging against a forest of trees with his lights off. He left her alone in the car and walked ahead into the shadows. He was back within minutes, slipping into the seat beside her and pounding the steering wheel in his fury.

"Always before there has been one Soviet sentry here. Tonight I see three. There is no way that I can take you across the bridge in the car. And now I am the one who does not want to let you go, for you must cross alone."

"I do not know anyone in Germany."

"You will soon. Someone will be waiting for you on the other side." His hand was firm on her shoulder. "His name is Anton. He is young but wise. He will take you to his home and shelter you there for two nights. And then he will help you make your way to Passau. And from there you will take a riverboat into Vienna."

He sighed wearily. "Don't fear, little one. I would not let you go if I did not expect you to reach your destination. It would be best for me to be back in Prague before my father realizes I am gone."

Again he stepped outside and slid beneath the car. He came back reeking with oil. "In another few yards, the oil will all leak out, the car will stall. I will create a disturbance so the guards will come to me."

He lifted her face toward him. For a moment she thought he was going to lean down and kiss her. She felt his warm breath on her cheek, caught the scent of peppermint on his breath.

"While I argue with the guards, you must slip under the barricade and cross quickly. Stay low and close to the rail. I will keep the guards busy. You will have time—and remember Anton will meet you on the other side."

He patted her hand. "Now take that violin of yours and go. Do not look back. I will see you again soon."

Halfway across, she realized it was not the bridge swaying, but her legs trembling beneath her. Ahead she heard raucous laughter and saw the German guards inside the sentry enclave drinking, oblivious to her. She slid under the rail, along a muddy embankment, around the sentry box.

"Pssst."

She stopped creeping and listened.

"Pssst."

A shadowed figure moved behind the trees. A pebble landed at her feet. Another raucous laugh pierced her ears. A hand tightened around her mouth. A string of German words followed. She recognized "Anton," nothing else.

Slowly he released her, a tall wiry figure, little more than a boy himself, but confident of what he was doing, where he was going.

"*Kommen Sie mit,*" he said, and though she did not understand the words, she knew what he wanted.

They did not speak again until they reached the safety of the farmhouse. He couldn't be more than twelve, sturdy as a rock, a visored cap shading his brooding eyes. His mother moved away from the stove to slip her arm around Anton's shoulder. And now in the light of the lantern, Kerina saw the boy's likeness to Franck, so much alike that he could be Franck's son.

But was that possible? At sixteen, these were matters that she could not reconcile, but thinking back on it, she knew there was a kinship between them and wondered where Anton might be now, and if father and son had ever recognized each other.

Seven

Kerina was still standing at the rail of the *Swiss Jade* when Nicole McClaren joined her. As she turned to face her friend, the eyes of other passengers focused on Nicole. Nicole was elegantly dressed in an Italian pantsuit that emphasized her narrow waist and hips. Her slick black hair was brushed back from her forehead, highlighting that charming oval face and those luminous green eyes as cunning as a Siamese cat. But beneath Nicole's need to be noticed lay a warmhearted person, a friend that Kerina had come to treasure and trust.

"Kerina, you'll end up with bronchitis in this chilly air."

"The fresh air feels wonderful. Join me. I'm just reliving my first trip on the Danube."

"Hardly as luxurious as this one, was it?"

"Quite distasteful actually. But it's pleasant this time."

"It's still too chilly out here."

"Nicole, the only thing wrong with me is a stiff shoulder."

"Well, if it's still troubling you, I'll have you see my doctor when we get back to Vienna." She looked around. "I thought Franck and Jillian were going back with us."

Kerina tucked strands of her breeze-blown hair behind her ear. "Franck is taking a quick trip to Moscow to work out the negotiations with Jokhar Gukganov about the VanStryker painting. I wish you would talk Elias out of buying it."

She shrugged. "Once Elias sets his heart on a prize, there is no stopping him. He prides himself at the thought of owning two of VanStryker's works. So—did Jillian go with Franck?"

"As usual, they're going their separate ways. Jillian went to Munich to pick up her Saab convertible. She'll break the speed limits on the autobahn and cruise into Budapest before we do."

"She's full of surprises."

"Has been ever since I met her."

"She's such a charming girl. Where did you find her?"

"She found me when she charged into my dressing room in Berlin seven months ago and said, 'I'm looking for a job. I know you need a publicity agent, Miss Rudzinski. So here I am.'"

"You hired her! You must have liked her right off."

"There's little not to like. And I needed a new publicity agent. Jillian is never intimidated by my moods. If things are tense before a concert, she keeps everyone at bay—even Franck."

Kerina squinted at the fading sun. "She promised to give me a year of her life. Told me she had the right contacts. Knew the right people. Could handle my public. She has— and well. I was sitting there wiping the bridge of my violin with a soft velvet cloth. I can still remember holding that cloth in my hand and asking her, 'And do you have any experience, my dear?'"

"Did she?"

"I don't remember. I don't think I really cared. She reminded me of myself. Impulsive. Determined. Willing to tackle any task. And she was so beguiling when she said, 'Not much experience unless you count my flunking out of charm school, Miss Rudzinski. Actually I quit. I wanted to travel with my father.'"

They faced the river now, watching the shades of blue change as the sun dipped lower: an azure blue toward the shore, a foamy blue as the bow of their vessel cut the water, a murmur of blue in the distance.

"I've always loved the Danube. More so since I play Strauss's *Blue Danube* in concert." She smiled, at no one in particular. "When I was sixteen and first arrived in Vienna I was supposed to meet a friend of Franck's near the Danube. He was late coming so I sat down on the stone embankment and cried. I was so afraid the police would find me there and send me back to Czechoslovakia."

"And who rescued you?"

"The waiter from one of the Bohemian coffeehouses took me inside and gave me something to eat. I looked like a peasant in my faded cotton dress, clutching my shabby violin case. I didn't look any more affluent than the clientele. One grubby guest peered at me over the brim of his newspaper and asked me whether I could play that fiddle of mine."

"And did you?"

"I was afraid not to. The buzz of voices suddenly stilled. As I played a second song, the waiter poured me a free glass of *Einspanner* with whipped cream brimming over the top. That was my first concert in Vienna. I still go back now and then to play in that coffeehouse. Even today, many of them cannot afford a black-tie performance, but no audience is ever kinder to me."

"Both the celebrities and the masses love you, Kerina."

"And I them."

"I'm so different. In some ways I don't like the crowds—just my special friends. And I could never stand living alone."

"You have your husband."

"Yes. Dear Elias. I don't mind him being twenty years older than I. He adores me. I feel safe with him. I can't think of life without him."

"You should have had children."

96

"He still talks about having a child. But by the time our son or daughter was in university, Elias would be an old man. Gone, perhaps."

But you would still have your child. They stared at each other for long moments. "You never regretted marrying Elias."

A tiny frown formed between Nicole's brows. "I look and tease and enjoy tennis with younger men. I flirt as Elias calls it. It never goes beyond that. Elias is my husband."

"And you love him?"

"Put that way—I believe I do. But you, Kerina. I have never understood why you stay single. Why don't you marry Franck?"

"Because I don't love him."

"I didn't love Elias when I married him." Half in jest, she said, "There must be some secret love of your life, Kerina, that you've never told anyone about."

For an instant, a crumbling ruin along the riverbank caught Kerina's attention. *Yes, there was a great love of my life and so much more.* Of late, her son and Bill invaded her thoughts, filled her waking hours, dominated her sleepless nights, thrust themselves at her in her solitary walks along the Danube. There would always be a part of her that belonged to them.

Once remembered, thoughts of Bill seemed to haunt her for days or weeks on end, as they had been doing lately. Taunting her. Swallowing up her waking hours with what might have been. Reproaching, rebuking, tormenting her. Whether it was rekindled resentment or the smoldering embers of anger that had never died out, she could not be certain. Rather, she thought it the fact that he had been her first love, her only love. For those first five years she had waited expectantly, confident that he would keep his promise to come back. During those months she remembered him with kindness, like a treasure trove that was hers alone. So strong were the recollections that she could hear him laugh, smell the woody scent of his cologne, feel his thumb passing gently over her lips.

"You should date more often, Kerina."

"I do date. My dressing room is always filled with flowers from admirers who see me as more than a concert violinist."

"That Spanish count for one?"

"Yes, Ramon." The handsome count who bore a Spanish title and family recognition whose lifestyle was lavish and unfamiliar. And the Italian tenor who sought her hand between wives. The reserved British curator in tweeds with a pipe in his vest pocket. The jocular pilot who had ferried her from concert to concert in a private jet, a quick-witted man more acquainted with the sky and mountains than with Bach and Beethoven. And always Franck. Each one seeking her hand, offering her marriage. And yet she had remained single, unwilling to risk loving again.

"Flowers are not good bedfellows," Nicole said. "They do not have broad shoulders to lean on."

"But they have pretty petals."

"Not enough."

"Really, Nicole, I am not unhappy."

"Then you'd better redefine happiness."

She met Nicole's gaze. "Music is my passion."

"Another lousy bedfellow. Music fills your world, demands all your time. Get a life outside the concert hall, Kerina."

Music energized her, brought her deep satisfaction. It remained her gift to others, her claim to recognition. But now and then a familiar sight or scent or sound stirred her memories of Bill and forced her to remember him. Like this moment. She could almost sense his presence here on the *Swiss Jade* beside her.

She turned to Nicole. "Nicole, you were right. There was someone else. It's something I have never told a living soul."

"Tell on," Nicole said lightly.

"Long ago when I was only nineteen I was very much in love with a man almost ten years older than I." The mist from the river sprayed her face, merged with her tears. "We had a child. A son."

Nicole's thin brows arched. "But you didn't marry him?"

"I was already pregnant when I found out he had a wife."

"I gathered as much. Did you think you would shock me, Kerina? That I would turn against you if you told me?"

"I didn't know how you would react. I only know that lately it has been an unbearable burden. I had to tell someone before I fell apart like that old castle on the shore."

"Where is he now—this son of yours?"

Kerina waved her hand toward the children racing on the deck beside them. "There. Everywhere. I don't know where. I gave him away. Sometimes I go for weeks or months and never give it a thought, never allow myself to think about him. And then at other times—on holidays and especially on his birthday in April, I cannot get him out of my mind. I grieve all over again. He becomes part of my heartbeat."

"Kerina." Nicole hesitated. "Does Franck know?"

She marveled at the calm with which she said, "Of course."

"Is that why he holds such influence over you?"

"You know he manages my career. He was always there for me, protecting me. I was sixteen when he helped me escape from Prague with just the clothes on my back. I never expected to see him again—didn't want to—but a week later he joined me in Vienna. He followed me everywhere, even to Chicago. He built my career."

"You don't owe him your life."

"In a way I do. In Chicago when I was pregnant and frightened with my family back in Czechoslovakia, Franck offered to marry me and give the unborn child a name. He told me he would take care of us, and I could go on with my concerts."

99

She gazed out at the river, remembering. That day she had looked into Franck's solemn eyes and palmed his bristled cheeks and told him he could no longer protect her. But he tried. In the fourth month of her pregnancy he had found her a place to stay, canceled her concert tours, made excuses for her. Afterward, he arranged for her to go back to the concert hall in Chicago and pick up her career where she had left it. He had stood on the sidelines, waiting for the audience to receive her. But as she lifted her Stradivarius and played the sweet music of Strauss, her thoughts were on Bill.

In silence Nicole and Kerina watched the *Swiss Jade* dip with the gentle swells of the river, the cobalt blue waters flowing leisurely. Far behind their vessel, the Danube wound from the Black Forest of Germany, across the plateaus and valley, around the bends that revealed the magnificent landscape and countryside of Germany and Austria. Far ahead of them, it flowed into Hungary and Romania and Bulgaria, finally emptying into the Black Sea.

"The father—does he have a name, Kerina?"

"Bill. Bill VanBurien. I loved him, but it seemed as though I had no rights. Franck and Bill reminded me that my career was at stake. That Bill's reputation would be ruined. That the child could not be raised in concert halls. I would have to raise him in shame or let him go and bear the guilt as I have done for a lifetime."

Her voice went flat. "Thanks to Franck, clever man that he is, I've played in concert halls all over the world. He tells me I made the best choice for the baby, the right one for myself."

"So, Kerina, why does the choice trouble you so now?" She didn't wait for Kerina to answer but said, "Because that baby will always be a part of you. That's not wrong."

"I guess that's why I keep playing my music for him."

"You played for him in Passau last evening, didn't you?"

"Yes, out there on the open court of the campus. At least three other times when I played the Brahms Lullaby this year—in the concert hall in Milan, in the Bolshoi Theatre in Moscow, in the opulent auditorium in Monte Carlo—I played my music for my son."

"Elias and I were in Monte Carlo that night. I remember how splendidly you played. We talked about it afterward."

"My son was much in my heart and in my mind that night."

"And your music was never sweeter, nor the critics' reviews more glowing. Now I know why! Kerina, when your son was born, didn't anyone ask what *you* wanted to do about him?"

"I was too frightened to make decisions. Everyone else decided where I would stay during my pregnancy. Where I would have my child. Who would adopt him. The lawyer chosen for me insisted on a closed adoption as he thrust the adoption papers in front of me." She bit her lower lip. "There is only one good memory in it all—the nurse who let me hold my son told me it was not too late to change my mind. I will never forget her kindness. If she had been there with me from the beginning, perhaps I would have made a different choice. The choice to keep my child."

The onset of a headache came with the remembrance of Franck's insensitive remarks. "As a single woman, you can have no ties to the baby. You must not disgrace your family in Prague. You see that, don't you, Kerina? It's for your own good. It's best for the baby." Even his promise failed to comfort her. "I will make you famous, Kerina Rudzinski. I will make certain that the concert halls of Europe open their doors to you."

She had wanted Bill to hold her and tell her that they would raise their son together. All he did—all he could do—was promise that he'd make certain the child had a good home; then he had driven her to the airport and said goodbye. Everyone had wanted her to go on as though she had never given birth to the child. How could she? She had left a part of herself behind in Everdale.

She spoke now, more to the wind that swept across the Danube than to Nicole standing beside her. "No one asked me to name my child. I have no idea what name went on his birth certificate."

"What would you have called him?"

"William Karol—after Bill and my father. I think of him as William. All I have of him is one tiny snapshot—the one taken after his birth at the hospital. It's stained with my tears."

Thankfully, Nicole did not ask to see it but said, "It's a good thing I wasn't there. I would have shot Franck and Bill."

Kerina smiled at Nicole's loyalty. "I kept a snapshot of Bill too. If I ever saw my son again, I wanted to be able to show him a picture of Bill and tell him, 'This is your father.' It must be awful not knowing. I know it is for me. I'll wonder the rest of my life where he is. What has become of him? Is he still alive? Happy?"

"Other women go on with their lives, Kerina."

"I know, but the child ties me to Bill."

"The child is a grown man now."

But an infant in Kerina's mind. Tiny fingers. Tiny toes. Button lips. A warm human form held briefly against her breast, always in her heart. An unnamed child that bore someone else's name. Not Bill's. Not hers. Haunting memories possessing her, coming back to burden and disturb her quiet.

She smiled wanly. "Now you know why Franck, who knew about the child, became my refuge. My retreat. My sanctuary."

"But never your lover. Never the man you would marry. I don't know whether to pity you or Franck the most."

In the darkness that had overtaken them, the ancient castles and monasteries stood like blackened silhouettes on the craggy hillside, the medieval history of these villages veiled in the night. The women stood in silence as an eerie swirling mist rose slowly from the dark water. Five minutes. Ten.

Then gently prodding, Nicole said, "Don't stop now. You have carried this alone for far too long. Tell me just one thing. Do you want to find your son, Kerina?"

Her headache blinded her for a moment. "It's impossible, Nicole. It was part of the Adoption Consent that my son would never know my name. I would never know his."

"Kerina, somewhere your son may be searching for you."

Sadly, she shook her head. "In the town where the baby was born, there's a ledger with an original birth certificate that bears the time and place of my son's birth and what should have been my name. Bill persuaded me to register as Kerry Kovac. And I never told the hospital the name of the baby's father."

"And why not?" Nicole asked indignantly.

"Bill begged me not to. He said he was known there in Everdale. That it might make it difficult for our son."

Nicole mumbled under her breath, something quick and explosive in French. "Something deep inside your son may be telling him that part of himself is missing. Everyone leaves a trace, some hint of where they've gone. We could find him."

She was touched by Nicole's offer. "Perhaps I will find his trail in Everdale. I never planned to go back. But when we arranged the fall tour to America with five free days, I knew that I must go back. I'm certain that a couple from Everdale adopted my baby. Perhaps by some chance, my son is still living in the town where he was born. I'd give anything to see him—to see his father. Not to interfere in their lives, but just to bring closure for myself."

"This Bill—when did you see him last?"

"Days after the baby was born."

"And not since then? No letters? No phone calls?"

"Not since he left me at the Montgomery Airport."

"In other words, he walked out on you." Another French outburst had the ring of angry words. "Then it's foolish to cling to his memory. If you won't marry Franck, find some-one else."

"There could never be anyone else."

Nicole touched her lightly on the shoulder. "It's cold out here. I'm going to our cabin, Kerina. Don't be long."

As Kerina stood alone, Nicole's words thundered in the night air. "In other words, he walked out on you."

Yes. One moment Bill had stood at the airport in Mont-gomery, watching her plane take off, his handsome face a blur in the terminal window. Then he was gone, walking out of her life with not another word from him all these years.

Moments before she boarded the 707, he had leaned down and said, "One day, Kerina, I will make you proud of me. I will have my name in gold on the door of my office; I'll be the president of my own company."

He did not invite her to share his success. No, he would climb alone, right to the top of the corporate ladder. She thought now of the man that she could not describe to Nicole. Bill, the go-getter, the ambitious climber; yet she had loved him. *William,* his colleagues had called him. The tennis champ of the office, an expert player in spite of that slight limp from his navy days. A man driven to succeed—to surpass Kerina's success—and yet a strange composite of warmth and caring, of sports and music and poetry. The White Sox and Beethoven and T. S. Eliot. Dear Bill. Living on the cutting edge, charming her with his empty promises.

As they stood in the terminal that day, he did not men-tion Everdale, the town they had left behind. He had gazed down at her with those solemn, smoky-blue eyes, an un-ruly lock of blond hair slipping across his forehead. As the boarding call came over the intercom, he gripped her hand to keep her from leaving him and quoted Noel Coward's words. Bill's spicy scent and the sound of his deep voice were so clear in her mind that it could have been just yesterday.

This is to let you know
That all I feel for you
Can never wholly go.
I love you, and miss you,
even two hours away,
With all my heart.
This is to let you know.

Words that Bill had no right to say to her. Promises that she had no right to hear. *He must have known as he left the airport that it was over between us, that a publicized scandal with a concert violinist would have ruined his ambitions. Surely he knew he could not risk seeing me again. If only I had known then. If only . . .*

She coughed from the dampness in the evening air. Still she lingered by the rail, her thoughts turning to the family that had loved and reared her son for her. *Their son. My son.*

She had entrusted a letter to the nurse who had been so kind to her, two sheets of scented stationery with eleven wishes scrawled in her own handwriting. "Love my baby for me," she had written to the couple who would raise him as their own. "Be kind to him. Take care of him. Let him be a happy child. Take him fishing when he is old enough and let him walk in the woods and climb mountains." As she had done as a child, but hers had been an escape from a barren childhood ruled by communists.

"Take him to baseball games," she had scribbled on the paper. *The White Sox games. Maybe his father will see him there.*

"Keep him healthy, but now and then let him eat a foot-long hot dog or an ice-cream soda. And please teach him about Europe." She dared not specify Prague or the people of Czechoslovakia. But Europe. Pointing her son toward his roots. Her roots.

With her flow of tears blurring the words, she had penned her last requests for her son. "Expose him to good music. I want him to hear music. I want him to play the violin."

Almost as an afterthought, she had added, "And if you find it in your heart, teach him about God."

Kerina no longer felt awash with self-pity. Talking with Nicole had been liberating and left her with an unusual calm as she turned from the ship's rail and made her way to the cabin. Tomorrow when she and Nicole awakened, they would cruise the tranquil waters of the Danube, Kerina comforted as she had always been by the river. They'd visit the Benedictine Abbey on a ridge 180 feet above Melk and the next day glide into Vienna. Then overnighting on the boat, they would sail on to Budapest. With the pearl blue of the early morning sky shimmering in the blue of the water, their river vessel would pass beneath the Chain Bridge into Budapest where they would disembark. That night she would lift her Stradivarius and bring music to the people of Hungary.

Eight

At Los Angeles International, Ashley scanned the overhead screen for her flight number and welcomed the sign: *On time.* The crowded airport hummed with activity and a monotone voice warning, "Attention, all international passengers. Do not leave your luggage unattended."

Thankfully, David was there, taking charge, relieving her of the last-minute responsibility. Short of ordering a wheelchair so he could oversee her arrival inside the cabin, she was stuck with his attention. It was David's way of saying he was sorry she was traveling alone, but his not going remained a bone of contention between them. Even before leaving the house, he had irritated her more when she hurried from the shower with cream on her face and little more than a towel wrapped around her.

"You're not going like that?" he joked.

"Of course not. My jeans and sweatshirt are there on the bed." The king-size bed they had shared for thirty years.

David glanced at the open suitcase and pointed to her new wine-colored suit. "I was hoping you would wear that." His eyes were bright with pleasure. "You'd look elegant."

"I bought it with my last paycheck."

"I know. I wondered how long you'd hide it in your closet. I kept hoping you'd wear it to church and stun them all."

"You wouldn't mind?"

"I'm proud of you, Ashley. I like it when eyes turn your way. But wear what you want on the plane. Be comfortable. No matter what you wear, you are a beautiful woman."

She thought about the look in his eyes all the way to the airport. Their timing was always off. At that moment she wanted to stay home with him, and she could see by the wistful smile on his face that he shared her thoughts.

They raced to Los Angeles in a driving rain with David telling her at least three times, "Take a taxi straight from the Schwechat Airport to the Empress Isle Hotel. No matter what the cost," he insisted.

"After a red-eye flight, where do you think I would go? Out to a disco?" In her distant past, she would have.

He snapped back, "Chandler should be there to meet you, not expecting you to arrive on your own in a foreign city."

And if you were going with me, we wouldn't be having this row. "Oh, David, don't blame Chandler. He's on standby. Why don't you just drop me off at the curbside check-in?"

"I'm going all the way to the boarding gate with you."

The whole route, giving one last minute instruction after the other. Inside the lobby, he demanded, "Let me have your ticket, Ashley. I'll take care of it."

At the check-in, he handed in her ticket and passport, confirmed her first-class reservation and asked about the weather en route, about the food on board. She worried lest he'd ask whether there was a chaplain in attendance. Ashley almost walked away from the counter, but the clerk smiled and said, "I fly these planes often. It's one of the perks in the industry. Don't worry, Mr. Reynolds, our company takes care of its passengers."

David flashed a sheepish grin. "I don't like my wife traveling to Europe alone."

"She won't be. The flight is completely booked."

"I wouldn't be traveling alone if you were going with me," Ashley said annoyedly.

They made it to the boarding gate without quarreling. As sleepy as David looked, she worried that he would drive too fast on the rainswept streets outside the airport. "David, go home. Don't wait for the boarding call. You'll just over-sleep in the morning."

Without her there to wake him, he'd be late for his breakfast appointment with one of the elders. And then she laughed to herself. *We've been married much too long, David,* she thought. *All we do is fuss over each other.*

He stood inches from her. "Ashley, I'll miss you."

"I'll miss you too." But would she? She could hardly wait to get away from David's commitments and crowded schedule.

"Honey, if you need more money, I can wire—"

"I'll be okay."

"Ashley, you have your ticket and passport?"

"You gave them back to me at the check-in counter. Oh, David, stop hovering. You're suffocating me."

"Am I that bad?"

"You're like an old mother hen. You're making me nervous. You know I hate flying over the ocean at night."

"Then sleep all the way."

"I'm too excited."

"About seeing Chandler?" Misgiving clouded his gaze. "Give him a bear hug for me. And the minute you get together, call me. No matter what time it is. I want to know that you're both safe."

You want to know if Chandler has changed, she accused silently. *If Bosnia or the army has changed him. He's still the same boy, David. The child you loved.* The love between them was still there if David could only express it. If Chandler would only accept it.

David touched Ashley's cheek. "I hate to see you go away."

The old David. The gentle David. They were inviting first-class passengers to board now. "That's you, Ash. My VIP."

He hugged her and gave her a long, impassioned kiss, his lips hard on hers. The old tender David. Then, his cheek against hers, he whispered, "Go, before I won't let you."

On board, she dropped into the wide, leather seat and fastened her safety belt. The fragrance of David's cologne clung to her sweatshirt as she gazed through the murky windowpane, but it was impossible to distinguish David's lanky form in the terminal window. But he was there—would be until her plane leveled out above the clouds and headed toward Europe.

She touched her lips, treasuring the memory of his good-bye, her eyes filling with tears. *We've had so much together. We can't throw all those years away. I can't—I won't let you go.*

As the aisle filled with passengers, she studied the faces of the strangers, praying that she'd have a likable seat-mate, one who wouldn't snore or chat endlessly, one who wouldn't overlap onto her space or fall asleep on her shoulder. As the line thinned out, a tall man ducked as he entered the cabin, winked at the flight attendant, and gave a quick appraisal of first class before striding toward the empty seat.

He was fortyish, physically strong and attractive like David, his sun-tanned arms muscular and bare, his faded jeans too short for his gangly legs. A Tom Clancy paperback bulged in his hip pocket, a wedding ring glinted on his finger. He tossed his shaving kit and wool, ribbed sweater in the overhead compartment, loosened his short-sleeved shirt, adjusted his belt, and slid into the seat beside her, his tangy scent crowding out David's cologne. When he turned to her, he ceased being David. His nose was crooked, his curious, dark eyes too closely set.

He gave Ashley an amiable grin, tapped his Citizens watch and said, "Here's hoping we take off on time."

By the time the jet rolled down the runway, he had flipped open his book and was lost in a political thriller. *All you need,* Ashley thought, *is Tom Clancy's red baseball cap with USS Iowa emblazoned on the front.*

The plane lurched and leveled out as a gray, swirling cloud mass engulfed them, and they headed for Vienna.

The man ate in the same manner as he had boarded the plane, comfortable with himself and his surroundings, fingering a morsel of steak and shoving the onions aside. After eating, he sucked at a fragment of meat caught in his even white teeth and settled back against his seat as the attendant whisked his tray away.

"Wine, Mr. Gramdino?" she asked.

"Not for me. But perhaps the lady—" He turned to Ashley. "An after dinner drink for you?"

"None. Thank you."

He crossed his legs and tightened the shoestring on his tennis shoes and was suddenly talkative, as though he had been in need of time to himself and a good solid meal to counteract a last-minute rush to the airport without dinner.

"Your first trip to Vienna?" he asked.

"Oh, no, but my first one alone. I usually travel with my husband." She sounded haughty even to herself, as though this trip were a bonus accumulated from frequent flying hours and not one of those fast turnaround flights to religious conventions.

"Me—I travel on business to Geneva. Milan. Paris. Vienna."

The flight attendant had called him Mr. Gramdino. Now he filled in the rest. "Joel Gramdino. Brooklyn-born. Housed in Los Angeles. My friends call me Joe. My wife calls me to dinner."

His joke fell short, but she allowed him to shake her hand. It was a strong grip, his skin smooth, not the calloused hand of the working class. "I'm Ashley Reynolds. I'm visiting my son in Vienna. He's in the army."

"Tough—unless he likes it."

She nodded and opened her magazine to dismiss him. Long after the movie, high above the Atlantic, she sat with her reading light still on, a music magazine spread across her lap with the face of Kerina Rudzinski looking up at her. She tried to remember the youthful Kerina and quickly saw the similarities. The lovely auburn hair. The fragile, feminine features, the slight tilt of her chin. That sad melancholy look in her eyes.

The hulk beside her shifted restlessly as Gramdino stuffed the pillow behind his neck and sighed wearily. "As much as I fly, I can never get the hang of sleeping on these big birds." "That's my problem. That's why I'm reading this article on Kerina Rudzinski. My son and I are attending her violin concert."

He handed her a business card. "I'm into art appreciation."

"An art theft registry, Mr. Gramdino?"

"It's our job to track down lost or stolen art objects and return them to the owners. Picasso. Michelangelo. All the biggies."

"Do you have much success?"

"Not as much as we'd like. We haven't found that Picasso stolen during one of Rudzinski's last concerts in Vienna."

"Stolen during her concert? You can't be serious?"

"But I am. Elias McClaren was one of the opera house patrons, a wealthy art collector with a season ticket. Had his home ransacked while he listened to Beethoven's Fifth."

"How tragic!"

"It was, considering its million-dollar value. But somebody probably wanted it for his private collection."

"You wouldn't be the thief, would you, Mr. Gramdino?"

"Me?" He laughed. "That would be a clever twist." He stood, grabbed his sweater from the overhead and pulled it over his muscled biceps. "Now, tell me about you. Where you from?"

"Southern California. Everdale, Alabama, as a child."

"The deep South? Me, I'm an Italian Yankee." He formed a horizontal line with his hand. "With some folks just the edge of the mother tongue comes off. But you now, you've almost made that complete switch between dialects—from the south to the southwest. Everdale, Alabama, eh? Never heard of it."

"Few people have."

Nostalgia swept over her. *It's just a little place on the far side of town*, she thought. *Past the railroad track, almost to the county line. To Mama's house with the wide front pillars and fresh-cut flowers on the kitchen table, and the big living room smelling of Old English furniture polish and lemon. Even more vivid was the screen door squeaking as Mama came out on the porch fanning herself with an apron, her chapped hands as bright red as the sumac bush. Mama coming outside to check on her linens air-drying on the clothesline or to delight in a dogwood tree in bloom or to sit a spell in the wicker rocker. Mama. Mama.*

How quickly this stranger had sent her spinning back in time to the old family home, to the swings by the gazebo and those happy hours with her twin brother in the place where they had been sheltered and loved by the dearest mom of all.

A distinct Southern drawl crept back from her childhood as she quoted Bill. "Everdale is nothing more than a dot on the map. You have to travel miles just to reach the freeway. We haven't been back since my son was three. Twenty-three years ago."

"A long time to stay away."

She laughed dryly. "There's nothing to go back to. My parents and brother are buried there. I don't even think my friends would remember me—and those who did might snub me."

Gramdino cushioned his head against the leather seat. "Sounds like you've lost some of the good memories of Everdale?"

No, the pictures were there, as lifelike as ever. The wisteria vine, its clusters of purple flowers clambering up the fence. The sweet scent of the honeysuckle bush on a warm spring day. And then like black strokes against the canvas came the memory of a farm and barn in the neighboring town just over the county line. She forced herself to think instead of the brilliant azaleas blooming in the yard in Everdale on the day they moved away—and of her last

113

glimpse of the swings by the gazebo where she and her brother had played. Where Chandler had played.

She sat very still, trying to recall the song of the mockingbird and hearing only the rumble of the giant jet around her. She knew the dog days of Everdale had ended forever, the darkness of an Alabama winter coming hard against her. "Sometimes life's canvas gets marred, Mr. Gramdino."

He ran his hand along an imaginary line, pausing here and there like an artist dropping dabs of color on the canvas. "Going back home can be a great healer, Mrs. Reynolds. It worked like that for me when I went back to my father's birthplace in Italy. Sometimes it lets us find that missing canvas of our childhood."

He leaned over, his face close to hers, and turned off her reading lamp. "Good night, Mrs. Reynolds. Pleasant dreams."

Her dreams were frightening. Over and over, she saw a tall man in a ribbed pullover sweater and tight jeans with the face of Joel Gramdino. He was running over the blue gilded dome of the Opera House in Vienna, swinging over gold statues, a Picasso painting clutched in his hand. He slipped, tumbling to his death as the youthful Kerina Rudzinski played her violin onstage.

When Ashley awakened from her fitful sleep, Joel Gramdino was just making his way back from the washroom, a shaving kit in his hand. As he sat down, he thumb-combed his hair the way David did early in the morning.

"Is your son meeting you, Mrs. Reynolds?"

"No, he's on military standby."

"Will you be all right alone?"

"Of course."

"You have my business card. My hotel number's on the back. If you have any problems, give me a call. I know my way around Vienna. We could have dinner—" he laughed— "at your hotel."

As the jet descended into Vienna, her stomach tightened. "I'm certain Chandler will be here in time for dinner."

In Bosnia, Chandler Reynolds waited on standby to catch a military flight to Vienna. In spite of Colonel Bladstone's promise to arrange a meeting between Chandler and Zineta Hovic, Chandler had not seen her since Randy's death.

He wondered how she was; where she was. Then, as he stood by his duffel looking across the tarmac, he saw Colonel Bladstone coming toward him, a young woman by his side. It was Zineta, her woeful eyes fixed on Chandler.

When he held out his arms, she ran to him. "I thought I would never see you before I left," he said.

"Where is Ran-dee?" she whispered.

Doesn't she know? "They sent him home."

"He never said good-bye to me."

"If there had been a chance—"

"The last time I saw him, he was running by the side of the house." Her lips quivered. "I heard the land mine explode."

He took her hands and squeezed them.

"Kemal kept me in the house. He would not let me look."

"He was wise." He rubbed the top of her hand with his thumb.

"The Americans came with spotlights and trucks. They took Ran-dee away. Rasim said he died. . . . Is he dead, Chan-leer?"

Chandler nodded. He kept her trembling hands in his, offering her his strength. "I begged the colonel to tell you."

Tears filled her eyes. "Your colonel would not tell me." She pulled free and patted her swollen abdomen. "I have something of Ran-dee that your Colonel Bladstone cannot take away from me."

"The baby?"

She nodded and then seemingly aware of the planes around her, she asked, "Chan-leer, are you going away too?"

"For a month, but I'll see you when I get back."

She shook her head. "I will not be here."

If anything happens to me, Randy had said, *promise me you will watch after Zineta.* "I want to take you to America with me. Would you go with me, Zineta?"

"To Ran-dee's town?"

"Randy won't be there." He looked beyond her to Colonel Bladstone. "Where are they sending you?"

"I do not know. Kemal says the French sector. But I have relatives in Zagreb—if they are still alive."

"I'll find you, no matter where. I promise."

He used her for a shield as he searched his kit bag. He flipped past the rose-scented letter from Kerina Rudzinski's office and came up trumps. An address card for the Emerald Isle Hotel. "Take this. It's my hotel phone number in Vienna. I've scribbled my mother's California address on the back."

Her lower lip trembled. "Your mother will help me?"

"No, I will. But you have to let me know where you are. I have a plan. We'll make it work. If necessary, I'll marry you."

She shook her head. "Marry me—without loving me? That is wrong for you. I will not let you."

"But we're friends. It would get you safely to America."

"A business arrangement?" she asked sadly. "Is there no other way?"

"I don't know."

She tucked the card in her plunging neckline. "It is safe there. The colonel will not know I have it." She reached up and kissed Chandler. "Ran-dee said we could trust you."

She turned and walked back to the colonel, the palms of her hands wide, empty. Bladstone led her to the waiting helicopter; the wind from the rotor blades whipping her skirt against her thighs. She turned, waved, and climbed on board.

Chandler's eyes fixed on the chopper as it lifted and turned northwest. *They wanted me to see you leave, Zineta Hovic. Their silent warning that I am never to see you again.*

116

Nine

Kerina awakened, feverish, with a chest cold and a stuffy nose. She stole from the comfort of her large bed and stumbled barefoot to the windows of her hotel suite. Pulling back the lace curtains, she cooled her burning brow against the windowpane. Outside it was that muggy blackness just before dawn. Dawn, the hour she loved, when the first streaks of day washed the sky with amber gold. But the sky hung like an ebony canopy over Vienna, the stars and moon bedded down now, and the familiar landmark of the South Tower of the Stephansdom a dark silhouette in the raven sky.

It had been inky black like this the last time she saw Bill, just before her jet left the runway. Incredibly, twenty-six years ago. Yet every detail remained etched indelibly in her memory: the 707 soaring through the leaden clouds into the breaking of day, the light coming through her plane window like the promise of a rainbow. Color. Light. Hope.

The blush of that early morning lit a tiny corner of Kerina's darkness, the shades of light bringing with it a glimmer of hope. She was homesick—a stranger in a foreign land. A young woman without the comfort of her parents in Prague. A mother without her newborn child. A musician heading back to Chicago without a song. She pictured herself, her chin nestled against her Stradivarius, on a violin that would only play off-key. She had felt like one sinking in quicksand, trapped in a marshland of sin and despair by a romance that had nowhere to go.

As she boarded that plane in Montgomery with empty arms, she was numb—her fingers icy, her body screaming at her. Beneath her navel she could feel the hard round mass of her uterus. Her swollen breasts were gorged with milk for the infant son that would never nurse there. She felt nothing inside except emptiness and guilt. She had left a divided heart—a shattered fragment in the nursery in Everdale, the rest at the Montgomery Airport with the one person that she could not, should not, have.

High above the faceless clouds she cried out, "Oh, God! Does no one care what's happening to me?"

At that moment the stewardess who had brushed past her in the terminal stood in the aisle with her beverage cart, an angel unaware in her navy blue uniform and starched blouse with its red-white-and-blue bow. Leaning down, she tucked her own linen handkerchief in Kerina's hand. "If you need me, ring."

She pointed to the button on the armrest and then lowering Kerina's tray, placed a steaming cup of tea on it. Kerina nodded gratefully. As tears coursed down her cheeks, she turned her face to the window. Beyond the stewardess and the jet, Someone bigger than herself washed away the darkness and flooded her flight with the pastel hues of a sunrise. Yet now God seemed out of reach, distant. Unknown. Unreal. She wondered, with the psalmist, how she could find him.

Standing now at her hotel window, she watched the edge of the sun poke its rounded head above the horizon, brushing the carbon darkness aside as the Vienna sky went from a pelican gray to a powder blue. Morning dew was beginning to rise in a mist above the Danube. Milk-white clouds drifted across the horizon. Dawn came like a blushing begonia with ribbons of orange and gold; streaks of saffron yellow and garnet red splashed across the heavens. Sun filtered through the windows. She pressed her hands against the pane and scanned higher, beyond the clouds. Day had dawned over Vienna again, a city gloriously different. Vienna! Kerina's adopted city.

Today will be a good day, she thought.

In the distance she heard the clang of the first morning trolley, below her the clippety-clop of a horse-drawn carriage wending its way toward the Ringstrasse, and close by the sweet ring of the church bells. The spiraling towers of St. Stephen's Cathedral jutted skyward as though they had clasped hands with God himself. And if God did not exist—and these days Kerina could never be quite certain—at least the Gothic architecture offered hope to those more confident of eternity than she.

In this brief moment of quiet, she was without the thundering applause that would echo through the Opera House tomorrow evening. The prospect of performing at the Staatsoper accompanied by the Vienna Philharmonic Orchestra loomed as the capstone of her career, the crowning moment, the culmination of sacrificial years of practice and devotion to hone her skill, a magnificent grand finale. If she never played again, she would have this memory, this marvelous opportunity of giving back to the city she loved some of her deep gratitude—the climax of a career in the city where it all began. It would be like giving her own standing ovation to the people of Vienna for all they had been to her. Her thank-you. Her tears. Her applause for how warmly they had received her.

Suddenly, she remembered what she had repressed on awakening—thoughts of Bill. Ever since Jillian had shoved the copy of *Time* magazine across the table to her, the soldier's picture had stirred old, irritating wounds. Bill kept stealing into her thoughts unwelcomed, with memories of their son cascading into her heart, tumbling like a waterfall into the aching void inside her. Drenching her with the past. Depressing her with what might have been. Drowning her with what she had done. Stirring the dull, dead roots of

Everdale and making even June one of the cruellest months. Each time she pushed them away by turning the music up louder or practicing more diligently.

Kerina felt shaky, her flesh tingling as she turned from the window and crossed to the telephone. She tried to remember who she planned to call. Chandler Reynolds? No, Jillian would arrange to meet Lieutenant Reynolds with the tickets before the concert. So why did he creep back into her thoughts? *Because you have awakened the loss of my own son.*

The phone? Yes, she was going to dial Nicole's doctor and confirm her appointment; then she would ring room service and order juice and a croissant. This done—and an appointment secured for four o'clock—she hurried off to shower before the breakfast trolley arrived.

Early mornings were the hours when other musicians slept or sought solitude in the quiet of their own rooms. Kerina, for want of fresh air and the sights of the city she loved most, often promenaded in the parks or browsed through the Gothic and Baroque museums on the Ringstrasse, but she reserved Wednesday mornings for her visits to St. Stephen's. This morning, though, she had a nine o'clock appointment at the Opera House where she would look out over the empty auditorium and play a Brahms lullaby—the practice run for the greatest performance of her life.

With her violin case in hand, she set out. As she passed the concierge's desk, he called politely, "Fräulein Rudzinski, I have a message for you."

Distracted, she crossed the lobby to him. He was in his late thirties, an efficient, nattily dressed man with a clipped mustache and eyes that appraised her as she reached him. She gave him her most engaging smile as he handed her the envelope.

"Fräulein Ingram left this."

Kerina slit the envelope with her thumbnail and read Jillian's familiar scrawl:

Friends in town. Having breakfast with them. Will be back to go over the day's plans this afternoon. Sorry. Jill.

Kerina turned to cross the opulent, carpeted lobby again and saw Franck Petzold cutting toward her looking impeccable in his Italian suit, its deep charcoal complementing his thick, black hair and gray-flecked beard. As he reached her, he leaned down to kiss her cheeks and took both her hands, crushing Jillian's note as he did so.

His dark eyes never left Kerina's face. "What is this?" he asked lifting the scented envelope and inhaling the fragrance.

"A note from Jillian."

Franck's black brows arched. "She's gone? She knows that the hours before your concert are demanding. Where is she this time?"

"Off to breakfast with old acquaintances. Don't look so worried, Franck. It darkens your eyes."

She reached up to straighten the silk paisley tie accenting his pearl blue shirt. "Jillian is free to go off on her own. You know that."

"Who is she with this time?"

Lightly, she said, "With a lover perhaps. Or a secret admirer. Or Santos Garibaldi might be in town."

"Then have her followed."

"Franck, dear, her private life is her own."

"Not if it interferes with her work." He plucked at the sideburns that framed his angular face then flashed a sly smile. "Gone, you say? Then you are free to go with me to see Elias McClaren's latest art exhibit at the museum."

She nodded at the violin case in her hand. "Franck, I have an appointment at the Opera House. I want to check out the acoustics in the auditorium."

"Wait until this afternoon and I can go with you."

"I can't."

His eyes snapped as he turned to the concierge and demanded the use of the phone. He spoke rapidly in Russian.

121

"I will be an hour late. . . . Of course, I made the arrangements with McClaren. . . . No! I must go to the Staatsoper with Kerina first."

Franck's eyes were hard as he took the violin case from her. He guided Kerina swiftly through the red-carpeted lobby, nodding curtly to the uniformed doorman as they left the hotel.

"You didn't have to change your plans for me, Franck."

"I don't want you to go to the Opera House alone, Kerina."

"But it will make you late meeting Jokhar."

"Does it matter?" He brooded in silence, his hand touching her elbow but his mind elsewhere. In muteness they crossed the wide boulevard to the ring of buildings that had replaced the ancient walls of the city. The magnificent Opera House lay ahead with its majestic arches and curving blue roof and Renaissance exterior. Beyond one of the tiered fountains, the director waited for them. He smiled down at Kerina with bright, alert eyes and shook hands with Franck, then escorted them past the box office vestibule and up the grand, marble staircase to the first floor.

The splendor of the Opera House was an artist's dream. The interior glowed, the regal oil paintings and floral motifs on the walls giving off a golden reflection. Reliefs of opera and ballet and the ivory busts of famous composers filled the panels. They climbed the stairs and walked to the center of the stage to look out on an auditorium ablaze in white and gold. Kerina glanced past the orchestra pit and the gilded chandeliers and scanned the high balcony and the frescoed ceilings. She had forgotten the opulent beauty of the auditorium.

Without even looking at the director, she said, "It's hard to imagine all of this gutted at the end of the war."

"We took a direct hit from the Allied bombings, as you know. It took months to clear the debris and shore up the walls—and years to rebuild. But that was before you were even born, Miss Rudzinski. Destruction was everywhere. London. Leningrad. Dresden. Paris."

"I was only a boy," Franck said, "but I remember the bitter cold of Leningrad, standing with my hand in my father's and hating war and weeping over my grandfather's lost art treasures."

Kerina patted his bearded cheek before turning back to the director. "Were you able to arrange box seating for my guests?"

"Elias McClaren agreed to seat them in his loge. Let me get the tickets for you."

"Guests?" Franck asked as the director walked off.

"Friends."

Frowning, he lightly touched her waist. She felt the old sadness for him and turned from those somber eyes to open her violin case. As she lifted the violin, he said, "Play something for me."

She chose his favorite and played the second movement of Mozart's Violin Concerto no. 2, knowing that as the music poured from her soul it would touch his. As she lowered her violin, he said, "Don't stop. Play something else for me."

She played the opening bars of a Strauss waltz, the music resounding in the empty auditorium, and then with her eyes closed, the last few lines of the Brahms Lullaby. On the last note, she opened her eyes and lowered her bow. The morose expression on Franck's face startled her.

"You didn't play that for me, did you, Kerina?"

"No—it was for my son."

His taut lips looked like rubber bands about to snap. "It does no good to remember, Kerina," he said savagely.

She placed her Strad in its case with excessive care. "Lately, Franck, I cannot forget him."

"You will make yourself sick."

"He was flesh of my flesh. I gave him away, but I will never forget him. He would be twenty-six now. Did you remember that?"

"I don't celebrate his birthday."

She tried to smile. "Please, the director is coming back. He must not hear us quarrel. And, Franck, I never blamed you."

"Didn't you?"

"As you told me, letting my son go was best for him."

Moments later, she linked her arm in Franck's and walked slowly down the stairs behind the director. At the door they thanked their host profusely and breathed in the fresh air.

"Are you all right?" Franck asked as they neared the curb.

"Of course."

"You don't mind walking back to the Empress Isle alone?"

"Oh, Franck!" She laughed up at him. "If I can't get that short distance on my own, I am in trouble."

He leaned down and kissed her. "Then I will go on to the Academy of Fine Arts. Jokhar will be quite impatient by now." His eyes sought hers, moodily. "I will be back for lunch. Will you have it with me, Kerina?"

She took her violin from him. "I think not. I will just rest until Jillian gets back."

Ten

Franck turned and strode off, the snapping click of his heels taking him forward, his thoughts in reverse yanking him back in time to that farm outside of Prague, Czechoslovakia, where Kerina had spent her childhood. Kerina was fifteen when Franck met her, and he, all of twenty-eight, a man about town more interested in his feminine conquests in Prague than his father's politics. But his father's politics, not the pretty women in his life, would come between the youthful violinist and himself.

He was drawn to her music at a time when he was troubled by his father's political power. Later, during one of the concerts in Vienna when Kerina was eighteen, he realized that music and soul and the girl were one. He discovered then that he had already given his heart to her and could never take it back.

Prague, 1969

Franck heard Kerina's music coming from the thatched cottage where the Rudzinskis lived—violin music as sweet as the song of a hundred thrush singing. He turned to his mother. "Tell me about the girl with the violin. She makes beautiful music."

His mother patted his hand. "So did you once."

"Once, but no longer. But, Mama, the girl. Tell me about her. Her music is glorious, masterful, peaceful."

"You have already made up your mind." She shrugged. "So what is there to tell? She is Karol Rudzinski's daughter, Kerina. You be careful, Franck. She is too young for you."

He glared down at his wrist, still scarred from one of his father's beatings. "What chance does this violinist have, Mama?"

"None, unless she leaves this country."

The sound of a hundred thrush singing stopped abruptly. Franck strolled to the farmhouse window and saw Kerina race across the barren fields to the outhouse; a scrawny sheepdog yapped and leaped beside her. He watched the door shut, and he waited—as the dog waited—until it opened again. She stepped out smoothing the long skirt against her legs; then she leaned down and hugged the animal before running off down toward the river, the dog setting the pace. In that moment something stirred inside him. He was intrigued by the girl's utter sense of freedom, a freedom that eluded him. She was long-legged and scrawny like the dog, both of them jetting across the fields, her gleaming, red-brown hair sweeping across her shoulders.

The following Tuesday he sat in silence at the table with his father, his mother nervously pouring breakfast coffee for them. His father broke the stillness with a roar. "Karol Rudzinski forgot to bring the milk this morning."

"I can go for it," Franck offered.

"You? Then take this deed to the property with you. I need Karol Rudzinski's signature."

"But the land belongs to the Rudzinskis."

His father scoffed. "The country is state-owned now, and I want what is politically mine."

Franck tucked the deed into his pocket, took his jacket from the hook, and trudged over the muddy path, his eyes to the ground, his dislike for his father intense. Halfway to the cottage he thrust his hands into his jacket pockets, miserable at the task at hand. He was almost there when he heard the magical sounds of Kerina's violin again. He stopped to listen for the final note of Mendelssohn's Concerto in E minor. He wanted to clap, to demand that all nature give her a standing ovation.

Her music drowned out his knocking. He forced the door back and walked into a large kitchen with a woodstove smoking in one corner and sooty utensils hanging from hooks on the wall. Off to his right lay a tiny bedroom where the girl sat leaning against an iron bedstead, her legs resting against the white, ruffled pillows as she plucked the strings of her violin.

He crossed the room to her. "Kerina."

Still she did not hear him. Her head was bent, her chin secure against the violin. She adjusted the tone, a horsehair bow in one hand, the fingers of her left hand pressed against the strings. She struck a note and listened intently at the squeal. He watched the frown crinkle between her brows. And then she powdered the bow, rubbing rosin across it.

"Kerina," he said again.

Startled, she pushed back shiny locks of hair from her face and cried out, "Who are you? What do you want?"

"I'm Franck Petzold, your landlord's son. I've come to see your father—and to collect our milk supply."

"Oh, I forgot about the milk. Papa will be furious with me."

"You're busy."

The rough board walls of her room had been painted into a garden of wild geraniums and daisies, buttercups and pink camellias. The flowers dwarfed the room. There was little space for anything but her bed, with the chamber pot visible beneath it, and a crate that held her clothes, with a washbasin on top.

He stepped closer and took the violin from her.

"Give that back," she demanded.

She was on her feet at once, not as tall as he had first imagined when he saw her sprinting across the fields on those long legs. "That belonged to my great-grandfather. Give it back."

He turned the violin in his strong hands gently, as though he were holding a newborn infant. It was marvelous craftsmanship with deeply polished grain. "It must have taken fourteen or fifteen coats of varnish to make it glow like this." She seemed less wary. "At least that many."

He had read stories about Antonio Stradivari, the seventeenth-century craftsman, a stately, angular man with a solemn face and a cluttered workbench, the varnish from his works in progress often staining his leather apron. How many violins had come from the man's hands? At least eight hundred, Franck knew, with far fewer still in existence. But this instrument in his hands was a Strad, genuine, simon-pure.

Franck calculated its worth and saw it as money in his own pocket. "This is a marvelous piece of workmanship, an authentic Stradivarius. Worth much on the black market."

"It is not for sale." Her narrow jaw jutted forward. He saw fear in her eyes again as she said, "Please, do not take it."

"But it is worth a lot of money, Kerina Rudzinski." He twirled his tongue around her name, savoring it, teasing her.

She flicked back long strands of flaming hair from her rosy cheek, her eyes blazing as hotly. "It is more than money to me, Franck Petzold. It belongs to my family."

He knew at that moment that he would not take the violin from her. He put it back in her hands. "Play something for me, little one."

She sat down cross-legged on the bed and obeyed, her head bent toward the instrument, her loose hair falling forward and hiding those brilliant dark eyes. As her bow touched the strings, the tones came out rich and warm as the lilt of a waltz stole gently into the room. He knew as she played that he must channel her gift. He knew music and loved it and, thanks to his mother, had heard both Jascha Heifetz and Yehudi Menuhin play.

"Who taught you to play so well, little one?"

"My grandfather. My mother."

"No other teachers?"

She shook her head. "We never leave the farm, not even for school. Mother fears that one day I will flee my country and play my violin in a free world. You could help me, Mr. Petzold."

He laughed. "Why would I do that?"

"Because you like my music. And I will never give up my music—never give up my dream."

There was no future for Kerina in her own country. Stay here and her music would die with her. He could not let that happen. He could be her manager. She was worth far more to him as a violinist than the instrument itself. Again he calculated the price on the black market, marveling. "You are lucky that no one stole your Stradivarius during the Nazi occupation."

A mischievous grin filled her face. "My family wrapped it in cloth and hid it in the trap door beneath the old oak table."

"So no one found it?"

"No. But my father said no one dared play it during the war. The Nazis stole everything of value—except the violin."

"Didn't your family know what would happen if it was found?"

"My father says, 'You can only die once.'" Franck heard triumph in her voice as she added, "The important thing is that the Rudzinskis still have the violin. Even your papa agreed to let me keep it if my family farmed the land for him."

"As long as my father doesn't know its value, you are safe."

"Will you tell him?"

"No." He knew enough about music and the art world to know that he had found himself a young prodigy, a personal gold mine.

"How old are you, Kerina?"

"Fifteen. I will be sixteen in a few months." As Franck turned to leave, Kerina said, "The milk jug is by the door, Mr. Petzold."

He took the property deed from his pocket and laid it on the table. "I will leave this in place of the milk. It is the deed to this property. Your father must sign it."

Her eyes snapped. "He won't do that. The farm has belonged to my family for generations." She slipped off her bed and followed him to the kitchen. "I will not give it to him."

She snatched it up, ran to the woodstove and stuffed it into the crevice. It caught fire immediately.

"That was foolish," Franck said angrily.

She folded her arms against her chest as he opened the door and nodded at the stove. "Will you tell your father what I have done?" she asked defiantly.

His father would have her beaten, her hand crushed. "You would not be safe. My father is head of the secret police."

"Do you work for him?"

Wearily, he said, "No. I am trained to restore works of art. But for now, my father has me working in the office of records."

A vast room that detailed the life and statistics of every Czech in and around Prague as well as the long lists of art collections missing since the war. Paperwork that he despised.

Too many of those names had disappeared from the files— Czechs who had fought against the Germans and now resisted his father. Many had been shipped off to work the mines or fill the graves. Franck did not want to see the Rudzinskis shipped off to the mines or gunned down in the streets of Prague. He would tell his father that he had lost the deed en route to the cottage. Later he would risk eliminating the name Rudzinski from the city records and fill in his father's name as the sole owner of the farmhouse. After all it was merely logistics, paperwork. The Rudzinskis would never know what he had done.

The next time Franck returned to Czechoslovakia, Kerina looked more lovely than ever, her face as sweet as her music, her hair more rusty-brown than he remembered as she crossed the fields to him. She was beginning to lose the gangly look of youth, her body flowering into womanhood and her lips soft and sensuous.

"Where have you been?" she asked.

"My father sent me to Moscow for six months."

"Did he send you because I destroyed the property deed?"

"I never told him." He smiled down at her. "Do you still play your violin, Kerina?"

"Every day. I want to play in the concert halls of the world, Franck. Can you help me?"

"How? There is little travel permitted across the borders."

"But you are free to cross them."

"My father's politics give me the freedom to come and go. Where would you like to escape to, little one?" he teased.

"To Vienna."

"I have friends there. But the borders are closed."

"You leave the country all the time."

He smiled patiently. "Because my passport is Russian."

"Then get me a Russian passport."

He took her hand and held it, and she, childlike and trusting, let him. "Perhaps I could if you married me—"

"I don't want to marry anyone. I want only to play my music around the world."

He cupped her cheeks. "And you will play before great audiences, little one. Someday soon, I will help you leave this country." *And someday I shall marry you.*

When Franck reached the Academy of Fine Arts, Jokhar Gukganov, a tall, brusque, hard-faced man stepped forward. "You kept me waiting, Franck."

Franck felt the man's displeasure but said evenly, "I am here now. Shall we go in? I am sure you will find the McClaren exhibit worth your visit."

Gukganov grunted. "Have you checked out his residence?"

"Thoroughly. Elias McClaren and I are friends. We meet at the club whenever I am in Vienna. And I dine at his home often."

"You have seen his personal art collection?"

"Many times. The works of Degas and Rembrandt and VanStryker have prominent locations in his home."

"And his security system?"

Franck forced a smile. "Elaborate. State-of-the-art."

The man grunted again. "An impossible one?"

"A challenging one. But I advise against tomorrow night."

"Are you threatening me, Petzold? My only challenge is to get the Rembrandt to you at the Opera House after the concert."

"Not there. Have it delivered to me at my hotel, the day after tomorrow. I'll take it from there." *Hidden between Kerina's lovely gowns as we pass through customs at Moscow.*

"You are certain this McClaren will be occupied at the Opera House tomorrow evening?" Jokhar asked.

"He never misses Kerina's concerts when she's in Vienna. He has a private loge. And after the concert, the McClarens have asked Kerina and me to have dinner with them. That will keep them occupied until well past midnight."

"Perfect," Jokhar said, and he led the way inside the Italianate building and up the imposing stairway to the Second Gallery.

Later that afternoon, Kerina sat in the examining room, grasping the sheet draped over her as the physician studied her chart. As he turned to her with a benevolent smile, she focused on his narrow face where a ridge of worry lines tugged at his mouth.

"Miss Rudzinski, I can give you something to calm the cough—and a shot to relieve the shoulder pain. This should see you through the concerts at the Opera House. But, I think you know you have a more serious problem."

Kerina nodded slowly as he said, "There's a mass in your left breast that must come out."

Her stomach tightened as she thought of the windowless delivery room where her son had been born. The utter loneliness, the hopelessness she had felt in that hospital. "Are you sure, doctor?"

"I never make mistakes, Miss Rudzinski."

He seemed as cold as the metal chart he held in his hand. *You are acting like I am nothing but a number,* she thought. *A nameless person like I was in Everdale.*

She allowed her finger to touch the lump. *What if my arm is affected? What if it takes a mutilating surgery to remove the breast lump?*

"I'll have my nurse schedule a mammogram and a CAT scan on that shoulder—but even without these, I am certain you will need surgery."

"I am committed to a concert schedule—"

He smiled patiently. "We must move quickly to rule out a malignancy or the possibility of a slow-growing bone tumor in that shoulder." He consulted Kerina's chart. "I see there is no history of cancer in your family. That is in your favor."

You're talking about me. About my body. About my breast. She cut off his argument. "I have told you I cannot schedule anything right now."

She would deal with it later. She hated hospitals. Hated doctors prying into her life. A wave of nausea gripped her as she remembered the hospital in Everdale. The starchy professionalism. The silent condemnation. The doctor barking his orders and only once calling her by name. Maybe the breast lump was there for a purpose, divine retribution of some sort. Who was she to fight the dictates of nature?

She slipped from the examining table and stood there clutching her drape around her.

His patience waned. "The biopsy is a simple procedure—"

"Later. I'll schedule any surgery later—back in Prague with my family physician." *With someone I trust.*

He stood there—his pen poised. "I'll send him my report. When will you be there?"

"In November after my concert tour in America."

His exasperation broke. "Miss Rudzinski, five months is too long to wait. You could have a malignancy. You're risking your life. Music can't be that important."

"Music is my life."

"It is your life that I am trying to protect."

Kerina needed time to think rationally. She didn't need a biopsy or this surgeon to tell her there was a breast lump, its tentacles possibly spreading like spiderwebs to her lymph nodes. And that shoulder pain was real. More than a muscle spasm. The last few days her throbbing shoulder had made it difficult to hold her violin through long hours of practice. The doctor's words were ominous, but no darker than her fears. Kerina knew chemotherapy or radiation would follow any cancer surgery—and if surgery involved her shoulder and chest muscles, her bow arm could be damaged and useless in the future.

Her thoughts raced ahead to her fans—to the humiliation of hair loss. How could she accept baldness from chemotherapy, no matter how temporary? She had to wait until after the visit to Everdale; then she would fly home to Prague for a second opinion. No matter what happened, she could never give up her music. She had let Bill go and walked away from his child, but she could not endure that kind of agony again.

Eleven

As Jillian stood on the bank of the Danube, the fabled river seemed to stretch like a dull, greige fabric between the banks. Its waters were a murky gray this morning with only a murmur of blue to them; a fine, feathery mist swirled above the surface like the steam clouds on a mountain peak. As the day grew brighter, the grayness would catch reflections of the sky, and then the poet within her would see the waters as a hyacinth blue like a spring flower or as swirling pools of chambray. The rhythm of the river flowed like an unfinished symphony toward its final destination. Barges cut the waters, heading away from Vienna. She ached to go with them, to chart a new course or to find her way back to glamorous Paris or even rain-drenched London on the Thames.

Plucking a pebble from the ground, she tossed it. It dipped beneath the surface sending ripples along the embankment, little stirrings like she felt inside. For six months, she had sent her reports into the Coventry Art Theft Registry to keep Brooks Rankin appraised of Kerina's schedule. Jillian's suspicions no longer pointed to Kerina, but the more she defended her, the more she fell into disfavor with Brooks. He insisted that Kerina was behind what he called the concert conspiracy. He was like a bulldog gnarling over a well-chewed bone, snapping at anyone who differed with him.

As she made her way back up the embankment, she wished that she were meeting her dad at the coffeehouse instead of Brooks. Her father rarely told her what to do—he'd given up on that one! But she could count on him to listen to her. She felt somewhat cheered just thinking about him as she entered the smoky coffeehouse and made her way to an empty table by the window. After ordering, her thoughts raced back to her dad. She measured all men by him; Franck Petzold, Brooks Rankin, and the apron-clad waiter only came ankle high.

"It's the eyes," her dad had often told her. "Hold the plumbline to a man's eyes. They are the window to what he is really made of."

Her dad's eyes were a brilliant blue like her own, filled with warmth and rollicking good humor whenever they met for dinner in Paris or London or at the European racetracks. Between races, he expounded on the evils of the world and politics, pulling from memory his mother's firebrand lectures. Theodore Ingram took his own sins lightly, counting on his political prowess and hard work to carry him through, but he warned Jillian against piling up sins of her own. He considered the racetrack a proper setting for teaching her what little he knew about God.

"After all," he reminded her once as the thoroughbreds had raced past them, "there goes one of God's greatest creations."

She had placed a bet on a horse three or four times from the sheer anticipated pleasure of having an opening line in her letter home. But more often she took refuge in one of the cathedrals of Europe to hash out the sin questions. She felt better for having done so, but she was uncertain of her own standing with God. She was convinced that he kept accounts, but she was not sure how the record stacked against her.

She started in on her *mohnstrudel* and mocha. Brooks was already late, reminding her of Santos. She still felt the singe marks from that fruitless romance in Rome two years ago. But she planned to marry when the right man came along. She wouldn't mind at all if he came a bit like her dad—tall and good-looking in a new Rolls Royce, someone who would literally sweep her off her feet. But she was cautious too; she wanted the man she married to be faithful, more single-minded than Santos had been.

She was two-thirds through her strudel when Brooks came puffing into the cafe, annoyingly late, his blowzy face bloated and red. He collapsed into the seat across from her, dropping like an overloaded sandbag. He was an obese forty-year-old with a rotund abdomen and heavy jowls. He snatched a piece of strudel from her plate and stuffed it into his mouth.

"We'll order more," he said, his mouth full.

"None for me, Brooks."

"For me then."

Surprisingly his hands were smooth and undimpled as he folded them on the tabletop and demanded of the waiter, "Black coffee and three pieces of strudel, please."

His eyes, his strongest feature, were perceptive as he checked out the room. "I have a man coming from our Los Angeles office. But Joel Gramdino won't like this crowded place one bit."

Outside, the Danube played its own whispering music. Joel Gramdino, Jillian decided, would find the coffeehouse quaint, the coffee extraordinary, and the river glorious.

"Brooks, we can chat here for hours, undisturbed. Talking politics or art theft won't even bother our neighbors. That's why we're here, isn't it? To discuss Kerina and art and politics?"

"Why else would I fly over from London? This is Miss Rudzinski's second time back into Vienna in a short period of time. That's the pattern—that's when the thefts happen."

She disliked defending Kerina over strudel and coffee. But common sense told her that another art theft was possible. Loyalty forced her to deny it. "Kerina is not a common thief," she said.

"I'm only interested in the concert thefts. And her concert tours tie in with the statistics. She's a clever thief—plans the robberies in conjunction with her performances."

She and Brooks had been at odds from the beginning, a total surprise to Jillian, who liked people and could number her enemies on one hand, three fingers down. How brazen she had been when she had first burst into the Coventry Art Theft Registry with her perfect seven-point plan for tracking down stolen art: Know the art world—she had cut her teeth on art since she was a child. Keep contacts with the art dealers on the European scene—she knew two middle men on the Black Market, more useful to her out of prison. Recognize authenticity, suspect frauds. Acquaint yourself with the brush strokes and colors of a given artist and know the paint media he used. Trust your instincts.

Brooks stirred. "There's Joel Gramdino now."

He directed his wave toward a lanky American in jeans and a yellow sweater barreling his way toward their table. His arrogant stride annoyed her. So did his greeting.

"Hi, sweetheart. Looks like we'll be working together."

When he took the chair beside her, however, his eyes were not flirtatious but warm and kind. She knew in that instant Gramdino was a likely confidant, someone who would not destroy Kerina's career without knowing the truth.

"I was afraid you didn't get my message," Brooks said.

"Didn't get to the hotel until an hour ago."

"Then you didn't oversleep?"

"No sleep at all," Gramdino said cheerfully. "Couldn't doze on the plane, and once the plane touched down, I caught a taxi to the Academy of Fine Arts. The curator gave me a special tour before they opened the museum. Met Elias McClaren before I left."

Brooks ran his stubby fingers through his tufts of frowzy hair. "So what do you think? Is the McClaren exhibit safe?"

"No one in his right mind will touch that security system."

"So you don't expect trouble tomorrow night?"

"I'm expecting it, but not at the museum—so I promised McClaren that we could put a double guard on his home."

Rankin steamed. "Who's in charge here? We can't afford to protect all the art collectors with season tickets to the Opera House. We don't even know where the thief will strike next."

"Better to safeguard the collections than to search for stolen art. But cheer up, Rankin. In time our work will pay off." Joel turned to Jillian. "Our thief has good taste. A portrait by Joseph of Derby. A candelabra from the Nazi trove at Weimar. A black-and-white drawing by Michelangelo. And a landscape straight off the wall at Boston's Isabella Stewart Museum. Left a faded spot on the wall where it used to hang."

"And McClaren's valuable Rembrandt," Brooks mumbled.

Joel leaned back in his chair and smiled. "Tell me about you, Jillie. Brooks tells me you know the European scene."

She relaxed a little. "I should. Dad's career with the State Department allowed us to live abroad most of my life. I grew up browsing in art museums and sitting through glorious concerts—part of Mother's developmental program for her only daughter. I was lucky. Even did my university studies in Rome and Paris."

She grinned at the surprise on Gramdino's face. "From Dad I learned about horse races and polo, from Mom an appreciation for the world of art and music. I admit it's a vagabond existence, but I have my father's traveling spirit. I only need a twenty-minute warning to pack up and catch a plane to somewhere new."

Joel took three sips of coffee. "And Brooks tells me you're a fair musician in your own right."

She liked his casual way of prying. "You could call it that. I learned the cello after a few effective swats on the bumpkin."

"Ouch," he said.

"It was okay. I practiced my music lessons in exchange for free ski trips to Switzerland and Italy. My language skills came in handy on the slopes. I'm really good in Italian."

Joel cocked his head. "I only know the Brooklyn version."

As they talked, Brooks ordered another cut of strudel. He looked sullen, the way he had the day Jillian sashayed into the Registry for her first interview. She had arrived fresh from a year at a university in Rome—the perfect measurements in a fashionable Italian suit. She gave him a courteous nod when they were introduced, but her side glance had taken in his size as too heavy; the state of his breathing as labored; and his facial scowl as directed at her. His art credentials were flawless, but she hadn't looked forward to working with him.

"No matter what Brooks tells you, Joel, I can handle any assignment the Registry throws at me."

"Except this one with the concert violinist?"

Her gaze lowered. She wanted to salvage her pride. "I didn't count on my friendship with Kerina."

"Trust me, Jillie. We've followed this concert conspiracy for seven years. If the statistics are correct, we can expect another theft to occur while Miss Rudzinski is in concert. So far the loss runs into the millions." He looked up from the report. "The thefts usually occur on her second visit to the city. It happened that way in Milan and Paris and Monaco. It happened in London at the Tate Gallery. And once in La Paz. Twice in New York. On Miss Rudzinski's last tour in the States, we had a theft at the Dorothy Chambers Pavilion in Los Angeles."

Rankins rasped, "It's one masterpiece at a time."

Joel's high brows arched above his bright eyes. "What Brooks insists on calling the concert conspiracy, I choose to call the Strauss Waltz." The corners of his wide mouth curled in a smile. "She plays a Strauss waltz and a painting disappears. So far we can't prove it. But there's a link somehow—a signal to the thief maybe. In the last three years, there was an occasional break in the pattern—like those times in Budapest and Rio de Janeiro."

"Break," Rankin scoffed. "The thief got bolder and got away with two paintings and laughed all the way to the Black Market."

Gramdino offset Rankin's harshness saying, "Jillie, you know our Registry has twenty-four information centers around the world all linked to our central computer system in London. We're tapped into Interpol, sharing information. We'd be informed the moment something sold on the Black Market or went under the gavel at an auction house. So far none of the missing pieces have shown up."

Brooks shot back, "Rudzinski is masterminding this."

Gramdino stretched his long arms in a relaxed, unhurried motion. "This is where Brooks and I differ. I believe we have a thief who works alone, then uses other innocent victims to transport the stolen masterpieces." Joel took his pen and sketched a picture on the notes in front of him. "This is not an ordinary thief. No, we have a much more sophisticated gentleman, a nonviolent person. A modern-day buccaneer in a tailored suit who moves in high society and makes friends with art collectors and museum personnel. Do you know anyone like that, Jillie?"

He went on sketching, his strokes sharp, definite. "He's unattached, most likely. He could not risk a wife or children betraying him." He squinted at his drawing and added another line or two and then looked up, his gaze meeting Jillian's across the table. "You may know the man and not know that you've met him."

Her voice wavered. "Do you have someone in mind, Joel?"

"Do you?"

Her thoughts fled unwillingly to Franck Petzold who spent his free time in art museums and flying to Moscow. *A shrewd opportunist. Cunning. Resourceful. But a thief, a modern-day buccaneer? Not Franck. He is not daring or clever enough.*

Joel held up his sketch, a silhouette in black ink of a stately, well-dressed man. "Well?"

"He's faceless."

He winked at her. "But I think we have the profile of a man who loves art as you do. And steals something that will

141

give him great pleasure in the privacy of his own home. Not a con artist."

Abruptly he said, "Many of these treasures once hung in the homes of the wealthy Jews of Europe." He scratched his nose with his uncapped pen. "Hundreds of them were probably stolen during Nazi occupation. Elias McClaren may have purchased a number of these at auction sales."

Brooks's leathery face tightened. "A VanStryker for one, but we can't confirm that without access to his paintings. McClaren and Miss Rudzinski's manager are close friends."

Gramdino said, "Jillie, do you have a problem with Miss Rudzinski's manager?"

She turned scarlet. "A personal one. I don't like him, but I doubt that he's a thief."

He nodded, not pressing her further. "Can you get me a copy of tomorrow's concert program? I must know if Miss Rudzinski has scheduled a Strauss waltz. That could be her signal—and if not one deliberately given, then one used by a very clever thief."

Bridling, Jillian nodded. "Strauss is one of her favorite composers. Of course she plays his music—especially in Vienna."

Joel referred to the list in his hands again. "Rudzinski is just back from concerts in Passau and Budapest. After Vienna, she goes to Salzburg and then to Milan for a three-day engagement at the La Scala. And in the fall she leaves for the States."

"I know her schedule. I arranged it. So put padlocks on the Metropolitan Museum and the Getty Museum when she's in town."

"The police departments in New York City and Los Angeles have special teams to deal with art theft. We'll alert them when Rudzinski is scheduled in their cities. But if her schedule changes unexpectedly, we need to know."

Jillian felt color drain from her face. "Her manager just arranged a brief visit to Moscow before the Salzburg concert."

"Immediately after Vienna?" Rankin snapped. "She could be fencing another painting in Moscow."

"Nothing has been stolen yet," Jillian reminded him.

"Jillian, I'm pulling you off the case now."

"Don't do that. Kerina needs me. I promised her six more months of my service. I intend to keep that promise."

"And if we pull you off the case today?"

In view of her mounting frustration, she was surprised at the calm in her voice. "Then you would leave me no choice but to resign, effective immediately."

As Jillian and Gramdino left the coffeehouse together, she glanced at her watch, her face still flushed with anger.

"Expecting someone?" he asked.

She hesitated, then feeling those kind eyes on her, said, "An army officer from Bosnia is due in this afternoon. A music critic. He has an appointment to interview Kerina."

"All the way from Bosnia? You have the strangest friends." He laughed as he flipped open a pocket notebook. "Let me have his name as well as any staff member working with Miss Rudzinski."

"You're putting the American soldier on your suspect list?" She felt flustered under that steady gaze. "Chandler Reynolds. If you want to see him, I'm scheduled to meet him in the lobby of the Opera House tomorrow evening to give him his loge tickets."

"Expensive seating for a soldier boy?"

"Kerina's orders. She always goes first class."

As he flicked loose strands of hair from his forehead, she thought again, *You are much younger than your silver hair indicates. Much kinder than Brooks imagines.*

"Does she do that often? Give tickets away?"

"She's very generous."

"I see," he said, and she wondered if he did.

Twelve

Ashley Reynolds checked into the Empress Isle Hotel hours before Chandler was due to arrive. Even with jet lag, she marveled at the opulent good taste in the nineteenth-century furnishings and the personal attention from the staff. The maids and the concierge, the desk clerks and the uniformed bell porters smiled pleasantly as they moved over the carpeted lobby on their soundless leather soles. She chose to walk the palatial cascade of steps rather than ride up to the third floor in the lift. Walking, she heard the music of great composers wafting through the halls and had time to gaze up at the lavish Impressionist paintings that hung on the walls: Monet, Pissarro, Auguste Renoir. The hotel was impressive and expensive and typical of her mother-in-law's lavish spending.

The bell porter led her into a capacious room with elegance beyond her imagination: a massive canopy bed, a golden oak desk where she could write to David, and a bathroom in sienna marble. Her suite was joined to the one Chandler would have, both rooms more elaborate and ornate than any hotel where she and David had stayed, even on their honeymoon.

Emptying her suitcase took forever. She stopped to glance out the windows at Vienna. Paused to run her fingers over the shiny oak bedstead. And just now she had called down to the main desk for the third time to ask whether her son had arrived.

"No, Lieutenant Reynolds has not checked in yet."

She went back to her unpacking, shook out her last garment and hung it in the spacious closet before toeing the suitcases out of sight. Reveling in the music of Mozart being piped into her room, she waltzed to the glass door, slid it back, and stepped out on the private patio. In the distance, St. Stephen's Cathedral rose from the center of Vienna, its tiled roof and tall spire brilliant in the sun.

Now she had time to worry about Chandler. She wondered if he had missed his plane. Weather would not hold him back. The clear Vienna sky was alive with fleecy clouds, puffs of white framed in the azure blue. In her childhood she had spent hours imagining the circles and polygons of the sky to be clown faces or snowmen or marbled statues napping on their backs. Now she played the childhood game again—seeing a clown face to her left, a ship with smoke stacks behind it. Another swirling mass of clouds looked like the back of David's head, his familiar face turned from her. Like the clouds, she and David were drifting apart, her secret still building a wedge between them. David thought it was Bill and Chandler. Ashley knew better.

The thick cloud swept closer, the face in her mind vivid now. It was no longer the back of David's head. It was Bill's attractive face laughing at her. How much she had loved him. He had been part of her life, part of her family. Part of her pain. How could she break through God's canopy for answers where there were none? Everything in her life was being blown away, her marriage threatened, her faith crumbling.

She was here in one of her favorite European cities with the glory of Vienna all around her—the past with its magnificent Hapsburg Empire, the present with its charming coffeehouses. But all she could think about was that day in her garden. She remembered the heat. The persistent ring of the telephone. The mad dash to reach it before the answering machine kicked in. And then Chandler's deep voice dancing over the wires.

She still heard the ring. No, it was the phone in her hotel room. She fled back inside and grabbed it. *"Guten Tag."* A polite voice came back, "Frau Reynolds, this is the reception desk. Lieutenant Reynolds has arrived. He insisted on going straight up to your room."

Frazzled, she ran her hand through her hair. Not Bill coming out of her past but Chandler. She stood up straight and tall.

"It's all right," she said softly. "He's my son."

Ashley ran with lightning speed down the corridor to the stairwell and leaned over the hand-carved banister. Chandler had reached the first landing, his polished black boots echoless against the red carpeted steps. Her son was here safe in Vienna. Alive. Coming up to meet her. She felt enormous relief at just seeing the back of his finely shaped head, his dark hair cropped to military regulations. As short as it was, it looked a gleaming red-brown in the light of the crystal chandelier that hung above the landing. Reddish-brown like Kerina Rudzinski's.

It didn't matter as long as he was here. Pride filled her heart. As always, Chandler was straight-backed, his army olive greens trim against those strong shoulders and narrow hips. His visor cap was tucked securely in the crook of his arm. He reached out to grip the rail, propelling himself forward. He was limping.

As he reached the second landing, he looked up and saw her. Suddenly his solemn face was bathed in a warm smile. "Mom. Hi!"

She waved. "Hi, yourself."

A young couple going down the stairs moved aside to let him rush by them. As he came, double time now, he grabbed the railing and visibly tugged himself forward.

He's favoring that leg, she thought, *limping the way Bill limped after his injury in the navy.* Bill had been a demonstrative man, but not Chandler. Chandler bear-hugged his grandmother, but was standoffish with the rest of them, nursing the dark void that he sometimes felt inside.

"Something's missing in my life, and I don't even know what it is," he had told them.

Ashley knew. Perhaps her son would find his answers here in Vienna. But then the void would become hers. Once told, would Chandler ever forgive her for withholding the truth from him?

It had seemed such a simple promise when he was born. "Don't ever tell him he was adopted," Kerry Rudzinski had begged. "I could not bear it if he knew that I deserted him."

Ashley braced herself, her gaze on his handsome face as she waited for him to make a move.

He stood steps from her, yet towering above her on those lanky legs. "I was afraid you wouldn't be here, Mom."

"And I was afraid you'd miss your flight out of Bosnia."

"I would have walked." He sounded like he meant it.

"Over land and sea—on that leg of yours?"

He tapped his thigh. "We'll talk about it later. Okay?"

He looked so different in uniform, his First Lieutenant bars shining on his epaulets. More mature and yet the same. Older and yet boyish. Striking and yet sad. She longed to wrap her arms around him—this son, this stranger in front of her. His face seemed thinner, making his Grecian-like features prominent. His shadowed eyes were hollow, deeper than she remembered them.

"Chandler, are you going to give me a proper hello?" she murmured. "I've been waiting for your hug for hours."

He opened his arms. "Mom," he said huskily.

The word flew airborne, straight-arrowed into her heart. She soared the three steps to him on that marvelous word and felt a surge of joy as her son's strong arms engulfed her. She stepped back laughing. "I've missed you, son. I'm so glad you're here. Why didn't you tell us you were hurt?"

"I didn't want to worry you."

"We worry anyway."

"I thought Dad preached against that."

"I don't. So you can tell me what happened."

"Just an accident."

An accident that he doesn't want to talk about. She patted his arm. "You're certain you'll be all right?"

"Good as new in a few weeks."

"Okay. I can wait."

The corridor empty just seconds ago now filled with people. A family with three children. An older couple—the man with a cane. A bell porter stepping from the lift with a cart full of luggage. Guests hurrying to their rooms. Doors slamming. Strangers laughing.

"Where's your luggage?" She sounded distracted by practical things, desperate not to let him read her fears about his injury.

"You're looking at it."

She saw the army duffel, the smaller kit bag, and a pair of crutches. "Your crutches, Chandler?"

His dark brows arched. "We'll talk about them later."

"Are you supposed to be using them?"

"They help," he admitted, grinning. "But I didn't want you to see me using them until we had time to talk."

He slipped his arm around her shoulder, and they turned to follow the porter. "This is my room," she said, pushing the unlocked door open. "You're in the room next to mine."

Inside, he stared in disbelief. "What a swank place."

"It is ostentatious, isn't it?"

He pumped the mattress. "This should be army issue. A king-size bed instead of a bunk."

There were autumn colors in the spread and three pillows propped against the headboard. His gaze strayed to the painting by a Flemish artist. He walked over for a closer inspection. "That's a nice scene. I always liked autumn at home."

"It was even more lovely in the town where you were born."

148

His head turned sharply, surprise on his face. "Everdale?"
She could have bitten her tongue. "There was a lovely
woods behind Mama's place. I don't suppose you remember
that?"

"Hardly. You scooped me out of there before I was three.
But deer used to come through the woods to the edge of
our property."

"You remember that?"

"That and not much else."

He prowled, looking at everything. Her suite had it all—
an ivory soaking tub, a dressing alcove, a mirrored dresser,
a bar she didn't need, a giant television she probably wouldn't
turn on, and a patio with its marvelous view of Vienna.

They began their old word game. "It is grand, Mom."

"Elegant."

"Grams knows the way to go. Top hat—Chesterfieldian
all the way." He laughed, but his eyes remained sad. "Army
quarters were never like this." He flopped on the bed and
stretched out, shoving two pillows beneath his injured leg.
"All we need is a piano and Dad here so we could have a
family songfest. Could even invite Grams to join us."

"Let's just leave your grandmother in Denver."

"So, things haven't improved between you two? What's
the big deal, Mom? Did she have someone else picked out
for her son?"

"Anyone else."

"You're the right choice for Dad as far as I'm concerned."

They talked nonstop now. "Seriously, how are Dad and
Grams?"

Questions and answers back and forth for an hour. Ashley talked about planting snow flowers and glads in her garden and about David's busy schedule. Chandler asked about
the new neighbors and her last days as a nurse. She admitted to tears the day she quit.

"I guessed as much when we talked on the phone."

149

She told him about spending her last paycheck on clothes. "I hung my new suit in the closet, waiting for just the right time to wear it, and your father knew it was there all along. He scolded me for not wearing it. Said he likes me to turn eyes."

"Dad was always pleased with how you looked."

Every time Ashley steered the conversation to Bosnia and army life, Chandler backed off or pounded the pillow to fit the curve of his neck. Finally she asked, "Chandler, what about that friend of yours from the university? Randolph. Randy something."

He'd been lying there with his arms behind his head. He sat up slowly and swung his legs over the side of the bed, his face turning ashen as he met her gaze. "Randy Williams."

"That's it. From Akron, Ohio, wasn't he?"

"He's dead."

It didn't sound like Chandler's voice. It didn't look like him. For a few seconds it seemed like he was chiseled from plutonic rock, his face harsh, unmovable, and then rage and pain flicked in his eyes.

"When? . . . What happened?"

He looked away and blinked. *He's not a little boy now,* she told herself. *You can't gather him in your arms and kiss away the hurts. Just listen to him.*

As she listened, he said, "Six weeks ago Randy stepped on a land mine. It was quick. He didn't suffer, Mother."

"He was only a boy."

"My age. Twenty-six. A grown man."

She accepted his rebuke without flinching. *Shall I keep questioning him?* she wondered. *Yes, don't let him escape into a pit of despair. Hear him out. Don't let him be like David now; David would want him to handle it like a man.*

Men should cry, she thought. *My son should be free to cry if he wants.* She imagined that he had not cried yet—that he had not fully admitted Randy was dead.

Chandler ran his thumb over his knuckles. He hadn't intended to tell his mother about Randy. This was to be a month in which he wiped the pain from his mind and heard only music and laughter. How could he have been so foolish?

He imagined her in her nurse's uniform, sitting by a patient's bedside, just listening as she was doing now. Waiting for him to crack emotionally like the doctors had waited. *Everyone is waiting for signs of my falling apart because my best friend is dead.* He glanced beyond her to the autumn painting. The storm clouds in the picture were billowing through the sky, ready to rain their fury down on him.

"Chan, did they send Randy's body back to Akron for burial?"

His body, Mom? "No, just his casket."

If she caught his meaning, she gave no indication. Softly she asked, "Why didn't you tell us? Your father and I would gladly have flown to Akron to be with them, to comfort them."

No, he thought. *Dad would have talked of heaven and peace. Of sin and salvation. Do you call it sin when a man drops on a mine and saves your life?* he wondered. Aloud he said, "It wouldn't have worked out, you and Dad going there. I don't know about his parents, but Randy was never a very religious fellow."

"All the more reason for us to show them we cared. His parents lost a son, Chandler."

And I lost a friend. Yes, you would have shown them love—the nurse in you going up to total strangers and wrapping your arms around them. "Maybe when you get home you could call them?"

"I will if you'll give me the address."

"As soon as I unpack." He hesitated. "Mom, if Dad is right—if there is a heaven and hell—"

"*If* he's right?"

Chandler ignored her, repeating, "If Dad is right, then I blew it with Randy. When he saw the rubble and devasta-

151

tion in Bosnia, he asked me where God was when the Serbs and Croats were killing each other."

He loosened the top button of his army shirt. "Randy always razzed me about being a preacher's kid. Said it was easy for me to swallow all that religious stuff. I didn't want to argue with my best friend, not when he kept telling me he had plenty of time to think about God when he got out of the army."

"Don't blame yourself, Chandler."

"Who else then?" He wiped the back of his hand across his mouth. "Randy died for me, Mom. Died in my place. Not on some cross. But in a way Bosnia was like Golgotha for both of us. We weren't in that country for the long war, or in the thick of the siege and ethnic cleansing. But in a way getting to war-torn Bosnia was like reaching hell after the long battle."

He expected her to scold him for being irreverent. But she understood. She leaned forward and put her hand gently on his arm. "You were there? You saw it happen? That's what you meant when you said he died for you. Is that when you were injured?"

The tears he had fought off for weeks burned behind his eyelids. "I still see him, Mom. He was running toward me when that cocky look came across his face—as though he knew what was happening—as though he were saying, 'Chandler, this one's on me. This is for you, buddy.' And then his foot came down and he fell forward on the mine and took the brunt of the explosion."

Her eyes coaxed him to trust her. He felt swallowed up by her love. She was not making excuses. Not saying it was Randy's time to go. Not mouthing that time was the great healer.

"Chan," she whispered, "I am so sorry."

"But I'll be all right." *When I can sleep again. When I can stop blaming myself. When I can stop seeing Randy blown to bits.* He sighed. "I never meant to burden you with this."

"That's what mothers are for. I'm here for you. We have a month to sort out all that's happened. What's happened won't just fade away." She studied the rings on her finger, then looked up. "I knew something was wrong when you called us. I couldn't believe the army would drop a leave in your lap for nothing."

"It's a medical pass," he admitted.

"And not just for the leg?"

He gave his knuckles another jab. He would not have to pretend with her, but he would have to explain Zineta Hovic before his mom flew home. *Later! We can deal with that later.*

She grabbed his attention, asking, "Will we have time for everything? A concert in the park? St. Stephen's? The palace?"

"Everything." A month sounded like forever.

"Chandler, can we cruise the Danube?"

"Why not?" he asked lightly. "We can catch a riverboat from Vienna to Budapest and Kalocsa."

"That would be too expensive."

"You're worth it. I'll even go shopping with you on the Karntner Strasse. You can blow your traveler's checks on clothes."

Her brows arched. "I had one spending spree when I retired. I brought a suitcase full of new clothes. You won't recognize me."

"I'll be proud of you."

She tilted her head and studied him. "I wish you had someone young and beautiful to take around Vienna."

He stood and gave her a quick hug. "I do. You."

"Chandler, on the phone you mentioned a girl in Bosnia."

"Did I?"

"You know that you did. Is she off-limits right now?"

He thought about it. "No, I just didn't know when to mention her. Her name is Zineta Hovic. She was Randy's friend."

"Randy's girlfriend?" He heard surprise in her voice, more uncertainty as she asked, "Does she know what happened to him?"

"I'm afraid so."

"And now?" she asked guardedly.

"Now, I'm free to marry Zineta." He ran his thumb across his dry lips. "As I told you on the phone, Mom—she's pregnant."

Ashley had taken the death of Randy calmly for his sake, but the girl's pregnancy touched a raw spot in his mother; the expression in her eyes was one of deep pain.

"Chandler, are you—are you in love with her?"

"Don't worry, Mom. You'll like her."

Her voice sounded strained. "Will Dad?"

"Dad isn't planning to marry her."

"Oh, Chandler, why didn't you wait? That poor girl."

"It's not my baby, Mother; it's Randy's."

She twisted her rings. "Then—why are you marrying her?"

"Randy's child deserves more than a war-ravaged village. But let's not argue. That's between Zineta and me." He pivoted on his good leg and headed for the door between their rooms.

"Do Randy's parents know about the baby, Chan?"

He glanced back. "I don't even know if Randy knew."

"They've lost their only son. They have a right to know about their grandchild. Aren't you going to tell them?"

He flexed his jaw as though it had frozen in place. "I'd better unpack. I'll have to buy some civvies tomorrow."

"No need. Your dad sent some of your good clothes with me. They're in your room."

"Great. But I'll need a tuxedo tomorrow at the concert."

"The concierge made an appointment for a fitting in the morning."

"Great." He paused in the doorway. "I wish Dad had come."

"There wasn't time to rearrange his schedule."

"I just wish his schedule included me."

A frown shadowed her lovely face. "I thought we weren't going to let anything spoil our time in Vienna, Chandler."

"You win." *But something's going on back home.* "Is everything okay between you and Dad?"

"Nothing that a little separation won't cure."

"He's not still mad about Juilliard?"

"Don't blame yourself for problems back home. Your dad is busy, that's all. Too busy."

"But he always found time for trips up to Arrowhead. I used to resent the two of you going off like that. I hated it when you left me home with Grams. I figured you didn't need me—or want me."

"We always wanted you, Chandler. But sometimes we needed to be alone. We still do."

"You know what? When I was a kid I dreamed of growing up and marrying someone I loved as much as Dad loved you."

"That's sweet."

She was chewing her lower lip, looking as though she would burst into tears. He couldn't let her do that. They had just weathered his news about Randy and Zineta. The slate was clear.

Still he said, "You sure nothing's wrong? I'd hate to be the one who came between you two. For whatever reason."

"Your father loves you, Chandler."

"I know." *But does he still love you?* he wondered. *And if he doesn't, what right does he have to stand behind a pulpit? His whole message would be a lie.*

He started to ask if she had packed his birth certificate and transcripts, but there would be time enough to discuss his future later. "Give me fifteen minutes to shower and change, then we'll go out to dinner."

155

"I'd like that." Before he could protest she added, "Your father insists that I pay for all the meals. We'll cash some of my traveler's checks at the desk. You pocket the money."

He looked relieved. "I'll pay you back."

"In your civilian life? No. Our turn now. Your dad insists."

As he walked into his room, he called over his shoulder, "We should call Dad when we get back from dinner."

Her answer trailed after him. "Yes, we'd better do that. He'll be sitting up in his study waiting for the phone to ring. Or maybe we should just wait until morning."

He found his gear beside the bed where the porter had left it. He unzipped the duffel, grabbed his clothes, and started to strip down as he headed for the shower. He had the funny feeling that calling home was the last thing his mother wanted to do.

Fifteen minutes later Ashley slipped the pierced earring into the lobe of her ear and walked into Chandler's room. She winced at the sight of the crutches leaning against the foot of the bed, the reminder of what had happened to him in Bosnia.

She tried to visualize David standing in this room with her, his face turning purple at the casual way in which Chandler had spoken of his intention to marry a girl pregnant with another man's child. In the clash of words that would pass between them, David would say, "A marriage of convenience? I won't hear of it. You don't love her. You can't marry her out of duty to a friend."

Ashley knew what Chandler would answer. "My decision, Dad. And she has a name. Zineta Hovic. Remember that."

When had they drawn apart—these two who had been such buddies? Friends. Father and son. Inseparable. Until when?

Oh, David, Chandler's friend is dead, but miracle of miracles, your son is alive. He needs you to weep with him. To sit and grieve with him. And if Chandler insists—to join him in marriage to the girl from Bosnia. Right or wrong, it is not our decision. We need to help him pick up the shattered pieces of his faith. But how can I when I am struggling with my own flaws, my own faith?

She braced herself against the doorjamb, her nerve endings all shouting at once. She would have to tell him the truth. But how could she tell her son that they had deceived him for twenty-six years? Behind the bathroom door, the shower water thundered against the glass. The floor would be sopping wet and Chandler's towels dropped in the puddle.

What would she say as he came through the door? "Sit down, son, I have something to tell you. No, no, this is not about the mess in the bathroom. This is something that will fill the aching void you have inside. Something that may turn you against your father and me."

She groped vainly for words to describe his birth parents to him. Parents that he did not know existed. "Oh, Chandler, you have your father's wide, pensive eyes. Your mother's gentle smile, her musical talent. But I see David's strengths in you too. And mine. You are our son as well."

Once started, she would say, "Look in the mirror. You are very much your birth father's son, but it is too late to know him. Your father made many mistakes—a long trail of pain that I have never forgiven. But he did one good thing, Chandler, one act of trying to right all his wrongs when he chose a country house for you to grow up in before he drove away. Whatever you do, don't ask me if he ever held you in his arms. As sensitive as you are, Chandler, you will feel that rejection."

Ashley rubbed her hands together. Would she have the courage to face her son with the truth as he came through the door or should she wait until they came back from dinner? Wait until the midnight hour and say, "I have something to confess to you—"

She imagined Chandler too stunned to repeat the word adopted. She pictured him wide-eyed, disbelieving as she

157

said, "Try to understand. You were born to a frightened nineteen-year-old. To a successful concert violinist from Prague. She was young and beautiful. I was there at the hospital nursery when your mother held you for the last time and said good-bye. I know that she loved you. I told her it was not too late to change her mind, even knowing if she did, my heart would break. Your father and I wanted a son. We wanted you."

Ashley didn't want to go to the Opera House the following evening and give Kerina Rudzinski a standing ovation. She wanted to turn to the audience and tell them, "This is the woman who gave her son away. What right does she have to him now?"

Her vengeance startled her. "Why am I so vindictive when my own sins lie hidden just beneath the surface?"

Above the erratic thumping of her own heart, Ashley heard the shower water still running and smiled through her tears at the trail of clothes dropped on the thick red carpet. Chandler had left the regimentation of army life and slipped back in time to the carefree, careless days of his boyhood and the clutter that he always left behind. His boyhood belonged to Ashley and David, not to Kerina or the father who gave him away.

"But who does he belong to now, God?" she whispered. "Tell me quickly before I face him again."

She knew the answer, felt it tugging at her heart. Chandler belonged to himself. To God. *Let him go, Ashley. Let him go,* she cautioned herself.

She strained to hear above the sound of water and her heart raced with sudden gratitude. The problem was out of her hands. And Chandler was whistling, whistling as he turned off the shower.

Thirteen

David swiveled in his soft leather chair, his eyes leaving the silent phone to stare out on Ashley's garden. Her flower beds were filled with brilliant colors—the cardinals and Dresden blues, the soft yellow petals on the roses. Brick paths wound around the yard past the neatly trimmed hedges and bushes. He pictured Ashley sitting on the white stone bench near the bird feeder—happily watching the hummingbirds feed or the robins splash in the marble birdbath.

Through the open window, he heard the low-pitched cooing of a dove pruning its white-tipped feathers and mourning for its mate as he mourned for Ashley. His wife had been gone less than a day and he missed her desperately—missed her because of the unspoken words that lay between them. Worse were those words he could not retract. How had he dared accuse her of withholding the truth from their son? He'd been party to it for twenty-six years.

As he yanked at his tie, the top button of his shirt tore free and clattered on his desk. It rolled and then spun out as it hit the brochure of the Opera House in Vienna. The cover page featured the renowned Kerina Rudzinski, her exquisite eyes visible even in the brochure as he stared down at it.

Why did you ever come into our lives? he asked; then he laughed ironically. If she had not come, Chandler would never have been his son. *Yes, Kerina Rudzinski, I have you to thank for my son. Not the son of my loins, but no son could have brought me greater joy. So where did I go wrong? Where did I lose Chandler?*

Exhaustion frayed David's nerves. He imagined Ashley getting lost on her way to the Austrian hotel or Chandler missing the military flight out of Bosnia leaving her alone at the Empress Isle. Ashley had promised to call the minute Chandler arrived and still the phone was silent. He picked up the receiver to check for a dial tone and heard the annoying hum in his ear.

His gaze went back to Ashley's yard, her private world, and definitely off-limits whenever they quarreled. David respected her need for a private sanctuary, but he felt like an outcast barred from entry. He couldn't name the flowers growing there except for the roses and only recognized a gardenia by its smell.

He leaned forward and opened a louvered window letting in that sweet fragrance. "Ashley. Ashley. I should hire someone to keep your garden weeded," he said aloud.

"Why, David?"

The voice was his mother's. He had forgotten her midnight arrival. She walked gracefully into his office, tightening the belt of her fleecy pink robe as she came, her pink slippers silent against the carpet. The aroma of her perfume grew stronger as she reached him, overpowering the scent of Ashley's gardenias.

"Why didn't you wake me? I told you I would cook breakfast."

He glanced at his desk clock. Almost ten. "I wasn't hungry."

His mother looked as though she had just stepped from the beauty salon. He imagined her bed unmade, her fragrances and hairbrushes scattered across the counter in the guest bathroom—every waking minute given to maintaining her perfect image. Not a strand of her salt-and-pepper hair strayed out of place. But he noticed more silver there now than on her last holiday visit and wondered why she had not dyed it.

"Why would you want a gardener?" she asked again. "Has Ashley left you, David?"

The room spun, his blood pressure surely spinning with it. His theology and archeology books looked like they were ready to topple from their shelves. The overhead light faded in and out, and he thought vaguely that he would have to change the light globe but didn't know where Ashley kept the seventy-five-watt bulbs.

"David, does your silence mean she has finally left you?"

He fought down his anger. "You know she's with Chandler."

"Do I? When I went to bed last night—and I had to make up my own bed—you were sitting there. Right there at your desk waiting for her to call you from Vienna."

"I know."

"Obviously, you haven't heard from her yet. You look distraught—hair disheveled; face unshaven. You're waiting for something that may never happen."

David tented his fingers and rested his bristled chin against them. At times he found it difficult to think of her as the mother who had reared him through an easygoing boyhood and those tempestuous teen years. At the moment she reminded him more of one of the women in his congregation coming into the church office for counsel with complaints about marital discord. When he tried to point these women to the basic problem of the lust of the eye, they often stormed from his office. He imagined his mother doing the same if he ever confronted her with her sin nature. She tolerated his beliefs but would not accept them. She was a good woman, a good woman without a Savior. Still, for all their differences, he loved her.

But her descending on him without warning aggravated him. She had been at the house waiting when he drove back from L.A. International in a rainstorm. He had found her sitting in Ashley's chair, a *Vogue* magazine in her hands.

She had lowered the magazine and said, "Is Ashley gone?"

"Her plane left two hours ago. Did you fly into L.A.?"

"No, Orange County. I caught a taxi and let myself in."

"Why didn't you let me know you were coming?"

"I wanted to surprise you. With Ashley going off like that, you need someone to cook your meals and keep your shirts ironed."

He groaned. "I've survived on frozen dinners and eating out before . . . and Ashley sends my shirts to the laundry."

"That should be a wife's responsibility."

"You're old-fashioned," he said lightly, leaning down to kiss her proffered cheek.

"I did those things for your father for fifty years."

"I'm certain he was grateful, Mother." He kicked off his rain-sodden shoes. "If you'll excuse me, I'll run up and change. Since you think I need care, why don't you put the coffee on?"

"I already did. And I made some tuna sandwiches. Oh, David, don't be sulky. I just wanted this time alone with you. You'll feel better about my coming in the morning."

She was wrong. He still felt annoyed at her coming.

"David, I thought you'd be off to work by now."

She had used that tone when he was a teenager. "You are not to see that girl again—whatever her name is."

Her name was Ashley, blond and wholesome looking, and David had fallen in love with her. He had gone to his grandparents' farm that long-ago summer, a disciplinary act on the part of his parents. "You'll be a farmhand for the summer," his father had told him. "A little honest work won't hurt you. Heaven only knows your grandparents could do with some muscle about the place."

David had flexed his biceps, mentally planning to leave the farm the minute he got there.

His mother had given her jabs as well. "Maybe it will be the making of you, David. Good preparation for going off to USC. At least it will get you away from those friends of yours." She had been on a spiel, adding, "With what it is costing your father and me, I just hope something good happens to you this summer."

Something did. Ashley happened to him.

He met his mother's gaze again. He felt responsible for her now that she was widowed, but he could not understand her lingering malice toward Ashley.

"Aren't you going to work, David?"

"I told my secretary I wouldn't be in this morning."

"You can do that as a pastor? And your university class?"

"Not until two today."

"Convenient." She sat uninvited in the chair across from him. "I haven't heard from Chandler since wiring the money for the hotel in Vienna. I assume the money arrived."

"You know that it did. He rarely writes letters."

"He rarely writes thank-yous. Ashley—"

"Ashley wrote thanking you, didn't she?"

"It was not the same as hearing from Chandler. I do so much for this family. Sometimes I wish you had waited for a child of your own. You deserved that, David."

"Chandler is a child of my own."

"David, you know what I mean. Instead of Ashley being in that delivery room as a nurse, she should have been there delivering your child. Not someone else's."

"That was impossible. Ashley couldn't conceive."

"Really? Sometimes I don't think you know Ashley at all."

"Ashley found Chandler for us."

"All wrapped up in a neat little package."

"I thought you and Chan were the greatest of friends."

His mother's face softened. "We are. But I can't help wishing he had been your son, David—our own flesh and blood."

He fought down his simmering rage. "From the day I held him in my arms he was my son, Mother. Surely you know that."

"Yes. Yes. I felt the same way the first time I held him. But, David, if we only knew who his parents really were."

163

"Ashley and I are his parents."

"I mean his birth parents, David. Can't you face the truth even now?" she asked. "Ashley comes home from the hospital at the end of her night shift and announces that you can adopt a baby. You knew nothing about the mother. Nothing about the father."

"We wanted that baby, Mother." He slid Kerina Rudzinski's brochure into his top desk drawer. "Chandler's birth mother was just a nice kid. A girl in trouble who wanted someone who would love her son. That's all she asked. That's what we did."

As Rosalyn Reynolds smiled, her lips parted, revealing her even, white teeth. "Yes, David, we have all loved him. But has it been fair to Chandler not to know that he was adopted? I would have told him the truth long ago. But tell him at this late date and it will alienate him from all of us."

"The decision to tell him is not yours to make."

"You and Ashley made that quite apparent over the years. It didn't matter to your father. God rest his soul. But it matters to me. But to not know a thing about Chandler's parents—"

David knew the girl's name. He could take his mother to the very place where Chandler's birth father was. But the truth would only make her dislike Ashley more. He felt oddly detached, as though he were no longer talking to his mother. This person sitting across from him, judging him with her eyes, was someone who ran in social circles and spent her Sundays playing bridge or golfing, a woman who took pleasure in making the society page in Denver. At the moment they were like total strangers, and yet it was his mother who had taken no part in the trail of lies that surrounded Chandler's roots. He was the pastor, Ashley was the pastor's wife, and yet it was his mother—who believed in nothing beyond this life—who urged integrity. A woman who loved Chandler as her own grandson but who even now despised deceiving him.

He started to smile at her, to tell her he was glad she was on board for a few days. But as the smile formed at the corners of his mouth, she said, "I asked you moments ago—I'm going to ask you again. Has Ashley left you for good, David?"

"Is that what you want, Mother?"

"I want the best for you."

"My wife is my best—and my son."

"Oh, David, it would take a blind person to miss how unhappy you and Ashley have been these last few months."

"We'll work it out."

"What if she goes away and influences Chandler to go with her? I will not be deprived of my only grandson, David."

"Moments ago you regretted that he wasn't your own blood line. I have no control over what Chandler does. You should know that after these last three years in the army. He's even talking about reenlisting or staying on in Europe as a music critic."

"That sounds like you, David. You were always your own man."

"I was a disappointment to you, wasn't I?"

"To your father the sun rose and set on you, David."

"I never figured it that way. It was make the football squad or the basketball team. Make your old man proud of you," he mocked. "Any talk of college other than USC was out. Remember, Mother, it was law school or nothing if I wanted to please him."

"He was always proud of you."

"Even when I went off to seminary?"

"That was hard for him to take," she admitted. "But in the end, he was proud of you for standing up for what you wanted."

"I wish Dad had told me."

The mid-morning sun beat against his back, coming in through the garden window and flooding the office with light. He had twelve hours until sundown, twelve hours to allow his anger at his mother to fester before he would have to be rid of his rage. As the sun touched her face, shadowed flecks of gray appeared in her eyes.

"David, do you ever tell Chandler how proud you are of him?"

The muscles along his jaw tightened. She was right. What his father had done to him, he had done in turn to Chandler. Pushing, cajoling, demanding that his son reach certain goals. David's goals. He had even taken the burden of choice for college from Chandler's shoulders. It would be David's alma mater or nothing.

"Mother, I had a thousand dreams for my son from that first day I held him in my arms."

"So like your father. Your dreams, David. Not Chandler's."

He nodded. "Chandler told me as much when we spoke on the phone last week. I exploded when he told me he was staying on in Europe as a music critic after the army. That's when he reminded me that a man has to find his own way."

"He really is like you, David. Almost like your own flesh and blood except for his love of music. He didn't get that from you." Her pupils widened, the emerald green in her eyes bright and shiny. "Ashley's brother was a music critic, wasn't he?"

She knows, he thought. "Ashley's brother was in business, investments mostly. He did music reviews in college, I think."

"I see."

Did she? She'd had twenty-six years to work out the puzzle.

"It was selfish on our part, David, but your father and I wanted so much for you. Dad wanted you to go into the law firm with him." Sadly, she said, "But once you met Ashley, the die was cast. She was all wrong for you—for us. The only good thing that came out of it was Chandler."

In spite of the hours she spent in front of the mirror, age lines framed his mother's eyes. The skin sagged at the hol-

166

low of her neck. As she sat facing him, her expression was proud—that same look of independence she had given him after his father's funeral. "Live with you and Ashley? Never. I'll make it on my own, David," she had told him. "I won't need a handout from my daughter-in-law. Good man that he was, your father has left me quite comfortable."

He tented his fingers again and rested his chin against them. "Why do you dislike my wife so, Mother?"

"I never said I disliked her, David."

"You can't be in the same room without showing your displeasure or correcting Ashley for something."

"It goes back a long time."

"Back to the summer I met her?"

"She was wrong for you. I told you that back then. How could Ashley and I be friends? We're from two separate worlds. You want the truth? Then let me tell you what I have known since the day you met her—she was never good enough for you, David Reynolds."

Mercifully the phone rang, taking with it the need to lash back. His fingered canopy collapsed as he grabbed the receiver. "Pastor Reynolds's residence."

"David! It's Ashley."

"Where are you?"

"In Vienna. Did you think I ended up in Rome?"

"I thought you were going to call when Chandler got there. I've been up all night waiting. Worrying."

"Oh, David, I'm sorry. We've been so busy. Talking and laughing. It was one thing after the other—"

She sounded happy, lighthearted, distant. "It's all right, Ashley. Is Chandler there now?"

"He's here. He's fine." She hesitated. "He hurt his leg several weeks ago, but it's healing nicely. Says to tell you he looks great in the clothes you sent."

And then Chandler was on the phone. "Dad. You old rock, why aren't you here? We miss you."

"I wanted to come—but this schedule of mine. There's the church and a book deadline and—"

"What about me, Dad?"

Before David could apologize, his mother left the room. He watched her climb slowly up the stairs, his guilt mounting with her. She seemed suddenly old, as distant as his son.

"Is someone there with you, Dad?" Chandler asked.

David wanted to say, *your grandmother.* The words caught in his throat. "In the office with me? I'm alone right now. Tell me about your leg injury, son, and tell me what you and your mother have been doing."

They talked for thirty minutes, the clock ticking away until noon with every other sentence about Vienna or the violinist. Twice Chandler said, "I'm okay, Dad. Let's not talk about Bosnia." And finally, "We'd better call it quits, Dad. I think Mom reversed the charges so the call is on you. We'll call after the concert, but don't stay up all night waiting. You hear?"

"Put your mother on the line, son."

"Can't. She's back in her room taking a shower."

David hastily said good-bye, then cradled the phone and pushed it back on the desk. The silent room screamed at him. *Ashley, Chandler. My wife, my son. My whole life wrapped up in two people.*

A movement in Ashley's garden caught his attention. He shot to his feet. His mother was kneeling by one of the flower beds, work gloves on her hands. She was tugging at the weeds, trying in her own way to tell him she was sorry for what she had said. But her words kept ringing in his ears. "Has Ashley left you, David?"

David showered, shaved, and dressed in twenty minutes and was back down in the garden, briefcase in hand. He knelt beside his mother. "I'm off to the university, Mother."

She looked up into his face. "When will you be back?"

"In time to take you out to dinner."

"I think I'll be gone before then."

168

"You don't have to leave."

"I'll come back some other time when you invite me."

"Come for the next holiday?"

She pulled unsuccessfully at a weed. "If you want me to."

"It's an open invitation. You know that."

"We'll see." She removed the garden glove and touched his face with her long, slender fingers. "I love you, David. I don't mean to interfere or belittle your wife."

He pressed her hand against his cheek. She looked as if she would cry, and he wanted to spare her the humiliation. "I have to hurry or I'll be late for class. We'll keep in touch."

Tears balanced on her eyelashes. "I learned something this morning, David. Something I didn't want to believe."

He waited, glancing anxiously at his watch.

"Ashley is in your blood, and you can never let her go."

Even as he slid into the car and turned on the ignition, her words haunted him. But what if Ashley did leave him? Where would she go?

Back to Everdale, he told himself. Yes, he was certain she would go back to Everdale, back to where it all began.

Fourteen

Even back in the 1960s, David Lee Reynolds was into politics and history. Knowing statistics pleased his father, and Clayton Reynolds's approval meant an increase in David's allowance. David kept up on the current hot spots in the world so he could engage in heated debates with his father at the dinner table. He could spiel off facts like words in a spelling bee.

John Fitzgerald Kennedy was President of the United States, Lyndon Baines Johnson his V.P., McNamara Secretary of Defense, and Premier Khrushchev in power in the Soviet Union. Concrete slabs had replaced the barbed wire along a twenty-eight-mile death trap known as the Berlin Wall—a wall that divided a city and made the Brandenburg Gate and Checkpoint Charlie names to be reckoned with. Young Prince Charles was heir to the British throne, and Beatlemania was just getting off the ground with four long-haired musicians from Liverpool taking the U.S. by storm. And high school senior David Reynolds of Southern California was almost eighteen.

David admired the man in the White House, but the Bay of Pigs remained a blot on Kennedy's presidency. Kennedy had other problems: Air America, the CIA airline that didn't exist, was flying daring supply runs into Laos and South Vietnam, and a conflict near the Gulf of Tonkin and the Mekong River was taking shape, with American losses slowly mounting in the jungles of Laos and Vietnam. U.S. Special Forces were serving as advisors to a poorly equipped army, ill prepared to fend off attacks by the Viet Cong guerrillas. An all-out war would force Kennedy to draft high school graduates for a military buildup that already had opposition from Congress and the Republicans. And from David.

David's real interests were the Yankee baseball scores, the latest model cars, and the conditions of the winds and surf off Hermosa Beach or Huntington Beach pier. At almost eighteen, life looked good. David intended to keep it that way. He had no intention of being one of the U.S. troops patrolling the Berlin Wall or one of the Green Berets dying in Vietnam. He had no desire at all to wear his country's uniform, not after seeing the news photo of the bullet-riddled body of eighteen-year-old Peter Fechter trying to scale the Wall into the freedom of West Berlin.

For once David was in full agreement with his dad. Clayton Reynolds had caught the tail end of World War II and determined at all costs to keep his son from the bloodbath on the Ho Chi Minh trail.

Nor would David be out on the streets protesting the war—his mother would see to that. Let the Peace Corps circle the world and astronauts lift off into space. David's sights didn't go beyond the U.S. border. He kept short-term goals—the prom in June and the university in the fall. Thanks to his father's legal maneuvers and David's outstanding GPA, his destination was a university campus, not the army's basic training camp.

But just before his birthday, in the last few weeks of his senior year of high school, David's defiance almost cost him his diploma. David wasn't dating much, and alcohol and smoking were out. He was saving every spare dime of his allowance toward insurance for a two-door Plymouth Fury or a Dodge Dart with heavy bumpers and tail fins.

That meant no girls. No drinks. No smokes.

He didn't have the car yet, but he expected one for graduation, a combined birthday-graduation present. It didn't even matter whether it was brand-new or not—although his dad could afford ten new ones. But as long as it was blue and shiny and souped up for speed, that's what counted. Then he blew it, and his dad pulled the dream out from under his feet. And for a few weeks David felt as if the president was breathing down his neck, waving draft papers.

It was his third straight night of breaking the family curfew. A guy almost out of high school and on his own had a right to break a few rules. Right? Wrong. That night as he turned the key in the front door, he came face to face with his father.

"I'll take that key," Clayton Reynolds said. He grabbed it and shoved it into the pocket of his plaid bathrobe.

"Why?" David shouted.

"You won't be needing it."

"Dad, I'm just a little late."

"A little later than last night," his mother said.

"An hour and a half late to be precise, Rosalyn. From now until graduation, there will be no nights out. Do you understand that, David?"

He looked to his mother to rescue him. "You can't hang this one on me. That's house arrest, Mom."

"Those are the house rules," his dad told him.

The fury in his father's face almost made David back off. "You can't do that, Dad. I'm not a kid anymore."

"You're acting like one."

"We're just hanging out at the cafe. Listening to the Beatles. Talking to the girls. School's almost out. The guys will all be going in different directions after that."

"Rock bands?" Clayton asked in utter disgust.

"And the girls—if they're nice girls—should be home in bed." His mother's comment only added fuel to the fire.

He glared at them both. "The two of you are too stinking old-fashioned. And I will go out if I want to."

That did it. His dad's face flushed a beet red. "There will be no car for graduation. You can count on that."

"Clayton, can't we talk about this in the morning?"

"No, Rosalyn. I've made up my mind. We'll talk about the car again in the fall when he goes to college."

David sulked in his room for a week, his grades tumbling with his mood. And then at the urging of friends on the basketball team, he struck out in the name of freedom. He took an extra set of his dad's car keys from the kitchen cupboard, waited until midnight, and climbed out the bedroom window.

His break for freedom began with drag racing on the streets of Brentwood and ended at three in the morning with an accident that left one classmate paralyzed, the town in an uproar, and his father pulling him out of school three weeks before the prom.

David wasn't driving the car, but on the next drag race he would have been at the wheel. The courts were ready to hang him on two counts: The Lincoln Continental was registered in his dad's name, and David had taken it without permission.

He would become his father's hardest case, his greatest shame. David tried to remember why he had aligned himself with the daredevils in his class. Tried even now, more than three decades later, to come up with a logical reason for taking his father's Lincoln that night without permission. He still recoiled at the memory of his father's punishment—no prom and a summer away from his buddies, working on his grandparents' farm. But it was better than the punishment meted to the driver of the car. Three years probation for the injury of their classmate.

When David tried to beg off from a summer in Alabama with his mother's parents, his father stared him down. "David, you need a summer on the farm. It will give you time to think about another young man of eighteen who will never walk again."

David's first glimpse of Everdale, Alabama, was blurry. He sat in the passenger train with his booted feet sprawled on the seat across from him and stared through the smoky windows out on the farm fields outside of Everdale.

As they pulled into the station he turned to his mother beside him and said, "I won't stay here."

"You will if you ever want to go to college. And if you don't, I think the army can use you."

USC had been his goal for years, a dream lost during those last few weeks of high school. Without his parents funding him, the dream was dead. It was dead anyway without his high school diploma. "That's out now, Mom. Dad pulled me out of school before I could graduate."

"You can be thankful he did. The scandal is hard enough on your father. It would have ruined you."

He unraveled and stood beside her. "So what do you expect?"

"There's a school in Everdale. It goes until the end of June. You can finish there. We've already arranged it."

"That's five miles from the farm. I'll need a car."

"No car. You have two good legs. That's more than your friend has now. So walk, David."

His grandfather proved less vindictive. He figured the school bus would get David home early for the chores. As it turned out, a pretty girl by the name of Ashley rode the bus for two miles each day. She lived on the outskirts of town in a large house with a big wraparound porch and a gazebo out back. And she had a mom who baked the best cookies and cooked the most marvelous dinners on Sundays.

To get Ashley's attention and to wrangle invitations to her house, David took a shine to her brother, a beanpole of a guy with an easygoing grin and a jalopy of his own. They had basketball in common and the desire to finish their sentences in Everdale. David only had to endure a summer there, but William felt he was on a life sentence if he didn't join the navy. They cruised around town in the old jalopy with David conniving every excuse to go back to the house to see Ashley. When he tired of slamming hook shots into the basket with William, he'd sit in the gazebo beside Ashley. And every time he did, he fell more madly in love.

They talked about growing up in opposite parts of the country. About their lifestyles that were so different. And they talked about the future when the war in Vietnam would be over. She wanted to be a nurse. He told her that his parents wanted him to become a partner in his father's law firm.

"Is that what you want to do, David?"

"What I want to do is stay here and marry you."

She turned scarlet. "You don't even know me."

"Then go out with me."

"Mother won't let me. She says you're going back to California for college soon, if the army doesn't get you first."

Ashley would be going to the community college in a neighboring town, three thousand miles away from USC. "Ash, I'll convince my parents to let me go to college here in Alabama."

Her laughter was musical. "I don't think they'd like that."

"You're probably right, but I want to stay here with you."

That day he trusted her with the story of drag racing on the streets of Brentwood and the tragic accident that had brought him to Alabama. He looked away when he admitted that he still had nightmares thinking about his friend who would never walk again.

She had reached up and turned his face toward her. "You weren't driving the car. You can't blame yourself forever."

He could still remember the kindness and sympathy in her eyes as she looked up at him, her eyes as blue as the sky above the gazebo. He thought of the natural wave to her long corn-silk hair and the sweet smile that had filled her face. Like a man trying to get everything off his chest, he had blurted, "I took my dad's car that night—and let someone else drive it."

"You stole it." It wasn't a question, but a correction of terms, an attempt to put it all in perspective. "We all make mistakes. My mama knows of only one Person who can forgive us."

"That's right," Ashley's mother said, coming up the gazebo steps just then with cookies and milk. "God forgives people who ask him. You remember that, young man, and you'll do all right."

But he ended up doing everything wrong from the day he stole his first kiss while they sat on the swings by the gazebo until that day on his grandparents' farm. Ashley had driven out in her brother's jalopy to buy some fresh eggs. She stepped from the car with the basket in her hands.

David ran over to meet her. "I didn't know you were coming."

"I didn't know my mother would let me. But she needed some eggs, and I offered to go buy them for her."

"They have eggs in Everdale."

"But you weren't there."

He took her basket and then her hand. "Then we'd better go out to the hen house and get them."

"Where are your grandparents?" she asked as they walked along, side by side.

"Gone to Montgomery—for the whole day, I hope."

"Gone? They're never gone. You told me they were too old and decrepit to get around much."

"That's why my mother came back early. Grams hasn't been feeling well lately."

"Then it's a good thing you're with her."

"That's what Grams says. She hates the thought of my going."

"You're leaving?"

"I don't want to. Mother and I argued all last night about my going to community college here, but it ended in a nasty row. By the time she left for the doctor's this morning with my grandparents, Mother looked more in need of a doctor."

"You're here alone?"

His lips went dry, his heart pounding against his chest wall. It scared him to even think that they were alone for the first time since he'd met her three months ago. His hand tightened around hers, and he felt the dampness in her palm.

He showed her the whole farm, walking end to end, not wanting to let her go. They laughed as he showed her how to pick eggs from the hen house, and after he set the basket down, they walked down to the river. That's where he stole his second kiss, but she pulled free and ran from him.

He caught up with her and took her hand again. "I'm sorry."

She smiled coyly. "I'm not."

His chest wall was about to explode. She slowed her pace to his. On the way back they stopped off at the barn. She allowed her eyes to scan back toward the river. "It's so beautiful here."

"I hated it when I first came. I hated getting up in the half-light of early morning. But granddad treated me like a man."

"You are a man," she said. Again she flushed a cardinal red.

He struggled to keep his emotions in check. "Do you know much about farming, Ashley?"

"Next to nothing. Only what you tell me." She tucked a strand of flaxen hair behind her ear, and he longed to reach out and touch those golden waves.

"It only took me a few days to catch on to the routine," he said. "Carry oats and corn to the horses; then put them out to pasture. And take the shelled corn to the cows. But it took me awhile to get the hang of the milking machines. Now I don't mind the chores at all. Not when I'm with Gramps."

"You're happy here?"

"Because you're here. And this is the first time someone really needed me. At least that's what my grandparents tell me all the time. It's not someone planning my life for me.

Gramps made me feel like part of the team. Like I'm really needed."

"I need you too," she whispered. "Don't go away."

He tried to shut out her words as he rambled on. "I've come to love the smell of the pasture and the hay in the loft and the river running by. I don't even mind the smells in the barn—especially when the cows are out grazing like they are now. That gave me the chance to hose the place down this morning. The barn and the farm animals represent my grandfather to me. And he's pretty special."

"And your grandmother?"

"She's a sweet old thing. Frail and getting a bit deaf, but she makes me feel at home. Gives me a great big bear hug when I remember to take off my boots before going into the kitchen."

"Your grandparents do sound special."

"They are. They never mention the accident back in California. It's as though it never happened, and I'm sure my folks told them about it." He smiled. "I think the best thing every morning is going back up to the farmhouse for Grams's ham and biscuits for breakfast and the sound of the skillet sizzling. It all grows on you. And then—then I met you, Ashley. If it hadn't been for you, I wouldn't have finished high school."

"That did take a bit of prodding," she said.

He slipped his arm around her waist, the blood roiling inside him. "I don't care what my parents want. I want us to be together forever."

"But we can't, David. You're going away."

"I'll come back someday. Once I finish university."

"You'll forget me by then."

He saw tears in her eyes and reached up to wipe them away. "I love you, Ashley."

She was in his arms and he was kissing her hard, hungrily, passionately. He wanted nothing more than to stay here and be with her, but by the next weekend at the latest, his mother planned to pack up and take him home again.

Behind them, the horse neighed. Gently, David took Ashley's hand and led her into the barn, saying, "I don't expect everyone back for a couple of hours."

She pulled away from him as they reached the horse's stall. He could still see her, holding the sugar cube in her hand for the stallion to nibble. Ashley half turned to smile at David, and every desire inside him was for her.

She lowered her eyes, the long lashes touching her cheeks. "We mustn't," she said. "We mustn't, David."

"But we love each other. Isn't that enough?"

He took her hand and led her up the ladder to the loft where the sweet smell of hay and the scent of Ashley's cologne merged.

Later, when they heard the car coming back to the house, they made their way out the back entry of the barn and down to the creek; when they saw his mother they were approaching the farmhouse from the creek bed trail.

But Rosalyn Reynolds held up the basket of eggs and said, "Is this what you're looking for, David? You left it in front of the barn."

That night she stormed into his bedroom and said, "You are not to see that girl again—whatever her name is."

But he did, more than once walking the long distance over the country road to her house. Ten days later, David and his mother left Alabama early in the morning before he had a chance to tell Ashley good-bye. He did not see her again for five years. His letters to her came back unopened. The more she ignored him, the more he buried the guilt that he felt. He had loved her—still did—but he had in his impassioned youth demanded more of her than she should have given.

He was in his third year at the university before he remembered what Ashley's mother had told him. "God forgives people who ask him. You remember that, young man, and you'll do all right."

On his own he found a church in Long Beach and sat on the back pew, listening to old-time hymns and to what he would later define as a message of forgiveness. It was an invitation to peace from a Man on a cross. David didn't know what it meant exactly, but he knew the Man hanging there had extended his arms to him. Telling his parents was the toughest job of all.

Twelve months later changing his career major from graduate studies at law school to a seminary didn't sit well either. When he faced his dad with his decision, he had said apologetically, "I'm sorry, Dad, but I think you know I was never cut out to be a lawyer."

His father had been too choked up to do much more than nod, but his mother had wrung her hands, saying over and over, "But a pastor in the family. What will we do with a pastor?"

At the end of his first year at seminary, his grandparents were forced to admit their frailty, leave their farm, and move into a nearby nursing home. David withdrew from seminary to be near them and moved back east to take up his first pastorate in the little town of Everdale. The church was an hour's drive from Grams and Gramps and a stone's throw from the house with the wraparound porch where Ashley still lived.

She was a nurse now, working the nightshift at the hospital in Everdale. It wasn't hard to find her, not when she sat in his congregation, week after week. But it was months before he could convince her to go out with him again. To trust him. And that wouldn't have happened if he hadn't run into her at the nursing home visiting his grandparents.

They married a year later, Ashley refusing to come down the aisle to him in a white bridal gown. It didn't matter. She was coming to him—his wife, his bride, his love. If need be, he would take a lifetime to make up to her for those stolen moments in his grandparents' barn.

In that small church in Everdale and in the cathedral where he was now the senior pastor, his message continued to be one of hope in the Man on the cross. He continued to encourage the young people of his congregations to maintain abstinence before marriage—never admitting that it was a flawed man who stood behind the pulpit.

Even now driving toward his university class three thousand miles from his grandmother's farm, he remembered as though it were yesterday the sweet smell of the hay and the prickle of the straw against his bare skin. And Ashley there with him. He gripped the steering wheel, his longing for his wife more intense than that day so long ago on the farm near Everdale.

Fifteen

When Jillian opened the door to Kerina's empty dressing room, the sweet fragrance of a hundred flowers assailed her. Bouquets from Kerina's fans and friends occupied every available space. Jillian glanced at some of the gift cards as she crossed the room: the usual three dozen red roses from Franck, a variegated arrangement from Elias and Nicole Mc-Claren, a massive pink azalea from the maitre d' at the Sacher, and a vase of yellow tulips flown in from Holland from the director of the Opera House. Almost lost among the larger arrangements was the orchid in a bud vase with a thank-you note from Elizabeth and Raquel.

But Jillian was drawn to the red carnations on Kerina's dressing table. She snatched up the card and read with surprise:

> Good luck and good music, Miss Rudzinski.
> Lieutenant Chandler Reynolds

Kerina's gowns for the evening's performance hung from a shiny brass pole. An elegant Valentino in a shimmering midnight blue with a tiered hem—its frills and lace scented with Guerlain from Paris. The form-fitting black silk purchased in Milan that she would wear with the diamond earrings Franck had given her. And Jillian's favorite—the low-cut, off-the-shoulder Parisian gown in a cranberry red with its spaghetti straps and long, free-flowing neck scarf.

Jillian turned her attention to the search for a white envelope marked with the lieutenant's name. She expected to find his concert tickets propped against the mirror or lying among the bottles of perfume. Instead she found Kerina's dresser drawer ajar. A sepia photo stared up at her, its reddish browns faded and yellowed with age. It lay on top of Kerina's journal—a picture of a young man, tall as a beanstalk, his hands thrust into his trouser pockets, strands of his thick hair windblown. He stood against the backdrop of the Water Tower, the stone landmark that had weathered the great Chicago fire. The Water Tower had survived. But what of this young man? Jillian picked up the photo for a closer look. It was not a handsome face yet it was striking, winsome with its dimpled grin. She guessed his eyes to be blue, the thick hair blond. Kerina must have caught him unawares for he had turned to look back, half smiling as she snapped the picture.

On the back in Kerina's brush script were the words: *Bill. Chicago*—and the date of her American debut in Chicago. Kerina would have been little more than eighteen. This must be the snapshot that she had not wanted to share. Jillian's own question came back as piercing as a shard of glass.

"Is he anyone I know, Kerina?"

What had she answered? "He was a long time ago." No, "He was long before your time, Jillian."

Jillian looked again at the casual pose. He wore a tie and dress shirt, dark slacks and a suit jacket. She guessed him to be a businessman meeting Kerina in the heart of the Windy City on his lunch hour. Or had they been stolen moments, a clandestine meeting at the Water Tower? His name was Bill. Bill what? Bill of Chicago—that someone special from Kerina's past? Jillian noted the high forehead and hooded brows. She bent lower, squinting. His face smiled but not his eyes. She had seen his face before. No, that was foolishness. The photo was ages old, yet those features belonged to the present as though she had faced him once, talked to him. Talked about him. Vague impressions that faded and came back. Receded and reappeared. It was that kind of a face. The face of a remembered past, of a living present. She tried to pluck from memory the rest of the conversation at the Sacher Cafe. She recalled begging, "Can't we squeeze Chicago in?" But Kerina was going on a trip alone—back to somewhere special. To *someone special?* Back to this man?

Is this Bill planning to rendezvous with you? No, you would do nothing to ruin your career or your reputation.

Jillian took one final glance at the prominent features: the firm jaw, wide eyes, aquiline nose, an almost impish, devilish grin. Something in his expression reminded Jillian of the way Santos had often looked at her in Rome. She had been blinded to his weaknesses, and when their romance ended in a fit of anger, she had torn Santos's pictures into bits and thrown them at his feet. But Kerina, more gentle-hearted and coming from more sentimental times, had saved this photograph.

Impulsively, Jillian eased the sepia photo behind one of the clamps that held the mirror in place. Something lingered on the edge of memory. "Did Kerina mention a last name?" she mumbled out loud.

"His name was Bill," Kerina said. "Bill VanBurien."

Jillian spun around. Kerina stood in the doorway looking pale and drawn, her ringed hands clasped in front of her.

"Kerina, I was looking for Lieutenant Reynolds's tickets."

"And found Bill's picture instead."

"I'm sorry. Your dresser drawer was open."

"Careless of me. I forgot to set the tickets out for you. I've—" She seemed to forget what she was about to say as she closed the door and crossed the dressing room to Jillian.

"You're late, Kerina. You'll have to hurry."

"I was talking with Franck."

"Arguing again?"

"Yes, about another trip to Moscow." She looked distraught, wisps of her hair falling over one brow. "I told him I couldn't go this time. He insists that I go."

"But you're exhausted."

Kerina rearranged a carnation and then rummaged in the drawer of her dressing table. She lifted her journal and opened it. "Oh, here they are." She handed an envelope to Jillian. "These are for Lieutenant Reynolds. But would you tell him I won't be able to keep that appointment this evening?"

"What? After we wrote and told him you would? You can't do that. The lieutenant came all the way from Bosnia."

"For an interview with me? I think not." Her eyes filled with pain. "Oh, all right. Have him come backstage for just a few minutes. You be here. I'll send him off with you afterwards."

"He'll have a guest with him."

"Have his guest come too." Kerina reached out and squeezed Jillian's hand. "It's best. You'll see. Just a quick visit. No more."

"Franck's idea?"

"Franck doesn't know about the lieutenant."

"Then why? It's not like you to break a commitment."

"Franck made dinner plans with Elias and Nicole for after the concert." Kerina sounded rattled. "Franck insists we can't disappoint them. Not when he's negotiating that art sale for Elias."

"A Degas?" Jillian asked.

"A Josef VanStryker."

"I didn't think VanStryker was that well known. Died in the thirties, didn't he, Kerina?"

"The early forties in a concentration camp. Franck is excited about the renewed interest in his work recently."

"And that makes the value go up into the thousands?"

Kerina eyed Jillian surreptitiously. "Into the millions now. And it means a sizable commission for Franck. There you go again, Jillian, showing a real interest in art. I thought you just pampered me when I wanted to browse in the museums."

"I told you. Your interest rubbed off on me. So Franck wants to get in on the ground level while he can afford a VanStryker?"

"It's for Elias—but Franck has resale value in mind too."

"I thought he just collected art. I never knew him to sell or negotiate for it. Franck usually takes what he wants."

Color rose in Kerina's cheeks. "Go, please. Don't keep the lieutenant waiting. I have to dress for the concert. Franck will be back soon. He can zip me up."

"But he's upset you. You're flittery as a hummingbird."

"He'll come back smiling."

"He never smiles."

"And he never stays angry long. He won't want me to either. This performance is important to both of us."

"Then what's troubling you? Moscow? The McClarens? Not the concert? You've played hundreds of times before."

"Nothing is wrong."

Jillian felt a deepening sense of gloom. Kerina and Franck's evening with the McClarens alarmed her. She had no way to let Brooks Rankin or Joel Gramdino know about the dinner arrangement. *Stop fretting*, she told herself. *It's just an innocent night out. Kerina and Franck dine with kings and queens, composers, and the wealthy of the world. Why not with an art collector and his lovely French wife?*

Her worry persisted, her thoughts on an unsuspecting art collector like McClaren sitting in the loge section, thrilled with Kerina's magical touch, and going home at midnight to find that a painting was missing. The Registry's hands were tied. How could they warn any of the rich of Vienna without alerting the thief?

As Kerina slid onto the cushioned bench, she blew Jillian a kiss that reflected in the mirror; the lights above the glass caught the glitter of her rings.

"Don't be fretful, Jillian dear. Remember, I promised I would give you the performance of a lifetime tonight."

Jillian nodded toward the man in the snapshot. "Will he be in the audience this evening?"

"No," she said in a whisper. "Bill will not be here."

She watched Kerina pick up her hairbrush and in long even strokes brush her russet hair back into a shiny chignon. Suddenly Jillian felt that this moment would linger in her memory in the months ahead, long after she left Kerina's employ: the glamorous Kerina Rudzinski with her back to Jillian in the simple act of brushing her hair, a vase of red carnations from an unknown soldier on her dressing table, and a faded snapshot of someone special tucked in the mirror's edge.

Ashley Reynolds turned from her mirror as her son came into her suite. He looked striking in his black tuxedo, his father's Giorgio scent wafting into the room with him.

Ashley scrunched the tip of her nose. "Smells familiar."

"Dad sent it. Guess he didn't want you to forget him."

"How could I? I've known him forever—and been married to him almost as long, it seems. Son, it would take more than the absence of Giorgio to make me forget your dad."

Chandler's dry chuckle drifted off. "Thought I'd buy some Givenchy while we're here in Vienna and send it home to Dad to try. And Chanel for Grams."

"I'll help you pick them out."

"I'd like to buy something nice like that for Zineta."

She nodded. He was giving her an approving appraisal now. "Do you ever look stunning, Mother!"

"I have an important date," she said lightly.

"Is that gown one of your retirement purchases?"

"No, I've worn it on two or three occasions, but no one in Vienna will know that. Are you ready?"

He held up his black tie and cuff links and pointed to his stocking feet. "Help."

She laughed. "Come here."

Chandler crossed the room to her. Her voice was still light, cheerful. "You are just like your father. With all the weddings he performs, he still depends on me to do his bow tie."

"He just likes being spoiled."

"And you?"

"Lack of experience," he admitted.

"It's easy—just like tying your shoelaces."

He bent down as she looped the strap around his neck. She crossed the two ends and made a bow and gave it an extra twist to straighten it. "There, that looks perfect."

He glanced in her mirror and eyeing her from there asked, "So Dad's still in the marrying business? Do you think he'd do the honors for me?"

Her heart skipped a beat. "Zineta?" She said the name without rancor, without even a tremor in her voice, but she couldn't meet his gaze even in the mirror.

"Could you handle your dad's premarital lectures?"

"I have trouble with his sermons."

"Believing them?"

"Just listening to them. Ten minutes in and I'm out."

She fussed with his bow tie again as she rose to David's defense. "He's a good preacher. Very precise. Honest."

"I just can't live up to his expectations so I tune out."

She understood. She shared Chandler's inadequacies. "You try too hard to please him; I like you the way you are."

"I wish Dad did. These last few years I feel like I'm falling short. Like a piece of me is missing." He thumped his chest, sending the tie askew again. "I've got a big empty hollow inside me, Mom. I blame it on Dad, and it really isn't his fault. No kid could have had a better father."

She forced herself to look up into his handsome face and noticed the shadowed half circles under his eyes. She longed for the freedom to say, "You have your birth mother's gift of music, your birth father's features."

188

But Chandler had David's strengths and integrity—and most importantly, with all of Chandler's uncertainty, he always had David's love. It was more than his birth parents had given him.

"If Dad married Zineta and me, he might like her better."

"I'll talk to him when I get home. He might agree to a simple ceremony at home but not in the church."

"Because she's pregnant? Wouldn't he bend the rules for me?"

"Would you want him to go against his convictions?"

Chandler dropped the cuff links into her hand. "Diamond cuff links. I found them in the suitcase from home."

"They belonged to your grandfather. Your dad wanted you to wear them," she told him as she snapped the second one in place.

"Barely remember Grandpa Clayton."

"Don't tell your grandmother that."

"Never," he promised. "Rosalyn ole girl thinks I'm sharp as two ice picks. We chat Gramps every time we get together."

"Your grandmother needs that. It's all she has left."

"She has you and Dad."

"I never counted."

"I've never understood why. You bend over backwards to give her a good time."

"Not your problem, Chan." *You have enough of your own,* she thought. "Now get your shoes on and let's go, or we'll be late."

"The shoes don't fit."

"But I ordered your size."

He grinned. "But you didn't order the swelling in my foot to go down."

"Is that why you had trouble sleeping last night?" She followed him into his room and picked up his trail of clothes from the floor. "I thought I heard you tossing and turning."

"I was dreaming about Randy and Zineta and the land mines. I woke up in a sweat." He smiled reassuringly. "And then I realized I was in Vienna—and I couldn't get back to sleep."

"I'll pinch you if you fall asleep at the opera."

"Good. Will these do?" he asked, pointing to his army boots.

They were ankle boots, black and shiny. "No one will notice, Chan. And you'd better use your crutches tonight."

"No way. I'm not hobbling into Miss Rudzinski's dressing room on a pair of crutches."

In spite of the crowd inside the Opera House, Jillian recognized Chandler Reynolds from his picture on the cover of *Time* magazine. He stood waiting for her near the foot of the grand marble staircase, his hand resting on the wide banister.

He was much taller than she had guessed, and she thought him handsome in his tuxedo, looking confident like a man with a purpose. He was alone and she felt hopeful. She drew his attention with a quick wave and navigated her way swiftly through the pressing crowd. She caught the masculine scent of his cologne as she reached him, a fragrance that she could not name, and yet she would in the future always associate it with this moment.

"Lieutenant Reynolds?"

His face lit with a beguiling smile, his gaze direct and friendly as he took her outstretched hand. "Chandler, please."

Even as he greeted her, she felt a touch of color reaching her cheeks. He had that fresh-scrubbed look, an all-American face too pale from the Bosnian winter; yet his profile was strong, his frame athletic, his hooded eyes shiny brown like an autumn leaf.

Those windows of his soul galvanized her. *Hold a plumbline to a man's eyes.* Her father speaking. Her own heart scudding, thwacking, doing crazy circular jigs inside her chest.

190

"I forgot to tell you I'd be out of uniform. It's packed away in the hotel closet." His voice was deep, utterly charming. "I'm just another concertgoer tonight, Miss Ingram."

"Jillian, please. And you look like one of the regulars."

"Good. I thought maybe we had missed each other."

"I'm late, lieutenant."

"You're here now." His voice seemed to say, *Don't go away.*

As she stood there with him, Brooks Rankin and his wife and Joel Gramdino strolled past her and started up the stairs. She felt their silence, their awareness, Brooks's disapproval. Midway up the carpeted stairwell, Gramdino glanced back and saluted.

She went back to appraising the lieutenant. His hair was post military, too short to slick down. Curly strands of auburn hair fell across his forehead as though he had just stepped from the shower before coming to the Opera House. Up close, out of uniform, he didn't look exactly like the face on the *Time* cover, and yet there was something familiar about him—as though she had seen that angular face, the firm set of the jaw, the captivating smile before. She recognized him. Knew him. And yet he was a stranger.

"Do you ever get used to this opulence?" he asked, gazing around. "I can hardly wait to see the paintings upstairs."

"You're into art?"

"From the minute I walked into the Opera House."

She conjured up a romantic entanglement, a flurry of activity showing the young soldier the highlights of Vienna. She started to say, "Do you know Vienna?" and caught herself dead.

Don't go goggle-eyed over the American soldier in a sharp-looking tuxedo, she warned herself. *He's here as a well-wisher to Kerina, and after tonight, he will be gone. No dinner and dancing with this young man. No strolling through the parks of Vienna. By the time the concert is over, he won't even remember he met you.*

"Hello!" he said. "I thought I lost you for a moment."

"Sorry, lieutenant, my mind is on a thousand things."

"Too bad it's not on me."

She held out the small envelope. "I brought your tickets for the concert."

"I have tickets—in the peanut gallery."

"Miss Rudzinski insists on upgrading you. You're in the loge with Elias and Nicole McClaren."

"Box seating? I can't accept that." He seemed serious, even when he smiled, his eyes intense and direct as he looked down at her. "What about the interview with Miss Rudzinski?"

"She can only spare a few minutes after the concert. She's sorry—"

He controlled his disappointment. "Just my luck."

"Chandler." A voice behind him. He turned, the expression on his face one of pleasure as he greeted an attractive, older woman and tucked her arm in his.

The spell had broken. Embarrassed, Jillian didn't wait to be introduced. "I must get backstage, lieutenant. Kerina—Miss Rudzinski—always has last minute things for me to do."

"Of course. Will we see you back—?"

She didn't let him finish, but slipped through the crowd, her cheeks florid. *You are one good-looking young man, Lieutenant Reynolds,* she sighed. *But your date! She's old enough to be your mother!*

A few steps from the entry to the Opera House, Jokhar Gukganov and Vladimir, his well-dressed bodyguard, awaited the arrival of a gray limousine. They were dressed in black tie and blended with the crowd, looking much like any concertgoers eager for a night of music in Vienna. A third man stood five feet from them, a smirk on his youthful face, his thick dark hair unruly, his restlessness growing with each passing second; Pierre had immigrated to Moscow from Paris with a questionable resumé, seeking quick riches. Tonight he wore the green jacket and britches of an Austrian, the outfit looking much like a uniform. It would pass as one, once Jokhar gave the signal.

Jokhar Gukganov was a survivalist, fiftyish, gray-haired, his face harsh, his skin sallow. His perpetual frown formed vertical ridges between his eyes. He had left politics, his position and profit among the Russian rich secured at the fall of communism. Since then he had taken over the ownership of his father's design company, a private enterprise that paid well.

Some considered his sudden wealth stolen money, Mafia-backed cash. Jokhar never explained himself to others. He considered wealth his right, the result of wise business moves. These days he drove Cadillacs and a Mercedes with tinted windows and a chauffeur at the wheel. He drank champagne freely, not the hard Vodka of his youth, and packed a revolver and expensive tins of red caviar whenever he traveled. He dined at five-star hotels near the Kremlin and owned a villa decorated with masterpieces for his third wife. Most people did his bidding.

But lately, Franck Petzold was being overly cautious, wary of the young woman in Kerina Rudzinski's employ. Yesterday at the McClaren exhibit at the Academy of Fine Arts, Petzold had said, "Jokhar, if you want any more paintings, you must steal them yourself. But leave the McClaren paintings alone."

Jokhar had scanned the marvelous display. "Surely he has enough for both of us. And even more in his home."

"His place is heavily secured. You can't scale the walls. The only safe way in is with the McClaren limousine. There's a code system in the dash that opens the gate."

"So I would need the McClarens' chauffeur."

Jokhar shifted his weight and smiled at Vladimir, his thoughts still his own. Until recently, Petzold had worked alone. The thrill of the chase belonged to him, but tonight— for the first time—Jokhar would remove the painting from the wall himself and experience that personal thrill of choosing a Degas or another Rembrandt.

He needed Franck to transport the masterpiece to Moscow, but he would have the thrill of taking the prize. What was it that Franck was trying to save for himself? It had to be the Degas or Rembrandt. Petzold wanted these artists in his own collection. Threatening Franck's exposure would do no good. Outwitting him was the only way—outwitting him like he was planning to do in the sale of the fake VanStryker. Jokhar liked daring moves. Surprises. With the crowd at the Opera House bent on an evening of music, who would even notice the kidnapping of a chauffeur?

Vladimir touched Jokhar's shoulder. "That's the car we are expecting, sir."

With an imperceptible move of his hand, Jokhar signaled Pierre as the chauffeur-driven limousine slowed for a stop. Pierre's muscles flexed. Jokhar saw the excitement in Pierre's eyes, felt it in the blood coursing through his own body. Pierre sprang toward the curb, stepped out in front of the McClarens' vehicle and passed in front of it to the driver's side.

Easy, Jokhar thought. *Not yet. Give the chauffeur time to open the door for the McClarens.*

Jokhar watched with pleasure as Frau McClaren stepped from the limousine and waited for her husband. Jokhar knew women and fashion, and Nicole McClaren was elegantly dressed in a Yves Saint Laurent velvet gown that revealed her excellent figure. Her jet-black hair was slicked back from her face; her smile was bewitching, her eyes catlike. She noticed Jokhar, even flirted briefly, and then she turned with a smile and linked her arm in her husband's.

Elias McClaren took obvious pride in his wife, strutting away in his black tie, pleased with the woman by his side. *No,* Jokhar thought, *we will have no trouble from them.* A woman like that thrived on attention and would be expecting it in the crowd moving toward the Opera House. He turned to signal Pierre again.

It was too late. The McClarens' chauffeur was unaware of anything unusual until the metal object crashed against his neck. One quick blow and he crumpled without a whimper.

"You fool, Pierre. You didn't have to hurt him," Jokhar said. "We needed him alert to get us through the gate."

Pierre was thirty years his junior, jaunty and defiant and given to using his fists and not his brain. "I could not risk him putting up a fight or calling out for help," he said as he braced the injured man against the car. "Here, help me get him inside."

They were holding up traffic, but they wrangled the side door of the limousine open and shoved the chauffeur inside. He slumped to the floor. Vladimir piled in behind him.

"Too much *Krugel*," Jokhar told the man in the car behind them. "He will be all right. He is our friend. We will take him home now and let him sleep it off."

Pierre cocked the chauffeur's cap on his own head and slid behind the wheel. "Too small," he complained.

"Your head is too big. Shut up and drive," Jokhar said.

"Fish the keys out of his pocket."

"Since when do you need keys to start a car?" But Jokhar wrestled the recalcitrant key chain from the unconscious man's hand. "A coded key," he said.

"Not if I push the right button. See—just like that."

It was a jerky start, but they were off, pulling away before the police officer who was cutting across the street could question them.

"Where to?" Pierre asked.

As they drove away, Jokhar pulled on a stocking mask and gloves. "To the McClarens', you fool."

"Just give me directions. And use my name."

Jokhar tugged a hand-drawn map from his pocket. "Right at the corner. The McClarens have an older mansion outside Vienna."

The chauffeur lying on the floor of the limousine was moaning now, struggling back to consciousness. Vladimir put his foot on the man's knee. "Move and I will crush your knee bone."

The eyes opened, stark fear in them. "Where are we going?" he asked in German.

"Home," Vladimir told him. "Just cooperate and nothing more will happen to you. Start by telling us your name."

"Hans."

For a second he relaxed, and then, twisting his body, grabbed for Jokhar's leg. Vladimir came down hard on the chauffeur's knee, and the yelp of pain amused Pierre.

"What was that about me hurting Hans?"

"Shut up, Pierre." Right now Jokhar feared two men out of control. The revolver was in Vladimir's hand, and that familiar tick along his jaw throbbed. His face hardened as he bent over Hans and shoved the barrel of his gun beneath the man's chin.

"You understand?"

"What do you want?" Hans asked hoarsely.

"A masterpiece from your employer's library."

As Hans's frantic gaze turned to him, Jokhar said, "Do as my young friend says, Hans."

Hans's nod was blocked by the barrel of the gun. Sweat poured from his face. He lay motionless, the seat of his pants damp now.

"You will get us safely through the gate at the McClarens' residence and into the house," Jokhar said beneath his mask. "Is anyone in the house, Hans?"

The answer came back slurred. "The maid—Anna."

"She will be safe as long as you help us. Fifteen minutes, that's all we need. You will get us through the gate and turn off the alarm system."

Panic mounted in the man's eyes.

"There she is," Pierre announced. "The gate is just ahead."

Vladimir's revolver wedged tighter beneath the chauffeur's jaw, the weight of the gun pressed hard against his neck.

Jokhar put out a restraining hand. "Ease up. His lips are turning blue, Vladimir."

"Good. Then he understands us."

"Now, Hans," Jokhar said, the excitement building in him, "you must do exactly as we say. If not, you and Anna will have a long rest."

Sixteen

As Chandler took his seat in the Opera House, he could think of no one but Jillian Ingram, the girl with the silken tawny hair and those magnificent sapphire blue eyes. Then, as the house lights dimmed, he did not think of her.

A hush swept across the audience as Kerina Rudzinski stepped onto the stage. For a second she stood there, re-splendent in a cranberry-red gown, a bloodstone locket in the hollow of her throat. He watched, spellbound as she glided gracefully across the brightly lit stage, the feathery tapping of her heels and the rustle of her gown echoing in the stillness. Adjusting his binoculars, he brought Miss Rudzinski's lovely face into focus. A delicate, oval face soft as silk, arched brows pencil-thin, perfectly formed lips a glossy vermilion. For just a second, he wondered what in her life had left the tiny twist of sadness at the corner of her mouth.

She seemed to be waiting for the tap of the conductor's baton. Or was she searching her soul for that moment of calm before she played? He seemed to know her so well without knowing her at all. But he knew music and knew what drove a musician. His own fingers itched to lift the bow and glide it over the strings of her violin. His grip tight-ened on the binoculars. Her auburn hair was almost the color of his own, the long-lashed eyes shining as she faced her audience, her smile warm and gentle as she cradled her Stradivarius. He had not expected her to be so elegant, so breathtaking, so ravishingly beautiful.

Stillness thundered in Ashley's ears. She guessed that the silence was for more than the anticipated concert, more than politeness. It was for the violinist herself, a legend in the world of music.

The stage lights fell softly on Kerina's face, highlighting her cheekbones and the flawless porcelain skin. Ashley recognized the long, reddish-brown hair, not falling softly over the pillow as it did in that hospital bed so long ago but pulled back in an elegant chignon, revealing that same fragile beauty and delicate features. She knew Kerina's eyes would be pensive, full of sadness, unchanged from that first meeting twenty-six years ago when a shy, frightened Kerry Kovac had met her gaze.

Kerry Kovac. Kerina Rudzinski. One and the same.

Kerina stood center stage now. The lights caught the glitter of her glamorous Parisian gown—a low-cut, off-the-shoulder, waist-slimming evening dress with a long, flowing, berry-red train. Kerina's charisma, that magnetic smile, the perfect fit of her designer's gown delighted the Austrians. She had not played a note, and yet her hold on the audience was complete. They admired, adored, respected her.

With graceful, sure movements Kerina tucked her violin under her chin, cupped her fingers over the strings, and placed her thumb on the finger board. The Vienna Philharmonic Orchestra sat poised, ready to accompany her.

The conductor tapped the music stand. All eyes turned to his gloved hands. Into the hushed auditorium flowed the magical sounds of the first violinists. The sounds grew more powerful as all the strings—the violins, the cellos, the violas, the bass—and the harpist joined together.

The conductor's baton dipped toward Kerina. She lifted her bow high in her hand, then gently, skillfully she fingered the strings and guided the bow across them. The conductor raised his arms and brought them together with a gusto. The entire orchestra obeyed. The thirty-four violinists. The woodwind instruments: the bassoon and oboe, the flutes and clarinets. The brass section with its French horns and trumpets, the trombones and the deep bellow of the tuba. The glorious sounds of "The Blue Danube" vibrated through the Opera House.

The conductor's baton lowered, lowered, lowered. The orchestra played softly now, their music muted, as the violin in Kerina's hand sang out in rich, warm tones. Kerina's fingers ran over the strings like a bird taking flight, like the fine drizzle of the first spring rain, like the gentle sway of a field full of golden tulips. Heart and musician were one.

The effect of her music was hypnotic—Chandler and the audience experiencing the music, caught up in it, lost in it. Kerina's lithe body seemed to dance with the lilting waltz, her instrument dipping and rocking with her body. The Austrians around Ashley swayed to the melody. Elias and Nicole McClaren in the box seats with them linked arms. Ashley's feet tapped to the music. Her heart sang, and yet she was on the outside looking in, shut out from the joy around her. But she knew from the happiness on Chandler's face and the glowing expressions on the faces of the Austrians that they had been transported back to those glorious days when Strauss and his waltzes had awakened music in the hearts of the Viennese.

A thousand acid thoughts crossed Ashley's mind. Her son was enchanted by the music of the woman who had given him away. The last time she saw Kerina she had knelt beside her in the hospital nursery in Everdale and unfolded Chandler's receiving blanket. Ashley had wanted that baby, yearned for him, and knew that he would be hers if the adoption went through. With mixed emotions and her own heart stretched to the breaking point, she had whispered, "Kerry, it's not too late to change your mind."

Now, once again, Ashley's heart stretched to the breaking point. If Chandler learned the truth, she might lose him forever. She glanced at Chandler sitting beside her, this attractive son of hers with his strong profile and classical features. He looked dashing in his tuxedo, his eyes glowing as he watched Kerina. Chandler was often so self-willed and restless that he could easily have been Ashley's own son. He seemed intent—he always did when he listened to music, as though he had moved to a different realm of pleasure. Ashley loved music; Chandler felt it, lived it. He let it stir his soul.

As they sat there high above the main auditorium, Chandler's arms rested on his lap, his long fingers gripping the program, his lips smiling. She wondered if he knew or whether the mystique of the violinist had caught him unawares. Ashley could not read her son's face. He had not come from her womb, but he was more her child, her son, than Kerina Rudzinski's. And nothing—and no one—could take him away from her, not even this gifted violinist.

He remained quiet, soft-spoken during both intermissions, his thoughts far away. She could not imagine what he knew. When she returned from the powder room during the last intermission, he seemed more withdrawn. She linked her arm in his. "What are you thinking about, Chandler?"

"About music. About packing my own violin away too soon."

"Maybe you should play it again when you get home."

"Maybe. First I have to decide what I'm going to do. But I know I want to stay on in Europe at least for a little while."

"You play the piano well," she said lightly.

"How many yardsticks did you break on my butt trying to get me to practice?"

"We didn't need the yardsticks when you took piano. You were born for it. But it took a little urging for violin practice."

He sighed. "Miss Rudzinski was born to play the violin. I played classical music in Bosnia until my cassettes broke. Randy teased me about that—even threatened to trash them for me."

"Didn't he like music?"

201

"We knew each other for years, and I don't even know. Sometimes he played rock and roll, but he joked about classical music."

"What about his girlfriend?"

"Zineta loves music. I remember that. Kemal Hovic— he's the one who took her in when her family was killed— he plays the cello. I wish he could hear a concert like this one. Maybe he would be well again."

"He's ill?"

"Depressed. Devastated by his losses during the war. Zineta says he rarely says anything. Just sits there playing the cello."

Tears welled in her eyes. "It's good that he has his music."

"I wish I could give him something else to live for. Randy was good for him. Kemal was just beginning to take interest in life again—and then Randy was killed. Enough," he said, "or I'll have us both crying. It's time to get back to our seats. Let's not miss a note of this performance."

I would gladly run from it all, Ashley thought. *I'm afraid of where it will lead. Afraid of Kerina Rudzinski.*

Kerina was beautiful and gifted; she had the accolades of the music world and already two standing ovations in this evening's performance. She had it all—all except the child she had given away. And after the concert tonight, would she claim him back—this handsome, young man with a piece of his life missing?

"Mother."

"Oh, Chandler. I was lost in thought."

"Well, I found you again." Smiling, he led her back to their loge seats in the McClarens' private box. He glanced around. The McClarens' seats were empty. "Why would anyone go home early?" he asked, incredulous.

"Shhh," Ashley said, her finger to her lips.

Kerina moved across the stage in a cloud of midnight blue—a Valentino gown with a heart-shaped bodice, its tiered skirt swirling around her narrow ankles. Under the stage lights her milky skin looked blue-white, her brushed hair like burnished gold. Dangling earrings and a glittering blue sapphire necklace sparkled as she walked.

Throughout the concert, Kerina had shown her versatility and skill as she played the glorious works of the sons of Austria, the sons of Vienna. But now as Kerina stepped to the microphone again, those sounds of Strauss, Haydn, Mozart, and Schubert continued to form only bitter, discordant notes in Ashley's mind.

She listened in disbelief as Kerina said, "Johannes Brahms' 'Lullaby' is not on this evening's program, but I would like to play it for someone special."

Closing her eyes, Kerina lifted her Stradivarius. The high gloss on the instrument gleamed as she held it. She began to play, and as she did, the concert hall filled with the sweet notes of Brahms' "Lullaby." *Could she be playing it for Chandler?* Ashley wondered. *Dear God, could anything done for Chandler out of love be wrong? Kerina, from your beauty alone,* she thought, *you could have had countless suitors or others flocking to you for your fame and fortune. Why, why then did you fall in love with my brother? And he with you?*

The romance should never have been. And yet without that short-lived affair, that stolen romance, there would be no Chandler. *My son,* Ashley thought, *loving him.* She had loved him from the moment she saw him in the delivery room. Nine pounds. Twenty-one inches long. Red face scrunched up; fists doubled; legs kicking. His first cry a long protesting wail as he entered the world. Then, as he was placed on the examining table, a little gurgle, a gasp as the cold stethoscope touched his chest.

Had Bill been Kerina's only love? Even back then she had loved her music, had carried her violin in a blue case into the hospital at Everdale. As she played now, it was obvious that music was still her life. It consumed her. She had sacrificed everything for it. But hadn't Ashley sacrificed too?

Unexpectedly, Ashley's bitterness was touched with sympathy. The program slipped from her hand. Did Kerina ever think about Chandler on April 15? Did she think back on the day he was born or count the candles on his birthday cakes? Did she think of a little boy growing up without her? Did she long for him at Christmastime or wrap presents that she could never send him? Did she ever wonder what kind of man Chandler had become? Surely these were things Ashley would have done.

She reflected back to that moment when Kerry Kovac held her son for the last time. Yes, Kerry would have thought of him as a little boy at a baseball game eating a foot-long hot dog or walking in the woods, or fishing with his dad. But did Kerina, the violinist, remember those dreams for her newborn son?

The orchestra hit a high note; it resounded through the auditorium and seemed to splinter the coves and inlets of Ashley's own heart. It stirred the ripples. Her past resurfaced and refused to sink back into the abyss. The Brahms Lullaby collided with the remembered strands of Schubert's Unfinished Symphony that often came to mind. Of her own unfinished symphony. She had her own day to remember, that day when summer and fall merged back in Everdale, when her own innocence was lost. She thought of her own unborn child. Of birthday candles that would never be placed on gooey icing. Of a little boy who would never be born, never cry. Never grow up. How dare she sit here in this magnificent Opera House and condemn Kerina when she had sins of her own? Splinters in her own eye. Not splinters, giant redwoods.

Chandler reached over and brushed a tear from Ashley's cheek. She had not even felt it fall. He squeezed her hand. She focused back on the concert, on the lovely violinist. Watching her now, listening to her, even Ashley found Kerina enchanting.

For seconds as the concert ended, silence again gripped the audience before the Viennese gave Kerina a standing ovation. Chandler leaped to his feet during the deafening applause, his eyes glowing. Ashley rose reluctantly beside him, her hands barely touching.

"Come on, Mom," he said excitedly as they left the concert hall. "Let's get backstage. Miss Rudzinski promised to give me a few minutes of her time."

That is all she has ever given you, Ashley thought.

Seventeen

Kerina sat on her cushioned bench, facing the three-way gilded mirror above her dressing table. Tiny globe lights framed the glass, reflecting the bouquets behind her and sending shadows across her face. Tonight the heady fragrance of a room filled with flowers stifled her, robbing her of her usual enjoyment. She leaned forward and outlined the quarter moons beneath her eyes with her fingers. Slowly, she touched her cheeks, her chin, her hands coming to rest on her slender throat, her elbows resting gently against her breast. That little twist of sadness at the corner of her mouth would not go away—it was as though she had been born with it.

She caught Jillian's eye in the mirror. "Should I change?"

"No, don't. The lieutenant will be here any minute. You look lovely as you are. Just freshen your makeup."

Kerina applied some eye shadow and a tea rose gloss to her dry lips. "There, that's better," she admitted.

"You must be proud, Kerina. This evening's concert was the greatest performance you've ever given."

"Then I kept my promise."

"And Vienna loved you for it." She gave Kerina a thumbs-up. "You should be up waltzing around. Singing. Dancing."

"I'm much too tired to sing and dance."

"Then call off your dinner with Franck and the Mc-Clarens, and I'll send the lieutenant away when he comes."

Kerina's laugh was brittle. "One minute you tell me I should keep my commitments, the next that I should break them." She turned and met Jillian's gaze. "This should be the happiest night of my life, yet the accolades seem so empty. Is that all I can look forward to for another twenty years? More applause?"

"I thought it was what you lived for."

Kerina reached out and touched the red carnations on her dressing table. "The lieutenant sent these, Jillian. My fans—even my critics—are so good to me. What do I give them in return?"

"Your beautiful music."

"It's not enough."

"And why not? Look—you're just tired. You have a few days between concerts. Why don't we go to your villa on the Riviera?"

That private haven in Italy. The very thought of going excited Kerina. The gated villa, high on a hill with the endless blue horizon and the silk-white sand on the beach; the olive groves and fruit trees; and her beloved housekeeper, Mia, who would fatten her up on pastas and fresh seafood and make up her bed daily with fresh, air-dried linens.

She sighed, some of her emptiness dissipating. "We haven't done that for a long time, Jillian. I was afraid to suggest it for fear Italy would remind you of Santos Garibaldi."

"I loved him once, Kerina. At least I thought I did. But now he sits on the edge of my memory so I can kick myself more often. Believe me, I won't send him an invitation to your villa."

"Why not? I might like him."

"He'd charm you all right. Can we go and not tell Franck we're going?"

"I would have to cancel my trip to Moscow."

"Oh, do."

"Franck will be furious—unless we go without telling him. But would you be happy with no one to swim with or play tennis?"

"You do both."

"Not this time. I will just sleep. Read books. Sit in the sun. And gorge on Mia's meals."

"Why don't you invite your parents to join us?"

"They dislike traveling. We might invite some friends of yours, Jillian. Perhaps the ones you met yesterday."

"They're both married. And rotten company."

"Who then?"

Jillian flipped her hair from her brow. "The lieutenant. Why don't we ask the likes of him?"

Kerina's touch of happiness faded. She turned back to her mirror and removed the hair clip, letting her hair fall loosely around her shoulders. She began brushing it with long strokes, her arm more tired than it had been in a long time; she was still untangling her hair when the knock came.

"Jillian, dear, that's probably the lieutenant. Get the door for me, please."

She heard the door swing back and glanced down at the picture of Bill on her mirror. "Wish me luck," she told him.

Kerina smiled at the excitement in Jillian's voice as she said, "Lieutenant Reynolds, we've been expecting you."

"Miss Ingram, I was hoping to see you again. You rushed off so suddenly this evening—"

"Well, I'm here now. Come in. Come in, both of you."

The lieutenant came limping around the maze of flowers to the center of the room. Kerina watched him in the mirror; then her world stood still. She felt the muscles in her throat constrict. The hairbrush slipped from her hand and clattered on the dressing table; she could not move. The lieutenant stood there favoring his right leg, a strange composite of shyness and friendliness. Tall. Lean. Eyes like Bill's. Her mirror seemed to fog leaving the tall figure veiled in a blinding mist. An apparition, a phantom of her mind, an illusion. In the mirror he was ghostlike in appearance, a shadow of her past, the image of Bill. It was Bill coming back at last, still limping. No, someone younger, young like Bill had been when they said good-bye.

208

Her throat locked. How could two men look so much alike? With great dignity she swung slowly around on the bench. As she looked up at her guest, her heart felt like a groggy sponge, pumping slowly, erratically. The apparition faded. His features became real. She found the strength from deep within her to meet the lieutenant's eyes. She was certain he was Bill's son. Only the set of his jaw was stronger. No one could look so much like Bill without being his child. A quizzical frown formed on his brow as he waited for her to speak.

But if this is Bill's son, he may know who I am. Perhaps he has come here to confront me, to punish me for going away.

The lieutenant smiled. Bill's smile. His piercing eyes held hers, bridging the twenty-six years from that long ago when Bill had met her gaze. "Hi," he said in a voice deep and rich. "I'm Chandler Reynolds."

No, you are my son. She found her voice at last. "I was expecting someone in an army officer's uniform."

"I left my army gear in the closet at the Empress Isle."

She felt riveted to the bench, at a loss for the right words. "I didn't know the army turned out music critics," she said.

He laughed. Bill's easy chuckle. "That's not the army's doing, ma'am. It's my personal goal—I was born into a family that loved music."

Her heart thundered in her ears. She had to know—had to be certain. "Where were you born, lieutenant?"

He seemed surprised, the woman behind him more startled. "In Everdale, Alabama, ma'am."

"A dot on the map."

"How did you know that?"

"I guessed." She stood and stole another glance at his handsome face. *Tall and charming like your father,* she thought. Slowly, she moved toward him, her soft hands outstretched. He took them in his and lifted them to his lips.

"Thank you for the flowers, Lieutenant Reynolds."

He waved his hand around the room. "You're smothered in flowers." He beckoned to the woman behind him. "Mom, come and meet Miss Rudzinski."

As she stepped forward, he slipped his arm around her shoulders. "This is my mom—Ashley Reynolds." Kerina heard pride in his voice. But she wanted to cry out, *No, I am your mother!*

She faced the woman who had raised her son for her and was shocked. Kerina remembered that nurse who took her baby away, remembered her eyes. She was looking into them again—an attractive woman with streaks of gray in her corn-silk hair and a quiet calm about her as she met Kerina's gaze.

Impulsively, gratefully, Kerina reached out and clasped Ashley Reynolds's hands and whispered in her ear, "The night nurse. I would know you anywhere."

The last time she saw her son, this nurse had knelt beside her and unfolded the receiving blanket. His pink toes curled; his legs kicked. She felt the grasp of those tiny fingers on her own. Gurgling, cooing sounds had filled the hospital nursery as the nurse said, "Kerry, it's not too late to change your mind."

It was an awkward moment as they took the chairs by the dressing table, Jillian sitting down with them. Ashley's gaze swept past the snapshot and then did a rebound; her eyes misted as she stared at Bill's snapshot. *She recognizes him,* Kerina thought. *But, of course. They grew up in the same town.*

As Kerina looked directly at Chandler, she traced his features in her mind. *The image of Bill—pensive brow, aquiline nose, those mesmerizing eyes. But my sensitive mouth.*

"Have you made the army your career, lieutenant?"

He glanced at his mother. "That's the big debate. Whether to reenlist or to go civilian. My best buddy was killed recently."

Kerina caught her breath. "Is that why you were in the hospital?"

His voice wavered. "Yes. A leg injury in the same accident. That's why I'm on leave. But whatever I do, I want to stay on in Europe. If I don't stay army, I want to pursue a music career."

"Jillian tells me you play a musical instrument."

"One or two."

"And very well," Ashley interjected. "The violin. The piano."

"Then your son inherited his musical talent?"

"His destiny," Ashley said. "He was born to it. My husband and I love music, but we make better listeners than performers."

"And you, Chandler?" Kerina asked.

"I started violin when I was four. But when I got to fifth grade and Mom wouldn't sign me up for a soccer team, I rebelled. By the time I reached puberty, my rebellion was in full bloom."

"We didn't want him to injure his arm," Ashley said softly. "We made a promise once to—"

Kerina cut in. "Couldn't you have both sports and music?"

"That's why I stopped playing the violin and took to piano. But I'm not professional enough for either one."

"Nor willing to practice enough?" Kerina guessed.

"Mom and Dad kept holding out for another Yehudi Menuhin or Paganini. But I was way past being a child prodigy." He shrugged, brushing off his brief push toward a musical career. "By the time I was a sophomore in high school, I buried my violin in the back of the closet. For all I know, it's still there."

Kerina's blue gown rustled as she leaned toward him. "You cannot make music that way."

"Chan studied piano for several months at Juilliard," Ashley defended. "You were a guest artist while he was there, Miss Rudzinski."

"You heard me play, lieutenant?"

"I didn't arrive until your last number." He grinned. "I was at the recruitment office. I left Juilliard for the army."

Sadly she said, "You left Juilliard? For lack of practice?"

211

He frowned, thoughtful for a moment—a look so much like Bill's. "I left because I was searching for something. For myself, I think."

Her gaze drifted to Ashley and back. "Did you find what you were looking for?"

He didn't answer. Instead he said, "What I really want to do is try my hand as a music critic. That's why I'm here."

Jillian broke her silence. "A full-time music critic! That's like throwing yourself to the sharks, lieutenant. You'll starve to death."

Kerina smiled. *Music reviews. Like Bill once did.* "You don't want to be a concert violinist?"

"I did while you were playing this evening. My folks pinned their hopes on me being a professional musician." He looked apologetically at Ashley. "But I can never achieve my parents' goal for me. Nor play as beautifully as you do, Miss Rudzinski."

Kerina lifted her violin from its case and handed it to him.

Chandler examined it carefully. "Wow," he said. "A Stradivarius. What an instrument!"

"It's my livelihood and also my life. It has belonged to my family for generations."

"Then you must keep it in the family."

"I will." As they talked, she powdered the bow with rosin.

"May I, Miss Rudzinski?"

She gave him the bow. "Play something for me and let me be the judge as to whether you should go on with your music career."

He hesitated only a second and then tucked the violin beneath his chin and ran the bow across the strings. His eyes teasing, he made squeals and grating sounds and then clearly the first notes of a Strauss waltz filled the dressing room.

She leaned forward and repositioned his fingers. "You must take your violin from the closet, lieutenant."

"That's what Mom and Dad tell me."

"So you're not the perfect son?"

"Hardly."

Alarmed, she asked, "You don't drink or—"

"Not with a pastor for a dad. He keeps me on the straight and narrow. And Mom here prays a house a'fire for me." Again there was pride in his voice.

He played another measure and then handed the Strad back to her. "You're the violinist, Miss Rudzinski."

"But you were born for music, Chandler."

As she placed the violin back in its case, she sketched imaginary lines over his features, outlining them in her memory. His hair was growing out, one unruly lock falling across his well-shaped forehead. His pensive eyes searched hers. "How old are you?" she asked.

"Twenty-six a few weeks ago. April fifteenth to be exact. Do you have a family, Miss Rudzinski?"

Ashley gasped. *Don't worry, Mrs. Reynolds,* Kerina thought. *I won't tell him. Your secret—our secret—is safe with me.*

"Chandler, the truth is I do have a son your age." She felt rather than saw the shock on Jillian's face. The fear on Ashley's. Her voice grew faint. "You are very much like—my son, lieutenant. It's strange how very much you—"

Her voice trailed, a miserable lump in her throat. She turned hurriedly back to her mirror, blinking back sudden tears.

"Miss Rudzinski, I—"

"Lieutenant, I am sorry, but I have a dinner date. I must ask you to leave. Now."

"But the interview . . ."

She began to twist her hair into a chignon. "There is no time for that now."

He stumbled to his feet. "I'm sorry, Miss Rudzinski. We didn't mean to wear out our welcome. I—"

"Please go."

Kerina caught his reflection in the mirror and winced at the bewilderment on his face. She felt like she had been swept back to Jackson Memorial—to that day when she held her infant son and heard him whimper as the nurse took him from her. Ashley was moving toward the door, the same night nurse taking her son away.

She cupped a red carnation in the vase beside her. "Thank you for sending the flowers."

"No big deal."

She put down her brush and turned to face him again. "I am sorry about the interview, lieutenant. But you do understand?"

With a cavalier shrug, he said, "Like I said, no big deal."

Kerina forced herself to stand and walk to the door with her son. *I may never see you again. And I am sending you away.*

She glanced up into his handsome face as more tears pricked behind her eyelids. "Lieutenant." She hesitated. "Perhaps we can arrange to talk again if you still want that interview?"

The corner of his mouth twisted to Bill's half smile. "Sure. If you can find time in your busy schedule."

He smiled at Jillian who had opened the door for them. Ashley went out first, Chandler behind her. He did not look back.

Jillian closed the door and whirled around, her face flushed. "Kerina, that was cruel. The lieutenant was in the middle of a sentence and you cut him off and told him to leave."

"I had no choice, Jillian. Franck will be here any minute."

"Oh, forget appeasing Franck. He always fusses about your guests! The lieutenant and his mother are here for a month. Franck will be around until doom's day."

"So what do you want me to do, Jillian?"

"Invite the Reynoldses for lunch on Saturday so you can apologize for your rudeness. I'll smooth it over. I'll tell him that you get on edge when you're late for dinner. That you want to make it up to him. Let him have that interview."

"Does it matter that much to you?"

"Yes. I haven't liked anyone so much since Santos Garibaldi. So please invite them to lunch. Give me a fighting chance."

Kerina fought back the tears. "Oh, Jillian, I can't. That soldier is wrong for you."

"That soldier has a name, Kerina."

Kerina felt faint, grief-stricken. *Jillian is right,* she thought. *The soldier has a name, more than I gave my infant son.* "Oh, Jillian . . . Jillian, help me."

Jillian was at her side at once, her arm around Kerina's shoulders. "Kerina, don't sob so. What's wrong?"

"I could not go on talking to him. Knowing who he was. Knowing that his mother recognized me."

"What are you talking about?" Jillian's eyes strayed to the snapshot in the mirror, then back to Kerina's tear-stained face. "What are you talking about?"

"I can't tell you. Please, don't ask."

Jillian crossed the room and snapped up the picture. "The lieutenant looks like this man, doesn't he? You saw the resemblance between them, didn't you?"

"Yes, the moment the lieutenant entered the room."

"I thought I had seen this face before. But it didn't click until now. The *Time* magazine. This snapshot. They look like the same person, but they're not. They couldn't be."

"I know."

"But the lieutenant and this man—they're related?"

"Yes, Jillian." She wrapped her hand around a rose and crushed its petals. "Yes, they are father and son."

The color drained from Jillian's cheeks. "This evening you said that the lieutenant reminded you of your son. I didn't even know you had a child. He is your son, isn't he?"

Kerina's voice quavered. "I knew the minute I saw him—and when I saw his mother, I knew for certain. She was the nurse in the delivery room the night that Chandler was born." Kerina's knuckles were bone white. "I haven't seen them for twenty-six years, not since I gave my baby away."

Eighteen

Franck stormed into the dressing room, his bearded face flushed. "Kerina, who was that young man in the hall with an older woman? He looked familiar. Mid-twenties. Wearing a tuxedo."

"Many of the guests this evening were in black tie."

Again, he demanded, "Who was he, Kerina?"

She gave him a carefree shrug. "A fan. A well-wisher. Jillian, what did he say his name was?" She didn't wait for the answer, but said, "Franck, I will be ready in a minute—here, unzip me. Never mind, I got it myself."

"Kerina, you look like you've been crying."

"Do I?"

He glared at Jillian. "Has Jillian upset you?"

"Of course not. Now, what time do we meet the Mc-Clarens?"

"Dinner is off, Kerina. Elias just called to cancel."

"Called?" She poked her head around the dressing screen. "I thought they were at the concert."

"They went home during the second intermission."

"Was I that bad?"

"No, my dear. You were magnificent as always." He paused, glancing toward Jillian again.

"I have no secrets from Jillian, Franck, so what happened?"

"McClaren's wife called their maid several times and got no answer. They always call when they're out—just to make certain everything is all right at the mansion. When they couldn't even rally their chauffeur, they rushed home."

Distractedly, Franck rubbed his bony hands. "They were robbed, Kerina."

She stifled her gasp. "Was anyone hurt?"

"The maid was restrained and gagged. The chauffeur beaten. But they will live."

Kerina faced him now, her voice ragged. "What did the thief want, Franck? Jewelry? Money? The McClarens' art collection?"

Franck tugged at his beard. "Three thieves. They stole two paintings. Nothing else."

"Two paintings?" Jillian asked. "Not the whole collection?"

"A Degas and a Rembrandt. Taking the VanStryker probably posed a greater risk." He paced the length of Kerina's dresser, his fingers still raking his beard. "It wasn't supposed to happen this way. The police promised to keep a guard at the house during the concert. I tried to warn Elias."

At the tremor in his voice, Kerina crossed the space between them. "Were you expecting trouble, Franck?"

"There was too much interest in the McClarens' exhibit yesterday. Strangers asking questions."

"Why would a museum complain about that? The Mc-Clarens always put on an excellent display."

"But calling off our dinner, Kerina—I'm sorry."

"We can have dinner with them another time. Why don't we drive over there and see if we can be of some comfort to them?"

As he scowled his thick brows slid up and down. "They didn't lose a child, Kerina. Just two paintings."

She flinched, her eyes pools of sadness. "Works of art that have always interested you. Worth millions, I would suspect."

"Believe me, my dear, I didn't take them."

"I am glad." She straightened his tie and kissed his cheek. "We must talk about that soon. Now come. Be a pet and take me to the McClarens' so I can see for myself."

He gripped her wrists. "I don't want you involved. The police will have the place cordoned off. We'd be in the way."

"I know Nicole will let us in. You will excuse us, Jillian?"

"Of course. I was going to run an errand anyway."

Kerina glanced at her jeweled watch. "Wait until morning, dear. That will be time enough to invite our friends to lunch." At the door, she glanced back. "Jillian, could you do something about the flowers? Send two bouquets to my hotel suite—the rest to hospitals."

"Anything special to the hotel?"

The sad twist at her mouth tightened. "Franck's red roses and the vase of carnations from the lieutenant. And it would be best if you told no one where I went this evening."

"Then why don't you take my car?" Jillian dangled the keys. "It's fully automatic. And handy for personal emergencies."

"And you think this is an emergency?"

"Isn't it?" Jill walked over and dropped the keys in Kerina's hand. "You know the car. It will probably be the only red Saab in the hotel parking lot."

Jillian listened to the steady thud of Franck's shoes and the lighter tap of Kerina's heels until the sounds disappeared down the corridor. Something stirred in her mind. Franck was always there, protecting Kerina, so Franck would know about Kerina's son. Was this the secret that Franck wielded to his own advantage? Even art theft?

Jillian hung the midnight blue gown on the brass pole and waited around until the stagehands emptied the room of flowers. Then she switched off the lights and followed them out of the dressing room, her thoughts jumbled with unanswered questions about the robbery. Why a Degas and Rembrandt when the mansion was filled with high-priced masterpieces? Could Franck really be involved in an art conspiracy against his friend? He was shrewd, cunning, wise in the ways of the theater, but hardly one capable of plotting art thefts. She tried to remember whether Franck had left the concert hall during the performance, but she had been too busy thinking pleasant thoughts about the lieutenant from Bosnia. For weeks now, she had hotly defended Kerina's innocence. But had she defended her too quickly? She should call Brooks Rankin and Joel Gramdino. And tell them what? She had nothing but questions. If Franck Petzold was the mastermind behind the concert thefts, she would be dragged deeper into the mess than she cared to be. She must wait, make certain. But what joy would it be if she was right? Franck was Kerina's stability, her constant companion for years. She would never marry him, but could she live without him?

Ruin Franck and Kerina's career would be over; she would never find strength to go on without him. Blow her own assignment with the Art Theft Registry and Jillian would be out of a job and taking off in a red convertible with no destination in mind.

Joel Gramdino left Brooks Rankin and his wife at a *kaffeehaus* near the Staatsoper; then he hailed a cab smaller than a New Yorker, and taxied to the McClarens' with the meter rolling against the Registry's expense account.

The concert had been okay in his judgment. High-brow stuff was out of his realm, but he recognized style when he saw it and good music when he heard it. Rudzinski lived up to the best in couture fashion and wore it well, and she surpassed her reputation as a world-class violinist. "The Blue Danube" still waltzed in his head.

During the program, Joel had used his powerful binoculars to keep Miss Rudzinski's manager and the art collector and his wife in constant focus. Petzold stayed backstage throughout the concert, but the McClarens—decked out fit to kill—left the concert early. Joel's interest in their box seating had mushroomed when he recognized the young man who had been standing in the lobby with Jillian Ingram.

The soldier boy from Bosnia. Out of uniform, but attractive enough to make Jillian take a second look. So Miss Rudzinski had arranged special seating, had she?

As the taxi sped toward the McClarens', he wondered why the American soldier had one of the best views in the theater and with one of the most prominent art collectors in Vienna? Was the soldier messed up in the art thefts? A point of contact? Someone placed close to the McClarens by Kerina Rudzinski? If so, why didn't the lieutenant follow the McClarens when they left the theater during the second intermission?

Joel slouched in the backseat of the taxi, rehearsing the evening. The concert began with "The Blue Danube." No other Strauss waltz was listed on the program. Then Kerina returned to the stage after the second intermission and dedicated a number to someone special. Someone in the audience? Her voice cracked as she spoke. A signal? He was on alert. Once the Brahms "Lullaby" ended, she went immediately into another unscheduled waltz.

Brooks Rankin had slammed his fist into his program with a bull's-eye in the middle as Joel scanned the hot spots with his binoculars. The visible exits. The McClarens' loge seating. He spotted Franck Petzold still standing offstage. But Kerina Rudzinski had signaled someone in the audience! His binoculars swept back to the McClarens for another check. They were gone.

He accomplished nothing by replaying it all in his mind. The concert was already a thing of the past. He paid the driver and stepped out into the shadows a half block from the McClarens' residence and took the half block with long strides. The place was flooded with lights. Police vehicles lined the street. A bad sign. He pushed his way through the crowd to the cordoned ribbon.

"I need to see Elias McClaren," he told the officer who caught him trying to duck beneath the barrier.

The officer sized him up head-to-toe, and then made eye contact. Arguing persuasively and flashing his ID, Joel crossed the cordoned line. Reporters occupied the McClaren driveway, gaping for a look inside. He made his way past them and into the McClarens' spacious sitting room.

"What did they take?" he asked as he reached McClaren.

Elias turned, scowled. "A Degas and my best Rembrandt. And the limousine. What happened to your security guards, Gramdino?"

"I expected Brooks Rankin to handle that."

"You left me wide open for a robbery."

"I'll talk to Rankin."

I'll have it out with him, Joel thought. So what happened? He didn't have to ask. Brooks liked giving orders. He didn't like an American investigator moving in. Gramdino could pull rank, but hadn't. He'd know better the next time. "I could call Rankin from here," he offered. But how? He didn't remember the name of the coffeehouse and Rankin never hurried a good meal.

"Why bother?" McClaren asked wearily. "The three thieves—"

"Three of them? That's not the usual pattern."

"Then they changed their game plan. Three men accosted my chauffeur, Hans, at the Opera House. Tried to kill him. Ask him."

Joel's frown deepened. *Never bodily injury before, not with the concert conspiracy.* "Where's Hans?"

McClaren pointed through the glass doors that overlooked the terrace. A lone figure sat on the terrace wall, staring into space. He was hunched forward, his back to the house.

"The police blamed him. Hans offered to resign. I was willing to take his resignation." A wry smile touched his lips. "My wife insisted that he stay on."

He decided that McClaren had been this route before. The younger wife. A young employee. "Do you think Hans was involved?"

"Hans is a good man. Been with us for three years."

"I'd like to talk to him, McClaren."

"Officially?"

"Strictly as a representative of the Coventry Registry. You do plan to list the stolen objects with us?" Joel whipped out a small notepad and pen. Chewing the cap from the pen, he left it dangling from the corner of his mouth like an unlit cigarette.

"I can't list them. I'm not going public with this robbery."

"With that crowd out there—and the television truck?"

"We told them there was nothing of value stolen."

"Then you won't list with the Registry?"

"Why? We are well insured. And the police say we will never get the paintings back."

"List them with us, McClaren. We can have an alert around the world in minutes. Time is your best chance for recovery."

"With a recovery rate of five percent?" Elias scoffed.

"Five percent back in the hands of the rightful owners is a step forward. Given time, our percentages will rise."

Joel glanced around. McClaren's wife was engaged in a conversation with a man in a tailored gray suit. Another woman stood nearby, staring at an empty spot on the wall.

"That's where the Degas hung," Elias said.

"Who's that couple with your wife?"

"You don't recognize the woman?"

"Not with her back to me."

"Kerina Rudzinski, the violinst; she gave her best performance this evening. She never played better. We've been friends for years. That's her manager Franck Petzold talking with my wife. He wants me to exhibit my collection in Moscow for a friend of his."

"You'd risk it after this? When?"

"This month." He shrugged. "Petzold is negotiating for another VanStryker for me. Not go and I miss the opportunity to purchase that painting."

"Worth the price?" *And worth Petzold's fee?* Joel wondered.

"The portrait by Vincent van Gogh is one of his last works. I want that one before someone else bids on it and sends the price soaring. The other is a VanStryker, an un-claimed masterpiece stolen by the Nazis and then confis-cated by the Russians at the close of war. That would be a bonus in my collection."

A legal sale? And what else have Franck and the lovely Miss Rudzinski been negotiating for? He pondered for a moment. *The Registry had no listing of an authentic VanStryker on the market.*

"McClaren, do you trust Petzold's judgment? And after tonight's theft, do you still trust Hans?"

His petulant grimace warned Joel to back off. "Given the position that Hans was in, I would have opened the gate too." He went from rubbing his jaw to hand-brushing his hair, his motions jerky, disjointed. "This is not a good night for me, Gramdino. Not the time for you to question my friends. My alarm system is state-of-the-art, and look what happened."

A police officer stood at McClaren's side now, demand-ing his attention. Joel made himself scarce, strolling around the room to admire the pictures still on the walls. Millions in value had been left behind. But why? He glanced through the terrace doors at the despondent Hans and made his way toward him.

When Joel passed the wall where the Degas had hung, he stopped to speak to Kerina Rudzinski. "Good evening, Fräulein Rudzinski. I'm Joel Gramdino."

She turned in deep concentration, her face, even up close, lovely, well-featured. "Yes?"

"A magnificent performance this evening. Your best ever."

A smile touched her eyes, her lips. He took her icy hand and held it momentarily in his broad ones. "You surprised me with those Strauss numbers not listed on your program."

"I know," she whispered. "I like surprises."

"You were playing for someone special."

"Yes, but that was a work by Brahms. For my son," she said. "I learned later that he was in the audience."

Her hand slipped from his. "Your son?"

But she had turned from his question, her gaze fixed on the vacant spot on the wall, her thoughts far away.

"They took a Rembrandt too," Gramdino said.

"They?" The word seemed lost in the room, in her thoughts.

"Yes, the thieves."

She glanced back briefly. "It has to stop sometime."

When he saw Franck Petzold and Nicole McClaren making their way toward Kerina, he moved off, casually, out through the terrace door. Hans jumped as Gramdino sat down beside him. His face was drawn and ashen, even in the shadows, and his hands were jammed into the pockets of his oversized Donegal-tweed coat.

"You've had a bad scare, Hans," Gramdino said.

"I talked to the *polizei*. I told them all I know."

"I'm with the Art Registry. We find stolen art. We can help you—and Herr McClaren. Tell me where you were abducted."

He looked perplexed. "I drove the McClarens to the opera. That's where—in front of the Opera House. Two men—three men."

With a crowd looking on? Kidnapping the chauffeur had been carefully orchestrated. "No one tried to help you, Hans?"

"It happened so quickly that no one noticed." He touched his neck. "I was knocked out, and when I came to, I saw they were wearing masks and carrying guns."

"An American soldier, perhaps? Anything to identify them?"

"No soldiers. No Americans. Tourists maybe, with strange accents. I think one called himself Vladimir. Another Pierre."

Not German then. "We'll find them," Gramdino promised.

"They could be hiding anywhere. Or driving south. They threatened me—that's how they got into the house. Poor Anna."

"Tell me about it, son. Tell me exactly what happened."

224

Nineteen

As the Reynoldses left the Opera House, Chandler hailed a horse-drawn fiacre. In the brilliant lights of the Ringstrasse, Ashley could see that the carriage was black, the wheels red. It offered a romantic view of the city that would hurl them back to seventeenth-century travel, the kind of evening that Chandler should spend with a girl like Jillian Ingram. Not with his mother.

Ashley eyed the horse, which was pawing the ground impatiently. Drawing back, she remarked, "Chandler, we could walk to the hotel. It's not far."

"Mother, let's do things the Austrian way."

She chuckled. "Most of them seem to be walking."

The coachman was a cheeky man with full gray sideburns that twisted and curled into his mustache. He wore what appeared to be traditional gear—a red jacket, baggy pants, a bow tie, and a black bowler hat that sat crunched over his balding head. His nose was bulbous, his chin double, and his carriage was ready for customers.

"Well?" Chandler asked. "What do you think, Mom?"

The coachman's heavy eyelids narrowed his eyes to merry slits, but he had a friendly smile. Ashley decided that the whip in his hand was nonthreatening. She nodded, still reluctant.

Speaking German, Chandler said, "We're staying at the Empress Isle, sir, but can you take us the long way home?"

"A little ride around the inner city," he agreed.

They settled on a fare, and grinning, Chandler and the coachman helped Ashley mount the narrow step into the carriage. She stepped cautiously in her strapped heels, her elegant gown restricting her movement. She wrapped her stole around her shoulders as the driver shut the door, and with another reassuring smile swung himself onto the high seat and took the reins in his hand. Gently he nudged his horse with the whip, and the carriage eased away from the curb.

As they turned from the Ringstrasse and merged with the Vienna traffic, Ashley rested her hand on Chandler's arm. "The concert was beautiful, Chan."

"It was great, but it was crazy thinking I could get an interview with a total stranger."

"Yes . . . a total stranger."

Ashley bit her lip and settled back in the seat to listen to the steady clippety-clop of the horse. *It was a simple request,* she thought. *Just an interview. Oh, you knew him all right, Kerina Rudzinski. I saw it in the way you looked at him, in the way you traced the features of his face.*

Ashley nursed her fury against Kerina. It was the one way she could bury her own guilt, her own dark secret of betrayal. The complete truth was too painful, too involved, a many-sided memory—a strange polygon.

The night air brushed against her face, cooling her cheeks. *I am angry at you. You recognized Chandler—of that I have no doubt. And you recognized me—I heard it in your greeting. I don't want you to know Chandler, and yet I don't want you to reject him again. But you did when you hurried us out of your dressing room this evening.*

"What's wrong, Mother? Tired?"

"I'm fine."

But she had just lied to him. One chamber of her heart had always been off-limits to her family, to her friends. The chamber of her heart where she had long harbored Kerina's secret, where she harbored her own.

Their carriage looped through the inner city, taking them back in time past Gothic edifices en route to their hotel. The midnight hour closed in on them, but the city of Vi-

226

enna was awakening, coming alive to celebrate the evening. The concert crowd walked leisurely toward the restaurants and coffeehouses. In the distance Ashley could see the Prater ferris wheel spinning around slowly. Their driver followed the flow of traffic, giving them a marvelous view of the well-lit Parliament, the City Hall, and the Palace. Chandler sat humming a waltz, musing, even smiling, but behind his dark eyes she sensed an unsettledness. Questions.

Chandler must be told the truth. For now he was still her son. But tonight, in the quiet of the hotel, she would tell him about his birth mother.

Chandler leaned down and kissed Ashley's gloved hand, his lips not quite making contact. "That's the way the Austrians do it," he said. "Thank you for coming to Vienna with me. But I'm worried about you. Are you missing Dad?"

"I should be—but we've been too busy."

He laughed dryly. "We promised to call him after the concert, but let's call in the morning. Are you hungry? We could have our coachman drop us off at a coffeehouse or at the Sacher, if you prefer."

"I'd rather go to the hotel. It's been a long day."

At the Empress Isle, Chandler helped the coachman lift Ashley from the carriage; then he paid the man, tipping him liberally.

"You shouldn't lift me, not when your leg is hurting."

"You were light as a feather."

But as they walked up the steps he was limping.

An hour later, Ashley tightened the belt around her robe and padded softly over the thick carpet in her blue slippers to Chandler's room. He lay in the middle of the monstrous bed, stretched out on his back, his bare arms on top of the sheets, two pillows tucked behind his head.

"Hi, Chan. May I come in?"

"Sure. Been waiting to say good night."

She pulled a chair closer and sat down beside him. "You enjoyed yourself this evening, didn't you, son?"

"Thoroughly. But I was disappointed about the interview."

"Perhaps some other time."

"We'll see."

Her heart lurched. His pensive gaze looked so much like Kerina Rudzinski's. Had he noticed the similarity? Or seen that snapshot of Bill on Kerina's mirror? No, there would be no reason for him to connect that faded snapshot with Bill VanBurien. And how long had it been since he had looked at the family photo albums with her? Three years? Five years? Why would he recognize Bill? He had never seen him.

"Miss Rudzinski liked you," Ashley said.

"I think she liked the flowers better."

"That was sweet of you to send them."

He shrugged. "I was trying to do everything right. You know, thanking her ahead of time for the interview."

"Don't dwell on your disappointment."

"I won't. It was a good evening and she was lovely."

Ashley's clasped hands tightened. *Tell him now,* she told herself. *Let him know why he was drawn to her.* But what if Kerina Rudzinski rejected him again?

He frowned, his gaze going from the ceiling back to her face. "Miss Rudzinski said she had a son my age."

"I heard her." Ashley wanted to clap her hands over her ears to prevent him from telling her that he knew the truth already. She braced herself for the inevitable.

He stretched, made himself more comfortable, buried his head deeper into the pillows. "She didn't mention her husband."

"Perhaps there is no husband, Chan."

"I can't imagine not having a dad in the family. What kind of an upbringing did the poor kid have?"

"Tutors," she suggested. "And nannies. He would have been well cared for—provided for. The best of everything."

"But hopping from country to country? Playing cars in the dressing rooms behind the concert halls? Talking to his mother during the intermission? Probably never in one place long enough to learn how to play soccer."

"I'm sure they worked it out, Chandler."

The room was warm, the air conditioner low. Ashley felt goose bumps prickling her skin. Her spine was rigid from a nervous chill. She rubbed her hands, trying to warm them; her right hand was frigid, as though the circulation had stopped.

Stop talking in circles. Tell him. Tell him that the young boy didn't play in the back rooms of a concert hall. Tell him. Tell him he is the young boy.

Chandler looked sleepy, his eyelids drooping as he watched her. She must tell him now before he slept.

He reached for her hand. "What's wrong? You're cold as ice." He rubbed it between his own, laughing. "You did this for me when I was a kid coming in from the snow. There, that should do it."

"It's late, Chandler."

"Then go get some sleep. I'm about passed out myself. I think—" His words were lost in a yawn. "I think we'd better sleep in late, Mom."

"Let's do. But first, Chandler, I—your father and I—"

"Hmm?"

No, she told herself. *Leave David out of this. This is between you and your son.* She felt frost-nipped; the glacial chill paralyzed her.

She wanted to blame it on Kerina Rudzinski and did. She remembered it as it had happened and thought bitterly, *Kerina, without ever knowing who we were, you shackled us to that promise.*

The conditions had gone back and forth from Kerry Kovac to the lawyer. From the lawyer to David and Ashley. *You forced us to sign that Consent Decree. No, you signed it. But we gave you our word. Our word to the lawyer, his to you—your last hold on your son, binding David and me to silence.*

"My son must never know that he is adopted," Kerry Kovac had written on the Consent Decree. "They agree to that or else—"

Or else what? You live a lie for twenty-six years.

Ashley tried again. "Chandler, I have a confession to make. But—I want you to know that I have loved you from that first moment in the delivery room."

"Good thing," he said, smiling groggily. "I came into this world on good faith. Depended on you."

She rushed on. "I never intended to hurt you—"

"No . . . problem, Mom. Go . . . get some sleep."

The room went stark still, not a sound. And then one sound. The low rumble of her son's muffled snoring.

"Chandler . . . Chandler."

His eyes were closed, his muscular arms stretched against the pillow. His lean chest moved rhythmically, up and down. His breathing became deep and even, his face untroubled, relaxed in sleep. She touched her dozing son, her fingertips grazing his forehead. *Some other time,* she whispered. *I will tell you then.*

Ashley went back to her own suite, closing the door behind her. She heard it click and knew that she was locked out until Chandler opened it again. She crossed to her bed in the darkness, slipped out of her dressing gown, and slid beneath the cool, crisp sheets. Even on this spring evening in May, she snuggled beneath the covers and felt as chilled as she had in Chandler's room. Sleep eluded her. She was too angry with Kerina. *You have ruined everything by coming back into our lives,* she cried.

But she knew it was her own unforgiving heart that stood in the way. She wanted more than anything to feel her mother's arms around her. Even though Mama had been dead for twenty-eight years now, she was as present in this room as she had been back in the house in Everdale. Always there singing, praying, laughing, comforting.

She thought of Mama saying, "Remember, Ashley dear, the forgiving heart goes a long way toward happiness."

But Ashley had forgotten how to forgive, how to be forgiven. As she tossed and turned, the luminous dial of the clock pushed the minutes ahead. One o'clock. Two o'clock. Three. When had she last been happy, peaceful? With David? Yes, joyous in the beginning, even content in these later years. She had loved him since the day she met him on the school bus. Two years ago some insidious thing had drifted between them. Memories partly. And guilt. Unasked, uninvited she let the distance grow, shutting herself away in her garden, shutting David out.

Even in those good days with David, had she ever really been carefree as in the days of her childhood with the smell of cookies baking in Mama's kitchen and the rich fragrance of pines and cedars in the woods behind the house? Memories. Mama coming into her room to say good night. The little church that David would later pastor. The old-timers always rehashing the Confederate battles of the Civil War and casting covert glances at any Yankee who passed through town.

The miserable blunders, the sins of that year she graduated from high school, lingered in the shadows. She pushed them away, once again assigning them to the abyss—refusing to allow them to erase the enchantment of her childhood in Mama's house.

Nothing could dim that memory, not even the bleak landscapes on the frosty mornings of winter. Nothing could steal her joy of being back in that old house with its high ceilings and no central heating, yet as warm as any place could be with Mama there.

In the darkness of the Empress Isle Hotel, the memories of Everdale played across her mind. Fire logs stacked against the shed, the smell of wood smoke in the evening air, the glow of the kerosene lantern on the table when the rare ice storms short-circuited the electric wires in Everdale. Outside, the howling winds wrapped around the old pillars. Inside, Mama, Bill, and Ashley sat huddled by the potbellied stove in the living room or curled by the wood-burning stove in the kitchen—Mama drinking coffee and Bill and Ashley sipping mugs of cocoa before going to bed. She remembered that mad dash from the warm kitchen into the bedroom in her bare feet and climbing in between cold sheets. Cold like the ones she had just slipped into here in Vienna.

As a child she had shivered on her feather bed, lulled to sleep by shadows from the dying fire flickering on the ceiling. At the close of winter, spring came, her favorite time of the year. Spring pushed its way into Everdale in late February with daffodils and flowering quince. In March the azaleas and the wisteria and the dogwoods would burst into bloom in Mama's yard.

You knew it was spring when Mama put up new birdhouses for the cardinals and bluebirds and kept her windows open so she could enjoy the evening air scented with honeysuckle.

The summers in Everdale came with lush greens growing everywhere. Life slowed down. Daytime was oppressive with heat. Bill and Ashley ran barefoot, waiting for the ice man to come around the corner with a twenty-five-pound block of ice on his back. The evenings were warm with what Mama called the smell of Southern summer. She'd sit on the porch swing, a tinkling glass of iced tea in her hand. Ashley sat with her, shelling peas for her and listening to Bill mimic the frogs and crickets out by the gazebo.

When the next-door neighbor would drop in to sit a spell and swing with her, Mama bragged (it was the only time Mama ever bragged) about the butter beans, black-eyed peas, okra, and summer squash in her vegetable garden.

Sampling Mama's fresh-baked cookies and fanning herself with her apron, the neighbor would say, "I'll trade you some. A bit of your okra for a bowl of my fresh, ripe tomatoes."

For long moments, Ashley thrashed on her hotel bed, her eyes swollen from lack of sleep. And then thoughts of fall in Everdale crept in with its smell of burning leaves and dead wood. Autumn back home had filled her with sadness—the dread of everything dying, of going back to school, of the bleakness of winter coming again, and of the cemetery ghostly with its headstones in the family plot. Bill went away in the fall and Mama died in the fall—that wonderful, laughable, lovable Mama. The sin of Ashley's youth came just as the seasons of summer and fall merged. But it was springtime when Chandler came into their lives and her twin brother Bill died.

In the darkness of the Empress Isle Hotel, Ashley thought about the two letters that Bill had left on the passenger seat of his car, letters that he had intended to post on the night he was killed in a traffic accident—only days after Chandler was born. One letter to Ashley. The other—addressed to the violinist—remained sealed, undelivered. It had been locked in the top drawer of Ashley's desk back home, but she had brought it to Vienna to give to Kerina Rudzinski.

Those letters were part of Everdale. Part of Ashley's unhappiness. And yet the good memories of life in Mama's house far outweighed the dread of autumn or the bitter pain of Bill's death. Bill's childhood had been happy too. Ashley scolded herself in retrospect. What had she done leaving all that behind, running away, and taking Chandler from that magical experience of growing up in Mama's old house?

She turned on the bedside lamp and stared at the clock again. Four A.M. She crawled out of bed and jabbed her arms back into her robe and padded barefoot—like she had done as a child—to the windows. She pushed the drapes aside. Some of the night lights of Vienna were still flickering, but it was the sky that caught her attention. A bright half moon wearing a skull cap and a host of dazzling stars spattered across the night sky.

David loved the starry host. Out of all of his sermons, she remembered one. She pictured him in his clerical robe, his arms outstretched, his fingers pointing heavenward. "Look," he said in his deep, rich voice. "Look up at the heavens and count the stars—if indeed you can count them."

Ashley could not count them. Except for the Evening Star and the Big Dipper she could barely call them by name. She left the drapes drawn and lay down once more to watch the sky over Vienna from her windows. Tears stung behind her eyes. She remembered a night much like this one twenty-six years ago with an almost full moon and the heavens bathed in brilliant stars. It was the night that Bill VanBurien had come back to Everdale for the last time.

Twenty

Everdale: April 13, 1973. Everdale was in the middle of nowhere, far south of Montgomery—a sleepy place with a railroad track running through the middle of town. The stores in the business district ran down both sides of the tracks. The brownstone courthouse and bank lay on the east side, the craft store and Barney's Hardware Store with the Confederate flag still hanging on the back wall to the west. The owner of the craft store was a Yankee trying to make a go of her business, but she was as welcomed as a bad case of Asian flu in a town where few strangers ever lingered.

The town had a worn look to it, but people took pride in their place in history. Streets were kept clean, lawns mowed, historical buildings preserved. Most folks were neighborly, taking time to chat a bit over a cup of coffee and meeting at the grange for Saturday night bingo. A white, steepled church on the south side had a long list of interim pastors until David came.

Freight trains rattled through twice a day right on schedule, and a twice-weekly passenger train seldom had need to stop at the railroad depot. Except for the curious faces pressed against the smudgy train windows, Everdale remained a community turned inward, a shunning town that had no need for outsiders. Seasons came and went—the hot summers, fall with bright leaves, winter with its bleakness. But this was a perfect spring day fragrant with blossoms, a snappy breeze whipping Ashley's wash and making billowy tents of the sheets and twisted coils of the towels.

The mockingbirds sang, and the wind scuttled flower petals across Ashley's path as she picked her way back toward the house. When she reached the gazebo, she set the laundry basket down and sat a spell, lifting her face up to the touch of summer that was only weeks away. A rush of tears came as she thought of Mama, Pops, and Bill. Her dad remained vague in her memory because she could not put a face to someone she barely remembered. Mama's face faded sometimes too, but never the sound of her laughter or the sight of her peering out the window as the school bus rattled to a stop in front of the house and Bill and Ashley piled out.

Growing up, the VanBurien twins were a puzzle to everyone. Ashley was considered the good twin—*that dear sweet girl;* Bill—*that brother of hers,* the erring one. Ashley fiercely protected him. Always had. But once, when she was the erring twin, he had helped her. Ashley's roots went deep, and except for nursing school, nothing short of a disaster could pry her away from the old hometown. The deep roots trapped Bill. Once he graduated from high school, he caught the passenger train out of Everdale and headed for the first navy recruiting station he could find.

As the sun dipped low on the horizon, she picked up the laundry basket and carried it into the house and up the narrow stairs to the second floor where she dumped the wash load on the old bed in Mama's room, the room that was hers and David's now. "The master bedroom," David called their nine-by-twelve breathing space.

David was the only other Yankee living in town, if you could call him that. His grandparents had owned a farm outside of Everdale, but David had been born and reared in Southern California. He found Mama's house too cramped compared to the modern complexes going up across town. Mama's place was good enough for Ashley, even though the creaky rafters refused to ring with Mama's old chuckle and Bill never came back anymore, not even for short visits.

Shortly after they married, they turned Ashley's old room into a nursery, painting it white with a border of colorful animals for the baby that would one day fill the room. But after those trips to the infertility clinics in Montgomery and Mobile (they were the rage now) and changing doctors, they knew they would never have a child of their own to fill the nursery.

Ashley could never bear another child. But how could she tell David when he didn't know about the one she had carried in her womb and aborted in Montgomery—the butcher job that left her barren? Someday, she had promised herself, she would talk to David about adopting someone else's child. Her arms ached from emptiness. And then six weeks ago, Dr. Nelson announced that he had found a baby for them.

She sighed and picked up a sheet, squared it, folded it, hand-pressed the wrinkles. Absently she folded the rest of the clothes, putting them in neat, systematic piles. Sheets and pillowcases in sets. Towels and washcloths together. Underwear in separate stacks. She dumped David's socks in the middle of the four-poster bed where he would match and fold them himself. It was one of those quirks of marriage, one of their first major battles. She chuckled, recalling that first clash like yesterday.

"Ashley, sweetie, these socks don't go together," he had said.

David had stood in the middle of the room, muscular and thick-browed, holding up a pair of socks for her inspection. He looked impeccable in his starched shirt and blue suit, a good-looking man who still made her heart palpitate. That morning it pounded in defiance. How dare he criticize her work! She had snatched the socks from his hand and held them up to the sunlight.

Coldly she had said, "Same color: brown. Same brand: from the Penney's catalogue, David. Same length: size 10."

"Yes, but they don't match," he had reasoned.

She had thrown them at him and made her first declaration of marital independence. "From now on, David, I wash them; you match and fold them."

She scooped up a pile of sheets and buried her nose in the air-dried bedding as she headed for the linen closet. "Oh, Mama, how did you ever find time to iron sheets and towels?"

The hours had gotten away from her. Hurriedly, she laid out her uniform and shoes for the night shift at the hospital. She heard the distinct roar of a car careening along the country road and then the screeching of brakes. She ran to the windows and squinted into the shadows. A car was parked in the gravel on the wrong side of the street with its lights turned off. She saw no one hurrying up toward their porch to ask for assistance, but she did notice two figures in the front seat. As she watched, the car's engine turned over again. The driver eased the car back onto the road and, with a grating of the gears, took the first winding curve with the headlights still off.

Forty minutes later—after scouring the sinks and the toilet bowls—she ran down the steps into the kitchen where David was browning steaks and steaming garden vegetables for dinner.

"Thanks for doing dinner. Smells good," she said. "And I'm starving."

He cocked his ear. "Is that someone running on the porch?"

Someone pressed the doorbell, demanding entry.

"I'll go, David. I don't want burned steaks."

She switched on the porch light, eye-balled the peephole, and could barely turn the key fast enough to swing the door open.

"Bill!" she exclaimed, her voice filled with pleasure.

She was smothered by Bill's lanky arms as he stepped inside, swept her up with a spontaneous hug, and whirled her around.

"Hi, Sis." Laughter rippled from him.

"Bill, what brought you to Everdale?"

"I needed the old hometown," he teased.

She stepped back so she could look at him. Six-foot-four, ramrod straight, his angular face deceptively attentive and guileless. She glanced past him. "Where's Celeste and the boys?"

"They didn't come. I drove down with a friend in my new Chevy."

"A lady friend?" she asked worriedly.

He cuffed her chin playfully. "We drove straight through from Chicago. So no lectures, Sis, please. Things will work out."

"They always do for you, don't they?"

He forced a grin. "Not always, Ashley. Not this time."

As she led him into the kitchen, David lanced Bill with his intent pulpit gaze. "I threw another steak on when I heard your voice in the hall. Medium rare, if I remember right?"

"I'm hungry as a mountain lion."

"You here for long?" David asked, turning the steaks.

"A few days—if that's all right with you two."

"Would have been better if you had come sooner," David said evenly. "Like two years ago, *before* your mama died."

"I just didn't get here in time."

"Why didn't you?"

"Look, David, I can sleep in the car if you want me to."

"No, you'll stay with us," Ashley said. "In your old room."

She glared at David. Let the sparks fly and Bill would walk out again. Her two favorite men had been good friends once. Now David, stouthearted as ever, saw everything in black and white. Bill was double-sided, double-minded, motivated by his own heartstrings. Bill had been brilliant in college. Successful at work. Climbing the corporate ladder, yet constantly struggling in his marriage. Everything was arbitrary with Bill, the middle line and gray okay with him, classical music his greatest relaxation.

Bill came from good stock, but he was like worsted cloth, a smooth, hard-twisted man, a rough fabric in a weave of many colors. Charming one minute. Bolting the next. Lose him and she would never know what had driven him back to Everdale at this precise time in his troubled life. She touched Bill's hand. "Let's not quarrel. Let's just enjoy our time together."

Minutes later, as they sat around the kitchen table eating steaks and sipping coffee, Ashley noticed the haggard creases that edged Bill's blue eyes. He was only twenty-nine, but graying temples added a distinctive touch to his thick blond hair. He was not just lanky but much too thin. He looked more like Mama with each passing year—dimpled cheeks, angular face with sensitive overtones. But he had broken Mama's heart when he married into one of the prominent Chicago families.

"How's Celeste?" Ashley asked as she warmed his coffee.

His cup rattled. "She moved back home with her parents."

"Again?" David asked. "You can't toss out nine years of marriage. Why can't you two work things out?"

Bill twisted his wedding band. "It's too late. Celeste has filed for divorce."

"On what grounds?" Ashley asked.

A crooked smile dragged at the corners of his mouth. "Infidelity. I've messed up. Blown everything this time."

Ashley rubbed the back of his hand and found it trembling. "Is that why you haven't written lately, or called? Not even one phone call in the last several months?"

"There wasn't much to say." It seemed an effort for him to lift his face to meet her gaze. "Ash, eleven months ago I thought I was going to be happy, really happy for the first time in my life. I met someone, fell in love. But even that was blown away." A bite of steak fell from his fork back onto his plate. "Don't say it, David. Another woman. Another affair. I know I'm married. I know it's wrong." He dropped his fork on his plate. "Man, I miss Mom. I knew I could always depend on her."

"David and I are here for you. You can call us anytime."

"Ash, I've been a disappointment to this family. But just once in my life I'm going to do something for all of us."

"We don't need anything. We just want you to keep in touch."

Bill's mouth turned at the corner, a pathetic twist that reminded her of his childhood when he was dreading punishment, expecting it. Ashley squeezed his hand. "I love you, Bill."

"I'm glad someone does. I hate Everdale, but when I'm away I constantly think about home. A few months ago I told my friend about my mother's home, my sister's home, my childhood home."

"And what did your friend say?"

"She said she wanted to go there someday."

"You're always welcome here, Bill. Bring your friends. Bring your boys. How are they by the way?"

Pride came into his eyes. "Skip's almost as tall as Jeff now. Eight and seven. Poor kids, they're skinny rascals."

"You should have brought them."

"They're with Celeste—staying with their grandparents."

"We'll have a son in our house soon," David said.

"Or maybe a daughter," Ashley reminded him.

Bill scanned Ashley's one hundred twenty pounds, frowning.

"Having our own child wasn't an option for us, Bill."

David sent her a reassuring smile. "When we found we couldn't have children, I wanted to adopt right away."

"And I fought it until Dr. Nelson told me he had just the right baby for us. It's a private arrangement with Dr. Nelson and a lawyer from Montgomery. The girl's coming here to Everdale."

The old cocky grin tugged at Bill's mouth. "To the middle of nowhere to have her baby? Sounds like something I'd cook up."

"A friend of Doc's referred her," David said.

Bill seemed remote again as he traced the patterns of the oilcloth with the cap of his ballpoint pen. A somber expression crossed his face. "You don't seem happy about the baby, Sis. I thought that's what you wanted."

"We're not comfortable with a closed adoption. The mother doesn't want to meet us or know anything about us. I'll be right there at the hospital when the baby is born, and I won't even be able to tell her who I am."

Bill scowled. "Is that so wrong?"

David stacked his dirty dishes. "It isn't honest."

"Honey," Ashley interjected, "we've talked this out with Dr. Nelson a dozen times already. It's the girl's decision, not ours. Not yours. She doesn't even know you're a preacher."

"But did we have to agree with it? I stand behind the pulpit every Sunday, and I'm about to lie to a little baby. Someday the child will want to know more—who his parents were. All we'll be able to say to the child is, 'Your father was a businessman, and your mother was a musician.' How's that for knowing your roots?"

"We can't tell the child anything, David. The papers will be sealed." Ashley searched Bill's face. "Bill, David and I want this baby more than anything, but why is that mother coming nine hundred miles to a place like Everdale to have her baby?"

"Maybe she knows someone here, Ash."

As the grandfather clock in the living room chimed ten, Ashley shoved back her chair. "I'm on the graveyard shift, Bill. I hate leaving you two with the cleanup."

David laughed. "We could save it for you until morning."

"Do that and I'll throw the dishes at you."

Ashley reappeared thirty minutes later in her nurse's uniform. "Bill, I left towels and bedding out for you."

Bill's chair scraped as he pushed it back. He chuckled. "Dave, you make up the bed. I'll walk Ashley to the car."

He limped beside her to the door, his old navy wound kicking up a fuss. "I've never understood why you like this dreary little town, Sis."

"Mama liked it."

"You and Mama were the only good things about it."

He stopped by the front pillar and stared up at the shadowed trees. A spring breeze brushed his face. "I'm glad it isn't fall. I always hated it when the old maple leaves started falling."

"Everything is beginning to bloom now. You'll see in the morning. We can go walking in the woods when I get home."

"You'll be beat."

"I like taking a walk before I go to bed."

"And crunching through dead leaves?" he asked bitterly.

"All your life, you've fought off the end of summer."

"And the barren woods and the turning of leaves to amber and burnt orange. I hated stacking logs for winter."

But most of all Ashley knew that fall reminded him of Mama. He had flown home when she was dying, but Mama—Bill's life support, his link with God—was gone before he reached Everdale.

When he left after the funeral, he asked, "If your God is so big, Sis, why didn't he wait? Why didn't he let Mama live until I got home?" Then he gave Ashley a firm hug before limping off toward the boarding ramp.

"Bill," she had called after him, "if you ever need us—"

Turning back he saluted her with his boarding pass. "If I ever need Everdale or you again, I'll whistle."

Bill was whistling now. He closed her car door and leaned in the window. "You've never forgiven yourself about that abortion."

"How would you know that?"

"I see it in your face. Have you ever told David?"

"No. I can never bring myself to tell him. But, Bill, don't hold that against David. You two were friends once."

"And don't let Montgomery destroy you, Ash. Once you adopt that baby, the pain of Montgomery will slip away."

The good twin, the erring one. "And don't let Celeste slip away. You need her and the boys."

"I know. Without them—without Mom—I'm nothing."

She turned the ignition. "I'm family too. Remember?"

He stepped back and winked. "Things will work out, Ash. For all of us. They always do."

He cupped his hands and gave the call of the whippoorwill, the way he always did when they parted as children.

Ashley turned down the winding street and pulled into the parking lot of the forty-four-bed hospital where she worked. The evening shift waited idly at the nurses' station, eager to be off duty. Selma Malkoski stood when she saw Ashley and handed her the key to the medicine cabinet. "I hear Bill's back in town, Ashley."

"Just for a few days. But how did you—"

Her brows arched. "Did he bring that sweet family of his?"

"No, the boys are in school now."

Selma's eyes mocked her. Selma was one of the scars that Bill had left behind with an irresponsible shrug of his bony shoulders. Selma had never forgotten. Never forgiven.

As Ashley pinned her cap in place—a habit she clung to—Beth Duran spun her chair around. "Ashley," she said gently, "Dr. Nelson told me to tell you his OB case is here now."

"Someone from town?"

Beth shook her head. "No, not Emma Garvey again. This one's a stranger, an out-of-towner from up North."

Ashley froze. *My unborn child.* "What's her name? What's the mother like?"

"The mystery girl?" Selma asked. "She's a fancy one—expensive luggage, the latest clothes. Looks like she's a violinist, at least she checked in with a Stradivarius. She calls herself Kerry Kovac but I doubt if she gave us her right name. She's as sullen and noncommunicative as they come. With her admission we have a full house—just three beds left for emergencies."

"Then I'm understaffed, and if the OB should deliver tonight—"

Selma patted her shoulder. "You can handle it. You may be busy, but you'll have violin music."

Beth's ebony face glowed. "Tell you one thing, if I were trying to hide my identity, I wouldn't come to Everdale. You can barely sneeze in town without someone starting a rumor. You know us; we specialize in curious eyes and quick tongues."

"The girl didn't come alone, Ashley," Selma said. "Someone drove her right to the emergency entrance in a brand-new car with an Illinois license plate. Bold as you please." She gave Ashley a piercing glance. "Then he sped away so no one could identify him."

"Go easy on her, Selma," Beth said. "The poor kid is single and scared." She flipped the kardex, ready to give her evening report. "The girl intended to come here. Right smack-dab to Everdale to have her baby. So now we're the Dale Motel for unwed mothers. She should have checked into the hotel over in Spruceville, but she was so depressed, Dr. Nelson insisted on admitting her. If nothing happens by the fifteenth, he'll induce labor."

Moments later, when Ashley made her rounds, she hesitated at the girl's door—afraid to face this girl who never wanted to know her. Kerry Kovac lay on her back, her hands clenched tightly on either side of the yellow spread. A shadowed hump rose and fell with her uneven breathing. She had a porcelain, doll-like quality to her features, her dark auburn hair intensifying her pallor. She was young. *Nineteen,* the chart said.

Ashley walked to the bed and leaned over the side rail. "Kerry, I'm Mrs. Reynolds, your night nurse. How are you?"

In the shadowed light, the girl's lower lip trembled; the fingers on her soft exquisite hands flattened against the spread. Ashley touched Kerry's arm. Her skin felt cold and clammy. "Kerry, do you want me to notify anyone that you are here? A friend? Your family?"

"No. No one." She turned away.

Ashley wanted to draw her back. The watch on her wrist, the clothes in her closet, the expensive violin were clues to the real Kerry Kovac. And yet she had chosen to come to Everdale, a town that was warm and friendly to those who belonged but cold and hostile to someone from the North.

"Where's your family, Kerry?"

"In Prague." A tear slid down her cheek. "They don't know about the baby. They'd be so ashamed. They think I am in Alabama on concert. But I have no desire to ever play again."

"You will—when this is all over."

"Will it ever end, Mrs. Reynolds?"

"Soon, Kerry." She quoted Bill. "Things always work out."

As the girl stared blindly out the darkened window, Ashley said, "The woods behind my house were beautiful today."

"It was too dark to see anything when we drove into town."

We? Ashley longed to take Kerry for a walk in the woods so she could get to know the beauty of Everdale where her child would live. Ashley wanted her to see the dogwoods and sumacs, the sweet gum trees, and the little leaf huckleberry. She wanted her to smell the honeysuckle bushes in front of Mama's house. She wanted Kerry to hear David's message on God's love, God's forgiveness.

"In the morning you'll see how beautiful it is in Everdale."

"It is pretty in Prague now too," Kerry said.

On the night Chandler was born, Pitocin dripped steadily from Kerry's IV bottle. She lay on the delivery table, her feet in stirrups. Beads of perspiration lined her forehead, poured down her neck. Between contractions, she fell back against the pillows exhausted, panting. Crying without tears.

Ashley ached for the emptiness, for the unexpressed grieving that was tearing Kerry apart. She would deliver a child, but it would not bring joy. Only separation. Even the squirming antics of her unseen infant that she had felt in these last months of pregnancy would be gone. Kerry seemed determined to hold back her screams, but her nails dug into Ashley's hand with each contraction.

Birth should bring you happiness, Ashley thought. But there was no gladness in the room, only the clanging of the metal carts and the squeak of the bassinet being rolled into the room.

As Selma bustled around the room, Ashley dabbed Kerry's face with a cloth, and reached out to steady the cold, trembling knees. "Dr. Nelson is on his way, Kerry. It will be over soon."

Kerry nodded, her eyes filling with tears. The hot, windowless room was oppressive. The skin stretched taut over Kerry's swollen, glistening abdomen.

Ashley heard Dr. Nelson's lumbering footsteps plodding down the corridor, heard the whack as his broad shoulders split the swinging doors. Kerry panicked as he barreled in. By the time Dr. Nelson settled himself at the foot of the delivery table, his gloved hands raised, she was in full-blown labor, ready to push.

"It won't be long, Miss Kovac," he said cheerily. "Your baby will soon be here. Go ahead. Push, Kerry," he commanded. "Push!"

The pungent smell of amniotic fluid filled the air. He peered at Kerry over his mask. "I see the baby's head. Hang in there, Kerry."

She cried out now as the slick, milky-wet baby slipped out between her legs. Moments later, Nelson gave another satisfied exclamation. "We've got a little boy, Miss Kovac."

There was a gasp, Ashley's gasp as a tiny baby filled his lungs with air and cried. *Kerry Kovac's baby. No, my baby.* Kerry fell exhausted against the pillow as Dr. Nelson held the baby up. Tears of joy filled Ashley's eyes.

"He's beautiful, Kerry," Dr. Nelson said. "Just beautiful. You have a fine son. Would you like to hold him?"

He held the baby up with the bluish cord still attached and pulsating with Kerry's blood. For a moment, Kerry's innocent infant lay wiggling in Dr. Nelson's palm, and then he was placed on her flattened abdomen, his body small and fair and his attempt at another cry lost in a yawn.

Ashley knew that if Kerry held her baby she might want to keep him. But as she watched the girl pull back, her eyes closed, she urged, "Would you like to hold him, Kerry?"

Now the tears fell freely. Kerry reached out and stroked the infant's cheek and silky, blood-matted hair, the pain of separation intense. "Take him away," she whispered.

The night Kerry Kovac was to leave the hospital Ashley found her standing by the nursery window in the middle of the hall. Her suitcase and violin case were on the floor beside her; the bold name tags on both of them read *Kerina Rudzinski.*

The girl watched the baby's every move, a look that would have to last her a lifetime if Ashley didn't intervene. Ashley struggled with reality: *Her baby, my baby.*

His eyes, almost oriental in appearance, flickered. His ears were close to his scalp and his hair thick and auburn like Kerry's. The glass between them shut out the sucking sounds that must surely be coming from his rosebud mouth as he tried to chew his chubby fist.

Kerry bent down and took two sheets of scented stationery from her violin case and handed them to Ashley.

"Will you make certain that the couple who take my baby get this? Promise me."

Ashley's throat went dry. "I promise. But, Kerry, before you go, would you like to hold your baby?"

She nodded and followed Ashley, accepting the surgical gown and the rocking chair in the alcove without a word.

It was a magical moment. Kerry hardly breathed when Ashley placed the baby in her arms. There were long stretches of quiet for both of them as Kerry took in the feel of him, the sight of him. The child was warm and unbelievably alive and real as he tilted his head in contentment toward Kerry's breast.

"I am so sorry. So sorry," she whispered as she rocked him.

Ashley knelt beside her and unfolded the blanket. The baby's pink toes curled; his legs kicked. Kerry touched his tiny hands with her fingertips. Muffled joy escaped her as she felt the grasp of his fingers on her own. "You are so beautiful," Kerry said.

As Ashley knelt by the rocker, her chest muscles tightened. "It's not too late to change your mind, Kerry."

Kerry kissed her son. "If I gave up my music, Mrs. Reynolds, I would end up back in Prague. It was difficult where I grew up. I don't want that for my son." She kissed him again. "I must go back to my music. I have no choice. My family sacrificed for my career. They are proud of me, but they would be so ashamed if they knew about the baby."

Gurgling, cooing sounds filled the room. Kerry gazed up into Ashley's face. "I travel a lot and live out of suitcases. I go from concert hall to concert hall, from country to country. That is no life for my baby. I want the best for him. I want him to grow up in this country, to have a good home. To have both a mother and father."

Gently Ashley asked, "Is the baby's father married?"

Kerry's body went rigid. In a barely audible whisper she answered, "Yes, but I didn't know that at first. I was on concert in Chicago when I met him."

She cupped the baby's hand and held it. "I grew up under communism, but my parents were godly people. They sacrificed for their faith. I wanted no part of that life, Mrs. Reynolds. I kept searching for something else—someone else—to belong to."

She smiled faintly. "Suddenly in Chicago, there he was—so tall he stood out in a crowd. Then he laughed that deep laugh of his as he gave me a dimpled smile and a bouquet of flowers."

"Roses?" Ashley asked, her brother's favorite flower.

"Yes. White ones." Her tears dropped on the baby's blanket. "When we knew about the baby, I wanted an abortion. But he said 'No, that happened to someone dear to me, Kerry. Never again. Two wrongs don't make a right. I'll think of something.'"

Kerry hesitated. "But my having a baby has changed him. Grieved him. He would keep our baby if I would let him."

Ashley felt embarrassed by the girl's honesty. Would the baby ever be truly David's and hers? Ashley was afraid and was certain that she knew why. She leaned down to take the child.

"Please, Mrs. Reynolds, could I have a few more minutes with him—before I let him go?"

Ashley left Kerry alone with her son so she could tell him she loved him. Alone so she could cradle him for the last time. Later, when Ashley took the baby from Kerry, she knew that some of that warmth of him would stay with Kerry Kovac forever.

She led Kerry out of the nursery alcove. The girl went back blindly to the hallway and picked up her suitcase and violin. "Thank you, Mrs. Reynolds."

Ashley squeezed her hand. Kerry returned the gesture. There was nothing left to say. Ashley couldn't tell her that the baby would have a good home—that the baby would be loved.

They walked down the long corridor together, pausing at the lobby door. Kerry's face was pale, her soul in turmoil. "Where will you go, Kerry?" Ashley asked.

"Chicago for a while."

Ashley glanced at the closed door, certain that Bill was waiting on the other side for Kerry. Bill had chosen Everdale for both of them. Ashley nodded toward the lobby. "Does he know that you are going back to Chicago?"

"He knows. He keeps telling me that he will find a way for us to be together, but he needs his wife." There was a catch in her voice. "I think if he tries—I want him to try. And yet."

She put her hand to the swinging door. "He's taking me to Montgomery—to Dannelly Field."

Her narrow heels clicked as she fled through the lobby door. From out of the shadows, Bill rose to meet her. His dimples seemed like hollows in his cheeks, his eyes forlorn in the dimly lit room. He looked at Ashley without a flicker of recognition.

"Good evening, nurse," he said, forcing a smile.

He took Kerry's luggage and opened the main door with his shoulder. Kerry slipped out and stood alone in the driveway.

With one longing glimpse backwards, Bill's blue eyes seemed to say, *You're not surprised, Ash. You knew all along.* Silently he formed the words, "I love you, Sis. Forgive me."

"Wait," Ashley called. "You've forgotten your raincoat, sir."

He came back in and picked it up from the empty chair. His expression filled with torment as their eyes met. "I'm sorry, Sis."

"Why, Bill? Why this way?"

"I needed Everdale, Ash. I needed you."

"Then please stay. Let David and me help you."

Kerry had almost reached the parked car. "It's over for me," Bill said. "But Kerry—Kerina has her career. What I did by coming back to Everdale, I did for you. For her."

"The baby?"

"You'll take good care of him? In Mama's house."

"I promise," she said.

Bill had come up short. There was no way out, but he had done the best he could to unravel the tangled web he'd weaved. Ashley was convinced that without Kerry ever knowing, Bill had arranged for the baby to have parents who would love him and a home in Mama's old house.

She opened her mouth to ask him, but Bill blew Ashley a kiss across the silent lobby and ran to catch up to the girl. He slipped into the driver's seat beside her, backed his car out of the parking space, and sped up the winding driveway, racing into the blinding rainstorm. Blasting as he had always done into the unknown.

Hours later as he drove away from the airport, he was still speeding on a rain-drenched road when his car went out of control. Two unposted letters lay on the passenger seat beside him. One to the young concert violinist and one to his sister, Ashley, asking her forgiveness.

Ashley lay wide awake on the king-size bed. Outside her hotel windows, the sky over Vienna was still awash with stars. The heavens glowed with them, their brilliance comforting her. She still missed her brother. She knew—as she had known all along—that something of the bond between twins never died.

Remembering Kerina and Bill together as she had last seen them in the hospital lobby mellowed Ashley's heartache. Love, not anger, touched her in the semidarkness of her room. She longed to right her own mistakes, not Kerina's. Not Bill's. But Ashley had forgotten how level it was at the foot of the cross, how easy it was to go there. She ached to go home to David. David knew about forgiveness. David. David.

 Twenty-one

Jillian rushed into the Empress Isle Hotel and went straight to the concierge's desk. She was accustomed to attention and second glances and was not disappointed. The impeccably groomed man blinked his dark eyes as if he had clicked a candid shot of her as she approached. Charm poured into his greeting, but a shadow crossed his face as she asked for Chandler Reynolds.

He directed her down the corridor, past the gift shops to the gym. Even at this early hour, seven hotel guests were pedaling and pumping their way back into shape, working off last evening's dinner. She was surprised to see one young man who had been standing in the lobby of the Opera House the night before, casting shifty, watchful glances toward the lieutenant.

The lieutenant lay flat on his back, his hair damp with perspiration, a determined grimace on his face as he puffed under the strain of leg weights. Instant recognition flashed in those hooded dark eyes as he gave her the same beguiling smile that had electrified her last evening. "Good morning, lieutenant."

"You're up early." He went right on exercising. "I open my eyes and there you are. Better than any alarm clock."

She glanced around and nodded toward the man on the exercise bike. "Do you know that gentleman over there?"

"No. He followed me in here, but he hasn't bothered me."

"I'm certain he was at the Opera House last night."

"And at breakfast this morning."

"You're not in trouble?"

"Not that I know of. But it's nice to have you here to protect me. Are you staying in this hotel?"

"No, Miss Rudzinski sent me over to invite you on an all-day excursion Sunday."

"Really? Will you be there, Miss Ingram?"

She hated it when she blushed, but an embarrassing crimson crept up her neck to her cheeks, blotching the tip of her nose. "Of course; we'll be driving to the Vienna Woods—the invitation includes your mother."

"I was afraid of that."

Jillian saw teasing good humor in his eyes and Kerina's strength and strong, sculpted lines in his handsome expression. She pressed for his decision. "So what about Sunday?"

"Why the red carpet?" he asked in his deep, rich voice.

"Because Kerina was rude to you last night."

"Go, please," he mocked. "I'll just keep my distance."

"I'm not here to beg, lieutenant. So what's your decision?"

"What I wanted was a crack at the interview."

"But the interview didn't happen," she reminded him.

He held up his hand. "I'd better accept that invitation before you change your mind. That way, I'll be with you."

She laughed. *Don't let this get out of hand,* she warned herself. *Remember Santos and the pain he caused you.*

Chandler closed his eyes and kept on pumping, a painful grimace running its course each time he bent his knee and started the rotation over again. "Do you pray?" he asked.

"I don't think much about it. Is it something like fate? Chance? Two hearts meeting and all that?"

"Better than that. A much higher connection."

"So you pray?"

"Just last night. Prayed that I'd see you again. Fat chance, I thought, when Miss Rudzinski tossed us out of the dressing room, but I prayed anyway. And here you are."

The be-careful alarm button went off. She'd been many things, but never an answer to prayer. What kind of a joker was he? But he *was* cute with that prankish grin and those eyes like pongee autumn leaves. No wedding band, she noted. No girl back home? Just a little Vienna fling and then like a quick gust of wind, he'd be back to Bosnia, forgetting her.

He sat bolt upright, flattened his bare foot on the floor, and rubbed his calf frantically. "Sorry. Another leg cramp."

Perspiration glistened on his lean body. Now she saw the jagged scar that ran from his thigh to his ankle. With a scar that size he had good reason to count on prayer.

"Picked it up in Bosnia," he said. "Nasty accident."

He seemed distant for a minute before saying, "My time in Bosnia gave me a sour view on life. Especially when my friend died." His mouth twitched. "I wrestled that for a while. But God didn't make a mess of that country or take Randy's life. I don't like the duty there, but I like the people."

He was like two people himself. One teasing and light-hearted. The other sensitive, caring. Old loves passed through her thoughts. Santos again with his swarthy good looks was better looking than the lieutenant, and Brian, her sweet, hot-tempered Irishman, had been more jolly. She stole a look at Chandler's eyes. They were more open and direct than Santos's had ever been, more sensitive than Brian's. "I'm sorry about your friend."

"Not your fault. Take heart. I'm back on track now. I'll be good company. I've given prayer a fresh start since reaching Vienna."

So he was back on that and flat on his back lifting weights. He was strong in spite of the leanness, and she wondered if he had dropped in weight lately. Wondered about that distant look when he mentioned the accident.

He distracted her with another line twenty kilometers long. "Jillian, you have the most beautiful sapphire blue eyes. Honest, every time you look at me, I go on meltdown."

She started to stomp off, but he was on his feet, blocking her way and jauntily tossing his towel around his neck. "Don't leave. I told you, you're an answer to prayer."

"You're crazy, lieutenant."

"I don't have much time to be serious. I'm only in Vienna for thirty days. I want to spend them with you."

"I thought you were spending them with your mother."

"She won't mind sharing me."

"Sorry. I'm heading for a week on the Italian Riviera."

He cast a side glance at the man on the exercise bike. "Do you think we could shake that man if Mother and I went with you?"

"You're not invited. It's Miss Rudzinski's private villa."

"What would I have to do to score an invitation?"

This was Kerina's son. He didn't seem to have a clue about that, but as much as she wanted to get mother and son together, he didn't have a chance. At the peak of her successful career, Kerina wasn't going to risk her reputation by recognizing him. She thought of Kerina's vast fortune going to so many charities and wondered if even a dime had ever been spent on Chandler.

"You're not listening to me, Miss Ingram. I'm serious about going to the Riviera with you. Can't you put in a good word for me? After all, Miss Rudzinski promised me an interview."

"Ask her yourself on Sunday."

"My mother would have fits. So what about today and the rest of the time you're in Vienna? Let's spend it together."

"What about the man over there?" She jerked her thumb in his direction. "I hate tagalongs."

"We'll dodge him. I think he's army. Keeping an eye on me."

"I thought you said you weren't in trouble."

His facial muscles tightened. "Not in the way you think. When my buddy, Randy, was killed in Bosnia—no, don't look at the man—there were some nasty rumors. There may be those who are interested in what I'm doing in Vienna."

He mopped his face with his towel and missed her sympathetic glance. What was the lieutenant mixed up in? She was a fool for getting involved but said, "Kerina did say I could take guests. We could outrun that man in my Saab on the way to Italy."

"You're sure?"

"I'll talk to Kerina."

"Don't mention the dodgeball game I'm playing. I don't want to worry her. Now what about today? Tonight? The rest of the time you're in Vienna? Will you spend it with me?"

"When Kerina is in concert, I work twelve-hour days."

"That still leaves twelve for me."

She swung her purse strap over her shoulder. "Those are the hours on either side of midnight and just before dawn."

"I'll set my alarm. Where can I meet you? Please, Jillian, say yes. You can sleep all next month when I'm back in Bosnia."

Before she could open her mouth to give him a firm forget it, he said, "We don't have all that long to fall in love."

He reminded her of a fresh gust of wind, blowing in, swirling around. She had always loved autumn when the golden brown leaves drifted with the wind. The lieutenant's eyes were like that. A brilliant, rich brown like autumn leaves. He was Santos, American style. No, Chandler was different. There were sadness and laughter, boyishness and utter charm tumbling over one another like autumn leaves. She sensed pain and loneliness—those things she saw in Kerina. She had no desire to ruin Kerina's magnificent career or bring any more sadness into her life, but could she bring the two of them together—this mother and son? Or would she only widen the wedge between them?

"So what about midnight, Jill?"

"What about a good night's sleep so you'll enjoy our trip to the Vienna Woods on Sunday?"

He dismissed sleep with the wave of his hand. "I can sleep when I get back to Bosnia. Where do I meet you?"

Her mental calculations clicked into play. "I'll pick you and your mother up for late dinner after the concert."

He looked mischievous now, his gaze locking with hers. "Mother needs her beauty rest. I insist on it. It's just you and me at midnight, Jillian. No backseat drivers."

"I'd feel safer with your mother along."

"We have that bodyguard over there. Besides, I'm harmless."

So was Santos. But as she looked at Chandler, she was confident that he was deep, more complex than Santos. "I'll pick you up in the hotel lobby, lieutenant."

"Not very chauvinistic," he protested.

"But I have the red convertible."

She had embarrassed him. A faint flush added color to his cheeks. He was too fair, but he had wintered in Bosnia, hardly the place for a suntan. Her own brows crinkled quizzically. A shadow had darkened Chandler's eyes as he looked at her—and then beyond her to the man on the exercise bike.

Kerina had wandered along the winding streets in the Stephansdom Quarter since dawn but was resting now on a park bench across from St. Stephens enjoying the beauty of its high Gothic spire and glazed tile roof. She considered the magnificent cathedral the center of the city, its very soul.

Her musings were splintered by a deep voice. "Kerina."

"Franck. You frightened me."

He was wearing a gray-vested suit with a gray-striped shirt, giving his skin a sallow cast in the early morning sun. Even his eyes were a granite gray. But she had long ago come to appreciate that angular face and his deep devotion to her.

"I was looking for you, Kerina."

"In all Vienna?"

"Jillian told me I would find you here. We should have your name engraved on this bench—you come often enough."

"But usually on Wednesdays—and then I go inside."

As he smiled down at her, she made room for him. "Sit with me a while, Franck."

He edged the seat, facing her. "I was worried about you. You shouldn't walk alone."

"Why not? This is one of the safest cities of the world."

"At least one of the most beautiful. I wanted to talk to you about our plans for Moscow, Kerina."

"I have no plans for Moscow."

He took her hand. "Let's have coffee."

"I'd like that."

He walked her to a coffeehouse near the cathedral, one of the smaller ones that lined the streets of Vienna. Kerina had tried them all—the Frauenhuber where Mozart had once performed, the Landtmann near the Burgtheater, the Kleines where she often sat and sipped a *kaffeinfreier kaffee*. No matter how elaborate or shabby the coffeehouse, it seemed a waiter always appeared in a tux as one was doing now.

"Strudel and coffee with whipped cream, Kerina?" Franck asked.

She preferred something less sweet but politely moved her arm when the waiter reappeared with a *schlagobers* topped with whipped cream. Franck's black coffee came with an egg yolk and brandy and the familiar glass of water.

"You are too pale this morning, Kerina."

"I didn't do my makeup."

He scolded gently, "You never forget your makeup, my dear."

He studied her with his perpetual sadness, plucking at his sideburns. She liked his dark beard and soft voice. But lately he had become a gruff stranger, his features distorted.

"The strudel is marvelous," she said, taking a second bite. "But what did you want to talk to me about?"

"I rescheduled our trip to Moscow. We must go after the concert in Milan."

Her thoughts raced to the magnificent paintings in Milan—to the endless theft of great works of art in Italy. She slid her hand across the table and touched Franck's. "Franck, I am going on holiday with Jillian."

Anguished, he said, "But I need your help."

"I don't know what kind of trouble you are in, but I will not let you use me. I cannot get the McClaren robbery out of my mind. I fear you are implicated somehow. Why I cannot even guess."

"Implicated? How? I was at the Opera House that night."

"I don't know the logistics. But I do know that I have made you a wealthy man, Franck. You could buy any painting you wanted. And if you needed money, you have only to ask me."

"Don't you understand? Jokhar could ruin your career."

"Jokhar Gukganov? I barely know him."

"Kerina, my grandfather lost his art collection back in the war. When he was ill and dying, he begged me to get his paintings back. Some of them were not for sale, so Jokhar helped me."

"The black market? And now it is payback time?"

He nodded miserably. "Just three or four more paintings, Kerina. Two of them for Jokhar. He won't bother us again."

"You are so foolish, Franck."

"I remodeled the house on the Black Sea. It's filled with art treasures. I did it all for you."

"Then perhaps you should move there now."

"Without you?"

She nodded. "Don't force me to betray you. The McClarens are our friends. There was no excuse for taking something from them."

"I am not a thief, Kerina."

"Then what are you?" Tearing, she looked away and saw Jillian entering the cafe. She caught her eye and waved.

"Jillian is coming," she said, relieved.

"Why do you put up with her? She will ruin me—"

Kerina smiled as Jillian reached their table.

"Kerina, we need to talk. But it's a go for tomorrow. The lieutenant accepted with pleasure."

"What lieutenant?" Franck demanded.

Kerina hesitated for only a second. Her voice held steady. "I have found my son, Franck; he is here in Vienna."

Color crept from the edges of his beard across his cheeks. He was furious. "Not that young man outside your dressing room? That's why he looked so familiar. How? How did he find you?"

"Fate."

He glowered at Jillian. "Kerina, send him away. An old scandal will ruin your career."

"And ruin your trips to Moscow as well?"

"Don't force me to involve him in the trips to Moscow. I will," he warned, "if you don't send him away."

Her lips tightened. "Don't ask me to do that again, Franck."

"Not even for his safety?" He shoved his chair with such force that it crashed to the floor. He righted it at once.

"It was sweet of you to come here with me, Franck."

Stiffly, he said, "My pleasure, Kerina."

As he left, she met Jillian's gaze across the table. "Franck is not himself, Jill. But don't ask me about it. Now—what was so important that you had to see me?"

"I already told you. I want you to invite the Reynoldses to the Riviera."

"What! I can't do that. It would never work out."

"Please. Just for a week."

"A week? For your sake or mine, Jillian?"

"Kerina, you owe the lieutenant an interview." She licked her lips with the tip of her tongue. "You owe him a lot more than that. He's your son, Kerina. It would be your chance to let him know who you are."

Her eyes filled with tears. "Do you think they would come?"

Jillian grinned. "I'm certain they will."

"Then ask them. But you heard Franck. He means what he said."

"You can put Franck out of your mind for a whole week. Don't let him go on controlling you, Kerina."

"Dear Jillian, I owe him my life, my career."

"You succeeded because you are good. If Franck hadn't been there to manage your career, someone else would have come along. Chandler is the important one now. He's your son, Kerina. You're his mother."

"No, Jillian. You're wrong. I am the person who brought him into the world. Ashley Reynolds is his mother."

At midnight, Chandler was leaning on his crutches in front of the hotel when Jillian's convertible careened to the curb. He was in and dragging his crutches behind him when Jillian sped away before the man standing nearby could pursue them.

Chandler peered out the back window. "We did it! The poor guy's trying to hail a taxi."

As she swerved around another corner, she shook her hair from the nape of her neck. "Did you get your mother tucked in?"

"She's a big girl now. But she's probably up on her balcony cringing at the way you drive."

He heard the soft rippling laugh well up from deep inside her. The girl in Bosnia seemed a long way away. Bosnia was Bosnia. This was Vienna. He needed someone, and right now he needed Jillian Ingram. He saw her profile reflected in the lights of the city and felt something beat wildly inside his chest.

Twenty-two

Five or six times a year Kerina slipped away to Bello la Fortezza, her gated villa on the Italian Riviera. Her bedroom and balcony balanced on a rocky promontory with an unobstructed view of the glassy sea and the sleek yachts bobbing on its smooth waters. She often arose before dawn to watch the sun rise over the sparkling aquamarine waters, but this morning she awakened to the phone ringing.

She snatched the receiver before the ring disturbed her house guests. "Buon giorno," she whispered. Then impatiently, "Santos Garibaldi? Please. You must not come here. I must warn you, my guards will turn you away." She stopped his flurry of Italian, saying, "Yes, Jillian has found someone else. I am sorry, Santos."

She jammed the receiver back in place. With Garibaldi's voice silenced, she heard the sound of muted voices on her balcony. Tiptoeing barefoot to the window, Kerina felt the warm breeze from the Ligurian Sea brush her cheek. Outside, Chandler and Jillian stood as one, silhouetted against the iron balustrade.

The cinereous night clouds had separated, the glorious light of dawn turning the blue of the sea into rippling embers of gold. As the dawn touched Chandler's face, Kerina noticed how much his strong, chiseled features looked like Bill VanBurien's. She held her breath as Chandler bent down and tentatively kissed Jillian, and then in a warm embrace, the two of them wrapped their arms around each other.

Kerina drew back into the shadows. Her thoughts winged back to Chicago and Bill's first tender kiss. She wanted the growing bond between Chan and Jillian yet dreaded the outcome. Would he flee back to his life in Bosnia, leaving Jill more heartbroken than she had been with Santos?

Ashley had dreaded coming to Kerina's private villa, but now on her sixth morning at the Bello la Fortezza, she took her breakfast on the balcony, savoring the beauty that surrounded her. The villa sat perched on a rugged cliff as white-rocked as the silk-white sands below. Beyond the harbor lay a coastline of sheltered coves dotted with tiny fishing villages, ancient castles, and steepled Romanesque churches. The sheer cliff rose from the blue-green sea up to the terraced villas where the hillsides were covered with a profusion of flowers and fruit trees, olive groves and grape-ripened vineyards. She saw Chandler and Jillian down in the vineyard, talking and laughing and carrying a picnic basket between them. She wondered if they had slept at all.

It was happening too fast; they were rushing from friendship into romance in the same quick way that she and David had rushed into their own relationship. She had no right to interfere, but she ached for the girl in Bosnia. Had Chandler already forgotten her? No, the truth was, Ashley objected to either girl.

In Vienna she had watched Chandler grab the moments with Jillian. She had known that day as they drove back from the Vienna Woods with Chandler at the wheel and Jillian stealing constant glances at him that something was happening between them. What should have brought her joy only added to her pain. Jillian was Kerina's friend. And then, as they drove along—Kerina and Ashley silent in the backseat—Chandler reached out and put his hand over Jillian's. He kept grinning at her until they almost skidded off the motorway.

After that it was breakfast the next morning at an unearthly hour, a noontime walk along the Danube, hours discovering Vienna at night, an afternoon browsing in an art museum that he had not even wanted to see the day before. Now Kerina and Ashley could not separate them. Chandler and Jillian filled their days on the Riviera enjoying each other's company—swimming in the bay, exploring the caves in the cliffs, meandering through the fishing village, climbing the ancient staircase to the castle, and listening to romantic ballads on Kerina's console into the wee hours of the night.

Ashley was forced to spend her days with Kerina, sitting on the balcony sipping hot tea or iced lemonade. It was Mia's good cooking that eased the strain between them. She fed them lunches of pasta with pesto sauce and delicately browned fish and focaccia, a salted bread that Ashley liked. With Mia's watchful eye constantly on them, Kerina and Ashley began to talk.

They talked about Florence and Tuscany, the Renaissance and Italian opera, about the Dolomites and the history of Liguria, about wine making and music, about Genoa and Christopher Columbus and the magnificent career of Michelangelo. Kerina spoke heatedly of the fascist government that once controlled these fun-loving people and with equal disdain about rich counts and countesses. She proved a wealth of information, her face animated as she spoke of the Italians who delighted her.

Kerina's lovely face was delicate, like the painting of a Madonna. Sitting so close to her these last few days, Ashley could not shake off the premonition that Kerina was not well. The fear was not clearly defined, but she saw the pallor, and saw her wince when she moved her arm.

Last night they had talked about the caves of Toirano and the concert in Milan where Kerina played Tchaikovsky's *Concerto in D major*. Kerina had played beautifully, passionately. But in five days, neither Kerina nor Ashley had spoken of Chandler's birth in Everdale, or of Bill VanBurien, the other name that lay like a chasm between them.

Behind her, Ashley heard Kerina on the phone in the hall, her voice tight with anger. "Please do not call again, Mr. Garibaldi. I told you already that we have guests."

Ashley glanced up as Kerina came out onto the balcony and slipped into the chair beside her. "Buon giorno, Kerina. Is everything all right?"

"It was Santos. Twice today. I cannot let him come here and upset Jillian—not when she's on the verge of happiness." She turned sideways in her chair, shading her eyes from the sun. "Where are the children, Ashley?"

Ashley laughed. "The last I saw *the children,* they were walking off, carrying a picnic basket between them."

"At least they won't run into that man any longer."

"The one who followed us from Vienna?"

"My friends at the police station are detaining him now."

"Can they do that?"

She smiled. "When they learned that he was constantly at our gates, they took him in for questioning. Chandler will be safely back in Bosnia before the police release the man." She shaded her eyes. "Do you think Chandler and Jillian are getting serious?"

Ashley frowned. "How can they? Chandler is planning to marry someone else, someone he met in Bosnia."

Kerina's face went rigid. "A girl in Bosnia? Then why—why has he misled Jillian?"

"I don't think he meant to." She met Kerina's gaze. "I don't even know what he plans to do now. The girl in Bosnia is pregnant. It's another man's child—Chandler's friend Randy who was killed a few weeks ago. For some reason, Chan feels responsible for the baby."

"Does he love the girl?"

"I don't think so, but he thinks marriage is the only way to sponsor Zineta out of Bosnia."

"What a strange thing for him to do then."

"David will find the idea deplorable."

A slight flush reached Kerina's cheeks. "Poor Jillian."

"Poor Chandler," Ashley countered, "to have met someone as lovely as Jillian and to care so deeply about her."

"Is there nothing we can do?" Kerina asked as Mia set steaming cups of tea in front of them.

"Us personally? We'd have a hard time getting through military red tape. Randy's parents live in Akron, Ohio, but they know nothing about their unborn grandchild."

Kerina gazed out on the sea and said quietly, "It was that way for my parents too. If we could get Zineta safely to my parents' farm, they would help."

"But Randy came from Ohio."

"Jillian and I have talked about going on concert in Bosnia. I have friends there, if they haven't all been killed. I could attempt to contact them—perhaps find a way to help Zineta—but I won't interfere unless you think it's right for me to help Chandler."

"I have another plan to suggest," Ashley said. She spelled it out as a backup plan and then, smiling conspiratorially, they toasted the grandparents in Akron, Ohio, with their teacups.

Kerina replaced her cup in its saucer. "Coming here hasn't been a very pleasant holiday for you, has it, Ashley?"

"The hardest part has been knowing who you are. You should know that Chandler and I argued about coming."

The trip had softened her heart. She was no longer blaming Kerina for ruining Bill's life or deserting her child for a violin. She had spent these days remembering that Mama had always said, "The forgiving heart goes a long way toward happiness."

And Ashley wanted Kerina Rudzinski to be happy. "Kerina," she said calmly, "I think it's time to talk about you and Chandler."

Kerina's eyes brimmed with tears. "I was afraid to mention Everdale—or Chandler. And what is there to tell of myself? I was born poor, but my family had a Stradivarius violin that passed down through the generations. Music became my life."

"You sent Chandler a violin when he was three, didn't you?"

A smile lit her face. "You did receive it? I played that one as a child. I sent it in care of the hospital where he was born, hoping you would receive it."

"We did. Kerina, we're leaving in the morning. You may never see Chandler again. Do you want to tell him who you are?"

Kerina's knuckles went white against the arms of the chair. "We must not spoil this time for Chandler and Jillian. It may be all they have. Right now, I have the joy of seeing him. I would lose everything if he knew I was the mother who abandoned him."

"Perhaps; you did what you thought was best."

Kerina shook her head. "For me it was always wrong. After the baby was gone, I could barely sleep or eat just thinking about him. I threw myself into my music. I had nothing else."

"You have a letter. I brought a letter with me, Kerina—it's from Bill VanBurien."

"You know Bill?" She laughed nervously, embarrassed. "Of course, you knew him. You grew up in the same town."

"Kerina—there is something you should know. I've been struggling to find the words to tell you ever since we arrived in Vienna. Even more since arriving at your villa. But, please, you must read the letter before Chandler comes back."

I'm going about this all wrong, Ashley thought. She took a deep breath and said, "I grew up with Bill. Bill VanBurien was my brother—my twin brother."

Kerina stared blankly, her eyes darting from Ashley's face to the sea and back again. The flush in her cheeks reappeared. "Your brother?" She was a mixture of anger and pain, her wound raw. "He arranged for you to adopt my baby. I was never to know, and he has known all these years. Why did he do that to me, Ashley? I trusted him."

Ashley thought of Bill, the man of rough fabric that had chafed so many lives. No matter how severely she judged it—no matter how much she disapproved—Kerina had loved him too.

"You were the nurse in the lobby at the hospital the night Bill picked me up. You didn't act like you knew each other."

"Bill didn't want me to know that he was the baby's father. I just happened to be on duty that night."

"He hurt you too."

Ashley nodded. "I worried when you left Everdale that night. You were depressed. I was afraid something would happen to you."

"I had nothing to live for," Kerina admitted.

"You had your music."

"But you had my son." Distractedly, she said, "I met Bill in Chicago. He was charming and friendly. I was pregnant when I discovered that he was married, separated from his family. I am so sorry, Ashley. I would never have destroyed his family.

"I considered an abortion, but Bill said he knew someone who had done that, and he would not let me go through that pain . . . Ashley, are you all right?"

"I just felt faint for a minute."

"Bill promised to find a good home for the baby if I would carry the pregnancy to full term. He told me he knew a doctor in Everdale who would help us."

Ashley understood. Bill had chosen his childhood home as the place for his son to live.

She said, "All his life, my brother made trouble for our family, but he made certain that his son would have a good home. Dear Bill! You loved him, didn't you, Kerina?"

"With all my heart."

Ashley pulled Bill's letter from her purse and handed it to Kerina. Kerina's eyes clouded with tears as she read it, silently at first and then aloud.

"I am filled with shame, my darling, for all that has happened to you. When you boarded the plane, I told you I loved you. I promised that I would find a way for us to be together forever. I think you knew that could never be— T. S. Eliot was right. April is the cruellest month. I am not even certain that God will forgive me for the twisted turns my life has taken. But if you can, Kerina, forgive me, and may God do the same." Kerina's voice trailed as she read, "The baby has a good home, my darling. They will take good care of our son. They will love him for us."

The letter slipped from Kerina's hands. "He never intended to come back to me, did he, Ashley?"

"He never had a chance to make that decision."

"Where is he now?" she asked softly.

Ashley's voice wavered. "He's dead."

"Dead? Bill—Bill is dead?" She swayed in the chair. "Tell me it's not true."

"Kerina—he was killed in an automobile accident on the freeway, two hours after he left you off at the airport in Montgomery—only minutes after he wrote that letter." *Minutes after he called his wife to ask for another chance,* she thought. "Bill's car catapulted over the guardrail into a deep gully. The back wheels were still spinning when the State Police found him. He didn't suffer."

Kerina pushed herself from the chair and stumbled across to the railing. She leaned so far over that Ashley feared she would topple. She stayed there, saying his name over and over. "Bill. Bill. Bill." At last she asked, "You are certain he is dead? You are not just protecting him?"

"He's dead, Kerina. We buried him in Everdale."

Kerina loosened her hair and let it fall softly to her shoulders, flecks of red in the gleaming gold. "No wonder I never heard from him again."

Ashley crossed the balcony to her. "The last time I saw my brother alive, he told me he had finally found happiness. That he truly loved someone. I have no doubt that you are the one Bill talked about. He loved you, Kerina."

Kerina lifted her tear-stained face and smiled. "It's good to know what happened. Good of you to have brought the letter to me. Until now I always hoped that he would come back someday. Even after all these years—" She bit her lip. "But that was impossible. Bill knew that when he said good-bye."

"It's over, Kerina. Let it rest." Gently, Ashley put her arms around Kerina, and they walked back into the villa together.

The next morning as Ashley finished packing, Chandler and Jillian walked in the garden. Chandler's eyes looked like dark sockets, as though he hadn't slept all night.

"I hate to see you go," Jillian said, smiling up at him.

"I hate to go."

"You could stay on and do the three-city tour with us."

"Budapest, Berlin, and Paris? I promised Mom more of Vienna."

She felt disappointment. "Kerina and I will be in Vienna before you fly back to Bosnia. Will you call me?"

He stopped walking and faced her, looking troubled. "I don't think we should see each other again, Jill."

Her stomach churned. "But I thought—"

He ran his thumb gently across her cheek. "What did you think, Jillian?"

"That you brought me out here to ask me to wait for you."

"I wanted to. But I can't do that to you. We can't go on with our friendship. We have to break up before it goes too far."

"Friendship? Is that all you call these last few days? Last night you told me—" Her voice cracked.

He looked even more stricken. "I told you I thought I was falling in love. I was. I am."

"Then what's wrong, Chandler? Don't tell me you're another Santos in my life. A little fling and you're gone?"

"You know you mean more to me than that."

He tried to grasp her hand. "The tip of your nose is turning red again," he said gently.

"Oh, don't fret, love. I've survived the best of you. So what's your excuse, lieutenant? A girl in every city?"

"There's someone else, Jillian. A girl in Bosnia."

The pungent smell of ripened grapes and the damp soil and wildflowers on the hillside pooled together, the sweet odor nauseating her. "Someone in Bosnia? Someone you just remembered?"

"The girl is pregnant, Jillian."

"Pregnant!" Choking, she said, "That dresses it up nicely. At least you're not leaving me that way."

"I respect you too much for that."

"Go, Chandler, before I slap you. Before I hate you."

He ran his hands through his hair. "I don't want to leave you this way. Just let me explain—"

"No, Chandler. I don't want to hear it. Just go."

He took off, running back toward the villa, favoring his injured leg. She stood in the vineyard watching him go, certain that he had taken her heart with him. She expected him to take the path around to the door, but when he reached the steep cliff beneath the balcony, he climbed recklessly up the rocky incline.

She watched, stunned at the fury at which he tugged his way up. He was almost to the balcony when he stopped abruptly.

Get over that railing, she thought, *before you fall back.*

But as suddenly as he had climbed, he was slipping and sliding frantically down the hillside. Her heart thumped wildly until he was safely at the bottom. He was coming back to her!

Her joy was momentary. He stood on level ground now. Looking up. Looking away. He jammed his fists into his pockets and limped slowly around the stone-flagged path, his eyes riveted on the ground. Something had happened at the top of the cliff.

She had to go to him. But seconds later she saw him again—fighting his own demons with his head thrown back, his eyes toward the sky, his fists beating the air. He shouted angry, incoherent words, bitter words like the ones welling inside of her. Then he ran, not toward her, but on the east side of the vineyards.

Kerina and Ashley leaned over the railing waving. "What's wrong?" Kerina called.

Jillian's throat felt tighter than a drum. "Everything's cool," she cried. "It's just Chandler running off steam."

Kerina went in search of Jillian and found her in the garden an hour later. "I thought you would come to see our guests off, Jill. It was embarrassing without you there. What happened?"

"I said my good-byes."

"Do you expect Chandler in Budapest tomorrow evening?"

"I don't expect him to show up anywhere. Ever."

Sharply she asked, "Why was Chan running in the vineyards?"

"Trampling grapes! No, nothing happened. That's what makes it so sad. One minute he acts like I'm the only girl for him, and this morning he tells me there's someone else. I'm afraid he's going to marry her."

"Oh, Jillian, didn't you tell him how you feel?"

"I really thought I wanted to spend the rest of my life with him, and he wants to spend it with someone else. I can't fight that kind of competition."

"You needed more time together. You barely know him."

"He told me it doesn't take all that long to fall in love. Oh, Kerina, if I thought he would change his mind about the girl in Bosnia, I would wait for him forever."

Like I waited, thought Kerina. "I did that once, but forever is too long. Did you tell him we'll be in Vienna this weekend?"

"He said it's over. Besides, the girl in Bosnia is pregnant." Their eyes met. "Chandler is not the baby's father."

"He isn't? How do you know that?"

"Ashley told me. He made a promise to a friend to take care of the girl. I will try to work something out, Jillian, so we can free him from that promise. Maybe I will play for the troops in Bosnia." Her gaze traveled back to Jillian's troubled face, those long lashes still wet with tears. "Chandler has a few more days in Vienna. Call him when we get there this weekend. Spend that time with him."

"I can't call Chandler."

"And why not? Women have been calling men for a long time."

"I don't think he wants to see me again, Kerina."

"If he loves you he will."

Twenty-three

It was a lovely June morning in Vienna with billowy white clouds drifting lazily across the Dresden blue sky. Kerina walked along the bank of the Danube and watched the breaking dawn filter through the rising mist, the fiery embers of gold reflecting against the dark gray water. Her city, the city of Mozart and Beethoven and Haydn. Her river flowing gently, waltzing, winding its way to somewhere.

This was the day that Kerina's son was going away, waiting at some unknown airstrip for a standby flight to Bosnia. She was losing him again. An hour before, she had called his hotel only to be told that the Reynoldses had checked out. In her disappointment the haunting memory of the house she longed to find came back. She captured it in her mind's eye as the rolling mist blew across the Danube. She knew that peace belonged to that country house with its heart-shaped dormer window in the attic and its narrow, wood-framed bedroom windows on the second floor. There came again the remembered scent of the sweet gum tree in the backyard, the thought of branches on the old maple hanging low to the ground, the clusters of purple flowers on the wisteria vine. She closed her eyes, trying to picture the swings by the gazebo, trying to hear the cry of the baby louder than the whippoorwill.

She felt certain that the longing for the house belonged to Everdale, to that moment in time when she sat in the nursery at Jackson Memorial and held her infant son in her arms for the last time. She had loved him then. She loved him now. The image of the house faded. Gone. The Danube flowed on. She turned from the river with her eyes to the rolling hills that surrounded Vienna. She found them beautiful at any season—sometimes a lush green, often a pale yellow, rusty-red in the fall, covered with snow in the winter. She kept walking, walking, allowing the soaring spire of St. Stephen's to guide her, the glazed roof tiles blinding in the sunshine. Shading her eyes, she glanced up where the Pummerin Bell hung high in the North Tower.

In 1945, at the close of a war she had never known, a fire had swept through the Stephansdom, plunging the bell through the burning roof into ruin. Years later, the bell that had made music was dug from the ruins and recast from the ashes. Kerina felt much like the bell, plunging into ruin, unable to make music.

Outside the cathedral, she found a discarded rosary lying on the sidewalk. Her parents' faith shouted up at her. She picked up the rosary and entered St. Stephen's through the Giants' Doorway and vestibule, her heels tapping against the marble as she went beneath the West Gallery into the nave.

Drawn by the familiar panels of the Mother and Christ Child she made her way down the narrow aisle to the front row. As she faced the High Altar, her fingers entwined around the rosary.

"God," she said tentatively, "I don't know where you are, but if you are anywhere, surely you must be here in this cathedral. If you hear me, please help me." Light from the windows reflected on the Mother and the Christ Child. "I have seen my son—as you saw your Son and agonized for him. Oh, God, if I could only see my son one more time."

Thirty minutes of silence engulfed her and then she heard sturdy booted footsteps coming down the long aisle and wished with all her heart that it would be Chandler. Someone slipped into the seat beside her.

"Miss Rudzinski."

She turned, breathless, overjoyed. "Chandler," she cried.

He wore his uniform, the lieutenant bars on his epaulets. He looked handsome, striking in his army greens. "I was hoping to find you here. Jillian assured me that you always come here on Wednesdays. I just wanted to say good-bye."

"I called your hotel." She brushed away the tears. "But you had checked out. I thought I had missed you."

"I wouldn't leave Vienna without saying good-bye to you."

She glanced around. "Where's Ashley?"

"I took Mother to the airport early this morning. If I know Dad, he's already at Los Angeles International waiting for her."

"But, Chandler, it will be hours before she arrives."

"He's anxious to have her home. Now I'm heading out."

"Will you ever come back to Vienna?"

"It depends on what I decide to do with my future."

Again she traced his features as she had done that day he walked back into her life at the Opera House. "What do you really want to be, Chandler?"

"A music critic someday."

"And not a musician? But you were born for music, Chandler. Why did you quit Juilliard?"

"I had to face the truth. I was never going to make the grade professionally. Going there was Mom and Dad's idea."

"You had to be good to get in."

"Lucky maybe. I had an uncle who was into classical music. I always figured they wanted me to go because of him."

She felt weak, disoriented, with memories of autumn leaves sweeping across a porch. "Tell me about your uncle, Chandler."

"There's not much to tell. He died right after I was born." Chandler shrugged. "Having Dad's favor was the important thing in my life. The army was our first big clash. I can't imagine what he will do if I reenlist or take that government job."

"The one that will take you back to Bosnia as a spy?"

He laughed out loud, his laughter echoing in the quiet sanctuary. "Hardly a spy. An intelligence officer. Dad won't like it either, Kerina. He's a big influence on my life, even though I rarely please him anymore." He looked away and then came back to meet her gaze. "Did Mom tell you he's a preacher? A sought-after speaker. He'd be national if Mom didn't oppose it. And he teaches archeology at the university. He's a smart man—makes a good professor. He's a great guy."

"But not wise enough to let you be a music critic?"

"We haven't talked that one out yet. Dad always thought he was raising a child prodigy. A violinist, no less. Now if I had the instrument that you have—"

Kerina stared down at her hands. "Someday, Chandler, when I no longer need my violin, I will send it to you."

"Your Strad? You're kidding, of course."

"I have never been more serious. Would you play it?"

"I'd be honored. But you should keep it in your own family."

"I will."

"But what about your son?" he asked unexpectedly. "Shouldn't it go to him? Surely he is musical?"

She had forgotten their conversation in the Staatsoper dressing room. They had been speaking in hushed voices; now it seemed as though her very words had reached the vaulted ceiling and echoed back like Chandler's laughter. "You remind me of him."

He grinned. "Is that why you are so kind to me?"

She patted his hand. "You remind me of someone else that I cared for deeply."

"Past tense?"

"He belonged to my past."

Now his sigh echoed through the chamber. "I have to go, Kerina. Jillian is waiting for me. And so's the army."

"Jillian is fond of you, Chandler—in love with you."

"I know. But I have things to work out in Bosnia."

He stood and when he pulled her up beside him and hugged her, she caught the scent of her son's cologne, the sweet smell of peppermint on his breath. She felt the smoothness of his freshly shaven skin, the strength of his hands on her arms supporting her. *Her son. Ashley's son.*

"Thanks for that week on the Riviera. I still can't believe you took in strangers like that. But we're grateful."

"Jillian insisted."

"Take care of yourself, Miss Rudzinski. And take care of Jillian for me."

"I will. And you—be careful, Chandler."

She watched him striding down the long aisle, straight and tall, his finely shaped head so much like Bill's. When he reached the door, he turned and waved. She felt numb. Even her tears refused to come. Moments later, she stepped outside where a summer storm had blackened the sky. She had gone inside with the sun reflecting off the steep slanted roof. Now dark clouds hovered above the North Tower. The leaden sky blotted out the daylight. In the distance, her son strolled hand-in-hand with Jillian, oblivious to the rain.

Drops of rain splattered around her as she hurried toward the shelter of the cafe awning across the boulevard. The downpour left glittering wet spiderwebs in her tangled hair. She felt a tightening in her chest, a struggle to catch her breath as she sprinted for cover. Drenched as she was, she risked another bout with bronchitis. Nothing must stop her fall schedule. Nothing. She looked forward to reaching New York and catching a train that would carry her over the rails to Everdale—perhaps to the elusive house and gazebo that constantly filled her mind.

August had not changed the bleakness of Bosnia nor the isolation of long confinement behind the locked doors at the top security command post. The electricity fed into Tuzla by the burning of soft coal, causing more low-hanging clouds and heavy mists. Chandler had forgotten how dreary it could be living in a town where the sun seldom shone. Even when it did shine, he was shut away in a windowless room, sifting through intelligence data and classified satellite photos of infantry training camps and the acquisition of weapons that exceeded the quotas for the Muslims and Croats.

Now after two months back from Vienna, he'd fallen into the routine where huge, brown tents still served as base camps and dissension came from American soldiers bored with bad weather, treacherous roads, and the slow reconciliation among the country's ethnic groups. Chandler stuck firmly to his belief that the separatist sympathies and guerrilla activity in the southern province was a cry for freedom. Even before his trip to Vienna, he had noted an increase in paramilitary units in the area and more Serbian helicopters and armored personnel carriers being moved in. The high command hadn't listened to him, not when the area involved was outside their military jurisdiction. Now he continued to keep his records straight, making detailed reports for his commanding officers.

He was putting in ten- to twelve-hour days. It kept his mind off Randy Williams, but it hadn't solved the problem of Zineta Hovic. Yet someone had pulled strings that permitted her return from the French sector. She was shy and reticent with him, but she was the same sweet girl whom Randy had loved, and she was definitely heavy with child. Steeling himself against thoughts of Jillian, he had filed more than one request, asking permission to marry Zineta. Two requests were tabled, the third lost, the fourth one buried under red tape.

Chandler would head home before the next Balkan winter, before the freezing cold swept over the area and hard snow made the search for land mines more difficult. It didn't give him much time to clear the military red tape that opposed Zineta leaving the country. And it didn't give him a wide margin between discharge from the military and flying to Washington regarding the government job that would eventually bring him back to Bosnia. In spite of all the plans he was making, Jillian Ingram stole into his thoughts continuously.

This morning Chandler sat in a strategy meeting as an observer, reviewing Washington's equip and train rule. The multinational group in the room were divided on the agenda. The biggest concern was not the Serbian crisis to the south but the foreign freighter sitting in the Adriatic Sea filled with weapons and tanks intended for the Muslim army and quarantined under heavy NATO guard. Chandler smothered his disgust. He was not expected to comment, but he knew why he was there. Colonel Bladstone had chosen him for the Langley intelligence team that would return to Bosnia with a new identity and a new job.

Unexpectedly, the commanding officer glowered at Chandler. "Lieutenant, I see by your reports you predicted trouble in Kosovo long before it happened. You've been critical of NATO's response time."

"Yes, sir."

"But that was outside our military jurisdiction."

"Yes, sir. But does humanity have a boundary line?"

A snarl cut across the man's crusty features. "We'll pass your suggestions on to Washington, lieutenant."

Like you passed along reports of my activities in Vienna? Chandler thought.

It was still a sore spot with him that he had been followed, a surveillance that Colonel Bladstone continued to deny. When the meeting ended, Chandler walked out of the room with Bladstone. "You see what kind of problems we're up against, lieutenant, trying to appease a multinational force."

"My job is to examine intelligence data, sir."

"Examine it, not interpret it." Bladstone rubbed his jaw vigorously. "That's why Langley wants a special team of operatives back in this country within the next twelve months.

Separate from the military involvement. That's why we handpicked you as one of them, Reynolds."

"Is that why you had me followed in Vienna?"

"I keep telling you, if someone followed you, it was not my doing."

"Tell that to the poor devil detained in Italy. But you are the one who turned down my reenlistment."

"You're more important to us out of uniform. NATO isn't here forever. We'll leave a team of advisors when we pull out, but we want an intelligence team made up of men with no family ties."

"Is that why you ignored my request to marry Zineta Hovic?"

"What would you do with a Bosnian wife on your hands, lieutenant? She wouldn't be welcomed back here. Besides, Miss Hovic may get a passport to America without a wedding ring."

Chandler stopped dead on the muddy trail. "What?"

"Someone advised Captain Williams's parents about the girl and his unborn child. And now Washington is on it."

"Sir, I didn't inform them."

They stood outside of Bladstone's barren office now. "That isn't another lie, is it, Reynolds?"

"A lie, sir? I haven't been in touch with Randy's family."

"Well, there's one lie that may hold up your future. Langley tells me one of your legal documents is in question. Seems your birth certificate lacks an official signature. Langley insists you could have been adopted."

"Me? Adopted?" The colonel's words sent Chandler into a tailspin, confirming his worst nightmare. A golf-ball-size lump lodged in his throat. He couldn't suck in air or blow any out. He stood there, wobbly as a newborn colt, his legs so unsteady that he feared passing out like those fool recruits had done back in basic training. The pounding in his head turned explosive.

"Well?" roared Bladstone. "What do you say for yourself?"

"As far as I know, sir, I am not adopted."

But the lump in his throat grew bigger. *A piece of himself was really missing.* A flash of memory took him back to that last day on the Riviera to an incident he had been trying to repress for nearly two months. He had just split with Jillian and left her weeping after telling her about Zineta. On impulse, he had taken the steep cliff up to Kerina's balcony like a rock climber, tugging his way up by gripping the shrubs.

He'd been ready to swing his leg over the railing and surprise his mother when he heard her saying, "Chan doesn't even know he's adopted, Kerina. How can I ever tell him?"

He had ducked down and almost toppled backwards, as shattered by his mother's words as Jillian had been by his. He slid and stumbled back down the hillside. Once out of sight of the villa, he ran with every ounce of strength through the vineyards. Exhausted at last, he had turned back to the house, certain that he had misunderstood his mother's words.

"Reynolds, it looks like I've given you quite a shock. But I need an answer. Could you be adopted?"

Chandler forced himself to meet Bladstone's stern gaze without flinching. "What difference would it make, sir?"

He answered his own question. *All the difference in the world if the two people I trusted most in life deceived me for twenty-six years.*

Bladstone said, "I told Colonel Daniels when he was here three months ago that it was probably just a mix-up, lieutenant. Daniels is hard to convince, so get that cleared up before you go for your interview in Washington."

The air coming from Chandler's lungs was nothing but a wheeze. "I'll try to do that, colonel."

"And forget this business about marrying a Bosnian."

"If you guarantee me she'll get to America. If not—"

Bladstone snorted. "Why not ask that violinist who's coming in tomorrow to play for the troops? Seems like she's a friend of yours. And she's pulled some political maneuvers to get Miss Hovic to America before the baby comes."

Chandler saluted. "I'll do that, sir."

283

The Apache helicopter lowered and came in for a landing at the military airport in Tuzla, rotor blades whirling. Moments later, Kerina was assisted from the copter, bending low against the dust and wind, and running toward Chandler.

He took her hands, his grin widening. "Miss Rudzinski, am I glad to see you. And I've got good news."

Kerina smiled. "That was my line, as Jillian would say."

"You first," he said, walking her toward the waiting Humvee.

Her gaze met his, her wide, hazel eyes anxious. "You haven't done anything foolish about Zineta Hovic, have you, Chandler?"

He looked embarrassed. "I've filed the papers so I can marry her. My last request is bogged down in military red tape."

She touched his arm. "Marrying Zineta won't be necessary now. We found another way for you to keep your promise to your friend Randy."

"Then the colonel wasn't kidding?"

"Once your mother notified Randy's parents about the baby, they stirred up support in Washington. They are doing everything in their power to get her to Akron before the baby is born."

"The Williamses really want her? Will it work?"

She laughed delightedly. "Chandler, your commanding officer was quite pleased about my coming to play for the troops, so he offered me anything I wanted."

"And you wanted Zineta's release? How can I ever thank you?"

She blushed. "You said you had a surprise for me, Chandler."

"I do. Zineta is coming to the concert tonight to meet you."

She tucked her arm in his. "Meeting Zineta was one of the stipulations of my coming. Now—I have another surprise for you."

284

She turned him back toward the helicopter where a young woman in camouflage pants and parka with a helmet tilted cockily on her head was coming across the field to meet them—her sapphire blue eyes on Chandler.

Chandler's jaw dropped. "Jillian!"

Jillian waved and started running. He met her halfway, his arms wide and ready when she reached him.

The military threw out the red carpet for Kerina, receiving her warmly and whistling and cheering as she played her violin. Chandler's pride in her built with each song. The following day he escorted her to Kemal Hovic's house. Once inside the bullet-pocked home, Kerina took Zineta's hands in hers and smiled.

Zineta glanced at Chandler. "It's okay," he mouthed.

She looked childlike and very pregnant. Shiny black-bobbed hair framed her flushed cheeks, but there was a brightness in those dark, soulful eyes as she looked up at Kerina.

"Are you happy?" Kerina asked her.

The girl nodded. "Am I truly going to America?"

"Soon. Your baby will be born in Randy's hometown."

Chandler swallowed hard and slipped his arm around Jillian's waist as Zineta asked, "Ran-dee's parents really want me?"

"They want you," Kerina said. "You will be happy with them."

"They want me—and my baby?"

"They have room for both of you."

Zineta's voice trembled. "But I worked for the Serbs during the war. And afterwards. Ran-dee—he never knew."

"The war is over, Zineta."

"I had to survive."

Kerina brushed Zineta's tears away. "It is over, Zineta. You don't have to be afraid any longer."

She led the girl to the table and sat down across from Kemal Hovic and his wife. "I know you feel bad about

Zineta going away," Kerina said through an interpreter. She studied him earnestly. "But I have a plan, Kemal, that will comfort you. One that will bring music to this village and to Tuzla."

She outlined a detailed plan, promising to fund musical instruments and offering Kemal the opportunity to teach a few village school children how to play them. "Later you can take your program into Tuzla," she said.

He hunched forward and adjusted his skullcap. "Impossible. I have never taught anyone."

"He can do it, Miss Rudzinski," Zineta said excitedly. "Kemal plays the cello well. He knows music."

Zineta pointed to Kemal's youngest son. "Rasim wants to play the violin like you do. He must play it. You see—he is too afraid to go outside since he saw Ran-dee die."

"I will send a child's violin for him." Kerina turned and met Kemal's worried gaze with a smile. "Kemal, are you acquainted with Luciano Pavarotti, the Italian tenor?"

He nodded.

"Pavarotti and his friends opened a music center in Mostar to unite the children of Bosnia. I have spoken to Luciano. He is sending guests from abroad to Mostar to teach the children to play and sing. Perhaps some of his guests would come here to help you get started—to show Rasim how to play the violin. We will bring music back into your village," she promised.

Chandler saw Kemal's face come alive, saw hope in the man's eyes for the first time since Randy's death. Chan took Jillian's hand and led her outside into the breezy midnight darkness. No stars. No moon shining on them.

"Jillian, I'm not certain about my own future, but I know I want you to be part of it."

"You're sure this time? You're settled about Zineta?"

He ran his fingers across her lips. "I'm crazy about you, Jill. I'm so glad Kerina brought you with her." He paused. "I don't know why, but she has done so much for us—for me."

"You'll understand someday."

"Right now, I can only ask you to be my friend. I want more—but for now I can only offer my friendship."

"Why, Chan? Why not more?"

Huskily, he murmured, "I don't know who I really am. I'm twenty-six years old, and I just found out I may be adopted. If the army is right, I'm not really Chandler William Reynolds. But whoever I am, Jill, I don't want to lose you."

She took a deep breath. "Who told you you're adopted, Chan?"

"The colonel. And I overheard Ashley and Kerina talking about it at the Riviera."

He felt her stiffen. "Then you know?"

"For weeks I told myself it couldn't be true. But now Colonel Bladstone tells me my birth documents are messed up. It seems like everyone knew I was adopted except me."

"Have you told Kerina?"

"Kerina? No. There's really no reason." His arm tightened around her. "Why would I tell her? I'm not even sure what I'm going to say when I get back to California and see the folks."

"Don't hurt them. Your parents love you. They have done everything they could for you."

"Don't hurt them?" His throat constricted. "If I'm adopted—if I'm really adopted—they've deceived me all these years."

Gently, she said, "They must have had their reasons for not telling you. Work it out, Chan. The truth is staring you in the face—as close to you as the breeze blowing against us now. Just ask Ashley for the truth when you get home."

"No, I'm going to find my own answers, and when I do— when I know who my birth parents are—you're the first one I'm going to call." He smiled at her in the darkness. "And then when you come to Los Angeles for Kerina's concert, we can celebrate."

And we can be more than friends, he thought.

Twenty-four

Ashley sat on the white stone bench in her backyard, the weeds in her heart and garden sprouting wildly. In the early years, the three of them—she, David, and Chandler—had been a triple-braided family full of happiness and sunshine and togetherness. She'd been the envy of many with her delightful child and her attentive husband. These days they were frayed, torn apart without words.

They still made an impression on outsiders—David striking and attractive with his silver-gray hair, Chandler more handsome than ever with his newly acquired California suntan, and Ashley holding her own with Lancome facials. But inside the family cord, their facade of oneness had eroded. Ashley felt naked and exposed, the guilt of Everdale surging to the surface—up from the abyss of her own heart where she had so long guarded her secret. How dare she condemn Kerina Rudzinski when the beam in her own eye was the size of a redwood.

She heard Chandler's strong, steady steps coming down the garden path to where she was waiting. He was wearing dark slacks with a new beige pullover, his army haircut all but gone. His actions since coming home two weeks ago had been perfunctory and polite, not warm like those days in Vienna. What was going on in his mind since arriving neither she nor David could imagine. No, that was not true. She feared what had come between them and dreaded the calculated, unrehearsed questions about Everdale and his childhood that had probed their family chats in the evenings.

Ashley noticed a sharp edge to Chandler's voice as he said, "Dad tells me you're not going to the airport with us."

She waved her hand blindly over the flower beds. "I need to weed before the next storm hits."

"The weeds will be there long after I'm gone. But it's not the weeds. You're ticked off about my seeing Grams."

Irritation awakened the anger she felt against her mother-in-law. "I have no qualms about your trip to Denver, Chandler. You should spend time with your grandmother."

"You know that I won't let her criticize you, Mom. I promise."

"Would it matter? I won't be there listening to her."

He fixed his gaze on the flower bed and bent down to pull up a weed and toss it aside. "She's not a bad sort, Mom. I'll only be there a couple of days. Then I have that interview in Washington and the visit with Randy's parents in Ohio."

Ashley leaned back on her heels, brushing the dirt from her hands, wondering whether Everdale was in his plans. "Kerina will be in concert in Los Angeles in three weeks," she reminded him.

"I know. Jillian called from New York. I promised her I'd be here for the concert. Can you ask Dad to order the tickets?"

She nodded.

"So—I guess Dad will drive me to John Wayne without you."

Eyeing him sharply, she saw only that guileless smile. She took a letter from the pocket of her jeans and handed it to him. "I'm sending this instead."

He glanced down and laughed, the resentment in his eyes softening. "Are you saying your good-byes in writing now? You do get choked up at the airports. That was quite a scene in Vienna with Jillian rushing off to find some tissues for you."

His effort to coax a smile from her fell flat. He studied the envelope, a frown forming between his brows. "Wait, this is addressed to you, Mom. It's from Uncle Bill."

"He wrote it the day he died. Twenty-six years ago."

"I can't nose into something between you and your brother."

"It's about you, Chandler. When you find time, read it."

A pulsating twitch ran the length of his jaw. He opened his briefcase and slid the letter inside. "Well, I'm off. Keep your fingers crossed about the government job."

Why? she wondered. *It will only take you away from us again.*

He leaned down and gave her a quick peck on the forehead. "No tears, Mom. Not now and not when I leave for Europe in a few months, with the government job or without it. I need to be with Jillian."

"Is it that serious between the two of you?"

"I'd like it to be. For now, we're just friends. Jill is giving me space. Time to myself. Time to thread through the past, plan out the future."

Rattled, she asked, "Will you need money? Your dad and I—"

"I'll be all right once I get a job."

"Why must you go away again, Chandler?"

"Do you mean this trip to Denver and all points east? I have to work things out for myself, Mom. To find out what's missing."

She took a gulping breath and said, "You know, don't you?"

He met her gaze. "I know. I've known for several weeks."

It was all that he said. He turned and went down the winding path. He was leaving, but for how long? In her heart of hearts she guessed that he was going off in search of himself—in search of his real roots—and as he went away she feared plunging into the cavernous pit of her own tangled yesterdays. Those days on the Riviera at Kerina Rudzinski's villa had only made Ashley keenly aware of her own shortcomings and sins. They came afresh now and weighed heavily upon her as she watched her son stroll back over the garden path.

When David came back from the airport, he and Ashley roamed around the house in silence; in the end they escaped to their separate sanctuaries—David to his desk piled high with paperwork, Ashley back to weeding in her garden. At dusk he called her back into the house and sent out for pizza for supper. They ate in the living room with the gas fireplace lit for coziness, sitting at opposite ends of the sofa, nibbling cheese and anchovies, pepperoni and thin browned crust.

David ran his hand through his thick hair dejectedly. "I can't concentrate on my sermon notes for Sunday. I hated seeing Chan go away again so soon. But it's more than that, isn't it?"

"Yes, it's us, David. No, it's me. I wish he were flying nonstop to Washington and not taking that layover in Denver."

"And skip the visit to my mother? He's fond of the old girl. Hasn't seen her since getting back from Bosnia."

"He's withdrawn since our time in Vienna."

"I know. He talks. Watches the games with me. Golfs. Helps me change the oil in the cars. Peeks over my shoulder at my book outlines. Shows an interest. But he's not communicating."

Like you, David, she thought. "I think he knows he's adopted," she blurted. "Kerina must have told him."

The muscles in David's neck grew taut. "Then why didn't he say something to us?"

"We never did."

David sat slouched against the back of the sofa, his long legs crossed, his hands clenched over his chest. Strands of his wavy hair fell across his forehead, black strands mixed with silver-gray. The past, the present! His dark brows twitched and his words came out derisive as he said, "What's wrong with you, Ash? You mean to tell me you were there with him, he insinuates he's adopted, and you didn't pursue it?"

"He's waiting for us to make the first move."

She let David blame, accuse. She took another slice of pizza, and broke off bits of cheese and ate them. His expression was like a changing reel: surprise, perfection, disgust, ridicule. As he raved she picked out slivers of anchovy and pepperoni and tossed them into the box.

"I didn't know what to tell him, David."

"The truth. You know, names like Kerina, Bill—we're sorry."

"You're the family speechmaker. You went to seminary. I didn't. You golfed together yesterday. Why didn't you tell him then?"

"I couldn't." He looked suddenly boyish. "It was the wrong time, Ash. My son and I—well, we were just getting reacquainted. I couldn't spoil our time together."

For several minutes, David went on defending himself, demanding answers. Now he looked weary, not unkind, but hopelessly unable to breech the gap between them. "Ash, I'll be in the library. When you're ready to iron this out, let me know. I don't like things standing between us. I love you—but that fact gets lost in your fury."

Ashley closed her eyes and felt the sofa cushion give as he stood, sensed him passing in front of her striding from the room. She stayed there alone, outlining the words on the pizza box with her finger and calming herself for five, ten, fifteen minutes.

Should she continue to let this wall of ridicule build between them? No. She would go to David. He wanted the truth. Demanded it. She would tell him the truth and heap her own guilt on him. Blame him as he had blamed her. Accuse as he had accused.

When she walked into the library, his Bible and theology books lay open on the desk. He glanced up. "Well!" He tapped his watch and grinned. "Only fifteen minutes this time. A record for us. I'm glad you're here, Ash." He looked sheepish. "I was just thinking about coming to find you to apologize—"

She wouldn't let him. Not now. "Stop it! You want the truth. I'm here to discuss it."

I love you, and yet I'm ravaged with guilt, she thought. *And you don't even know why.* "I want to talk about Everdale, David."

He pitched his pen on the desk. "That goes back a long ways," he said stiffly, his attempt to humor her gone.

In that minute he was marvelously controlled. He had not been that way in his youth when his passions and dreams ran freely. The crinkle lines around his blue-gray eyes ridged deeper. "Are you going back to before we were married?"

"Yes, to when we first met."

"To when we fell in love?" Anxiety curled the corners of his mouth. "So that's it. That's what has come between us all these months. The past! Oh, Ashley, the past is forgiven."

"How can it be forgiven if you don't even know it exists?"

He leaned forward, his gaze piercing. "In the beginning, I tried to talk to you about Everdale, and you always shut me out. But you've never forgiven me, have you? After all these years of marriage, you still hold it against me."

She let him struggle and grope for words, flinging her own pain back in his face. "I don't know what you're talking about."

His color turned pasty. "Don't you, Ashley?"

She knew. She had agonized over it many times, often when she felt on top of the world, the ashes of the past drifted across her memory. Her chin jutted out defiantly as her impeccably groomed David fingered the papers on his desk, spread them, restacked them. His smooth hands moved restlessly as though by the sweeping motion, he could rid himself of a damaging past.

"While you were in Vienna, Ashley, I could think of nothing else but the memories of Everdale."

"I've shouldered them often."

His voice turned bitter. "Ashley, do you hate me for that one moment in our lives? Is there no credit for the good years with you? Will you go on forcing me to bury myself in my work?"

He still couldn't bring himself to voice the truth. She wouldn't let him off the hook now. No, she was pushing him into a confessional box, almost gloating over his defeat. He sprang from his chair and gripped her shoulders. "Say it, Ash. Get it out in the open. You blame me for robbing you of your virginity before our marriage?"

"Seven years before to be exact. And I was willing to let it go. Eager." She thumped his desk with her fists. "Do you hear me, David? I wanted you to make love to me that day on your grandparents' farm."

His hands fell to his sides. "I'm so sorry, Ashley. I've tried so hard to make it up to you."

"No, you've tried to clear your own conscience, but not for me." She couldn't stop her angry flow of words even though she knew that ridicule could destroy a marriage. "You did it for your church. For your God."

"Your God too, Ashley." He was back in control, his words even, his gaze unblinking.

"So you could be that upstanding man to your congregation. The perfect sin-free pastor with a faithful wife by your side."

The control wavered again. "Ashley, no man is more aware of his imperfections than I am. I live with them when I stand behind the pulpit. Think about them in the classroom. I never went back to my grandfather's farm without going out to the barn and begging God to forgive me all over again."

He paced restlessly behind the desk, his face flushed, his anguish unbearable to both of them. Haggard ridges formed deep gullies by his mouth. She had gone too far and regretted lashing out at him. Regretted the whole sorry affair.

"David," she whispered, "maybe you never forgave yourself."

"I didn't give much thought to forgiveness until my life turned around—until God became both Savior and Shepherd to me; then I remembered Everdale."

"And worried that it would keep you from seminary?"

"I never told them. Never told anyone."

"What kind of an application did you fill in? No wonder the barn was your only sanctuary."

"I tried to talk to you about it. You always waved it off."

He seemed swallowed up in his own despair. "I always wanted a child of our own. Partly for Chandler. He wanted a brother."

"But I didn't want another child."

"I did. Even before the fertility clinics, I saw the doctor. I thought it was my fault that you couldn't get pregnant."

"No, it wasn't your fault, David. You were okay. But I wasn't; I couldn't have *another* child."

He seemed stunned, his eyes and mouth twitching at the same time. "Another child? I don't understand."

"I was butchered from the first one."

As the truth set in, he collapsed back into the desk chair and stared up at her. "You . . . had a baby?"

"An abortion—long before we were married."

She had never seen his face fill with such rage. His voice went rigid with accusation. "Do I know the father?"

"You were the father, David."

For several moments the room was entombed in a deafening silence. He stared at her, disbelief etched in his handsome features. "Ashley, what right did you have to keep the truth from me all these years?"

David didn't wait for her to answer. He stumbled to his feet, shoved his theology books aside, grabbed his car keys from the desk, and stormed out of the room. The front door slammed shut. Car tires squealed as he backed out of the driveway. Once again, overwhelming silence engulfed her.

On his second day in Denver, Chandler put the phone down and walked back into his grandmother's kitchen where the good smells of a pot roast filled the room. She stood by her shiny, white stove, stirring gravy as he entered.

"Did your call go through?" she asked.

"Straight through to New York. I put it on my phone card."

"No need."

He squeezed her shoulder. "I was afraid I'd be long-winded talking to Jillian."

"Someone special?"

"The girl I want to marry. But right now I can't."

She put the roast on a platter and shoved it toward him. "Be a dear and carve that for me."

"Grams, aren't you going to ask me why?"

He saw her hand tremble as she spooned the carrots and onions and potatoes into her best china bowl, saw again the added lines on her face since his last visit. The gravy boiled and burned as she stood there, frowning. "I forgot to make a salad."

He wanted to say, "Grams, I'm not hungry." But she had gone to a lot of effort to fix his favorite dinner. He switched off the burner. "Looks like plenty without the salad."

"But you like my salads."

"I'm more interested in spending time with you. I thought you could tell me about Everdale."

Redness crept over her cheeks. "I haven't thought about Everdale for a long time."

"Can you think about it now, Grams?"

"Please, let's not talk about it until after dinner."

Last night she had put him off with a different excuse. He had to ask his questions while he had the chance. Tomorrow or the next day he was leaving for the east coast.

Dinner was not to be hurried. On the last bite, he turned down dessert and when she attempted to clear the table, said, "The dishes can wait, Grams. We have to talk."

Again he noticed a tremor as she pushed the dishes aside and folded her ringed hands on the table. She sat stiffly in the high-back mahogany chair, a proud old woman with a handsome, stoic face and a proud tilt to her chin. Whatever religious convictions she had, she kept them to herself. But she talked for hours about the girls at the bridge club and her volunteer work at the historical society and about the library committee she chaired. She was clearly a gregarious woman.

"Who is this Jillian, Chandler? Is she good enough for you?"

"Perfect."

"Then why can't you marry her?"

"Because I don't know who I am, Grams."

"You don't know who you are! Dear boy, what's wrong?"

"Two months ago I thought I knew all my statistics. Parents. Family background. My history three and four generations back. Now I'm not certain of anything. I'm not even sure I was born in Alabama. Tell me about Everdale, Grandma. Was I born there?"

"Such a ridiculous question. Of course, you were."

"Then tell me the names of my birth parents."

She steadied her hand as she covered her mouth. "I don't know much about Everdale. I haven't been there since I sold the old farm. Since my parents died. I went back then, of course."

"But you were there when I was born?"

"No. A month later."

"Why? I'm the only grandchild. Grandparents can hardly wait to see their first grandchild. Didn't you want to see me?"

Tears washed the faded blue eyes. "Not at first, Chandler."

"Because I was adopted?"

"Who told you that?"

"It doesn't matter. I know now. That's why I came—because I trust you to be honest with me. I want to know the names of my birth parents. I want to know why your son and daughter-in-law have never seen fit to tell me the truth."

She slipped the rings from her right hand and placed them in a row on the linen cloth. "I don't know their names, Chan."

"Then it's true. I'm adopted. I'm somebody else's kid."

She went on the defensive. "Don't ever let your father hear you say that. He reminds me over and over that you are his son."

"His only son?"

She hesitated. "They wanted other children."

"And I always wanted a brother."

She countered, "I suspect that you had one sibling, maybe more."

"What does that mean?"

"Your birth father was a married man."

"Then you know who he was?"

"Only that he came from Everdale—that there would have been a scandal if you had been born in the city where he lived and worked."

"Mom told me she was in the delivery room when I was born."

"She was, Chandler. She was the nurse on duty that night."

"And you never came to see me because I was adopted."

"I'm a proud woman, Chandler. I thought David would have consulted me on a matter of such grave importance. Finally, your grandfather and I flew to Everdale and from the minute I held you, I loved you. And from that moment, your grandfather and I would have defied anyone trying to take you away from us."

He believed her. Felt sorrow for her. "I've got to know the truth, Grams. Why didn't—why didn't my parents tell me I was adopted? Why did I have to wait to hear it from someone else?"

"I don't know. You will have to ask them."

"I can't hurt them. I have to find my own answers. Until I know who I am, I can't ask Jillian to marry me."

Quietly, she said, "David and Ashley must have had their reasons for not telling you. Whatever happens between you and your parents, you are my grandson, Chandler. Don't ever forget that. I'll always be here for you."

"Always?" he teased, watching the tired wrinkled face across from him. "That's good, Grams, because I want you and Jillian to know each other."

"Will I like her?"

"I think so. She can charm the socks off anybody."

"Even me?"

"Even you, Grams."

"What will you do, Chandler?"

"I don't have a choice, do I? I've been on the Internet. I've checked all sorts of records. Sent for vital statistics from Everdale. Short of going there myself, I won't have the answers I need. I won't rest until I know why your son and daughter-in-law lied to me."

"Will you call your father and let him know what you're doing?"

"No."

"But as soon as you're gone, I will have to tell David."

He reached across the table and patted her hand. "You understand, don't you, Grams? I have to find my birth parents. And if I have siblings, I want to meet them."

"What if your birth parents reject you again?"

"That's a risk I have to take."

Twenty-five

For three days David nursed his grudge against Ashley, rationalizing the injustice he had suffered and finding escape in his university classes. As Thursday's class hour came to an end, Anna Weinstad pushed her way to the front of the room, her dark wiry hair bouncing against the weighted knapsack strapped to her back. She was an attractive young woman with a good mind and a quest for answers. Of all David's archeology students, she held the most promise.

"I'm switching majors," she announced.

"You're quitting my classes?"

"No, I'm going for all the courses that will put me on an archeology dig someday."

"That's splendid, Miss Weinstad. I'll do everything I can to help you reach that goal."

As they left the classroom and walked down the corridor, she said, "Tell me about your church, Prof. Do you do any singing over at that cathedral of yours?"

"Me? Personally?" He laughed out loud. "I'm known to bluff my way through congregational singing." *Or booming loudly and happily off-key in the shower,* he thought. "My son is the one gifted in music." Even Ashley's love of music had found its way into Grace Cathedral, her influence strongly felt, but her presence was no longer visible. *My fault,* he acknowledged.

"We have a music director at the church," he continued. "The result has been quality music. Three adult choirs. A children's choir. A string orchestra. A cellist and two violinists in the congregation always willing to play a solo in the Sunday services. And a host of music guests throughout the year."

"Impressive. Maybe I'll check it out."

"You do that." He couldn't cross the line between church and state or tamper with university policy, but he did ask, "What about next Sunday?"

"What time?"

"Take your pick. Eight, nine forty-five or eleven."

"Don't you get bored saying the same thing over and over?"

"God's Word is never boring—not when the message is based on eternal truth."

Outside, she squinted into the sun. "Maybe I will come hear you sometime. What do you talk about?"

"God's love. God's forgiveness, mostly."

"Forgiveness," she exclaimed. She rushed off ahead of him, then turned back and waved. "That's a tough one, rabbi."

He didn't correct her but headed straight to his car. He wanted to call Ashley on the cell phone and ask her to have lunch with him so they could smooth over the last three days of animosity. But no, she would be in her garden tying back the larkspurs or pruning her rose bushes. She would not thank him for disturbing her, and in these last few days— these last few months—he had forgotten how to cross back into her world.

Forgiveness. That is a tough one, he thought as he drove home. He hadn't warned Anna Weinstad that his computer file for Sunday's sermon remained a blank page. He couldn't even fall back on an old standby: "The Pilgrim's Triple-Braided Cord." How could he preach on sacrifice, truth, and trust with unforgiveness in his own heart? He had to have Ashley's forgiveness, had to break down the wall between them. He shot through the yellow light; getting home to Ashley was the most important thing he could think of.

At the house, Ashley made a decision. She would not let the silence go on between David and herself another day. She paraded up and down the garden path. "Oh, God," she cried, "I wounded my husband when I told him the truth about the abortion. You know I love David. I want his forgiveness. I want your forgiveness."

Twenty minutes later, she made her way into the house as she heard David's car pull into the driveway. She waited expectantly in the hallway. David was the only man she had ever loved, the only one who left her breathless. David was a jute and tartan personality, the fabric of the man tightly woven and strongly twilled, a man whose spirit was linked indelibly to family and friends. To her. Like his maternal Scottish ancestry, David was determined, self-confident, always striving for success. Ashley could not change him, yet in the quiet seclusion of their lives together he had always been a tender, compassionate lover, a faithful companion. Three days ago, she had almost torn the fabric of the man apart. In her own disquiet, she had almost destroyed him, almost broken his spirit.

She heard his key turn in the door, watched the wide, carved door swing back. "David, I have to talk to you."

He nodded. "That's what I came home to tell you." He pushed the door closed behind him, his solemn eyes fixed on her. "These last three days have been the most miserable ones in my life."

"Mine too."

"Ash, I had to come to terms with what you told me. I had to come to accept my own guilt."

"Oh, no, David—"

"Hush," he said tenderly. "I must take responsibility for putting you in an untenable situation. You were so young. We both were. I should have known when my letters to you came back unopened."

"It's all right, David."

"No. We have to put it all out in the open so we can start again." His back arched against the door. "Ash, I've made a mess of being a good shepherd. On the way home I decided to resign my position as senior pastor—"

Alarmed, she murmured, "No. You can't quit, David. You love what you're doing."

"I love you . . . and I'm afraid I'm losing you."

"I won't let you go. And I won't let you quit."

"Ash, I've prided myself in keeping short accounts. At least I thought I did. I preached it from the pulpit, encouraged it in my classroom, practiced it in my daily life."

His hand ran jerkily through his hair, tousling it like it looked when he stepped from the shower. His face twisted into a crooked half smile. "I was so certain I had a handle on short accounts. So certain that the sin of our youth was forgiven."

"And I unraveled the past and put a barricade between us. I'm so sorry, David. But, I must tell you. I never slept with another man. Only you."

"I know that now." He walked to her and ran a thumb over her chin, touched her lips. The scent of his cologne wafted in the air around them. "I don't want it to go on this way, Ash. I want us to start over again. I want you to tell me everything."

"Here in the hallway?"

He smiled and led her into the living room and stood by the fireplace, his hand resting on the mantel. "Why didn't you tell me you were pregnant? I would have married you."

"You did."

"But a long time afterwards." He buried his face in his hands, strands of gray hair slipping between his fingers. She went to him and put her hand on his shoulder, the softness of his cardigan reminding her of that day in the barn when he had thrown his clothes on top of a bed of hay for her.

"You were only eighteen, David."

"I knew right from wrong. I talk to the kids in our parish about accountability. I was of the age of accountability."

"We both were. But you were so charming, the intriguing outsider from California. You wanted me. My friends envied me."

His effort to smile fell flat. He looked grieved and ten years older than he was. His voice was very gentle, the old David reaching out for her. "You should have told me. I had a right to know. I had a right to be there for you."

"I didn't even tell my mother. Just Bill. Bill knew."

"Your brother took you to the abortion clinic?"

"He went with me. He couldn't stop me from going. I was desperate; I had my whole life ahead of me. A baby out of wedlock was a disgrace. I couldn't hurt Mama. She trusted me."

"I would have quit university. I would have married you."

She rubbed the back of his neck. "Dear David, I did what I thought was best—but I will regret it the rest of my life."

He took her hands tentatively. "My mother knew about us," he confessed. "But, Ashley, she didn't know about the baby. I swear she didn't know."

"I've never been comfortable around her."

"She never meant for you to be comfortable. If we had had a child of our own—I think things would have been different."

"We did." Her voice caught. "But I chose to wash him away."

"A boy? It was a boy?"

"That's what the doctor said."

"A son!"

"You have a son, David. Chandler is your son."

"I know. But—"

"We can't undo the past. I've tried. Oh, how I've tried."

"Must we go on suffering for our one mistake?"

"You tell me, darling. You're the theologian." Her voice wavered. "And it wasn't one mistake. We went back to your grandfather's barn four times."

"I am so sorry, Ash. I always loved you. Even back then."

She brushed her cheek against his sweater. "I wanted to hurt you for getting me pregnant—to punish you. But it never worked out that way. I only compounded our sin when I aborted the baby."

"You bore all this pain alone? Is this why you awaken in the night sometimes, crying, and won't ever tell me why?"

"I didn't want to lose you. You always comforted me. And always held me until I could sleep again—and forget."

"You've born all this alone," he said again. "All this time? Is that why Bill made certain that Chandler came into our lives?"

"I think so. That's what he implied in his letter. But he didn't live long enough for me to ask him. And after his death, I had no one to confide in. It was too late to tell you. I kept thinking that Chandler would fill the void—and make it right."

She glanced out the window toward her garden, twisting her wedding rings over her knuckle, leaving her finger blanched.

"Put those rings back on, Ash. You're still my wife. Don't run from me now. We need each other."

Turning to face him, she said, "Chandler used to tell me a piece of himself was missing. I understood what he meant. I have a missing piece in my life—the baby that never had a chance to see the light of day or breathe the fresh air or grow up to know Chandler or us."

"Don't torture yourself, Ashley. Not when you know the One who carries heavy burdens."

"We lost one child—because of what I did. What if we lose Chandler too?"

"He's stronger than that. Once he works through this adoption business—and we'll help him—he will come through."

"Will you tell him about my past?"

He looked surprised. "Our past. No, darling, what happened so long ago has nothing to do with Chandler. It's just between us. Let's put it to rest and go on with our lives."

"But what if Chandler chooses Kerina Rudzinski?"

Smiling down at her, he said, "I never knew anyone who could worry and fret so much. Kerina is part of his life too. We'll work it out. Ash, let's go away for a week or two."

"But the church. Your classes. Your responsibilities."

"I've been neglecting my greatest responsibility—my family. My wife. I'd like to get away alone with you. To talk together. And laugh again. And pray together. And—"

She actually saw him blush. "But your mother is coming for a visit again this weekend, David."

"I'll call and ask her to put it off. She'll understand."

David pulled her against his broad chest, and her tears soaked the front of his shirt. "Can you ever forgive me, Ashley? I want to start over again. You and me. Only this time we'll ask for God's direction and blessing."

"And forgiveness?"

"Somehow, I think we already have that." He leaned down and kissed the top of her head, her cheek, her neck. "I love you, Ashley," he whispered in her ear. "I have always loved you."

For a long time they sat on the sofa, comfortable in each other's arms, enjoying the glow and warmth of the logs in the gas fireplace. Finally David prayed in his deep rich voice, thanking God for his mercy, speaking longingly of the son who had never been born, and gently giving him back to God. Afterwards—hours after David placed a brief call to his mother—he and Ashley talked about the days ahead and the rest of their lives together.

And long after that, David said gently, "It's past midnight. We'd better turn in, Ash."

Unrushed, unhurried, he switched off the lights, checked the locks on the doors, and smiling wryly at her, unplugged the phones from the wall. Hand-in-hand they climbed the stairs, the wall between them gone. They were young again.

As they reached the second floor, fragments of their wedding vows made so long ago came back to Ashley. *For better or worse; for richer, for poorer; in sickness and in health, until death do us part.* She meant that pledge more at this moment than she had on that day when she said the words aloud to David.

Moments later, for the first time in months, Ashley slipped willingly, gladly into David's arms, loving and being loved.

At three A.M. on Friday—the very weekend they were to go away—the doorbell rang persistently. David eased Ashley out of the crook of his arm and was out of bed at once, running down the stairs in his blue-striped pajamas with his silk robe tossed over one shoulder and his slippers flapping against his heels. He unchained the door and swung it back.

"Mother!" he exclaimed. "What are you doing here at this hour? I thought you agreed to put off your visit for a week."

"Don't send me away, David."

He frowned at the desperation in her voice. "We never have."

He jammed his arms into his robe, reached for her icy hand and drew her into the parquet entryway. He grabbed her luggage and dropped it just inside the door. "Now," he said, chaining the door again, "what's this all about? Traveling around alone at night all the way from Denver. It's not safe, Mother."

"It's Chandler, David. He's gone."

"Yes, we know that. He flew to Washington to apply for a government job. After that he's visiting friends in Akron."

"He knows, David. He knows everything. I knew you were going away this weekend. That's why I came—to tell you he's in Everdale."

David stiffened. "You flew all the way here to tell us he went to Everdale? Why didn't you call us?"

"Because I didn't want to be alone. I'm so afraid he won't come back, David, I never saw him so distraught. He said two months ago he knew who he was—and now, he can only guess."

For a minute David said nothing. He slipped his arm around his mother's shoulders and led her into the living room. She sank gratefully into an overstuffed chair, looking lost and forlorn as he gazed down at her. He kicked the ottoman in front of her chair and sat down facing her. She looked older than her seventy-five years, her tired eyes faded and anxious, the proud face lined with wrinkles. *When did old age sneak up on her?* he wondered.

He smothered his anxiety and took her hands in his. The once smooth hands were dotted with age spots, bulging with blue veins. He hated age creeping up on her, but no more than she dreaded it herself. He massaged her fingers, warming them with his own.

"What does Chandler know?" he asked, knowing.

"About the adoption."

"It had to come out someday."

"But not this way. Not with that young woman in Europe telling him it was time to face who he really was."

"Jillian?" David asked.

"That was her name. She has him wrapped in her clutches."

He smiled patiently. "That's what you told me when I fell in love with Ashley."

"Who is this Jillian, David? What right did she have—?"

"The girl is in love with my son."

She mocked, "Whose son is he, David? Jillian seems to know."

"Jillian works for Chandler's birth mother, but she had no right to tell him."

"I don't think she did. Not in actual words. Chandler called Jillian from my place."

"Tell me what happened, Mother," he urged. "Chandler said nothing to us before he left for your place."

"He won't. He doesn't want to hurt you, but he said it was up to you and Ashley to be honest with him—to make the first move. I assured him you had your reasons for never telling him. But Chandler is determined to find his own answers."

David wanted to lash out at Ashley again, to hide from his own responsibility. He calmed and said, "Kerina Rudzinski broke her promise to Ashley then."

"Kerina? The violinist?" His mother's color turned ashen. She pressed both hands against her chest. "David, you will be the death of me. Don't tell me that violinist is his birth mother?"

"Yes, Mother."

"You've always known, David?"

"From the beginning."

"And his father?' she whispered.

He looked away. "Ashley's brother."

"*Chandler William*. I should have known. I guessed as much and then thought it so improbable that I pushed it from my mind. Oh, David, you and Ashley have covered for Bill all these years?"

"It was a closed adoption, Mother. We were obligated to do as Kerina asked. When Bill died so soon after Chandler's birth, we didn't want Celeste and the children to be hurt anymore."

She pulled away. "All his life Chandler wanted brothers."

"And he had them. But we couldn't tell him."

"I did tell him that his birth father was a married man—that there might be siblings. As upset as he was, he will go to the ends of the earth to find them." Her voice grew shrill. "You and Ashley should have had a child of your own."

He had heard this more than he cared to remember. "Chandler is our son. How many times do I have to tell you that, Mother?"

"It was Ashley, wasn't it? Unable to bear a child."

"That's between Ashley and me. It always has been."

Arrogantly, she said, "But Ashley wasn't honest with you. She deceived you. She had an abortion; did you know that, David?" Her voice shook with remembered rage. "I had flown back to see my parents again. I heard the rumors in Everdale. I had to keep you from going back to Ashley so I followed her to that abortion clinic. I know. I have known for years. What she did was disgraceful, a black mark against our family name."

"And you have punished her for it." He ran his hands through his silver hair, wearied by it all. "It was my child," he said.

She gasped. "Yours? Your baby?" She looked white-washed, frightened, old. "It was your child? You were the father? Oh, no. I put all the blame on Ashley all these years! Oh, David, will she ever forgive me?"

"Of course, Mother Reynolds." Ashley came quietly into the room, walked over to David's chair and slipped her arms around his neck.

"Oh, Ashley, what an old fool I have been."

"You just wanted to protect David."

"And to blame you. Forgive me, Ashley? I beg you—don't leave my son over this."

"I thought that's what you always wanted, Rosalyn."

"Not any longer. I'm sick of this family being torn apart. You have been so right for David. I just didn't like losing him."

"You never lost him. He's always been here for you. We both have. We always will be."

Twenty-six

Five days ago when he arrived in Everdale, Chandler did not recognize the streets, could not put a name to a face. Rather, it was the sensation of familiarity, the feeling of having been here. Stirrings that came at the sight of goldenrod waving in the fields and the smell of burning leaves in the crisp, fall air. The feeling of going back in time to his post-toddler days. Vague impressions. Gut perceptions. His roots were here, his beginnings. More than the family photograph albums. More than the gilt-edged steeple against the Everdale skyline or the awareness of his dad carrying him in those strong arms of his or his mom pushing him on the backyard swing. Coming back was like hearing an echo of the past. Like having the missing piece of himself within grasp.

But he was convinced of one thing. As a kid, he never liked grits for breakfast, plain or mixed with eggs in the Southern way. He knew he would have spewed them out if his mom had spooned them in. He surely didn't like grits back then. He didn't like them now. And if Kyle Richardson's wife at Richardson's Bed-and-Breakfast gave him ham hocks simmered with okra and black-eyed peas for one more dinner, he'd have to plead the flu and dash for the bathroom.

Chandler awakened on Thursday morning to a rainstorm pelting the Richardsons' house, with rain coming in the open window. He showered and dressed in a cold bathroom and then used his towel to mop up the rainwater on the floor. He left the house fueled with a bowl of grits piled high with sugar and cream and set out for another day of searching for his identity.

His first stop was Dr. Malcolm Nelson's private residence, one of the older, well-preserved homes in town. The housekeeper led Chandler into the library where the doctor sat at a large oak desk scowling as Chandler crossed the room to him. Dr. Nelson didn't stand to greet his guest even when Chandler extended his hand.

"Thank you for seeing me, sir."

Nelson nodded, solemn and slack-mouthed. Even sitting, he looked tall and distinguished with his curly gray hair and unblinking gray eyes. But his face was the same shade as his cream shirt as if he had been ill and hadn't yet recovered.

"I won't keep you long, sir. I'm Ashley Reynolds's son. At least I was until a couple of weeks ago."

With effort Nelson lifted his limp arm and braced it on the desk. It was then that Chandler realized he was in a wheelchair, that the droop of his mouth was medical. The doctor couldn't be more than sixty-five, seventy at the most, but right now he was having a painful twist of an old man's body as he shifted in the chair and focused on Chandler.

"Did I come at a wrong time, sir?"

"There is no right or wrong time anymore," a woman said, entering the room. "Malcolm has few visitors since his stroke." She walked behind him and placed her hands on his shoulders. "How can my husband and I help you, young man?"

"My mother worked for Dr. Nelson some years ago."

Haltingly Nelson said, "Yes. I think I remember her."

"Of course, you do, Malcolm. She married Pastor Reynolds."

"Ashley? Yes . . . yes. A good nurse."

"That's why I'm here, sir."

"I can imagine why," he said, his words slurred.

His wife's back went rigid. "Oh, no—you're not—"

"Afraid he may be, Abby. Sam Waverly over at the Court House called me. Said Reynolds here was in town, asking to meet me."

"Then you know why I'm here, sir?"

"I have trouble remembering these days, but Waverly says you're looking for your father."

"Pastor Reynolds is the boy's father," his wife said.

Wearily, Nelson cut her off. "He's not a boy, Abby. He's a grown man. Sit down, son."

And I'm not your son either, Chandler thought as he sank into the chair across from Nelson. "I can't fight the bureaucracy. I talked to the attorney involved in my adoption, but he has no files on me. I met briefly with the Probate Judge. Says he wasn't here twenty-six years ago—needs time to look over my records. I've been to the Court House three days in a row. Sam Waverly refuses to open my court papers. He says they're sealed."

"Then leave them that way," Nelson's wife advised.

"I can't, Mrs. Nelson. I have to know who I am."

Her grip on Malcolm's shoulders tightened. "Please leave."

"Not without answers."

"If the court refuses to help you, why should my husband?"

"Because he delivered me and arranged for my adoption. It was his idea. I do know that much."

"It was your father's idea," she said. "Brought some rich Yankee down here with him. But she was just another woman with an unwanted pregnancy."

Chandler's throat burned. "She was my mother."

"She had few options back then. Adoption was one."

"Hush, Abby. Hush. We both know I was fool enough to go along with it. The baby's father said nothing would go wrong."

"Malcolm, you don't owe Mr. Reynolds an explanation. You're getting upset. We both are. I don't want you ill."

"I already am."

"Why did my mother give me up, sir?"

Nelson's twisted mouth pulsated. "How does anyone know another person's reasons? She was young, frightened. Unmarried."

"I wouldn't have held it against her."

"And how would you know that, young man? From hindsight?"

Chandler pressed his case. "You took advantage of her fears. Had her come all the way to Everdale."

"We had nothing to do with her coming," his wife said.

"But your husband arranged for my adoption. I've been thinking about that. A small town. A small-town doctor. Not much money in that. Arranging adoptions could be profitable. And then along comes the opportunity to put a baby into the hands of a couple who desperately wanted a child." His words dripped with sarcasm. "You chose the right couple, Doctor, didn't you?"

A flicker of protest crossed his face. "The baby's father chose the family you would live with."

"My own father?"

"We were friends once. They were friends."

Chandler's fists doubled. He wanted to shake this man and force the truth from him. He was glad for the desk between them, for the wheelchair that kept him from hitting the man.

"Why did you choose them? Because Reynolds was a preacher, the nurse someone you worked with? People who would never tell on you. Is that the way it went, Doctor Nelson?"

What good were unfounded accusations? He'd never get his answers that way. But he worried. Had this town turned their back on wrongdoing? Had the doctor arranged other adoptions for a fee?

Nelson leaned back against his wife's hands, a proud man defending his decision. "I did your mother a favor, Reynolds. She couldn't have any other children."

"She never had any," Chandler said.

"It seems she kept more from you than your identity."

The doctor's words were more difficult to comprehend now. He was visibly tired, his mouth sagging. His wife wiped the corner of his mouth with her handkerchief. "It was legal. We had an attorney. Rovner dealt with the courts."

"Mr. Rovner of the Rovner, Bates, and Grimwald Law Firm? I've been to his office. Like I mentioned, Rovner has no record of my adoption. It was amazing how short his memory was."

"Like mine. I have trouble remembering since my stroke. But Rex Rovner—" he laughed.

Chandler nearly lost control. "Then check your records. The law required you to record my birth parents. Both of them."

Slowly, he said, "I have no records. I sold my practice. The man who took over saw no need to keep records back that far."

"How much was I worth to you and the lawyer? Five thousand dollars? Ten thousand?"

Nelson looked smitten, as though Chandler had stolen his dignity. "Your father and I were friends. The lawyer charged a fee. I didn't."

"I wasn't worth a dime, eh?"

"Your mother was young—your father married."

"Keep still, Malcolm. He will drag us into court over this."

"I know that isn't any fun, Mrs. Nelson. I went to the courts for my answers and they are merciless."

Chandler faced the doctor again, ignoring the man's wife. "A month ago I knew who I was. I had no doubt that David and Ashley Reynolds were my parents. I could trace my family heritage back three or four generations on both sides. Back to General VanBurien on the Confederate side. Right now, sir, all I have left is the date of my birth."

"There's nothing my husband can do—"

Nelson waved her off with his good arm. "Hear the boy out."

"The courts can't tell me, but you can, Doctor. You know who my father is. I want to find him. Did he come from Everdale?"

Nelson nodded. "He did. A longtime resident." The pale gray eyes closed, opened again. "One might say he's still here."

"Please, I have to find him."

Mrs. Nelson bridled. "Sam Waverly is the one to help you."

"I've been there, three days in a row. He treated me like I was a criminal—for searching for my own roots."

"What right do you have to know?" she asked.

He thumped his chest with doubled fists. "Those records are all about me. The courts know more about me than I know myself. They won't even give me a copy of my own birth certificate."

Her face turned livid. "Your birth mother came into this town and asked my husband for help and he gave it. Don't come back here now accusing us of doing something wrong. You must leave. You're upsetting my husband."

"It was Chandler's father who asked me for help, Abby."

"How many other children did you put up for adoption, Doctor? I wasn't the only one, was I?"

Mrs. Nelson's blanched skin matched her husband's now, an ashy gray. "Leave, please."

"Mother used to trace my footprint on my birth certificate and tell me how tiny I was when she first held me. I figured it was just Mom being sentimental."

"Ask her for your answers."

His voice wavered. "I have to find my own answers, Mrs. Nelson. I've already checked the Internet. Nothing. I've gone back over my parents' tax records. I checked with the Library of Congress. Before I came to Everdale I contacted the genealogy department of a local Mormon church to see whether they could trace my roots. I've been to the newspaper office here in town."

"Why don't you hire a private detective? And leave my husband alone."

"Ma'am, I couldn't afford that until I get a civilian job."

"You don't work?"

"My army pay didn't leave much reserve."

Nelson rubbed his limp arm, a bemused smile on his face. "Your father was my friend. I can't—I won't betray him."

Chandler stood and made his way to the door. "Can you tell me one thing, sir? Did my mother want me?"

"I don't know, son. I—I don't remember."

"Good day, sir. Ma'am."

The doctor stopped him. "Where do you go from here, Reynolds?"

"I'm going to put flowers on my uncle's grave."

"Bill VanBurien?" From across the room Chandler saw the surprise on Nelson's face, saw those faded gray eyes dilate. "That uncle of yours was a good man. Shame the way he died."

Chandler nodded. "On a rain-drenched day like this."

"Heading back to Chicago that night, wasn't he?"

"Yes, sir. I believe he was. That's what my mother said."

His scowl softened. "Reynolds, I'm sorry I can't help you."

Won't, Chandler thought.

"But—your mother had a friend, a nurse . . . who was in the delivery room . . . the night you were born." He struggled for each word, obviously determined to be understood. "I don't . . . I don't remember her name, but Abby, you do. Give it to young Reynolds here."

Chandler guessed that Kerina was in town by now. But where? Did she have personal friends she could stay with? He'd never find her. Perhaps she had signed into the only

317

motel in Everdale, a row of eight units chipped and time-worn, on the other side of town.

"Imagine finding you in town," he would tell her. No, he'd be up-front. "Jillian called me. Told me you'd be here. I was coming anyway. It was a good chance to see you again."

Logical. Honest. Straight to the point. He'd ask her to go to dinner, but Everdale had no fancy restaurants, no restaurants at all unless you counted the fast-food chains. With any luck she'd like the novelty of French fries, chicken nuggets, and a milk shake.

He pulled into the Everdale Cemetery where the roads were muddied by the rain. He parked near the mortuary, checked on the lot number for the VanBurien family plot, and struck out on foot, armed with the Richardsons' umbrella and two bouquets of flowers.

Perpetual care kept the plots looking good, the lawns mowed; there was serenity all around him. Something seemed familiar, a sensation of having climbed over the headstones in the VanBurien family plot when he was a child. He placed the bouquet of yellow roses on his grandmother's marker, the white ones on Uncle Bill's grave. He was doing this flower thing for his mother. He stepped back, gave the setting a proper silence, then whirled around and walked briskly away over the rain-soaked ground.

Just ahead, a woman came toward him, her eyes downcast as she walked through the cemetery. The rain fell steadily, but her head was bare. He stepped aside to let her pass by and, startled, exclaimed, "Miss Rudzinski! Jillian told me you were taking a few days between concerts."

She glanced up, her sad eyes lighting with recognition. *Jillian was right,* Chandler thought. Kerina looked pale, thinner, a dark circle under each eye. Her clothes were soaking wet, her hair sopping. Quickly Chandler drew her under the protection of his umbrella.

"Chandler, what are you doing here?"

"I was going to ask you the same thing."

"I'm here to visit a friend's grave."

"A special friend?"

"Quite special. I didn't know he had died until a few weeks ago."

"Hold this." He shoved the umbrella into her hand, whipped off his raincoat and slipped it around her shoulders. "You'll catch pneumonia," he scolded, taking back the bumpershoot.

"I wasn't thinking. I left my coat in the car."

"You'd better make your visit here quick—and then we'll get you back to your car. Let me go with you. Which grave?"

She consulted a map in her hand, streaked with rainwater now, and then led him to a grave with fresh flowers lying on top and placed her own beside them. It was the Van-Burien family plot, and the tears that Kerina shed were obviously for his uncle.

Closure. She was looking for closure. Chandler stood back, giving her privacy for her grief. His uncle and Kerina Rudzinski? A thousand questions. Where had they met? When? What kind of torch had she carried for a man who had been dead for so long? Why hadn't his mother told him?

She turned at last. "Thank you for coming with me."

"You shouldn't wander alone in a cemetery, Miss Rudzinski."

She smiled at that. "Someone was here before me. Bill liked white roses."

"Then why did you bring red ones?" he asked gently.

"Because they are symbolic of love."

He tucked her arm in his, shielding her with his umbrella once more. "Let's get back to that car of yours."

She nodded gratefully. "Yes; then you can have your coat back. . . . Chandler, which grave were you visiting?"

He waved his hand vaguely toward a different tombstone, a different family plot.

As they reached the cars, he asked, "Would you have dinner with me this evening? We could drive over to Spruceville."

"I'm tired, Chandler. I need to be alone."

He offered her his handkerchief. "I can't let you go. Not like this. Let me take you for a drive around Everdale."

"I've been doing that all day."

He considered carefully and then said, "I know one place you didn't see—the house where I spent a brief span of my life. It's been in the family for years."

"Drive around in this weather? We'd better not."

He glanced at the drifting clouds. "These rain squalls pass over. Come back to my bed-and-breakfast. My hostess always has a pot of okra and black-eyed peas on. Or turnip greens."

"Sounds awful."

He grinned. "They're not my favorite either, but it will pass time while we wait for the sun to come back."

They were standing by her car, rain dripping down on both of them. "Let's just drive around. I'm not up to visiting anyone right now, Chandler."

"Suits me," he said. "We can leave your car here and pick it up later."

"Did you reenlist?" she asked as they drove back to town.

"No. I'm out of the army now."

"Good. Then you can take your violin out of the closet."

"Have you forgotten? Or maybe Jillian didn't tell you. I have an interview in Washington about that Bosnian job."

"The one with the government—yes, but what happened to being a music critic?"

"That's still on. Might be delayed a bit. I asked to be assigned to London. When needed, I'd fly into Bosnia from there."

"Will Jillian like that?"

"I didn't ask her. We'll have to settle that after the interview in Washington. Now let's talk about you and your concert in Los Angeles. I hope to get home in time to hear you."

She looked surprised. "But once I get back to New York—"

"Don't disappoint me. I'm counting on seeing Jillian."

"Once we get to Europe, she's moving back to London."

"She's leaving you?"

"Her year is almost up. And Franck wants to go back to Moscow. He'll be much safer there."

"And you?"

"Back to Prague for a few weeks. I'm cutting back on my schedule. I want to leave while people are still honoring me. The accolades don't mean as much to me anymore," she said. "I want to retire my Stradivarius while people are still giving me standing ovations."

He leaned over and brushed the rain from her cheeks. Or were they tears? "Honor belongs to a power greater than a musician."

For a second she looked puzzled. "God?" she asked.

By the time they reached the VanBuriens', the rain had stopped. A calm swept over Kerina as she stepped from the car and took the winding path up the hill to the house. It was like coming home. She belonged. She was at peace. Surely this was Bill's home. It had that look about it. The woodsy smell. The cozy feeling. The wraparound porch. In her heart, Bill was there, walking beside her, showing her his childhood home, giving her a glimpse of that person he had wanted to be.

Wood smoke poured from the chimney on the sloping roof of the two-story house. Blue shutters framed the narrow windows and lace curtains covered the panes. Round white pillars framed the porch and straggling wet vines of the dead wisteria still tumbled over the picket fence. The flower beds had been pruned back for winter, the soil soaked from the rain.

Chandler stood beside her, saying nothing. She put her hand on his arm. "Chandler, who lives here?"

"I don't know who owns it now, but until we moved away it belonged to the VanBuriens. Generation after generation."

"Bill's home! Bill grew up here, didn't he?"

"And you are comforted by that?"

"Yes, it is that kind of house."

"Have you been here before?" he asked.

"No, not this close. Yet I have been here a thousand times. This is the country home that I have dreamed about, thought about, searched for. There has to be a gazebo in the back."

"There is," he said in surprise. "Out by the swings. And trails lead right into the woods. You can see the trees above the roof. Pines, cedars, and the old oak trees."

Her eyes misted. "And deer come down to feed in the winter."

Chandler unlatched the gate and allowed Kerina to enter ahead of him. She waited for the rusty hinges to creak, listened for the sound of the mockingbird in the treetops or the call of the whippoorwill. Listened for the sound of a child.

A tangle of damp bracken scratched her legs as they passed the hedges. Chan urged her up the flagstone steps, through the rain puddles, along the winding cobbled path to the arched trellis. "In spring and summer, the trellis is covered with roses and bees. Funny I remember that. I was three when we moved away, but I recall running from the bees and up that porch into Mom's arms."

Touching Kerina's elbow, he urged her forward. As they crunched over the burnt-orange leaves drifting across the walkway, Kerina said, "I can't smell the honeysuckle."

"Autumn is the wrong time of the year."

"There should be a rocker on the porch and a baby crying in its mother's arms—as you must have done, Chandler."

He stopped at the porch, one foot on the first step. "It's still there in the corner. See?" He laughed. "It's not the one Mom rocked me in, but it serves the purpose."

Grasping the railing, he turned to face her. "I didn't realize until I saw you at the cemetery that you knew my uncle. Kerina, why didn't Uncle Bill ever bring you here to the house?"

"We parked at the bottom of the hill once," she whispered. "On the gravel by the side of the road near where you parked. Bill said this old house was his favorite place in the world when he was a boy. Because he loved it so, it must have lingered in my memory."

She looked up at her son, wanting him to understand. "I knew if I could find this place, I would be at peace. Can you understand that, Chandler?"

"Yes. I've been looking for a missing piece in my life too," he told her. "Mom always said the house was special because her mama was there. Once her mama was gone, her laughter went with it. But why didn't Uncle Bill take you inside?"

Tears balanced on Kerina's lashes. "Your uncle was married, Chandler. He had a wife and two children, and I was traveling with him. He didn't want to embarrass any of us. Himself especially."

"That would be my Aunt Celeste. She married again after my uncle died. I've never met my cousins. That side of the family wanted nothing to do with us after my uncle died."

"My fault," Kerina said.

"Uncle Bill had no right to hurt you."

"Love is always painful, Chandler." She sighed. "I wanted to come back and see the house in the daylight. Bill promised me that one day he would buy the place for me so I could be happy. But talking like that was wrong and we knew it."

"Would you really be happy here? It would be filled with memories. And the townsfolk don't always take to strangers."

How well I know, she thought. She allowed her gaze to wander over the property toward a gate that led to the side of the house. It was then that she saw the For Sale sign propped against the railing, almost hidden behind a faded purple bush.

"Look. The place is for sale. I should buy it."

"What would you do with a house in Everdale?"

"Keep it for a summer home."

He frowned. "It's steamy hot here in the summer time, and there are lots of mosquitoes to contend with."

"I will buy much repellent."

"A house like this has to be lived in, Kerina. It's like part of the family. It needs kids running through the kitchen, poking their skates through the screen door, exploring the woods behind the house. You can't buy this place and leave it empty. It would become a thicket of weeds and disrepair."

Like the house in my dreams, she thought.

They were on the porch now, peering through the window into a room full of old-fashioned furnishings that had to be hand-me-downs. But there was warmth there, that lived-in look. They stayed for an hour while Kerina ran her fingers over the picket fence, slid her hand down the banister railing, rocked in the rocker on the porch, smelled burning leaves from the neighbor's yard, picked at chipped paint on the gazebo, and sat on the swing where Bill had spent so many happy hours. After Chandler pushed her higher and higher in the swing, they walked around the house, hiked a pace in the woods where Bill had hiked, then ran through the garden where a very young Chandler had picked a bouquet of flowers for his mother.

Kerina felt as if Bill was there. And Mama, the woman she had never met—Bill's stronghold. As she sat and rocked, Kerina imagined Mama laughing and Bill's deep voice quoting T. S. Eliot.

"You're smiling," Chandler said.

"I'm just remembering. That's all. You are right, of course. There is no place in Everdale for me. I've come back. I have said my good-byes." She glanced back pensively as they walked down to the car. At the foot of the hill, her gaze went back to the house once more, sealing it in her memory. Bill and memories. Mama and her twins had made this place. But Bill and his mama were gone.

The late afternoon air was chilling, another rain squall threatening in the sky. "Miss Rudzinski, do you want me to get a camera and come back and take some pictures for you?"

Her fingers grazed his arm. "No. I have seen this place in my mind and heart for years. I will never forget it. Bill used to tell me that we would share it together one day—when I retired from the concert hall." Her voice filled with wistful happiness. "I knew it would never happen. Must not happen. But this house has belonged to me as far back as I can remember."

Twenty-seven

The next morning, with the nip of fall pushing him on and the cold rain soaking him, Chandler took refuge under the eaves of the craft store. He wiped the rain from his face with the back of his hand and checked the street numbers against the e-mail from home.

He had hit the 300 block, a high number for a town crunched together in the middle of nowhere with a population that barely numbered 3,000. Right now, he'd settle for locating Selma Malkoski at 593 Carstone Lane. He poked his head into the craft shop and asked for directions.

"Carstone? Close enough to walk," the shopkeeper said.

Chandler took the time to buy a box of candy and then plodded on, the mist-laden rain coming down harder now. *Good for the evergreens,* he thought, *but not for me.*

Ashley's friend Selma lived on a narrow residential street north of the hospital and not far from downtown. Behind her house the fields were covered with purple flowers drinking in the rain and hundreds of goldenrod—with enough pollen to send anyone into an allergy attack. As Chandler knocked on the door, a freight train rattled over the tracks in the center of town.

He knocked again. This time Selma Malkoski opened the door.

"Hey," she said.

"Hello, Mrs. Malkoski. I'm Ashley Reynolds's son. I called—"

"*Miss* Malkoski. Been looking for you. Where's your car?"

"I left it by the depot."

"And walked in the rain? I thought any son of Ashley's would be smarter than that. Come in. Take a load off those wet feet."

Selma was not the slim, trim nurse his mother had described. It was apparent she didn't need a box of chocolates, but he handed her the candy anyway.

"Bribery? Dr. Nelson warned me that you were a smooth one."

She pointed to a chair and sank down on the sofa across from him. The gift box was quickly opened and sampled, the lid left upright on her lap. "You look a bit different than the last time I saw you, Chandler. Three then, weren't you? A cute little kid."

He glanced around. It was an old-fashioned room with a high ceiling, and no visible central heating. Logs blazed in the stone fireplace, but the heat didn't reach him. His gaze strayed from the logs to the half-empty wineglass on the end table beside her and back to her face.

State your business and get out of here, he told himself.

"Dr. Nelson said you could help me locate my biological father."

"Me? Try the Court House."

"I did. But Nelson said you were my best bet. You were friends with my family."

"Don't placate me. Ashley Reynolds and I were coworkers, not really close friends."

"The doctor sees it differently. He's certain you can help me. Said he was having a bit of trouble with memory."

"Sounds like Nelson. He forgets what he wants to forget. He was an excellent physician. About the only one we had in town back then. But he is an utter coward when it comes to dealing with people. Makes it a point not to get involved."

"Meaning finding my father?"

"What makes you think I would know any more than Nelson?"

"He said you and my—birth father were close once."

"Lovers back in high school," she said bitterly. "Engaged once. That was our charming William."

William! A name at last. But he needed the last name, the whole name. He leaned forward, silently blessing the distracting box of candy. "I don't want to waste your time. Please, could you just tell me where I can find William?"

She snapped back, "I'll tell you what the good doctor was too coward to tell you. William is on the other side of town. Go dig him up."

"I need an address. Just tell me who he is—where he lives."

"Your father?" Selma's laughter trilled without mercy. Her mouth gaped open, her tongue coated with melting chocolates. "The whole town knows who your father was. Surely you've guessed."

"I wouldn't ask if I knew."

"Beanpole. That's what we called him in high school. A scoundrel. A loser. That's what I called him. Ashley idolized him." She selected another chocolate from the box and popped it into her mouth, licking her fingers before saying, "William hated Everdale. Could hardly wait to move away."

"Did he?"

"He left town all right. Joined the navy. Nearly broke his mother's heart, I'll tell you. And that wasn't the only heart he broke. The daahling of Everdale with that charming way of his and that dimpled grin. Easy come. Easy go."

An uneasiness settled over Chandler. *You were one of the broken hearts left behind,* he thought. *One of the broken hearts that stayed single.*

Chandler felt himself drifting toward despair. *William. The navy.* No, the idea was crazy. "Miss Malkoski, have I come all the way to Everdale for nothing? The doctor who delivered me isn't talking. The attorney who arranged my adoption kept no records on it. I was told you would help me, but you're hopscotching around the facts."

"Know what, Reynolds? I think you're backing down. You're afraid of the truth." She tossed an unfinished bon-bon back in the box. "If not, try the Court House."

"I told you, I already did. After being shafted from office to office, the Court House records remained sealed like some top secret at Langley. Do you know what Langley is, Miss Malkoski?"

"Central Intelligence," she said.

"For two days I've dealt with nothing but strangers. Power hungry strangers controlling the facts of my birth and spiel-ing off state laws that forbid me to know what my own file contains. Me—my origin is top secret."

"That's not fair," she admitted. "But let it go. I can't be-lieve that Ashley and Pastor Reynolds have not been good parents to you."

"The best until I found out we've all been living a lie."

"Do they know you've come to Everdale?"

"We've been in touch by e-mail. That's how I got your address and Dr. Nelson's name."

"Did you talk to Kyle Richardson over at the Court House? He was a personal friend of Pastor Reynolds."

"I know. I'm staying at the Richardsons' bed-and-breakfast."

"Crazy business," Selma said. "Not more than two dozen guests all year and most of them Yankees from up north."

"Richardson just referred me to someone else down the line."

"Sam Waverly?"

"He was the worst of all."

"Careful," she said, smiling for the first time. "Waverly is running for city mayor."

"I hope he doesn't make it."

"He will. He's the only one running."

"Waverly told me my birth records are none of my business. He had the paperwork right there on his desk. The files in his hands were mine, Miss Malkoski, but I couldn't touch them." Chandler indicated the size of his file with his thumb and forefinger. "Couldn't have been more than a dozen documents including a copy of the Order of Adoption and a thin form that Mr. Waverly held up and referred to as the Consent Decree."

"That would be the form your biological mother signed."

"I figured as much. A miserable piece of paper that tossed me out with the dirty bathwater."

"Try the new City Hall. Most of the records since 1970 have been transferred there. Births. Deaths. Marriages. Divorces."

"What good will it do? Waverly says my original birth certificate—if there is one—would be under seal of the court."

"Did he tell you that City Hall is closed until Tuesday?"

"Yes. Some Confederate holiday. And I'll be gone by then. I have an appointment in Washington that I can't break. I only have a couple more days in Everdale."

"Not much time to trace twenty-six years."

"Not your fault. You said my father was in the navy. If I only had a name, perhaps I could go that route. Tell me, Miss Malkoski, after his stint in the navy, where did my father go?"

She winced. "He told me he'd come back to Everdale. That's what he said in his letters. But he settled in Chicago."

Chicago? The navy? William? Chandler's uneasiness was back.

"Went to university first and then stayed on for some highfalutin job." She drummed her polished nails on the lid of the candy box, the sound like an Uzi emptying its rounds. Selma Malkoski was soured on life and men—especially William. "But he came home, all right. Back here when he needed us."

330

"Were you classmates in high school?"

"We all were. Nelson was ahead of us. But Ashley and her brother were in my class. Star basketball player that William."

His shirt felt clammy. He had passed the high school when he pulled into town. He'd drive there next and head straight to the library and the yearbooks mildewing there. He'd check out every William on the basketball team in the '70s. One of them would be his uncle. The greatest basketball player of all times according to his mom.

"Dr. Nelson said my father resides in Everdale now?"

"I guess you could say that. So Ashley never told you?"

He gambled on the truth. "She never wanted to hurt me."

"Or was she too ashamed to admit the truth?"

Suddenly he didn't want to hear the truth. He stood, the chair scraping across the floor. "I have to leave. I'm sorry I troubled you."

"Where are you going?"

"I came to Everdale to find my father."

Her face twisted, a mixture of pity and pain. "It won't do any good to keep looking. You won't find him. He's—he's dead."

Chandler gripped the chair back. "Dead?" he repeated.

She nodded. "I told you he always came back to Everdale when he was in trouble."

"Was he ill?"

"He came here when you were born and was killed in an automobile accident near the airport on his way back to Chicago."

He felt absolute fury. No wonder his parents had deceived him. Uncle Bill had died in a car accident days after Chandler's birth. *During a rainstorm. A muggy, misty, rain-drenched day like this one. For twenty-six years Uncle Bill had been not much more than a name.*

His back was soaked with perspiration. "Uncle Bill?" He said the name aloud as if for no other reason than to admit the truth to himself. "My mom's brother?"

"I am sorry, Reynolds. Them keeping it from you all these years. What's wrong with Ashley?"

"I'm the one who should be sorry. Forcing your hand. I didn't have a clue when I came here. I just thought I could find him and through him find my birth mother."

"She wasn't from these parts. Not Southern at all. I've been trying to remember her name ever since you phoned me. Ashley's brother brought the girl here. To the middle of nowhere. It was foreign sounding. Kovac, I think." A scowl deepened the ridges on Selma's forehead. "Kerry Kovac—that's it. But don't go looking for someone with that name. Kerry Kovac was something she pulled from the hat just long enough to birth you."

He stared at her. "That Consent Decree Mr. Waverly wouldn't show me—that's a legal document?"

"That's right."

"But was it legal if the name she gave was false?"

She stacked the empty candy wrappers. "I'm not a lawyer. All I can tell you is that I was on duty the night she was admitted—and the night you were born."

He had passed the Jackson Medical Center out on South Main. It was an impressive, two-story hospital with a large wing. Doctor's offices, a drugstore, and a gift shop surrounded it. If he remembered correctly, it had ample parking out in the front. "Do you remember the night I was born?"

She gave him one of her trilling laughs again. "Back when you were born it was just a small forty-four-bed hospital perched on an open field. Looked like it was out in no-man's-land, but we caught the highway victims from three communities. Unlucky patients. We did well to have one R.N. on duty per shift. Back then we were rarely full. That's why I remember Kerry Kovac. The mystery girl. Figuring her out put a spark in our dull lives."

Chandler closed his eyes, trying to shut out the moment. He had come here for two names and had them. *Kerry Kovac and Uncle Bill.* Bill VanBurien. Knowing was more painful than not knowing.

"Ashley was in the delivery room when you were born. We both were. Ashley wanted to be there to bond with you right away."

That close. Two mothers. One delivery. His mouth was dry, the taste bitter like gall. "I never knew I was adopted until recently."

"Thought Ashley might pull a fast one like that. Knew it for certain when they suddenly packed up and moved away from Everdale. She said her husband was finally going back to seminary—Pastor Reynolds always talked about doing that." Selma was on a roll, her voice rising. "But I knew better. I knew that wasn't their only reason for running out on us. I'm telling you, Chandler, it was a mean thing to do. They left us short a nurse at the hospital and the church without a pastor. Two-day notice. Just like that. Guess Ashley was going to keep her promise to Kerry Kovac or die."

"What promise, Miss Malkoski?"

"That you would never know who your biological parents were. The lawyer made Ashley and Reverend Reynolds promise. That's what the girl wanted. I was there. I heard it."

"Why would Mom and Dad make a promise like that?"

The harshness in Selma's face softened. "Bill was always in trouble—his whole life. And Ashley covered for him. Loved him. They were twins, you know. Really close. Ashley would have done anything for her brother Bill."

Even raise his son. "Why didn't my uncle marry the girl?"

"Marry her?" She was watching him intently now, no longer interested in the candy. "Have you forgotten? Your uncle was already married. Still had a wife and two sons. Three if we count you."

Chandler's shirt suddenly felt tight. He crooked his finger at the collar and tried to relieve the burning pressure on his neck. "So I'm illegitimate."

"Not uncommon," she said kindly. "Happens a lot these days."

"Not back then. Not in a small town like this. No wonder Mom never told me the truth. Anything to protect her brother."

"And to protect you."

"Deceive me, you mean." He shook his head. "All my life I wanted a kid brother to roughhouse with. And all Dad and Mom would say was they couldn't have any more children."

"They didn't have any of their own as far as I know."

"But I have two brothers?"

"Half-brothers," she corrected. "Lived in Chicago or thereabouts. Don't know where they'd be now. They were little boys at the funeral. Be in their thirties by now."

Truth was sucking the air out of his lungs. The brutality of the word mocked him. All through his childhood, Ashley had said, "You must always tell the truth, son."

David had preached it from the pulpit. *Talk is cheap,* he thought. Truth was to mold Chandler's life but not their own.

There was too much to swallow. Pride. Disappointment. Anger. Shame. But he kept his voice casual as he stood and said, "Thank you for seeing me, Miss Malkoski."

"No skin off my teeth. And thanks for the candy. You'll be all right, won't you?"

"I'll make it." *But how can I face Mom and Dad when I get back home?* he thought.

He was at the door when she said, "Your uncle—your father—he's buried in the VanBurien family plot."

"I know. I put flowers on his grave yesterday."

My father's grave. Bill VanBurien. Kerina Rudzinski! He knew he had found his birth mother without searching for her. Five months ago he didn't know she existed. He rehearsed everything that Kerina had said in Vienna and at the cemetery here in Everdale. Little phrases. Nugget comments. How blind he had been.

"I have a confession to make," Ashley had said in Vienna, and he had fallen asleep on her words.

He knew now that Ashley had recognized Kerina. Kerina had recognized him. He knew the truth, and he was the worse for knowing. "Miss Malkoski, what was Kerry Kovac like?"

"Quite striking, elegant. A face that you would never forget, it was so fragile. Sad eyes. Hazel, I think. It's been so many years I can't say for certain. But they were lovely. And her hair. A beautiful reddish-brown. Long and shiny." She reflected for a moment. "The girl had an accent. European, but she listed Chicago as her residence. I remember that. That's how we put two and two together and came up with Bill VanBurien."

"That's odd mathematics."

"Not odd when you consider that Bill made an unscheduled trip to Everdale after a two-year absence. He was here in town when you were born. Gone again right afterwards. To tell you the truth, I always thought his dying like he did in that car accident was justified punishment."

"It was an accident. He was driving in a rainstorm."

"That's what the police called it. But people in a small town like this have their own opinions."

"Miss Malkoski, did the girl play a violin by chance?"

"I'd forgotten that. She had one of those famous violins. A magnificent instrument and stylish clothes. She was quite young, but I think maybe your birth mother was a musician and well off financially."

She still is, he thought as he closed the door behind him. *A gifted violinist. And wealthy.*

Out on the sidewalk he stopped to take great gulps of air and realized he had not even said good-bye. But the void inside him was like a deep chasm, a black gaping hole. He knew who he was yet he felt as if he was no one at all. For an instant he wanted to go back to the VanBurien family plot and destroy the flowers he had placed there yesterday.

He clenched his fist at the rain-drenched sky. "My uncle? No, my father," he cried. "What right did you have to die when I never even knew you?"

He set out, walking blindly toward the depot in the center of town. Back in his rental car he picked up his cellular phone and dialed the motel where Kerina was staying. "I'm trying to reach Kerina Rudzinski," he said.

He could hear the rattle of the registry and then the motel manager saying, "No one here by that name."

"Check again. It's important."

"I'm fixin' to do that." Seconds dragged. "Nope. No Robinski."

"Rudzinski," Chandler said. "You're certain she's not a guest there?"

"I swanney . . . I swear it. You got a better idea, young man? Another motel, maybe?"

"Is there one?"

"Down the road a piece in Spruceville. Twenty miles, give or take a mile. The Dale Motel—we're it for Everdale."

"She has to be a guest at the Dale. An attractive woman in her mid-forties. Reddish-brown hair. Unforgettable dark eyes."

"Ohhhh. Why didn't you speak your piece before? You mean Miss Kovac. She checked out this morning. Let me see—yes, Kerry Kovac. Said she was catchin' a plane back to New York."

"Kerry Kovac. She's gone?"

"Yep."

Chandler mumbled his thank-you and disconnected. His birth mother. Gone from Everdale. Out of his life again. Gone forever this time.

Twenty-eight

Chandler tossed back the covers on the brass bed and, gripping one of the highly polished knobs, swung himself to a sitting position. He whacked the alarm button on his travel clock before it rang and was showered and packed by dawn. Outside, a glowing, rose-ribboned sky promised the first sunny, fall day in Everdale since he arrived. He settled his bill with a sizable tip, refusing breakfast even though his sleepy-eyed hostess stood in the narrow hallway insisting he not leave on an empty stomach.

"Won't take but a minute to cook your grits," she told him.

No grits, Mrs. Richardson, he thought.

She stood there in a woolly, yellow bathrobe with her arms wrapped around her ample bosom. Fringes of gray peeked out from her hair net and smudges of night cream whitened her face. She wrung her hands. "I never let my guests go away hungry," she murmured. "And my husband never starts a day without grits and coffee. Without them, he's a grumble all day."

Chandler could tell by her expression that he had offended her Southern hospitality. "I have a plane to catch, but the next time I come back, okay?" he offered.

The promise placated her. She turned the key in the front door with her red-knuckled hand and opened it for him.

He leaned down and kissed her cheek and came away with the taste of lilac face cream on his lips. The kiss was symbolic. *I have no desire to come back here,* he thought. *Everything that really matters to me lies in the cemetery.*

He strode off, the dappled sun making rainbow reflections on the wet walkway. Throwing his luggage into the backseat, Chandler slid into the car and, with a brisk wave to the woman in the doorway, roared off on his way north, racing like a speed demon through the quiet streets of Everdale, hell-bent at the wheel, like Bill VanBurien had driven.

Last night's scant sleep had left him with bitter thoughts against the man in the cemetery. Images and impressions churned over in his mind, coming at him like darts from every direction. Bill VanBurien's hometown. The high school where he led the team to a basketball championship two years in a row. His name engraved on the war monument in the park, names from every war the township could cook up. The Court House that held Bill's vital statistics: birth and death.

As Chandler's foot hit the floorboard, the car skidded. He steadied the wheel. Sweat dotted his brow as he thought of his father's car skidding out of control on a rain-drenched highway near Dannelly Field. The void inside him seemed larger than life. He had come to Everdale seeking his identity. Now what did he have? A cemetery plot. But nothing tangible.

Chandler couldn't grip his dad's hand and say, "So there you are." Or clamp his shoulder, saying, "Let me look at you."

He couldn't phone and ask, "Dad, how about the ball game tonight?" Or hear his dad answering, "Sounds like a winner, son."

Chandler felt betrayed. Cheated by his own parents. Renounced at birth. Hoodwinked by those who had adopted him. Intimidated and misunderstood at times by David's mother, the only grandmother he had ever known. The desertion was complete, as if he had been given a Judas kiss in the family garden.

He took the road that led past the VanBurien homestead and slammed on his brakes when he reached it. The engine on the rental car hiccuped. He turned the motor off and stared at the house where his dad had grown up. All his life Chandler had heard bits and pieces about Uncle Bill and had taken little interest in him. The man was dead, as dead as Randy Williams. Now it was like looking at a framed photo with the picture turned to the wall. You knew the person was there, but the face was missing. No one could fill in the features for him except his parents. His parents? In his anger, he thought of them as Ashley and David, but in his heart as Mom and Dad. What should he call them now? Who were they? Who was he?

"Dear God," he breathed, "what an ungrateful wretch I am. What a rotten Christ-follower."

What's the matter with you, man? he argued with himself. *They cradled you from the time you were born. Saw you safely from kindergarten to Juilliard. Paid every bill. Sat by your bedside through mumps and measles and an appendectomy and that fractured ankle in a skiing accident. Cheered you from every corner. Loved you all the way. So you hated being a preacher's kid. Was it really that bad? Going to church was just part of the bargain. Ashley and David were everything parents could be.*

The next move was Chandler's. Things were in his ball park. He had two choices: split from the family forever—the choice he leaned toward—or go home and face them. Demand answers. Have it out with them and then pick up the pieces—and if they could, go on from there as a family. He had no doubt that Grandmother Reynolds had told them everything he had shared with her. They knew he was seeking answers in Everdale. Why else had they sent him the address for the Richardsons' bed-and-breakfast and a check for his expenses that he hadn't cashed? When he saw them—if he did—he'd get it off his chest, give it to them straight.

339

"You lied to me all my life. Just tell me why," he would demand.

His conscience jabbed him. He wished that Randy were sitting here beside him. Randy always took giant-size boulders and made pebbles out of them. "So what would you do, buddy?" Chandler asked aloud.

Clear as a fast-running trout stream, Chandler knew. *Throw out the line. Take a gamble. Play the odds.* Randy's philosophy.

Chandler gave it a stab. His birth mother was a musician. He reasoned, if Ashley and David wanted to hide that one, why did they put a violin in his hands when he was four? Why expose him to good music all his life? Why encourage, even mandate, that he develop that innate ear for music? Christmas and his birthday never lacked for a new cassette or CD of one of the great violinists, Kerina Rudzinski included. By touching his life with music, they had given him part of his birth mother.

Here on a country road in Alabama, drumming his fingers on the steering wheel, he remembered Ashley giving him his first Rudzinski CD. Her voice had fractured when she said, "Dad and I thought you would like Miss Rudzinski's music."

It had gone into his growing pile of gifts—of little interest to him back then. He was into Zuckerman and Perlman. Idolized the work of Menuhin playing the Beethoven and Brahms concertos and took to Anne Sophie Mutter the first time he heard her in concert. And now for Chandler, Kerina's work surpassed them all. But she had grown on him slowly, as though he were being drawn irresistibly to someone he should know and respect.

And what of the family trips to Europe and the wall map in his father's library, a map marked with red dots for each European country they had visited or studied together? True, David never pointed to Prague in particular, but thinking on it now, Chandler knew Czech history back for decades and had without knowing it been drawn to his mother's country. As he rested his elbow on the car's window ledge, a brisk October air chafed his skin. What pain it must have cost Ashley to withhold the truth about her brother, Bill.

A promise, Selma Malkoski had called it.

Kerina swore them to secrecy to guard her own identity, not mine, he thought. *To protect her own career, not my future. She recognized me in Vienna and Everdale and never said a word.* The cold reality of her rejection came like a slap in the face.

In their own way, Ashley and David had done their best to tie him in with his heritage. Chandler had spent these last few weeks thinking about them as liars and deceivers. Yet all they had done was love, protect, and stand by him from birth to manhood. He craned his neck and looked in the rearview mirror. "Do I look like your brother, Mom?"

Of course. She had told him many times, "You're like the VanBurien side. Lanky and quick and ornery like Bill."

But give me a face, Mother.

She had tried. How many times had she taken out the family albums until he was bored when she grabbed for one? To Chandler, snapshots of fraternal twins—Bill the tall, lean one with an easy smile—had been fragments that did not form a whole.

"Oh, he was a charmer, all right," Grandmother Reynolds had said, voicing her disapproval. "A corporate climber. Definitely not a family man."

He could recall a dozen or two references to Uncle Bill's navy days and the injury on board his ship. "Bill wanted to go professional," David had told Chandler. "But that injury in the navy cut the dream of pro basketball from the slate. A great player. I think he could have made it."

You could have done a lot of things, Chandler thought. *Like stay alive. Like be my friend. Like admit that I was your son.* A knot of anger twisted inside him. *Mom loved you, Bill VanBurien. But I hate your guts, man.*

His life since Bosnia had become a deep, gutted chasm as though an avalanche had permanently split his yesterdays and tomorrows. He would have a thousand questions for Ashley and David when he got back to California, but all he could do was hammer away at the same one: Why hadn't they told him the truth?

In the painful silence that followed, Chandler remembered the letter Ashley had given him when he left for Denver. Grabbing his briefcase from the backseat, he snapped the locks open and rummaged through the papers. Nothing. Where was the letter? He was certain he had packed it. He sorted through the paperwork carefully this time and finally found it jammed in the fold of the lid. "It's about you, Chandler," Ashley had said.

His mouth went dry as he opened it. *April 18,* Bill had written in his bold scrawl. *Three days after my birth,* Chandler thought.

Dear Sis,

There is a torrential rain outside the airport. In a few minutes I will be out there driving in it. But I had to write to you first—to try and explain. Sis, I needed Everdale. I needed you. But can you ever forgive me for my deception? It seems I've been begging your forgiveness all my life, yet you never demanded it. Never asked it. It was always there, free for the taking.

You are so much like Mama, Ash. Mama was my lifeline, and you were the hinge that always swung me back toward Mama and home. Without you two believing in me, I would never have had the courage to tackle the university and reach for the stars. Anything I've accomplished for the good is with thanks to you and Mama for standing with me. I still treasure the memory of the two of you shouting from the sidelines during my basketball games. What a lucky guy I was to have you cheering me on.

Sis, when I saw you in the doorway there at Jackson Memorial I knew that you knew. I never wanted you to know that the baby was mine. I thought I could slip back into Everdale and make the final arrangements for my son to have a good home, a permanent one with you and David. Dr. Nelson assured me that the adoption would go through.

I have no plans to ever come back to Everdale, so I will not interfere in the way that you raise the baby. But send me pictures. Tell me about him. Ash, as we faced each other in the hospital lobby, I wanted to ask you to show me my son. To let me hold him just once. But I knew if I held him, I could never let him go. The kindest thing I could do for my child was to walk away. Celeste knew about Kerry, but she doesn't know about the baby. I've hurt her and the boys so much already that I couldn't add to their pain. Nor did I want to add to yours and David's.

When I married Celeste, Mama opposed it. She told me not to marry anyone unless I was in love. But Celeste was everything I thought I wanted. Social position. Money. Success. She was so glamorous to this small-town boy. She told me if we stayed on in Chicago, her father could open doors for me and save us years of climbing to the top. I no longer needed Everdale. I was out of the navy, doubling up on my studies at the university, determined to make it big in corporate America. Celeste offered me a chance to succeed. She was fun to be with; I was so proud of her. I figured love would come with the package.

Mama was right, Sis. It was never a good marriage. I didn't fit in. Mama was so sure I would meet someone someday that I would fall in love with. And when I did, it was too late. Celeste and I were at odds a lot, and one night I went alone to a concert in downtown Chicago to hear a violin soloist from Prague. Never had I heard such magnificent music; it stirred those old longings to work in the field of music.

Afterwards I bought a dozen white roses from the vendor outside the music hall and then pushed my way through the crowded lobby, backstage to Kerina Rudzinski's dressing room. I never intended anything more than to thank her for her concert. But I couldn't take my eyes from her face. She was beautiful and charming and, as we talked about her music, something clicked between us.

I never meant for it to go beyond my thank-you, but in the excitement of the moment, I invited her to have dinner with me. After that we were together whenever she was in town. I never meant to hurt Celeste and the boys. Never meant to hurt Kerry, that's what she wanted me to call her. When she told me she was pregnant, I worried that a scandal would ruin her career.

I was in so deep, Sis. I had nothing to offer Kerry. I was still married, even though Celeste had packed up the month before and gone back to the family mansion for the third time. She offered to call it quits, but all I could think of was Mama and her God and the way she used to get down on her knees when we were kids, night after night, and pray for us. There were the boys to think about, and I didn't need the court to tell me incompatibility with my wife was no excuse. It was up to me to make my marriage work.

Moments ago—just before Kerry's plane took off—I promised Kerry that I would find a way for us to be together forever. Ash, I cannot tell you how much I love her. I'd give anything to take her back to Mama's old house to live. But it's all wrong. I could never merit God's approval that way. It would never work out. I just walked out on my infant son. Just saw Kerry fly off. I couldn't shatter the lives of Jeff and Skip too.

I called Celeste from the air terminal and asked her if we could try to patch up our differences—for the boys' sake. She doesn't think so—doesn't want to, but she agreed to meet with me and talk it over with her father and the lawyer present. I'm going to drive all night, straight through to Chicago.

When all of this is settled, I will write to Kerry again. She is young. She needs a chance to go on in her career, to find someone who will love her and care for her more honestly than I have done. But as long as I live, Sis, right or wrong, I will remember how much I love Kerry. Yet the best thing I can do for my newborn son and his lovely mother is to set them free.

For now, I know that Kerry has forced you to a pledge of silence in the adoption consent. But someday, will you tell my son that I loved him? Tell him that his mother was very young, frightened, beautiful. Tell him that I had to let him go, knowing that two of the neatest people on earth would love him as their own son and raise him in a godly home. In Mama's home. Mama would like that.

Can you ever forgive me, Ashley? Can I ever forgive myself? I will keep in touch from time to time. Ever yours,

Bill

For a long while Chandler sat there gripping the letter, banging his fist against the steering wheel, too choked up to drive away. He was beginning to put a face to the man now, someone with deep emotions like Ashley. Someone who had never held him. Someone who broke his last promise.

"You didn't keep in touch," Chandler said aloud. He shook the letter in the air. "You didn't stick around long enough to tell me you loved me! All you did was fold this letter and seal it in an envelope, and an hour later you were dead. You never even saw me."

Chandler folded his father's letter with great care and put it back into his briefcase. In his anger, he longed for someone to talk to, someone who would understand. He thought of Randy Williams bullying his way through any disaster, taking a gamble on life and losing. No, Randy never lost anything that he set his hand to do. Even in that dying second, he dove face-down taking the land mine full blast to save others. *To save me,* Chandler thought. *Randy, the winner. Randy, my friend, who met problems head-on.*

Chandler pushed back his cuff and checked the hour. Avoiding grits for breakfast had given him ample time to drive the seventy-five miles to the airport. Add the rental car return and check-in at the airline counter and time was marginal. But he could not leave Everdale this way, not without going back. He switched the engine on and accelerated. The tires spun in the gravel, spinning like his emotions and splitting his boulders into pebbles. He risked a U-turn on the country road and broke the speed limit back to the Everdale Cemetery. His birth mother had walked out of his life again, but at least he could say good-bye to his father.

The cemetery gate was locked, a caretaker just arriving. "I have to get inside," Chandler told him.

"Sorry, don't open for business until nine."

"But you're going in, sir."

"Yep. Got another grave to dig."

Chandler's gaze glanced off the man's name tag. "Please, my dad's buried here, Rob. I'm leaving town. Won't be back."

"I'm acquainted with everybody here. Who's your dad?"

"VanBurien. William VanBurien."

Rob scratched his head. "You're new to me. You one of his younguns from Chicago?"

"No, sir. They're my brothers. I'm the son from California."

"Letting you in now is against the rules."

"I just want to say good-bye."

"Have to leave your car outside the gate."

"Whatever you say."

"Hop in then," Rob said. "Bounce you over the ruts to the VanBurien plot. They've got one of the best views in town."

His truck rattled to the familiar stop, high on a quiet knoll. Two oak trees formed a natural arch over the VanBuriens. The rains had turned the lawns a forest-green and washed mud over the gravesites. Autumn leaves skittered across the plots. The roses on the VanBurien headstones lay bruised and wilting.

"Be removing those later today," Rob said. "The gate's chained, but I left it ajar enough for you to slip through when you're done. Let yourself out."

Chandler slid down from the passenger side and shook Rob's dirt-encrusted hand. "I appreciate this."

Rob nodded. "Every man has to say his good-byes."

He trundled off and moments later joined his crew by the bulldozer, leaving Chandler facing the family plot, his feet leaden on the gravel path.

He moved at last, stepping over the small wrought-iron rail that surrounded the VanBurien resting place. Two days ago he hadn't noticed how many VanBuriens were buried here. He counted eight of them now, two of them small children. So three of Mama VanBurien's children were buried here, not just Bill. Chandler read some of the markers. *Our little angel sleeps* for a child born and dead the same day. *Our sunshine in heaven* for a boy of three. Mama Van-Burien's headstone said: *Mama the joy of our lives. At rest now.* And on his father's inscription the dates that made him twenty-nine at death—twenty-nine now—and the simple message from his family: *We love you.*

The song of a mockingbird broke the stillness. He knelt down on one knee by his father's grave and fingered the red roses Kerina had laid there. Red roses because she loved him. Then he ran his hand over the cold marble.

"I didn't know who you were the other day," he said aloud. "I'm sorry. All my life you've been just Uncle Bill. Someone who died before I knew you." His fingers traced the name. "I never shed any tears over you. You were just a faded photograph in the family album. Someone that Mom missed. Yet all my life I searched for you, trying to put a name and a face to that void inside me."

Tears pricked behind his eyes. "I never thought it would hurt so much to find you. I think you loved my birth mother. God help me, I hope you did. She sacrificed everything for you. She was here the other day—weeping for you. Still loving you."

His finger stopped on the inscription: *We love you.*

"I should hate you, having an affair like that. Ruining it for those two little boys in Chicago. Robbing me of my brothers. Breaking your vows to Aunt Celeste."

The noise of the bulldozer reached him—the ground being dug for another burial. "What hurts most is you never looked at me, Bill VanBurien. You never picked me up. You never held me. Why didn't you want me? Why didn't you hold me?"

He wept now for the father he would never know, for the emptiness he still felt—that big gaping hole lodged inside him. The white roses had wilted, but Chandler found a single red rose still in bloom in Kerina's bouquet. He tugged it free and pressed it against his father's marker.

"My—my mother left red roses because she loved you." His hand pressed against the inscription. A sob shook him. "I have to leave now. I have a plane to catch. But I had to say good-bye. David Reynolds would say that I have to forgive you. Remember him? You were good friends once."

Chandler wiped the marble free of the twigs and leaves that had blown across the family plot. "But how can I forgive you? Oh, God, how can I forgive this man?"

"The way Mama would have forgiven," Ashley would say.

Mama, the joy of Ashley and Bill VanBurien's lives. The woman who knew how to love, how to forgive. Chandler felt more related to her now than he ever had. Double-barreled. Ashley's mother, the woman who had reared him. His birth father's mother. So Mama's ability to forgive ran in his blood. Surged there now like a spiritual renewal, like an eternal turn-around.

"I forgive you, Dad," he whispered and felt relief flood over him. He rested his head against the headstone and struggled for the courage that he needed. At last he sat back, his eyes glistening. "Dad—Dad, I just came back . . . to say I love you."

Twenty-nine

Chandler's taxi careened through traffic toward his Washington hotel, jostling for right-of-way as it passed the president's residence in white-painted sandstone and the Capitol with its brilliant cast-iron dome. Here he was in that city on the Potomac River where ambitious politicians came out of anonymity and rose to power, and where cherry blossoms and scandal broke on the scene with equal flurry—a city where the laws of the country were made and the fate of the nation cemented into time, where the applause of men turned sour overnight and valor and virtue were swallowed up in a media frenzy.

In this town of monuments and war memorials from The Wall to the Eternal Flame, he kept wondering if Washington immortalized peacekeepers. If so, would Randy's name ever be engraved in marble or granite? Or was this business of applying to the CIA's Career Training Program a waste of time? He wanted to go back to Bosnia for Randy's sake and to help men like Kemal Hovic stay alive, but going back as an intelligence officer might be under false documents with a false birth certificate in his pocket. But would that be any different than the last twenty-six years of his life? He'd gone to Everdale in search of his past; he had come to Washington in search of his future.

By his third day, his eyelids were red-rimmed from hours in the lecture hall, his fingers cramped after filling in a thirty-four-page application form, his head spinning from the polygraph experience and a battery of psychological tests with their dumb questions. Give the address of your mother-in-law. That one was easy: not applicable. Employment history back to age seventeen: with all the mental gymnastics he couldn't remember the drugstore where he had clerked for six months. Military experience: three years, U.S. Army. Residences for the last fifteen years: the family home in Southern California, a flat near Juilliard, and army tents in Bosnia. Are you accident prone? Yes; I swim in snake-infested rivers, walk in fields with land mines.

By the end of the first twenty-four hours, the packed-out room had thinned, some of the Ivy League candidates more interested in annual incomes and a social life than in adventures on foreign soil. What remained was the cream of the crop: ambitious, aggressive, goal-oriented men and women who had been lured in from a dozen recruitment offices across the country.

Secrecy was the key word, intelligence gathering the objective, but Chandler could see that obtaining the objective made them expendable. Before the last lecture hour, the young woman who had sat beside him permanently vacated her chair.

"No way, Reynolds," she told him. "Who wants a phony birth certificate or forged documents? I'm not living a lie the rest of my life. I've got a perfectly good birth certificate in my bank box. I don't want to be one of those memorial stars in the lobby at Langley." She seemed perfectly calm as she said, "I don't go for this remaining nameless for security reasons or dead in the line of duty with my cover blown on a covert assignment."

They shook hands and she was gone—off to seek a less demanding job that paid better. She didn't even take her yellow memo pad with her. Chandler hung in and completed the last interview. As he stood to leave, the man across from him said, "Reynolds, Paul Daniels is waiting to see you in the next room."

Colonel Daniels had dropped his army fatigues and looked like a businessman in his three-piece suit and silk tie. But his grave eyes were as unfriendly as they had been in Bosnia.

"So you've made it this far. Sit down, Reynolds."

Chandler kept it respectful. "A tough three days, sir."

He wondered how long it would take Daniels to bring up Tuzla and their first visit. It took seconds. "Off the record," Daniels said, "we didn't like Miss Rudzinski pulling strings in Bosnia to get Zineta Hovic released. That woman was an annoyance."

"That woman," Chandler said evenly, "is my birth mother."

They sat in a spartan room, the only comfortable chair the one Daniels sat in. He leaned back in it, looking like a man ready to light up a stogie, his cat-like eyes triumphant. "I didn't think you'd admit that, Reynolds."

"Then you didn't check my polygraph results. They asked about my parents during the test. And I told them."

"With yes and no answers?"

"The lady turned off the equipment and demanded an explanation. It was simple. I was adopted right after birth—born to a mother who was a musician, to a father who was already married. He's dead now." He voiced the facts without shame, facing them now as one of those things in life he could not change.

Daniels remained thoughtful. "You may be useful to us after all. You've been straightforward with us, except in Bosnia."

"I didn't know I was adopted then, sir."

"Odd. We knew." Daniels exhaled, the imaginary stogie puffing away. "That girl—Zineta Hovic—worked for the Serbs during the war as one of their couriers. But according to our intelligence reports, she refused to carry any messages out of Tuzla after our peacekeeping forces arrived."

"I doubt Captain Williams knew anything about her war background. He was a today kind of guy. No yesterdays. No tomorrows. Tell me, will Miss Hovic arrive in Ohio before the baby is due?"

"I'd like to delay it, but the captain's father is pressing to get the girl out so his grandchild can be born in America. With the White House on his side, they'll make it. But what right do they have to have that child born in America?"

"Every right, sir. Captain Williams was an American."

Daniels's eyes looked dark as charred tree roots as he scanned Chandler's file. "You still have your own agenda, Reynolds. Not Langley's. If you don't come with our Career Training Program, what then?"

"London by spring or summer and marriage to the prettiest girl on the Thames."

"Marriage? That wasn't in the picture when we talked last."

"I met her in Vienna."

"We prefer single men for the team for Bosnia. You'd be away for long periods at a time. Not healthy for a married man. If we don't take you, what then?"

"I'd write music reviews. And if I'm good—and I will be good—I'd do the European circuit. The concert scene and all. I'd still plan trips to Bosnia to help Kemal Hovic get back into his music. Miss Rudzinski arranged funding for music programs for the children. I want to be certain her wishes are carried out."

The feline eyes narrowed. "An ambitious undertaking. We're looking for single-minded candidates. Men committed to our Agency—our purpose, our goals. Not to their own agenda."

"The sacrificial lamb?"

"We prefer to call it dedication. We don't want wives on the phone calling to find out where their husbands are. You wouldn't consider delaying this marriage for a while?"

"No, sir. I've got my dad lined up to marry us already." *As soon as my girl says yes,* he thought.

"You disappoint me, Reynolds. I thought you were serious about this job. You need to make a decision, lieutenant. A music career or this mission in Bosnia."

"I can't have both?"

Daniels thumped his fingers together. "Perhaps you could still be useful to us in London. On a voluntary basis."

"But with no direct ties to the Agency? Right?"

"You do think quickly. We gather intelligence data from people and events worldwide—satellites, human spies, foreign broadcasts, publications of all types. Why not from music articles and reviews? If you travel the European circuit—and with your mother on the world circuit—you just might serve our purposes better in the music world." He scratched his temple. "You expressed an interest in seeing Langley the last time we met. Is tomorrow okay?"

"Not this time, sir. I leave for Chicago this evening. Save your gated buildings and barbed wire fences for another time."

Daniels's sardonic chuckle rippled through the room as he stood and held out his hand. "We are much more sophisticated than that, lieutenant. We even have an impressive array of art hanging in our corridors that would appeal to your sensitive nature."

Chandler's brows furrowed. "I trust Langley will get back to me with the outcome of my interviews?"

"Of course, lieutenant. In a few months. Don't look so surprised. We do a thorough check on our candidates. This is a highly sensitive mission."

Chandler kept his question friendly and lighthearted. "If you reject me, I hope you give a good reason, sir."

Daniels matched Chandler's mood. "We never give a reason for rejecting our applicants. That's classified information. But we will be in touch, Reynolds."

Three thousand miles away David strolled out into the garden looking for Ashley. He saw her kneeling in the impatiens bed, patting the soil around her plants. She had that fresh, wholesome look that had drawn him to her the first time he saw her on the school bus in Everdale, pretty and long-legged even then. He had stared at the back of her honey-blond hair as he was doing now, wondering about the color of her eyes and whether she was going steady. He had saved a seat for her the next day and she took it coyly. He soon discovered her to be passionate about gardening and the war in Vietnam, a defender of women's issues and creative with a needle and thread. She was like a dark velour pattern, with contrasting shades of brightness and darkness to her personality, but tough and durable like brocade. In their marriage, though, he had seen that fine cambric quality about her—a strength of character that made her a good nurse, a good person.

He crossed the lawn to her, pleased at how sharp those form-fitting jeans looked on her. "It's chilly out here," he scolded, but he smiled as he leaned down to kiss her dirt-smudged nose.

She flashed that remarkable smile of hers—the one that said everything was fine between them again. His heart skipped a beat as her cornflower blue eyes met his. She fussed about being fifty-four, but she was still beautiful to him, her dark lashes the color of the violet pansies in her garden and her cheeks still smooth and rosy like the day he met her.

"David, I heard you drive in an hour ago."

"The house was so quiet, I thought maybe you were out shopping."

"Just gardening. My car's in the garage. How did your classes go today?"

"I have one student who drinks in archeology like diet Cokes. But come in and have some coffee with me."

"Did you make it yourself?"

"Yes, and I want to enjoy some time with my wife."

"Hum. I baked cookies this morning."

"I found them. Chocolate chips." He swiped his teeth with his tongue, trying to make certain the evidence was gone. "I set out a plate of them on the table with our mugs from Vienna."

She dropped the trowel in the dirt bed and allowed him to help her to her feet. "Sounds good. And it is cold out here. Whatever happened to sunny California?"

"It'll be back by spring."

"Not soon enough. I'm getting the garden ready for Chandler's return. Now, don't scowl, David. He'll come. Right now he needs space."

"Three thousand miles should be enough," he said ruefully.

She paused along the path, distracted for a moment. "Look, darling, my daffodils are budding. And I pruned back the rose bushes and planted some bare roots by your office windows."

"Then I can expect bees and roses at the same time. What are these orange and yellow critters?"

"My Iceland poppies."

"Nice." He flicked at the dirt speck on her nose.

"I'm a mess, eh?" she asked as they walked into the kitchen.

"A pretty one, Ash."

"But there's a problem brewing. I can tell by the coffee and compliments. So out with it."

"I tried to call Kerina Rudzinski in New York City."

She dropped into a chair. "About Chandler?"

"Now wait—don't get upset." He poured her mocha cappuccino. "I tried to get tickets for Kerina's concert. It's been canceled. So I've been making phone calls for the last forty minutes."

He didn't burden her with the details of calling The Lincoln Center and the New York Philharmonic, the ticket agencies, the Chamber of Commerce, and Kerina's manager without success. She'd catch on when the phone bill arrived. He couldn't even remember which one gave him Kerina's hotel number.

"The hotel concierge told me she was in the hospital."

The sun freckles seemed to fade from Ashley's cheeks. She reached for a sweater and slipped it around her. "What's wrong?"

"She's at Columbia Presbyterian Medical Center."

"An accident? Is Chandler with her?"

"I don't know on both counts. We'll have to call the hospital. I wanted you with me—in case Kerina asks for you."

Ashley pushed her coffee away. "Make the call, David."

After a frustrating hold and another long delay, he was transferred to Kerina's private room at the Harkness Pavilion.

"Hello." The voice was young, sad. "This is Jillian Ingram."

"Jillian, David Reynolds here. Chandler's father. I'm trying to reach Miss Rudzinski."

"She's in radiology for X rays. She's had pneumonia."

David felt overwhelming relief. "I was afraid it was something serious. Does Chandler know she's hospitalized?"

"He's still in Washington. I couldn't reach him. He'll be upset—they were in a horrible rainstorm in Everdale."

"Jillian, my wife wants to talk to you."

Ashley's knuckles blanched as she took the phone. "Jillian, David says Kerina has pneumonia. What's going on?"

"I'm afraid it's more serious than that. Kerina has cancer."

The thudding of Ashley's heart vibrated in her ears. "What kind of cancer, Jillian?"

"Breast. She refuses surgery. But they've done bone scans and located another slow-growing tumor. Her cancer is spreading."

Ashley glanced at David for approval as she said, "Do you want me to come, Jillian?"

"No, don't. Franck insists we leave for Europe at once."

"Is Kerina up to traveling?"

"She's gritty. Plans to see her own doctor in Prague for a second opinion. But Chandler will be so disappointed. We counted on that time together in Los Angeles."

Ashley hesitated and then found the courage to ask, "You know, don't you, that Chandler is Kerina's son?"

"I've known since Vienna."

Ashley's mouth felt dry. "Jill, does my son know who Kerina is? If he doesn't, Kerina should tell him before she leaves."

"Why, Ashley? You never told him."

She deserved that. Her cheeks felt like branding irons. "Surely Kerina wants him to know someday?"

"But not while she's ill; I am certain she wants him to remember her as he first saw her in Vienna."

Ashley recalled Kerina's breathtaking entry into the concert hall in her Parisian gown. "That will be easy to do. Chan is still talking about that lovely red dress."

"Oh, Ashley, they're coming with Kerina right now. I'm sorry. I must hang up and help them."

"Keep in touch, won't you, Jill? Call us with any news. Call us collect."

Kerina looked pale against the cream-washed walls and even more pallid as the orderly transferred her to the bed. But she was gracious to him and radiant with a smile for Jillian.

"Jillian, you should have gone back to the hotel and not waited for me. You look as exhausted as I feel."

Jillian flipped her pillow and brushed Kerina's hair back from her forehead. "How are you?"

"Frayed and worn-out like a cloth rag. And my shoulder aches."

Jillian propped Kerina's arm on another pillow. "You don't look like frayed cloth. You're lovely. Radiant as always."

Kerina's laughter sent her into a coughing spasm. She tugged at the hospital gown. "I don't call this fashion."

"Then let's put you in a gown of your own."

357

"And five minutes later they'll want another X ray. Let's put me in my clothes and get me out of here." She coughed again. "I can't stay here. Hospitals wear me out."

As the coughing eased, she gazed out the window at the towering Manhattan skyline. "The river's there. But it's not the Danube. Not the Vltava. I want Franck to take me home, Jillian."

"Back to Vienna?"

"To standing ovations and applause? They are so transitory. My dear, the doctors—if they can be believed—have just handed me a death sentence. Surgery or else." She waved her ringed hand as though to dismiss their advice. "Ever since Chandler was born, I have been afraid of hospitals and doctors and of falling asleep in surgery and never waking up. While I waited in radiology, I realized that I am a woman without hope or faith in anything eternal." Her eyes filled with unshed tears. "No surgery, dear. Two more concerts and then Franck must take me home to Prague. I want to be with my parents. I want to hear my mother pray her Rosary again."

"Do you want me to go to Prague with you, Kerina?"

"Oh, will you? Will you stay that long?"

"I'm not walking out on you while you're ill. But Vienna first. And the concert and maybe a ride on the gray Danube."

"Not gray in the song. Not in my heart. We see things the way we want to see them. And for me when I see that river, I hear the song. Strauss was right. The beautiful blue Danube."

Kerina was making an attempt to bounce back with that old stretching quality that allowed her to give her best to her audiences. But the diagnosis left her vulnerable, close to a breaking point. "Where's Franck?" she asked.

"He should be here with you."

"He hates hospitals like I do. Does he think I'm wrong—refusing the surgery here? Insisting that I go home for care?"

"He doesn't like you waiting another two or three weeks."

"But I trust my family doctor in Prague."

"How long have you known?"

"For a while. I thought I'd finish this year's schedule and then take care of the problems. But it doesn't work that way."

"Kerina, you weren't punishing yourself because of Chan?"

She closed her eyes and lay without moving. The television hummed. The phone rang at the nurses' station. The chair squeaked as Jillian shifted. "Someday would you tell Chandler how much I loved him? How many times I thought about him?"

"Kerina, why not tell him yourself?"

"I can't. I am the person who plays the Strad the way he likes it played. Now—if what the doctors say is true—I'm on borrowed time."

"Borrowed unless you do something about it."

She shook her head. "Jillian, please get me my lipstick— the vermilion red. I don't like the way I look." She applied it and then said, "Stop fretting. I have done the things I wanted most. Playing my Stradivarius around the world. And going back to Everdale to say good-bye to Bill." Her eyes glistened. "And finding the house that was always there in the back of my mind."

"The country house on a hill—the one with the gazebo?"

"Yes. It was just like I pictured it, with a wisteria vine growing over the fence. And the gazebo by the old swing." Her face glowed with unexpected happiness. She laced her fingers contentedly as she said, "The autumn leaves brushed across the path. I stood beneath the trellis where the roses grow in the spring and summer. And I heard the wind whistling by the porch. Have you ever heard the wind whistling, Jillian?"

"Sometimes. I think it's whistling outside now."

"Not like it did in Everdale." Another coughing spasm seized her. Jillian wiped her brow with a cool cloth.

Kerina pushed her hand away. "I'm all right. Oh, Jillian, have you ever smelled wood burning in the air? The forest lies behind the house where Bill hiked as a boy. I felt like Bill was there with me—like I was a young girl again. Like maybe soon, I will see him again. Does that make sense?"

Jillian nodded as she smoothed the bed linens. "Was it Bill's house?"

"Yes. The one where he grew up. And Chandler's when he was a little boy." She turned toward the windows again. "I was there once before—when Chandler was born. I think that's why the house lingered in the back of my mind as something good and peaceful."

In spite of her pallor, her eyes glowed. She had stepped back in time, away from her hospital room. "In a way that house brought my son back to me. We sat on the porch together and watched a cloud burst and the rain pour down. And when the rain stopped, we pretended we heard the whippoorwill. It was beautiful, Jillian, to find my son—to sit there with him. To know how well his parents have raised him. To know what a fine young man he is. He is so much like Bill."

"Then tell Chandler. Tell him how proud you are of him."

"I cannot do that. And you must not tell him as long as I am alive. I want to go on living—but in case I don't see Chandler again—I want him to remember me the way he saw me in Vienna."

"And if he calls me? Is he to know you are ill?"

"No, just send him my love."

Thirty

Jillian left the hospital and walked the two blocks to the subway, brushing shoulders with strangers and jumping at the sound of her own footsteps. The eerie wait in the underground and the deafening roar of the train speeding into the station rattled her nerves. She sank into the first vacant seat and dozed with her head bobbing against the grubby window until she reached her destination.

From there, it was another block to her hotel. Wearily, she unlocked the door, hurried inside, and bolted the door. A dim bathroom light cut a path across the rug. Her covers were turned back. A mint lay on her pillow. And the phone was ringing.

Not Kerina! she thought. *No more bad news today. And not Franck.* She didn't want to argue with him.

She grabbed the receiver. "Jillian Ingram."

"Jillian, it's Chandler."

For Jillian the only breath of kindness the whole day was hearing his voice. Picturing his face. Caressing him over the long distance wires. She burst into tears.

"Honey, what's wrong?"

She couldn't tell him. She said, "It's so good to hear from you. Where are you? Are you here in New York City?"

"I'm in Washington. About to catch my plane to O'Hare."

"You're not coming to New York?"

"Can't. Too many loose ends to tie up. Don't cry, Jill. We'll see each other in Los Angeles. I can hardly wait."

She couldn't tell him the concert was canceled. Couldn't tell him Kerina was ill. "Did Everdale go all right?"

His voice changed. "I'm glad it's over."

"Did you find what you were looking for?"

"I know who my birth parents are, if that's what you mean. My father is dead, and my mother walked out on me again. So the search is over. Done with."

Kerina? Were they talking about the same person? The woman who had glowed when she said she had seen her son again?

"Now I have to go home and tell Mom and Dad what I did."

She wanted to say, "They know."

"I have to go, Jill. That's my boarding call. I love you."

Had she heard him correctly?

"Jill? I have something I want to ask you when you get to Los Angeles. It may be rushing things a bit, but I'm sure—"

She was left with nothing but the dial tone. Her tears came in torrents. She kicked off her shoes and flopped on her bed, weeping into the pillow. It was too much with Kerina ill and Chandler expecting her in Los Angeles next week.

Two hours later the phone rang again. She still lay on her bed, bathed in self-pity. Perhaps it was Chandler calling from O'Hare. "Hello," she said breathlessly. "Chandler?"

"Miss Ingram, this is the concierge at the desk. You have a guest. A Mr. Joel Gramdino."

Gramdino here at the hotel? "Does he want me to come down?"

"He's already on his way up."

She leaped to her feet, splashed cold water in her eyes and rubbed them dry. The disaster in her room came into glaring focus. She swept the rumpled spread with her hand, shoved the loose items of clothing back into her suitcase, picked up the wet towel, and swung her door open as

Gramdino stepped off the elevator. He came toward her in a brisk stride, a wide grin on his face, his glistening silver hair adding its touch of dignity.

"What are you doing here, Joel?"

"Had to see you."

"Lucky for you, Franck and Kerina are not here."

His smile faded. "I know. I'm sorry about Miss Rudzinski. Will she be all right?"

"We don't know. It's very serious."

"I know that too." He shoved the wrinkled bedding aside and sat down, his long legs stretched out in front of him. "I have two men over at Harkness Pavilion. They're keeping me informed."

"She's sick, Joel. She's not going to walk out of this country with a painting."

"Granted. But Franck Petzold might."

"What are you talking about? The rest of the concert tour is canceled. So you can call off the guards from the art museums and the hospital. We're heading back to Europe."

"Commercial line?"

"Franck arranged for a private jet from one of his friends."

"An art collector from Moscow?"

"I don't know, Joel."

"I'll alert Kennedy International."

"Don't. Franck always uses a private field in New Jersey."

"So he has all the bases covered."

"He usually does."

Gramdino whammed the mattress with his fist. "That man is constantly outwitting me. You'd think I'd be wise to it by now."

"Don't blame yourself. We had no idea we would have to fly home early. I can't remember Kerina ever canceling a performance. She's gone onstage with a raging fever and miserable migraines."

"At least it will keep some unsuspecting art collector from getting a headache. We blew it when Petzold caught the subway at Forty-Second today. Got off at the next stop. Our man lost him."

"It's not unusual for Franck to catch a train and switch destinations two stops later. Or take three taxis to go a mile. That's just Franck. But no paintings were stolen this trip."

"One." Joel turned his kind gaze on Jillian. "Petzold didn't need a concert this time, nor Kerina playing a Strauss waltz."

She looked down at her hands. "What's missing?"

"A Rembrandt etching taken from a major auction house. A flat copper plate that was about to go on the auction block for a high sum—but stolen during a blackout. It was dark long enough for Petzold to walk out the front door."

"A dozen others must have left at the same time."

"Petzold was caught on the surveillance cameras in the side room where the Rembrandt was on display."

"You can't plan a robbery based on a power outage."

"He just took advantage of it. Crazy as it seems, Jillian, I don't think of the man as a thief. He's obsessed with art."

"That's no excuse for stealing to fill his coffers now." She picked at a thread on her slacks. "Joel, he won't risk taking a painting out of this country. How could he?"

"Aboard that private jet."

"Then you'll arrest him at the airport? Think about Kerina."

"Forget her. I'm depending on you. You'll be with them the whole flight. Brooks Rankin wants Petzold back in Europe. Arrest him here and we'll never recover the rest of the missing pieces."

"You're using me and the Rembrandt etching for bait."

"That's right, sweetheart."

Earlier that morning at the auction house, sweat beaded Franck Petzold's forehead as he studied a Rembrandt etching. He circled the display case. On one side was a painting of an ancient harbor by an unknown artist. On the other was the unsullied etching by Rembrandt. Desire for ownership sent an adrenaline rush through his body. As it peaked, the electricity went out. The room went black. He reached blindly into the display case, tore the plate from its base and tucked it inside his trousers, flat against his abdomen. He notched his belt and buttoned his jacket.

Panic gripped him. He wondered how he could get out of the auction house without a security guard stopping him or the copper plate tripping an alarm. Urgency forced him to feel his way in the darkness. He had only as long as it took the in-house engineer to reach the fuse box; then lights would flood the room. Or an emergency generator would kick in and the theft be discovered. He inched along the wall, stumbling through the darkened room into an auditorium filled with disgruntled clients.

"Be calm," the auctioneer shouted. "We'll have the lights back on in moments. Keep seated. Everything will be all right."

A woman grabbed Franck. He recoiled at the clammy hand clutching his and at the stench of so much perfume in one room. They were in the hall now, light from the windows making it easier to move through the lobby. The woman dashed for the door. He followed, the copper plate slipping an inch as he ran. A guard grabbed him.

"My wife. She's ill."

He pointed to the woman fleeing through the doors. The guard stepped back, and Franck was outside hailing a taxi, his shirt wet with sweat, but the thrill of escape empowering him.

Back at the hotel, he called the airfield in New Jersey and confirmed that the ultrafast business jet would be ready for departure by ten. "Do you have a nurse standing by?" he asked.

"Yes, and food on board. How many will be traveling, sir?"

"Two passengers. I won't be able to accompany them."

He called the second pilot and said, "I want to leave by eleven o'clock this evening. Midnight at the latest."

For seconds after alerting the pilots, Franck stared into space. My *plan will work,* he decided.

Separate planes. Separate destinations. The arrangement was only temporary. He would take refuge in his home on the Black Sea and find quiet and comfort surrounded by his paintings. But he refused to remain in exile. Things would calm down. Jillian had never trusted him, but to have Kerina ill and no longer believing in him, that was the worst. Stealing the Rembrandt added to his problems. He had lost the man who had followed him onto the subway at Forty-Second Street, but someone else might take up the chase.

Another plan sparked, a plan that would take the Rembrandt plate safely out of the country. Franck ordered a sandwich and a pot of black coffee from room service. He called the bell captain to arrange for a limousine at the curb by seven, a bellhop to collect the luggage ten minutes earlier. Then he dialed the concierge's desk and requested fabric glue, an X-acto knife and thick tape to be sent to his room immediately.

Impatiently, he said, "Try a stationery store or a sewing center. Or if you have a seamstress in the hotel, ask her."

The small packet from the seamstress arrived shortly after his sandwich. He tipped generously so the tip would be remembered instead of the fabric glue. He had already opened Kerina's violin case. The Strad lay cushioned on the pillows; the bow, the extra strings, the small wrap of rosin, the mute beside it.

With the Do-Not-Disturb sign hanging on the doorknob, he closed the room door and locked it once again. He loosened his watch, removed it, and placed it where he could keep abreast of the hour. Pouring himself a third cup of coffee, he set it on the bedside table, away from the velvet lining.

Removing the thin, lightweight Rembrandt etching from beneath his mattress, he studied it again. Touched it. Ran his hand over Rembrandt's signature. Visualized the very spot in his home on the Black Sea where the plate would one day hang. He had rescued it from the auction house, kept it from the hands of some collector who would bury it like a lost treasure.

Casting one more admirable glance at Rembrandt's work, he wrapped the copper plate in tissue paper. He, who rarely smiled, smiled to himself. He had come into possession of a masterpiece. Its worth lay in the eye of the beholder. He had felt that way in the side room of the auction house. He felt that way now.

Eyes narrowing, he bent over Kerina's violin case. He prided himself in his steady hands as he took the X-acto knife and worked the velvet lining in the lid free, each movement of his hand precise, fractional—the opening just wide enough to slip the copper plate behind it. Meticulously, he taped the plate securely in the lid, double-checking to make certain that the metal and the beautiful velvet lining did not touch.

His gaze strayed to the watch. Time was still in his favor. He was a careful, methodical man. Still smiling to himself, he secured the torn edge with fabric glue. Pressed it gently. Stepping back, he inspected his work and was satisfied.

Genuine sorrow stirred as he picked up Kerina's violin. The Strad and Kerina were one. Gently he lowered it into the case and locked the bow in place. He had ordered the bow for her in Paris. It cost him thousands of dollars. He had no regrets. She treasured it as she had always treasured his friendship. Putting it down was like letting her go. She who had brought him such joy.

He closed the lid and twenty minutes later left the hotel, glancing over his shoulder and out the back window of the limousine as they drove to the Harkness Pavilion. Jillian and Kerina were waiting for him in the hospital lobby.

"You didn't forget anything?" she asked as they drove off.

"Kerina, if I forget all else, I remember your violin."

When they reached the New Jersey airfield, Franck stared out the window. No cars followed them. His confidence perked as he spotted the two jets ready for takeoff. They slid cautiously past some vintage war planes. Parked beside them was a Piper Malibu Mirage with white leather upholstery, a Cessna P210, and an old Beech Starship with its futuristic nose.

He ordered their driver toward the company jet where the pilot waited for them. The pleasant-faced young man was a capable type, his grin easy and reassuring, his leather jacket zipped midway. He escorted Kerina from the limousine, half-carrying her up the steps into the luxury and safety of the jet.

When he reappeared moments later, Franck handed the violin to him. "This is gold to Miss Rudzinski." *Gold to me.* "Would you stow this safely on board until you land in Vienna?"

"As you like, sir. I'll keep it up in the cockpit."

Kerina would rage with the violin out of her sight, but the transatlantic flight would allow time for the glue to hold securely. Once the concerts in Austria were over, he'd have Kerina ship the Rembrandt to him. She owed him that small favor.

When he joined Kerina inside the plane, her long fingers caressed his hand. "I could have flown commercial, Franck."

"You'll be more comfortable this way. Less publicity."

"Jill sent out a press release before we left."

"The publicist to the end," he said bitterly.

Kerina lay on a French daybed with stuffed pillows behind her head and a comforter tucked around her waist. "Sit with me, Franck. I don't relish flying over the ocean."

"I want you to rest. Jillian will stay in here with you. If you need pain medication or sleeping pills, just ask."

She looked around. "Franck, where's my violin?"

"It's stored safely with the other luggage."

She yawned and eased back against the pillows. "I won't need anything to sleep. What are you going to do?"

"Finalize our concert plans. Talk with the customs agent."

He wondered whether she believed him. Her fingers pressed deeper into his hand; those dark eyes searched his face. She suspects, he thought. She has guessed that I am not going with her. He wanted to hold her hand against his cheek and never let her go. Always Kerina had been the joy of his life. What right did she have to be ill? To die? To be anywhere without him?

"After the concerts, I want to go home to Prague. And then you must go away to Moscow, Franck. For your own safety."

"Go with me—"

He wanted her to understand. Every beautiful art piece had been stolen for her, displayed even now in his well-secured home on the Black Sea. His soul agonized that she thought him a common thief. How else would she describe what he had done? No display of Rembrandt and Degas and VanStryker gracing the home he had prepared for her would dim the truth of how he had obtained them.

I did it for you, he thought. *The concert halls of the world. Your success. Your acclaim—all my doing.* But now—now he accepted what she had always known. They would never be one.

As she closed her eyes, he leaned down and kissed her forehead. Her eyes fluttered open. "Where are you going, Franck?"

"I told you. To make certain everything is under control."

"And after that?" Her hand felt like ice on his as she said, "You're not going with us, are you?"

"Not this time, my dear. I'll join you later."

She smiled, knowingly. "Will you ever come back?"

"When you really need me."

He stopped at the cockpit and said, "Have a safe journey, gentlemen. And take care of Miss Rudzinski for me."

"We will," the pilot said. "We have a nurse on board. Don't worry, Mr. Petzold." He patted the instrument panel. "I've flown this baby for years. We deliver our cargo on time and safely." He reached back and shook Franck's hand. "We're ready for takeoff."

As Franck prepared to leave, Jillian caught his eye. She did not ask about the violin, nor why he was not flying with them. But she said, "Franck, the customs agent checked the luggage."

"And you passed inspection?" he asked.

"Of course. Isn't that the way you planned it?"

Outside in the cool evening, Franck watched Kerina's plane taxi and soar; then, with his eyes to the tarmac, he walked the few yards in the darkness and boarded the second private jet.

Jokhar Gukganov wore his seat belt and his perpetual frown as he watched Franck drop into the seat beside him. Jokhar was a business man who dealt in art and fraud with equal pleasure and yet maintained a successful and thriving design company in Moscow. Owning a private jet was part of his company image.

"Did you lay the groundwork for a branch company in New York?" Franck asked in Russian.

Jokhar pulled out a tin of caviar and opened it. "I don't like the American tax system. But business talks give me a legitimate reason for being here. I do not like doing business with Americans, but," he said, "I enjoy their art museums."

Their jet was safely airborne and Jokhar's eyes hard and cold as he turned to face Franck. "Did you bring it?"

"The Rembrandt etching? Of course not. It's packed securely in the lining of Kerina's violin case."

"Then you are a bigger fool than I thought you." His skin looked sallow in the dim light of the cabin. "Or do

370

you plan to let them arrest Miss Rudzinski for robberies you committed?"

Franck would never harm Kerina. Sending the Rembrandt in her violin case was the only way to keep it out of Jokhar's hands. He closed his eyes. If he said anything, Jokhar would know how deeply he cared about Kerina.

Thirty-one

Chandler had walked away from the Everdale Cemetery at peace with his father. But he had half-brothers, brothers without faces. He wanted to touch base with the VanBuriens and bridge the gap their father had left behind. Calling Chicago from his hotel room in Washington, he blurted out his identity to the woman on the other end and asked that her family meet him when his plane touched down at O'Hare the next morning.

"Never!" she told him.

A man took over the phone. "Who is this?" he demanded.

"Chandler Reynolds—Ashley Reynolds's son."

"We don't know any Reynoldses."

"Celeste VanBurien does. Ashley was Bill VanBurien's sister."

Neither name set well with the man on the other end. "I'm her son. What do you want from us?"

A better reception than I'm getting, Chandler mused. "I want to meet you. I'm your younger half-brother."

Moments later, the man demanded the flight information and without saying good-bye slammed the receiver in Chandler's ear.

All through his boyhood, Chandler wanted a brother. For a while Randy Williams filled that void. Now as he stepped off the plane at O'Hare and glanced around at those in the waiting area, he had a sinking feeling that Celeste Van-Burien—Sanborg now—and her sons were not coming to meet him. Just when he was ready to strike out for the gate to catch the flight to Akron, he spotted a man with sharp blue eyes and a thick blond mustache who looked like the pictures of Bill VanBurien. Their eyes locked.

"Skip?" Chandler asked.

"No, I'm Jeffrey. Jeff VanBurien."

Chandler glanced around again.

"I'm alone. Mother said she didn't know you existed until last evening's phone call. She'd like to keep it that way."

"So she didn't know about me?"

"No; my dad didn't stick around long enough to tell us. But after three glasses of wine last night, Mother was sorry too—for you. She said Bill left too many black marks on the world."

"And Skip?"

"He doesn't know what your game is. If it's money, he'll have his lawyer meet with you."

Thanks for the welcome mat, Chandler thought. "No need for a lawyer. I just wanted to meet you and apologize."

"Apologize? For what? Not dropping in on us sooner? Believe me, we didn't know there was a little black sheep in the family."

He had been called a lot of names, but this one felt like acid tossed in his face. He braced himself for the man's darts. "All my life I thought you and Skip were my cousins. The side of the family that didn't want any part of us."

"You should have kept it that way. My mother will drink herself sick over this one." Without a flicker of warmth in his expression, Jeff said, "I know my way around O'Hare. Why don't we catch the Airport Transit System to your transfer point? That way you won't be running in the wrong direction at the last moment."

And that way, you make certain I leave town, Chan thought.

As they rode the conveyor belt, they shouted above the noisy crowd around them. Pushing their way into the Transit System, they kept exchanging barbs.

"Too bad you don't have more time, Chandler. I'd take you down by the old Water Tower. Kind of symbolic here in Chicago. It withstood the fires a hundred years ago—better than our family handled the flames that my father set."

"My birth mother had a picture of Dad standing in front of it." *Mother. Dad.* The words flowed easily.

"The violinist?" Jeff snarled. "I remember her. Young. Pretty. Played with the Elgin Symphony Orchestra here in Chicago. That's when Dad met her. And after that, our lives tumbled."

"I thought she played with the Chicago Symphony Orchestra."

He shrugged. "You may be right. Doesn't matter much with him dead now. Nothing mattered until my mother found out they were meeting at the Millhurst Inn. A limestone bed-and-breakfast in Oak Park. A romantic spot that overlooks the Fox River."

"I'm sorry."

He wanted to knock the boulder-size chip off Jeff's shoulder as he said, "You wanted to know about my side of the family. Mother lives in Oak Park in one of the fine old homes in Chicago. If Bill VanBurien had lived, we might not have fared so well."

And she might not be drinking heavily.

"I was just a kid when my grandfather hired a detective to follow Dad. Seemed to make my mother feel better somehow. Your mother," he said bitterly, "and my father had strange tastes. The planetarium. Hemingway's Museum in Oak Park. Old mansions, like the Cantigny. Sometimes they just rode the Downtown Loop."

"Were your parents in love?" Chandler asked.

"The charming Celeste and handsome, ambitious Bill from nowhere—in love? My mother thought so in the beginning. She adored him. Thought he was going places in the corporate world. That fit in with Mother's plans. She ignored the fact that he came from a little town in the South.

She hadn't been around for the Civil War. Didn't think they'd end up fighting." Jeff gave his firm jaw a vigorous rub. "Sometimes I wonder how they ever got together. They had different agendas. Like my brother and I."

When they reached the boarding area, Jeff jammed his hands into his pockets and paced by the terminal windows. In the reflected glass, he looked like a blade-thin weed that had blown free from the edge of the swamp and been carried by the wind through thirty-four troubled years. If they had been kids they could kick and scream and throw their toys or wrestle each other to the ground. But they were grown men unable to hide their smoldering resentments. Still Chandler wanted to bridge the gap.

"You're my brother. Doesn't that count for something, Jeff?"

Jeff glared at Chandler, his slouching six-foot-four frame carrying the weight of the world. "Is it money you want?"

"Money? No, your friendship." *Your respect,* he thought.

"I don't buy that. You must want something."

As Jeff's voice rose, a woman passenger vacated her seat, not waiting to snatch up all her parcels. An older lady stayed where she was, head bobbing, her wobbly fat legs crossed at the ankles. Chandler expected security guards on the double—an arrest instead of a boarding pass. He had to give it one last try.

"I didn't plan to dump the past on you, Jeff. I just wanted to be friends. To trace my roots."

Suddenly Jeff stopped in front of the old woman and faced Chandler head-on. His fists were still jammed in his pockets, his lips tightly drawn as he fought off thirty years of bitterness, but he said, "You're really okay, Chandler."

The woman shook her head. "Then stop making fools of yourselves in public. Hire a lawyer if you have to and settle this thing between you. You're big boys now. All grown up."

Jeff grinned down at her sheepishly. "I am a lawyer."

"The lawyer your brother would hire if he didn't trust me?"

"That's right, Chandler. One of my associates, most likely. Reynolds here is my brother," he told the woman.

"All the more reason to be friends. So shake hands."

"She's right, Jeff. And I'm not here for a cut in the insurance or Dad's stock assets. I didn't know he had any."

"It's all gone anyway. The stock money reinvested."

"I have no claims on a dead man. I just wanted to put a face to him." His own facial muscles worked overtime. "All my life, I wanted a brother, Jeff."

"Me too." His voice was as thin as his lips. His eyes darted toward the boarding gate and back to Chandler.

"You have Skip."

"They left the wrong parcel at my house. He's like our mother. Proud. Rich. Making a mess of his second marriage. We've never been close. We're at opposite poles."

"But you're his lawyer."

"Because I'm good at it and he needs me."

Something stirred in Chandler's blood too, a part of himself that could be redefined by knowing Jeff better. Brothers. The same blood. The same genes. "I need you too, Jeff."

The boarding call came. "All first-class passengers—"

"I hate to see you walk through that door," Jeff admitted.

"Then let's stay in touch." Chandler scribbled his phone number in exchange for the business card that Jeff offered. "Let's give this brother thing a chance, Jeff."

He made the first move. He dropped his briefcase, stepped forward, and, awkward as it seemed, gave Jeff his first real bear hug from a brother.

In Ohio, Chandler pulled the Williams's van smoothly up to the curb marked for loading and unloading only. He ignored the clamor and honking horns around him as passengers spewed out of cars, tugging their overweight luggage.

He took a deep breath and smiled at Mabel Williams who looked even shorter than her five-two sitting beside him.

She was reticent and shy with a freckled nose—a home-spun woman in a fluffy blue sweater that matched her eyes. She had welcomed him with tears and was still crying. Her husband's absence made the visit harder; Russell and their son's pregnant girlfriend wouldn't be back in Akron until the end of the week.

Chandler had come too soon, spreading Mabel Williams's wound raw again. He cut his visit down to three hours, but she had insisted on driving him to the airport. He offered to take the wheel when he realized freeway driving panicked her.

"Guess this is it, Mrs. Williams. Are you sure you're okay, driving back to your house alone?"

"I'd rather have Russell driving, but with him in Bosnia waiting to fly back with Zineta—well, I'll just have to take a firm grip of the wheel and do it myself."

"I should have taken the airport limo."

"You should have stayed on until Russell and Zineta arrived. You could have used Randy's room—except it's a nursery now."

He had seen it, a room transformed for their grandchild and highlighted in pale shades of blue with little red, white, and blue soldiers painted on the wall.

"Another time." He leaned across to the passenger side and kissed her gently on the cheek. "If I'm going to catch my flight I'd better go. Besides, we're about to be moved on."

She clutched his arm. "It's unbearable to lose a son."

"I can't imagine your grief. Randy was a great guy. I'm so sorry."

Her hand stayed firm on his arm. "Your plans to leave home for good—they're wrong, Chandler. I know we talked about it already—but I had to say it again. Your parents love you—you've told me they do. Walk out, Chandler, and it would be unbearable for them, as though you were dead. I know. Promise me—"

"I'll think about it." But she was right. It was time to go home and set things right with his parents.

He swung out of the car and around to the passenger side. She was already stepping out. "Get your luggage, Chandler, before they make me drive off with it still in the trunk."

He popped the lid and did as she told him, but he made certain she was safely back in the car and belted in. "I'm sorry about Randy. I wish it could have been different."

Her knuckles went bloodless as she gripped the steering wheel. He leaned toward her. "Drive carefully, Mrs. Williams. And remember, what you're doing for Zineta and the baby is special."

"Randy thought she was special too. And if it weren't for you, Chandler, we would never have known about her."

The guard breathed down his neck. "Give us another second," Chandler begged. "She lost her son recently in Bosnia, and we were just talking about him."

The guard backed off. "Try to hurry her along," he said.

"Mrs. Williams, maybe the baby will be a boy."

"I pray so. We decorated the nursery for a boy, hoping. Randy always wanted a son."

"And if it's a girl?"

Her eyes watered. "It will still be Randy's child. Chandler, will Zineta like us? Russell and me?"

"How could she not?"

She blew her nose heartily and said through her tears, "You will come back soon? We'd like you to be the baby's godfather."

"That's quite an honor. I'll come back. That's a promise."

While he waited for the flight to Los Angeles, Chandler called home. "Mom, it's Chandler."

"Chandler." Her apprehension winged over the wires to him. "When are you coming home?"

"I'm flying into L.A. this evening."

"We were so afraid you weren't coming."

"But I am."

"Let me grab a pencil and take down your flight number."

"It's probably there by the phone," he reminded her.

"Yes. I have it. Flight 805. Dad and I will meet you." She sounded rattled, unlike herself. "I'll go to the market right now and buy some steaks for dinner. Or do you want pot roast?"

"Don't cook. I'll take you and Dad out to dinner. You know the Beverly Hills Hotel on Sunset? Join me there at eight."

"That's too extravagant!"

"Grams sent me some money. I'll even have enough for a tip."

"I'll be there, Chandler, but your father, I'm not sure—"

"Tell him we're having dinner together. My treat. So tell Dad I expect him. We have things to talk about."

And with that, he disconnected, smiling.

The jet touched down in Los Angeles, winging through a late afternoon sky rippled with layers of clouds in margarine yellow and flushed with tea rose pink streamers. The color pattern was framed with shades of gray—pelican toward the patches of blue, a familiar threatening lead gray on the horizon. The clouds would alarm Ashley but were insignificant from the pilot's report.

Chandler's upgrade to first class allowed him a speedy exodus. The prettiest of the flight attendants stood primping by the kitchenette, the same one who had smothered him with attention during the flight. He caught her flicker of disappointment as he ducked his head to exit the cabin alone.

As he strode briskly up the ramp, pain shot through his leg, reminding him that healing after all these months was still in progress. Minutes later as he waited at the baggage claim, the turnabout started spinning. He snapped up his suitcase and was out of the terminal in line for a taxi ahead of other passengers.

Chandler whistled. "Taxi!"

"Where to?" the driver asked as he flagged the meter.

Chandler tossed his luggage on the backseat and tumbled in behind it. "The Beverly Hills Hotel on Sunset Boulevard."

Ashley checked her polished nails for the tenth time, biting back the desire to check the speedometer. David stayed in the fast lane, keeping with the flow of traffic, then inching above the sixty-five limit. She glanced at him, determined to warn him to slow down, but the lines at his well-shaped mouth were tight. Advice from her corner would only anger him.

She hunched in her seat. "David, I'm frightened."

"Of our son?"

"He may not call himself that any longer."

David's square jaw clamped. "He's legally ours. Has been since the day he was born. Nothing can change that."

Points one, two, three—like his disciplined sermons. She visualized him in his clerical robe, expounding boldly from the pulpit, the smooth orator preaching to others about family relationships. She saw none of this boldness in the man sitting beside her. It was the old David groping his way through a crisis. Proud and determined, yet struggling.

"David."

He shot her a glance, his heavy-lidded eyes too bright.

"I keep thinking of Chandler when he was a little boy."

His grip tightened on the wheel, his eyes catching the traffic through the mirrors. "But he's a man now."

"He was little once. He needed us then."

"We don't know what Everdale has done to him."

I know what it did to me, she thought. *It brought me my greatest joys and my deepest shame. But it was once a happy place in my childhood, and Chandler had his beginnings there.*

380

"He's like you, David. He'll reason things through."

"And you think that's why he asked us to drive into Beverly Hills for dinner so he can tell us everything is fine? He could have done that at home over one of your dinners."

"Maybe he likes dining out."

"Maybe he wants to tell us good-bye in a public place. What right did that woman have to come back into his life?"

She rested her hand on his arm. "Don't be bitter about Kerina. I know she regrets giving him away."

A tremor shook David's deep voice. "Oh, Ashley—how I love that boy."

"When he was little you used to tell him that. Why don't you tell him again, David?"

He grabbed her hand, his fingers locking with hers. "He should know that I love him. We've been over all of that."

He took the off-ramp at a good clip. Now he threaded his way through the traffic on Sunset Boulevard, traveling several blocks, going past the Los Angeles Country Club toward their date with Chandler.

When they saw the hotel to their left and the Will Rogers Memorial Park to their right, he said, "There's no turning back. If we want our son in our court, we have to listen to him."

Stately palms, potted plants, brightly flowered vines and lush foliage surrounded the well-lit, luxurious hotel, its blinding pink color a landmark in Beverly Hills. Ashley rummaged in her purse for her lip gloss as David stopped for valet parking. He swung around behind the car to open the door for her.

She straightened her St. John jacket. "Do I look all right?"

"You look lovely. Stop fretting."

"But we're not exactly royalty," she whispered.

"Honey, we're the famous Reynoldses. We'll fit right in with the celebrities. You'll see." He took her hand. "Hungry?" he asked as they walked up the red-carpeted entry.

"Scared."

He tucked her hand in his. "Whatever happens, Ashley, we still have each other."

She took a deep breath as they stepped into the glamorous lobby. "And whatever happens, David, we must tell Chandler how much we love him."

Chandler stood as the maitre d' led his parents to his candlelit table, elegantly set for three with a vase of roses in the center. A chilled bottle of Martinelli's Sparkling Cider lay tilted in the wine basket beside him. He kissed his mother lightly on the cheek, shook David's hand. Once seated, David flicked the napkin on his lap and glanced around for a waiter.

"I've already ordered dinner, Dad. To save time."

"I thought this was to be a leisurely dinner."

His mother's anxious voice intervened. "David, please."

Chandler sent her a ghost of a smile. It was not going the way he planned. He shifted uneasily. "This is a celebration."

"Really?" David asked.

"Yeah, we're celebrating our family. Mine especially. Two mothers. Two fathers. With nobody fessing up to the truth." The pain on his mother's face was more than he could swallow. "Sorry, I didn't mean it that way."

"We had it coming, Chan. Not telling you before. But the longer it went, the harder it was to admit what we had done."

"What *you* did? Doesn't the finger of blame go to Kerina and your brother Bill? All you two did was pick up the pieces."

"What we picked up was the most beautiful baby boy, and we were willing to do anything to keep from losing him. We wanted you, Chandler Reynolds," Ashley said. "We still do. So what are we really celebrating?"

"The truth. I didn't ask you to come here to hurt you. I thought the hotel would be neutral ground—a place where we could start building our lives together again."

"Is that what you want, Chandler?" she asked.

"Of course, Mom." He moved his arm so the waiter could put the salad plate in front of him. "Maybe some good food will loosen your tongue, Dad. You've barely said a word."

David pushed aside his soup bowl and peppered his salad. "You've had a long journey. Do you want to tell us about it?"

"Everdale was tough, but could we talk about that later? Tomorrow. Next week. We have plenty of time to sort things out. And before you ask, I won't know about that government job for months. They do thorough checks on their applicants."

David gave a short chuckle. "We've already had the FBI at our door. I couldn't imagine what your mother had done. But don't ask us to wait until tomorrow or next week to talk about Everdale. We've already had twenty-six years of not telling you who you are. Not telling you how much you mean to us."

"Why the big secret?"

"We promised Miss Rudzinski—"

"My mother."

David's jaw jerked. "We promised—your mother—that we would never tell you that you were adopted. And we regretted it the minute she left town. And then when Bill—when your birth father died so suddenly, well, son, we didn't know what to do."

"So you did nothing?"

"Please don't, Chandler," Ashley begged. "I'm the one who didn't want to tell you. David has always wanted you to know."

"You're a nurse. You knew the emotional impact of hiding this from me. I couldn't do much about a dead father, but it really hurt when Kerina walked out on me again."

Chandler stirred his salad, thick with ranch dressing. "The only good thing that came out of this was finding out I had brothers. Half-brothers, not cousins. Why, Mom? I remember being a little kid, telling you that I wanted a brother to horse around with and grow up with."

David arched his thick brows. "Someone to bully, maybe?"

Chandler bantered back, flexing his muscles. "I would have been the big brother. King of the mountain."

"We wanted a brother for you. It just didn't work out."

"And you weren't about to bring in some other stranger—some other nameless kid without roots, eh, Dad?"

The candlelight reflected the flush in his mother's cheeks, the pain in her eyes. "You did have cousins, Chan."

"Come on, Mom. Cousins in Chicago—a family that wanted nothing to do with us?" His voice cracked. "That's why Randy Williams meant so much to me. We were grabbing a little of the brotherly horseplay we missed as kids."

"Son, it seems to me that Randy was better than a brother."

"Yeah, Dad. You're right. And when he died in that Bosnian countryside, I felt like I'd lost my own flesh and blood."

Ashley twisted her watchband on her slender wrist. "Randy's child is going to mean a lot to you, isn't he?"

"Yeah. I don't want to lose touch."

"Your mother told me what you were willing to do for Randy's girlfriend."

"You mean marry her to get her to the States? That would have caused a riot in your church."

"That would have been a family matter, not something for the deacons to hash over." David flipped his fork up and down on the china plate. "Chandler, I admire you for what you wanted to do for a friend."

"You would have stood by me in a marriage of convenience?"

"I would never have counseled you that way. Marriage has a deeper foundation than that. But I would have stood by you. You are my son, no matter who brought you into this world."

384

He stared, disbelieving. "You blow my mind, Dad."

"The way you blew mine the first time I held you in my arms. You were the son I always wanted. You still are."

Chandler marveled at the control in David's voice as he asked, "Chan, do you think we can work through this maze of the silent years? Tomorrow we'll take out the paperwork we have in the vault. Your birth records, scanty as they are. We'll lay all the cards on the table, son. All we ask is that you forgive us."

Chandler drained his water goblet. "Jillian keeps reminding me that I owe everything to the two of you." He beckoned to the waiter for more water and drank lustily. "But it was my visit in Akron that turned me around. Mrs. Williams has a big hole in her heart since Randy died. I didn't want to do that to you."

He cleared his throat, but not the traces of anger still there. "I told her about my adoption—told her I was going to write you two off and bury our family relationship."

They sat there stoically. Not even a muscle twitched on David's jaw. "Mrs. Williams said the pain of losing a son is unbearable. She would give anything to have Randy back."

Chandler cracked his knuckles and saw Ashley's gaze slip from his face to his hands, then back to meet his eyes again. "Randy's mom said if I left home angry, I would be as good as dead to you, lost forever—so I came home to work things out."

"Will it work out for the Williamses having Zineta there?"

"Mom, Zineta and the baby are exactly what the doctor ordered. They fixed up Randy's old room. It's an old-fashioned house, but Zineta will think she moved into the Hilton."

He chewed at his lip. "My showing up was rough on Mrs. Williams, but she insisted on taking me to the cemetery." He glanced at David, hesitating before saying, "Randy believed that life—like the buck—stopped here. You got on. You got off. If he believed anything beyond the exodus, I don't know what it was. And if he considered eternity or cried out for it in those final seconds, we'll never know."

David's elbows edged the table, his hands clasped.

"I know what's coming next, Dad, but don't throw words like the sovereignty of God at me. I can hardly say the word, let alone understand it."

"I don't have it all down pat either, son. That's why I spend so much time between Genesis and Revelation."

"That's why you're the solid kind of man you are." Chandler wiped his lips with his napkin. "For all of Randy's not knowing, a part of him will go on living in his child."

He felt the corner of his mouth twist into a wry grin. "Mrs. Williams asked me to be the baby's godparent. That way my next visit won't be so hard on her."

Through soup and salad, they had skirted the real issue of what had brought them to the legendary Polo Lounge. Chandler faced it now. "What you really want to know is what happened to me in Everdale, right? You don't want to wait until tomorrow."

They exchanged guarded glances and nodded. He told them. Between bites of the rest of their five-course dinner, he choked down both the tender meat and his stretched emotions. An hour later, he said, "That covers it. I think Kerina found some of her answers in Everdale too."

He had said Kerina's name without rancor, without revealing how deeply she had hurt him by rejecting him again.

"How was she?" Ashley asked. "I gave her quite a shock when I told her that Bill was dead. I think she always thought she would see him again one day. I don't know why."

"When she stood at your brother's grave, she seemed to let go, laying down both the memories and the red roses on his headstone at the same time. I had a feeling she was putting everything to rest. The dreams. The might-have-beens."

"She really loved him. Did she say anything about Bill?"

"She didn't say much, Mom. We were caught in a cloudburst. You know what the downpours are like in Everdale.

She just took time to put the roses on the grave. How she stood the cold and rain without a coat, I'll never know." He paused, reflecting. "She didn't seem to notice even when I put my raincoat around her shoulders. She cried a little, but I gave her space, and when she turned back to face me she seemed at peace. Kind of proud too. Head thrown back, her face washed with rain and tears. Then she clutched my arm and hung on until we reached the cars."

He peered at them over the rim of his glass. "I didn't know who she was then, but she knew that I was her son, didn't she?"

"Yes. She knew for certain backstage at the Opera House."

"Why didn't she tell me?" Neither parent moved. "Never mind. Right now, I have to grapple with her rejecting me again."

Ashley held him with her eyes. "I don't think you can even comprehend how much she did love you. Does love you." She lifted her hand to keep him from arguing. "I was there the night you were born, Chandler."

"So you told me. I used to think it was a dumb statement. Mothers are usually on hand when their babies are born."

David moved the vase and stared at his son. "Not every baby has two mothers there at the same time. Ashley was there for you, Chandler, from the first cry you ever made."

"I know. But why didn't Kerina want me?"

"We could give you reasons, son, but they would only be excuses. Our own beliefs. She was young. Unmarried. Frightened."

"My brother influenced her decision. Bill didn't always make good choices, but he meant well when he arranged for David and me to adopt you. It was Kerina who insisted on a closed adoption. We would have agreed to anything to have a child in our lives."

He wanted to wrap his arm around her. "It's okay, Mom. Selma Malkoski told me about the closed adoption. She said you and Dad had no choice. We can talk about this later. We'll have time to unravel the mess before I go to London."

"Chandler, what Bill did was not right, but I loved him. He was my brother, my twin—a part of me. Your father was a good man. Strong in so many ways. Fun-loving and musical—that's why he was drawn to Kerina. He was hardworking, caring, but not always dependable. In his crazy, mixed-up way he was giving us part of himself when he arranged for us to adopt you."

"I know. I finally read his letter."

"Then you know he loved you—loved Kerina. Three days after you were born—the day Bill died—he came to the hospital to pick Kerina up. I wanted to confront him, but I didn't. Bill died before I had a second chance."

"Last week when Kerina was in Everdale, she registered at the motel as Kerry Kovac."

"Oh, Chandler, it was the name she used the night you were born. She went full circle—back to where she had left you. Back to the place where she held you for the only time. She loved you, Chandler."

The waiter was there with suggestions for desserts that would melt in their mouths. Chandler had no desire to add sugar to the bitter taste of bile still in his mouth. But he asked, "Mom, Dad—what's it going to be? Mousse? Cheesecake?"

David waved both hands and put his napkin down. Ashley said, "It looks like no dessert for either one of us."

"Well, then!" Chandler glanced up at the waiter. "We'll just have our sparkling cider and call it an evening."

Expertly, the waiter plucked the Martinelli bottle from the wine basket, broke the white seal, popped the lid, and filled the three goblets with bubbling cider before he left the table.

"It's been a painful evening for all of us," Chandler said. "I wasn't sure I could do this when I came here tonight. I can now. During my flight from Chicago, I thought about your sermons, Dad. Especially the ones on forgiveness. There's a lot more to say, but we have time to work out the problems before I move to London. There's just one more thing I need to tell you—"

David gripped Ashley's hand, their eyes focused on Chandler. He saw tears brimming in his mom's eyes, doubt creeping into his dad's. Chandler pushed back his chair and stood.

"I'd like to propose a toast," he said.

A romantic ballad played softly in the background. The muted lights reflected on their faces. He smiled at them, grateful for their years of sacrifice. For the trust they had placed in him. For the truth they had kept back for so long, not out of cruelty but out of their deep affection for him. He knew there would be rough days ahead. Bad moments. Disagreements. But wasn't that part of the triple-braided cord that bound families together?

Ashley and David waited, still holding hands, their eyes never leaving his face. Wrapping his fingers around the stem of the crystal goblet, Chandler saluted them. "Mom—Dad, thank you for loving me from the day I was born."

The lamp light behind them caught the amber glow in the glass. For a moment his mother's gaze seemed fixed on the bubbly effervescence of the cider. Slowly, comprehending, she lifted her face, her soft blue eyes wide with joy again.

Chandler brought the goblet to his lips. "Mom—Dad, I love you."

Thirty-two

January blew in over Southern California with wind and rain and high surf. The storms damaged many homes and toppled electric wires, putting sections of the towns in blackout and turning the hills and slopes into muddy runoffs. While the lowlands dried out, Chandler rode the ski slopes once again. His leg was nearly good as new, gaining strength as he put it to the test. His three months at home looked as pristine as the slopes. The Reynoldses had worked at settling their differences, learning to trust again as a family, disagreeing now and then, but cooling the air before sundown. They were giving each other space. David had full run of the library. The men stayed out of Ashley's garden when she was planting. And Chandler had Saturdays on the slopes at Big Bear.

He didn't know what had happened between his parents. Whatever it was, they were back to overnighting at Lake Arrowhead and seemed at peace with each other, laughing more, loving more. If they were falling in love again—and he suspected they were—his move to London would come easier. He stored up good memories for the days ahead, memories like Thanksgiving and Christmas and his grandmother contentedly baking cookies with Ashley.

The birth of Zineta's son and Thanksgiving turned out to be days worth celebrating, and Christmas rolled in with the taxi driver struggling up to the front door with his arms loaded down with Grandmother Reynolds's suitcases and holiday parcels. Chandler climbed the ladder expecting to hang the traditional star but was handed a glittering angel to hang on the top spike.

Without misgivings, Ashley had said, "We don't need the star this year."

Chandler's schedule was full. He was playing third baseman for a local team and had taken a part-time job driving for Federal Express, the temporary job stretching to thirty-two hours a week. He still had his Saturdays on the slopes and Sundays sitting beside his mother on the front pew rooting for David as he preached on forgiveness and love's triple-braided cord—sacrifice, truth, and trust.

He was not without his gray areas and bouts with hidden rage, but he was slowly coming to terms with the fact that one of the world's most accomplished violinists was his birth mother. Sometimes he awoke in a cold sweat in the middle of the night and lay in the darkened room thinking, *I am Bill VanBurien's and Kerina Rudzinski's son.*

But his loyalty remained with Ashley and David, the mom and dad who had reared him, and his best days included a phone call to Jillian in London or Paris or Prague or a thick letter from her. He had no reason to think that things could be anything but improving when he flipped the calendar to February.

February coasted in with sunny days for Southern California. The worst winter storm of the season hit the East Coast. Kansas waited for meltdown from an ice storm, and the Pacific Northwest braced for the blizzard blowing in from the Gulf of Alaska. According to Jillian's last letter, London was wet and rainy, but she didn't care; she and Kerina were back in the Czech Republic watching a blanket of snow drift softly over the farm outside of Prague.

On the first Thursday in February, Chandler was in the kitchen drinking his morning coffee, wondering how long it would be before he would see his girl again. He folded back the newspaper to the weather report and scanned it, but his thoughts kept wandering back to Jillian—and reluctantly to Kerina.

"Are you deaf?" his dad asked, coming into the kitchen.

Chandler peeked out from behind the weather report. "Huh?"

"The doorbell just rang."

"Did you get it?"

"Thought you would."

"Never mind, you two. I'll get it," Ashley said. She called back, "Chan, you must be moving up in your company. A FedEx truck just pulled up in front of the house."

"You expecting something, Dad?"

David glanced out the kitchen window. "Bad weather. No, looks like a sunny day this time."

"Chandler. David. Come here."

Chandler sloshed his coffee racing his dad for the door. "What's up, Mom? You okay?"

Her creamy cheeks had paled, her usually warm voice seemed too carefully articulated. She pointed to a large, well-wrapped parcel and said, "It's for you, Chandler."

"Wasn't expecting anything, Mom."

"It came from Prague."

He heard the uncertainty in her voice. Saw it in her eyes. "Mom, Jillian didn't say she was sending anything."

"She didn't. It's from Kerina."

Chandler took three strides to the sofa and jabbed the ends of the package with his penknife. He tore away the tissue and each layer of protection and lifted a violin case from the box.

He opened the lid. "It's Kerina's Stradivarius."

For a minute Kerina's words thundered in his head. "Someday, when I no longer need it, I will send my Stradivarius to you. You will play it, won't you, Chandler?"

"Is there a note with it?" Ashley asked.

Chandler pawed through the packing again, and then held out a sheet of pink stationery to Ashley. "Here. You read it, Mom."

Ashley's voice was strained as she read, "This is for you, Chandler, with all my love. Kerina."

Chandler's gaze drifted past Ashley to his father. "It must be her way of saying, 'Sorry, kid, for running out on you.'"

Ashley shook her head in protest. "Chan, don't you remember? She wanted you to have it when she stopped doing her concerts."

"Why would she quit playing? She's still young."

Gingerly, he lifted Kerina's Strad from its case. As he cradled the violin and ran the bow gently over it—much like Kerina had done at the concert hall—Ashley said, "It took a lot of love for Kerina to let you go. She gave your dad and me everything when she gave you up."

He didn't feel strong enough for her tears. "It's okay, Mom. You don't have to explain her. I know it hurt you when she walked out on me again. Believe me, there's no love lost between us."

"She must have had a good reason for letting you go."

"Mom, she never gave me a reason for the first time." He took a deep breath and felt his ribs tighten. "Guess she didn't want to be strapped with an illegitimate kid."

"Don't," Ashley cautioned. "You're only hurting yourself."

His voice wavered. "She recognized me back at the Opera House, didn't she? And she knew who I was when we stood by Bill's grave and didn't say anything. Bet she was too embarrassed to acknowledge me."

David crossed the room to Chandler's side and pressed his shoulder. "Perhaps she thought you weren't ready."

The muscle along Chandler's jaw pulsated as he placed the violin back in its case. "What makes her think this violin will make up for twenty-six years without her?"

He felt out-of-control, the way he did the day Randy blew up in front of him and died. His voice was tight with anger. "Kerina didn't want me when I was born, and she doesn't want me now. She gave me as much of herself as she could when she sent this violin. Well, she can have the old thing back."

He turned from the parcel and stormed toward the front door. Chandler's hand was on the doorknob when he heard his father say, "Let him go, Ashley."

"He can't run forever, David. He has to settle this thing before she dies. Kerina needs him."

"And Chandler needs time to work it out. He'll come through. I'll talk to him."

"No sermons this time, David?"

"He doesn't need a sermon, Ash."

Chandler yanked the door open and slammed it with such force that the living room windows rattled. He took off for the beach and stared gloomily at the ocean that separated him from his birth mother. He tossed his fury back to the horizon, back to God, back to the woman across the ocean who had deserted him so long ago. What did Ashley mean—before Kerina dies? What did he care what happened to her? You live. You die. He had lived without her for a lifetime. She'd been as good as dead all those years. Big deal. She had sent him her violin. For all he knew it could be a fake. Like his mother had been.

He sank down on the sand, a hard-packed sand dune to his back. The wind whipped across the ocean, sweeping in on him like the tide. Still he sat there fighting his demons. And then he closed his eyes and saw Kerina in a beautiful red gown, crossing the stage in Vienna with the Stradivarius in her hand. And he remembered the sad twist at the corner of her mouth and groaned, his wail crashing with the waves and sweeping into shore.

It was dark by the time he went home again. He found Ashley and David waiting for him. "Come join us, Chandler. I've made cocoa and brownies. And your father called your supervisor—told him you couldn't be in today."

"I guess I was so upset I forgot about my job."

"You did have other things on your mind, son. Have you worked them out?"

"Dad, I'm not sure. I'm angry that Kerina thinks she can buy me off with a violin."

"She's ill, son. She went back to Prague for medical care."

"Ill?"

"Seriously ill," Ashley said. "Jillian asked us not to tell you. She said Kerina had the right to be remembered as you saw her in Vienna. She was afraid of losing you if she told you who she was."

"Kerina told me that when she no longer needed the Strad—when she could no longer play it—she would send it to me. But I urged her to keep it in the family."

"She did, son," David said.

As Chandler turned and ran one knuckle gently across Ashley's cheek, she said, "Bill used to do that. You're a lot like him."

"Your Mother's right. You remind us of Bill often. He had his good points, you know."

"Mom, if she had sent the violin to Bill, would he have gone to her?"

"We don't know. He wasn't free, Chandler."

"If he had been free. Divorced. Whatever. Would he have gone then?"

Ashley ran her hand along the back of the chair. "I wish things had been different for Kerina and Bill. But if they had been—and if he were still alive—Bill would already be on the plane. I'm certain of it."

"Then by not going, I'm running out on her. Is that it, Mom? But how can I possibly face her with all of this anger?"

David caught his eye. "You know the answer to that. You know the One who carries burdens."

Chandler stared out the window, seeing nothing but darkness. At last he turned back to them. "Maybe I should thank her in person for the violin. Would you mind if I went?"

Ashley and David exchanged glances. "Go to her. The trip's on your mother and me this time."

"You're not worried about my not coming back?"

Ashley shook her head. "No. You will always be our son."

Chandler's jet touched down for a brief layover in Heathrow before starting on its last ninety-minute flight from London to Prague. After a sleepless flight, he felt jet lag as the plane came in for a bumpy landing at Ruzyne Airport. The terminal looked functional and clean, its interior modern and well-lit, its customs agents polite. He showered and changed in the business lounge and stowed his dirty, wrinkled clothes in his suitcase. After cashing traveler's checks at the money exchange, he took time for roast duck and baked dumplings at a stand-up counter before hiring a red Skoda at the car rental for the last lap of the journey.

When Chandler turned on the ignition, the Skoda took a sputter or two and then rolled smoothly. In spite of the lack of sleep, he drove the nine miles out of his way for a quick overview of the city that had shaped Kerina's life.

A light snowfall capped the city in white. Ice floes churned through the River Vltava. Prague was Bohemian, medieval in architecture, historic with its jutting spires and castles. Wenceslas Square stood as a reminder of the Czechs' quest for freedom. Chandler considered Prague modern in its music and its youth.

As he drove through the city, he smiled at the young people who were strolling through the parks and crossing bridges over the Vltava with snowflakes clinging to their hair and eyebrows.

Turning west in the direction of the White Carpathians, his thoughts geared toward the farm an hour outside of Prague. Kerina had finally come home. He couldn't even guess whether they would ever be free to acknowledge each other. He passed through a charming village and on to the outskirts where the Rudzinski farm still stood. Smoke poured from the farmhouse chimney, and a worn cottage sat on the knoll toward the river. With the ground crackling under his tires, he pulled to a stop near the front door. He knocked and was surprised to see Jillian standing there when the door swung open.

"Jillian!"

He lifted her in his arms and put his frostbitten cheek against hers. "I've missed you," he said and smothered her answer with a kiss.

She pushed him away. "You're cold. Put me down," she said, but she was smiling. She took his hand and pulled him toward the warmth of the old fireplace. "I'm so glad you came. I have hardly slept since you called to say you were coming. And then I worried that you might not find the place."

He looked around. "Where's Kerina?"

"She went out an hour ago."

"Because I was coming?"

"She's uncertain how you will feel about her now."

"Am I supposed to feel some special way?"

"Don't you?"

"I'm just worried about her health."

Jillian's sapphire eyes lost their luster. "If that's your only concern, Chandler, you should have stayed at home." Jillian brushed her cheek against his sleeve. "So far, you can't get past the thought of her giving you up for adoption. I see her for who she is today. And that is someone special. Someone caring."

"Jillian, I came because she sent me her violin."

"She told you she would."

"She told me she would keep it in the family. That's how I knew she was finally acknowledging me. But I didn't want to come at first, Jill. I dragged my feet until my mom said that Bill would have already been on the plane rushing to Kerina's side."

"Wise woman that mother of yours." She squeezed his hand. "Just be kind to Kerina. Don't pretend. She wants you to be yourself." She reached up and turned his face toward hers. "Kerina is dying. That's why she sent the violin. The cancer has spread to her spine and lungs."

"Isn't anything being done for her?"

"She finally had surgery two months ago, but she waited too long."

He rubbed his gloved hands together. "Then I'd better go to her." He still sounded duty-bound, as though Kerina were his project. "Where is she?" he asked.

"Out walking by the river."

"Out in this miserable weather? She'll get pneumonia."

"She doesn't care, Chandler. The prospect of dying the way she's going to die is not an easy one. You're not going out by the river to see some violinist. She's the woman who brought you into this world."

"That's the woman who gave me away. I've spent a lifetime staring in the mirror and thinking that Chandler Reynolds was staring back at me."

"He was."

"Was he? I was living a lie. I am almost twenty-seven years old and only recently found out I was born out of wedlock."

"Big deal," she snapped back. "That wasn't your doing. And it certainly didn't bother Ashley and your dad when they adopted you. You're legal. Adoption makes you legal." Her sapphire eyes were blistering hot. Sparking. "They did a good job raising you. And whatever pain and loss and mourning Kerina had to live through, you didn't. She did what she thought was best for you." Jillian tossed her head, her long, tawny hair swinging back from her angry face. "Grow up, Chandler. The fact that you were born is proof enough that Kerina wanted you from the beginning. And the fact that two of the nicest people in the world adopted you is worth a million."

He started laughing.

"And what's so funny?"

"You." He shrugged, buttoning up his coat. "I'm wondering if you will always be this hard to live with."

She looked beyond him, avoiding his gaze, her cheeks turning scarlet. "Do you want me to go with you, Chandler?"

"No; like you said, this is between Kerina and me."

"But first there are two people who want to meet you before you go."

"Kerina's parents?"

"Your grandparents, Chan."

Grandparents!

She led him into a kitchen that was warmed both by the wood-burning stove and by the sweet smile on the face of Kerina's mother. If he had expected a plump woman in a black shawl or a tottery old man in overalls, he had guessed wrong. The man, an alert eighty-year-old, sat in a pair of jeans and a thick wool sweater with his thin legs crossed and an unlit pipe bobbing from his mouth. He scowled from under heavy brows, daring Chandler to be anything but polite to his wife. To himself.

Chandler's gaze fled back to the woman in the chair beside him, her skin tissue-thin like her body. Their chairs were inches apart, her wrinkled hand grasping for her husband's. She looked like she had weathered a long, tough journey through life and had triumphed over the fate thrown her way. As late as these last few weeks since Kerina had come home to them ill, Chandler was certain they had traveled to hell and back, agonized in the journey, and found peace on the return.

Chandler could not take his eyes from his grandmother's face. Though she looked fragile, she was strong—he saw it in her expression. Looking down at her, he felt as though he had come home, home to part of himself. Her name was

Gretchen, and she was as lovely as Kerina with silver hair and kindly dark eyes and a smile of welcome on her wrinkled face.

He wondered if they knew about him, and Jillian solved that by saying, "Darlings, this is your grandson Chandler."

He whipped off his gloves and dropped to one knee between their chairs. He felt the old man's strong grip on his arm and the tender gesture of the woman's hand on his head. "We've waited a long time to meet you," she said.

Chandler spoke apologetically in English. They seemed to understand. "I didn't realize until minutes ago that Kerina's parents would be my grandparents."

"And do you mind?" his grandmother asked.

"No. No, it's nice. Nice having more grandparents."

Odd, he thought. *I can accept my grandparents much more readily than the mother who gave me away.*

"Call me as you please," the man said gruffly. "But my name is Karol. Tell me, do your parents know that you've come here?"

"Yes, sir. They sent me with their blessing."

"Young man, if you cannot love our daughter—cannot forgive her, then go. Go back home now before she knows you are here."

"Don't, Karol," Jillian said. "I told Kerina he was coming today. She wants him to stay. Let them work it out together."

Chandler heard his grandmother's stifled sob. As her hands cupped his face, he sensed more than the warmth of her skin against his cheeks. He felt loved. "Go to Kerina," she murmured. "My daughter needs you."

He nodded. "If Jillian sets me in the right direction, I'll be on my way."

He stood, shook the man's firm hand, and kissed his grandmother's cheek. "You're certain you have room for me here?"

Jillian turned to Chandler with a relieved smile. "Your grandmother told me that she's had your room ready for twenty-six years."

"I didn't know they knew about me."

"They guessed—and then Franck confirmed it a long time ago. We'll have soup simmering in the kettle when you get back."

As he put his hand on the knob, she said, "I'm sorry about Los Angeles. I couldn't tell you that Kerina had canceled the concert there. But on the phone you were going to ask me something when I got there."

"You never got there," he teased.

Disappointment shadowed her eyes. He smiled. "I told you then I might be rushing things, but—I love you. Right now with Kerina sick, it may be the wrong time to ask you."

"Go on," his grandfather said from the doorway. "Ask her."

Chandler cleared his throat. "I want you to marry me, Jill."

Jillian stood there blushing, speechless. He brushed her cheek with a kiss. "Never mind, sweetheart. I'll catch your answer later," he said and went out the door on a run.

Chandler found Kerina huddled on the steep embankment, wrapped warmly in her winter Burberry, a thick woolen scarf around her neck, and long, black boots snug against her legs. She seemed unaware of him as she watched great chunks of ice and time slowly floating from her. She half turned as he approached, startled when she saw him.

"Chandler." Her heel slipped on the wet concrete as she tried to push herself up.

"No, don't get up," he warned. "I'll come to you."

He slid down on the hard stones beside her and wondered why she was here alone so close to the deep, icy waters. A hazy winter mist swirled above the river, leaving frozen diamond ringlets in Kerina's hair. That sculpted, oval face was thinner now, the hazel eyes dull and hollow from illness.

"What are you doing sitting out here in the middle of winter, Kerina? You'll freeze to death."

"I've only been here a few minutes."

"Jillian said you left the house an hour ago."

"Oh, yes. But I've been walking."

"Jillian said you hated the winters."

"Not anymore. It's so peaceful here. Everything so still."

Everything frozen, he thought. *Your hands like ice.*

She hugged her knees and wrapped her coat more securely around them. "I grew up along this river. Did you know that?"

"No, but we weren't talking about the river."

"I was. I like the Danube best, but this is peaceful too with the blue mist rising. I've always wondered where the mist went. I think it is much like life. Lifting. Drifting. Something lovely and mysterious that we can never hold on to." She turned to him. "Why did you come, Chandler?"

"I wanted to thank you for the violin."

"All the way from California just to say thank you?"

"And to see you. How are you?"

"Better—now that you're here." Her lips were turning blue. "If you've come all this way to see me, then you know who I am, don't you?"

He blew on his hands and nodded.

"Do you mind?"

"Does it matter?"

"It has always mattered to me, Chandler."

She looked grieved. Awkwardly, he reached out and put his arm around her shoulders. "Even on my birthdays?" he asked.

"Always on your birthdays. I used to wonder what you were doing. What you looked like. Whether you were happy."

Snow began to fall again, the tiny flakes melting as they drifted across her face. "Kerina, you're cold. We're both cold."

With exquisite care, he unraveled his own wool scarf and placed it around her head and tight against her cheeks, tossing the end flaps over her shoulders.

Her tears fell with the snow. "I wanted you to walk in the woods and climb mountains and play a musical instrument."

"I know."

"I wanted your parents to love you, Chandler."

"They did. I've done all those things you wanted me to do." The chill burrowed through to his spine. "Kerina, we can't stay here. We'll both freeze to death."

He pulled off his leather gloves and tugged them gently over her slender hands, making them look bulky and big, those same smooth hands that had written eleven wishes for him on scented stationery right after he was born. He moved closer, putting his arm around her again, allowing his body heat to warm her. "There, that's better, isn't it, Kerina?"

She couldn't take her eyes from him. She seemed to be drinking him in, filling memory's cup with mental snapshots of his face. "I never thought I'd see you again," she whispered.

"I didn't think you wanted to see me."

Her lower lip quivered. Perhaps from the cold. "We can't sit here another minute," he insisted. "We'll get pneumonia. Let's go."

She didn't budge. "There's a letter in my pocket you must read."

Oh, God, he prayed. *Not a suicide letter.* He pulled it free and opened it with numb fingers. "My darling Kerina," it began.

"This is a personal note, Kerina. I can't read it."

"You must. It's from your father."

Chandler glanced at the date. The letter had been written three days after his birth. He felt slack-jawed as he read through the three pages, embarrassed in places, angry at others. His uncle, his father pouring out his love to a woman he had no intention of seeing again. Could not see again. How much pain she had borne for daring to love Bill VanBurien. Chandler was ready to shove the letter back in her pocket when he reached the last few lines.

"Someday," Bill VanBurien had written, "our son will know who you are. I can only hope that by then you will both find it in your hearts to forgive me. My mother always said that a forgiving heart goes a long way toward happiness. My dear Kerina, I want nothing more than for you to be happy again."

Chandler folded the letter and put it back in her pocket. "I didn't know he was my father when I saw you in the Everdale Cemetery. All my life, he was Uncle Bill. Nothing more. Nothing less. I didn't know him. I didn't care about him."

The gloved hand went over her mouth, leaving only the pain visible in her eyes. He drew her hand away. "Don't cry, Kerina."

"I never meant to hurt you. Can you ever forgive me, Chan?"

"I haven't thought much about it," he fibbed.

"Will you?"

"Yes." The damp cold fractured his smile. "But I'm not sure I can forgive you for not doing that concert in Los Angeles. I barely saved face with my parents."

She gave a throaty ripple. "Jillian begged me to reconsider. I didn't have the strength. But, I'd give anything to play my violin in Vienna one more time—in the city I love best."

He stood and balanced himself on the slanting embankment, "Perhaps you still can, Kerina. But come. Let's get you back to the house. Jillian has some soup simmering on the stove."

404

Together they trudged up from the river, back toward the old farmstead, Kerina moving with a slow, painful gait.

As they crunched over the cold ground, her arm tucked in his, he said, "I didn't know I was adopted until months ago."

"But you were searching for answers in Everdale."

"Because I heard you and Mom talking on the Riviera. I had just reached the patio railing when I heard Mother say, 'He doesn't know he's adopted, Kerina. How can I ever tell him?' I figured she was talking about me."

He felt her flinch as she whispered, "That was the morning you left the Riviera. And I said, 'Then don't tell him, Ashley.' How awful that you heard it that way."

"There was no easy way to find out."

"I was so ashamed, Chandler. You seemed to like me as the violinist. I was afraid if you knew the truth, you wouldn't like me anymore." He strained to hear her say, "And I didn't want Ashley to tell you. Not then. Our being related might have interfered with getting Zineta Hovic out of Bosnia."

"I didn't realize—"

"Can you ever forgive me for denying you a second time?"

"A third time," he corrected, his gaze focused on the farmhouse. "You walked out on me in Everdale twice. The last time—in October—I called the Dale Motel once I realized who you were. And they told me that Kerry Kovac had fled again."

She doubled forward. "My dear boy."

"Don't, Kerina."

"I wanted you when you were born, and yet I deserted you. I've had to live with that for all these years."

"For me, one of the tough things was finding out I had two brothers. I tried to contact them in Chicago." Again he felt her flinch. "It didn't work out exactly."

"I am so sorry."

"Aunt Celeste wanted nothing to do with me. She said she didn't know I existed and wanted to keep it that way."

"Because you were *my* son."

The words sounded strange to Chandler. He wanted to shrug them off. "Skip wanted nothing to do with me either, but Jeff came. It was funny talking about our relationship and having nothing to say, but Jeff and I decided to keep in touch and give our friendship a chance even though we had so little in common."

"You had Bill." Frosty vapors rose in cloudy white puffs as she spoke. "You had your father," she said again, as they approached the house.

Jillian met them at the door. "I was just about to send out a search team. Why were you out so long on such a cold day?"

"I was finding myself," Kerina said. "And talking with God until Chandler came. I have these little chats now and then in case God wants to hear me."

"He does," Chandler said.

"You seem so sure."

"I am."

She touched her gloved fingers to his lips. "It's still a private matter for me."

"So you told me in St. Stephen's. Someday, if you want me to, I'll tell you about him."

Dear God, when it comes time, help me to know what to say. I blew it with Randy. Don't let me mess up this time. Not with my mother.

"What's wrong, Chandler?" Jillian asked.

"I don't want Kerina to wait too long."

"I won't," Kerina said softly.

It wasn't until they finished supper and Chandler was feeling warm from the soup and the fire in the woodstove that he was aware of Franck Petzold's absence. "Kerina, where's Franck? No one has mentioned him all day."

"He is in Moscow."

"But you need him. When will he be back?"

"He's not coming, Chandler. It wouldn't be safe for him."

"Not coming!" She turned at the sharpness in his voice, tears brimming on her beautiful, dark lashes. The quick twist of her head sent a tear down her cheek. Gently he wiped it away. "Why isn't Franck coming back, Kerina?"

"They would arrest him for suspicion of art theft."

"Art theft!"

Jillian began stacking the dirty dishes. "He may have been involved in the theft of McClaren's Degas and Rembrandt—and a host of other paintings."

"Who told you that?"

"Franck did," Kerina said. "The night he left for Moscow, he admitted that he has been stealing paintings for seven years. Taking them through customs in my luggage. The great Kerina Rudzinski. Who would do more than a cursory inspection of her luggage? I didn't know until this past year. But that night in Vienna when the McClarens were robbed, I told him, 'Never again, Franck. Get another courier.'"

Chandler caressed her hands. "And what did he say?"

"When he realized who you were, Chandler, he threatened your safety." Her eyes were downcast. "In New York, he asked me to help him one more time, and then he would go away and never come back. That's why I had Jillian cancel my concerts. I had to protect him."

"You were ill, Kerina. That's the reason we canceled your concerts."

"That too, Jillian, but I had to send Franck away."

"Kerina," Chandler said gently, "that makes you an accomplice."

"I told you once, if it had not been for Franck, I would never have played in the concert halls of the world. In a way, dear Chandler, your father gave me you—a very precious part of himself. But Franck gave me my music."

"And you shared it with the world. Share it with them once more, Kerina. You can't give up your music because of Franck."

She shook her head, freeing more tears. "I'm in pain when I lift my arm. I had to stop playing before people pitied me."

"Pity you? People will always love you, Kerina. But does Franck know you're ill? He'd want to be with you."

"I cannot ask him to risk arrest just to come to me."

"He'd come, Kerina, if he knew."

"Don't send for Franck," Jillian begged him. "Kerina is right. If he comes, they will arrest him."

"Not if they don't know he's here."

"I'll know," Jillian said.

He frowned, perplexed. His gaze settled back on Kerina. "Will you play in concert one more time just for me?"

"In Prague?"

"In Vienna. Here too if you'd like."

Jillian dropped the silverware she was holding. "Chan, a full concert is too exhausting. Wait until she's feeling better."

"What about just one song or two?" he asked. "I brought your violin back so I could hear you play again." He pulled the case out from behind the chair and opened it for her. She lifted the Strad and the bow with stiff fingers and then, with her eyes closed, slipped into the joy of her music again.

That night long after the others had gone to bed, Chandler stood with Jillian by the old woodstove. The wick on a kerosene lantern burned low, the unsteady light dancing on her face.

"Jill, Kerina can't go on protecting Franck. If he's a thief, she will have to turn him in. Or you will."

"The Art Theft Registry and Interpol know about the paintings. But Franck's confession to Kerina is not proof enough."

"The Art Theft Registry?"

"They're headquartered in London. They search for stolen art. Don't worry, Chandler. Once Kerina is gone—"

"You seem so sure."

"Interpol knows that Kerina was never involved; Franck would be the first one to admit it. I've bargained with them. If they wait until Kerina's death, I will help them track Franck Petzold down to the ends of the earth."

"I think you're wrong, but you've been a good friend to Kerina. Would you do one more thing for her? Arrange a concert in Vienna so she can play her Strad one more time?"

"Chandler, she's too sick."

"I want my mother to go out with a song, Jill. That's what she wants. Let her have that chance. You heard the way she played this evening. She can do it. She'll find the strength somehow. Just think about it. That's all I ask."

"Let me sleep on it."

He reached out and ran his finger across her lips. "I love you, Jillian."

"How can you be so certain? We barely know each other."

"Falling in love with you didn't take that long. You're that special someone I've waited for all my life. You haven't given me your answer yet. Will you marry me?"

The spigot dripped, time ticking away, a new day breaking. She looked up, searching his face. Hers was shadowed in the darkness. He felt he was losing her. "It's no, isn't it?"

"For now."

"Why?"

"Kerina needs us. And I want to know whether you can accept me once you know who I really am. What I've done."

"That makes you sound more intriguing," he said.

"I had plans for my future long before I met you."

"London?" And then worriedly, he asked, "Not Santos?"

"No, that was over before I met you. But I planned to go back to London before Thanksgiving. I had an old job waiting for me. But with Kerina so ill, I couldn't walk out on her."

"Will that job still be waiting for you, Jillian?"

"My boss will hold it for me a little longer."

"You're so sure of your future."

"And I want to know what you plan to do with your life. Before it was the army. What now? That government job—the one you can't tell me about? If you take that I'd never know if you would be home for dinner. Never know whether I would have to lie alone at night worrying about you."

"I won't know for several weeks. They do a thorough check on our background. FBI and all."

The fluttering reflection of the lantern caught the tilt of her nose, the thrust of her jaw, the softness of her lips. He touched her chin—that stubborn, jutting chin—and turned her face back to him. "I want to do the right thing with the rest of my life. To take the right job."

"Are you taking it for Randy?"

"I want to help the people of Bosnia."

"And what happened to music?"

His arm tightened around her narrow waist; her head nestled under his chin. "It's still there, Jillian. Waiting in the shadows. I know I can never play professionally as Kerina does. Doing music reviews won't guarantee a salary. Or health benefits. Or job security. And I won't have my wife supporting me."

Her eyes glistened. "What happened to that two shall become one stuff? At least I'd have a husband home for dinner—even if we had to eat macaroni and cheese."

"Go lightly on the cheese, sweetheart."

"Chandler, doesn't it worry you—my not growing up in your father's church, not always believing the way you do?"

He smiled. "But you do now, don't you? I don't know how or when, but you're different somehow, Jillian."

She flushed with pleasure. "Your mother talked to me when she was in Vienna."

"Sounds like she ran interference for me."

"Ashley meant well."

"Mom didn't corner you with hellfire-and-brimstone, did she?"

"What's that?"

"Never mind. Dad's got the corner on that one every Sunday."

"So the two of us becoming one does worry him?"

"He's not the one proposing. So tell me what happened."

"After those glorious days on the Riviera—in spite of Santos almost showing up—I was so sure you liked me. But the day you flew back to Vienna, you told me it was over between us."

"That's when I told you about Zineta."

"Yes; I cried for four straight hours."

"Is that why you wouldn't talk to me on the phone?"

"That's why Ashley came to see me. I was a mess. I blamed her for standing in our way. She said she was pleased—my loving you—but there was something more important to settle first."

"And she gave it to you both barrels?"

"We argued. We talked. I cried. She kept me supplied with tissues and stood her ground. I almost threw her out, but before she left she gave me a little book called *The Man Called Saul*."

"Good choice."

"I threw the book down the hall after her. But ten minutes later I went out and picked it up. No one else wanted it."

He grinned. "We've had rows like that. Mom always wins."

"I spent the next three hours drenching that book with tears. I told God I didn't want him interfering and messing up my social life or killing my chances with you. I gave up finally and read the words your mother had underlined for me."

"About Saul seeing a blinding light?"

"How did you know?"

"She pulled the same one on me when I was twelve."

"Then it worked for both of us," Jillian said. "I was so scared alone in that hotel room. I was sure God was asking me the same question he had asked Saul. I figured I really didn't want to fight his Son. So I quit fighting."

He pulled Jillian tightly against him. "Did you tell Mom?"

"No. I wasn't trying to impress her. And I didn't want you to think I was trying to impress you."

"I know you better than that, Jillian. I can wait. You are dear to me. Worth waiting for."

His lips came down hard on hers, insistent, demanding. She slipped her arms around his neck, drawing him closer, her response long and passionate.

 Thirty-three

Jillian stayed by the phone for the next forty-eight hours, placing calls to Vienna that would have been easy in Franck Petzold's capable hands. Exhausted, she leaned back in the wooden chair and smiled across the room at Chandler. He had such an attractive face: the well-defined bone structure, one of strength; the sensitive, finely shaped mouth like his birth mother's. He was clearly Kerina's son. His head cocked her way as he stoked the woodstove.

"Nothing?" he asked. "No invitations?"

"The concert agents can't schedule Kerina for six months. I can't tell them she doesn't have that long—that her strength would be gone by then. But everyone wants to book her."

Chandler capped the stove with its iron lid and prowled around the room. He stopped at the oak sideboard to examine the Bohemian china and crystal glasses before picking up a thin copper plate. "Where did this come from?"

"It's an authentic Rembrandt etching—perhaps a cottage where Rembrandt once stayed. Kerina found it hidden in the lining of her violin case when we came back from New York."

He inspected the plate again. "What was it doing there?"

"Stolen, we think. Franck called Kerina several times asking her to ship it to him. She refuses."

"Jill, if it's a hot item, it can't just sit here and put my grandparents at risk. If you know it was stolen, turn it in."

"No; I promised Karol I wouldn't as long as Kerina is alive. And, Chan, when she's gone, I want that copper plate."

"That sounds crass," he said. "Did you want it for a little memento? You know value when you see it. It's certainly worth more than her diamond earrings. You're not planning to hang it in our flat in London, are you?"

"When I go back to London, I'm turning it over to the Art Theft Registry. That's the agreement. I hand deliver it."

Guardedly, he asked, "You won't ruin Kerina's reputation?"

"She wasn't involved. It will go back to its owner and from there probably to the auction block. It will sell well with Rembrandt's signature and date etched there. Don't worry. No thief expects to find it sitting here with Gretchen's china."

Chandler eased into his grandfather's rocker, his long legs stretched out, his ankles crossed. Jillian forced herself to meet his gaze, dreading the questions that lingered in his sleepless, bloodshot eyes. She ached for him, thinking, *I'll marry him and put the smile back on his face. Be his comfort, companion, lover.* As quickly, she knew her love for him had to be stronger. They had to find their own peace, rake over their beliefs and lean on the only One who could help them.

"I love you, Chandler. I want so much to help you."

His brows twisted at a rakish angle. "Does that mean things have changed since two nights ago?"

She remembered that night with a blush—sitting here in this room, nestled in Chan's warm embrace, and responding to his lips on hers. "Everything is still on hold as long as Kerina needs us. You will stay, won't you?"

"FedEx is holding my job until I get back. And," he said, admitting something new, "my parents wired me two thousand dollars to help out. Not bad, eh? Guess they're crazy about me."

So am I, she thought. She studied him, loving him. She wanted to spend the rest of her life with him, but once he knew that Franck's exile to Moscow was her doing—that she had been planted in Kerina's world to take Kerina down—then he would despise her. Yet she could never marry him without telling him the truth. And once he knew, would he still want her?

She lifted the phone to dial another music agent, but felt distracted by Chandler's smile. She could not pinpoint the exactness, the likeness between Chan and his mother, but it was there in undefined lines: in the twist of his head, in the pensive, searching gaze that met hers; in the way that he smiled. Yet having met Ashley, he was clearly her son as well.

"Are there any other music halls we can try, Jill?"

"I just tried and you wouldn't let me."

"I didn't say a word."

"You didn't have to—I guessed what you were thinking."

"I will have to restrain myself or you will have to come over and sit beside me so I can show you how much I love you."

"That's a tempting offer," she said and prayed that he did not know how erratically her heart was beating.

The phone rang. She snatched it up, glad for an excuse. "Yes, this is Jillian Ingram. Helmut, you *did* get my message?"

From the other end of the wire came the resolute, seductive, voice of Helmut Manchurin, the tenor soloist that Kerina had helped ten years ago when his career was floundering.

He said, "*Liebling,* I just this minute picked up your message on my answering machine. How special of you to call."

She filled in his features from memory. Dark eyes. Dark hair. Five-feet-ten. A blade-like nose. At thirty-six, he swooped onto the stage these days to a thundering applause. But best of all, he was Kerina's dear friend and maybe he could help them.

"*Liebling,* have you decided to marry me at last? We can run off to Italy tomorrow."

"I'm busy tomorrow." She laughed. "Besides, I'm thinking about marrying someone else. An American this time."

He groaned. "My dear girl, I knew I was too late. How is my friend Kerina? Maybe she will fly to Italy with me."

"Helmut, Kerina is ill. Seriously ill."

He slipped back into his strong German accent. "What's wrong? I thought she looked unwell when we dined in Munich recently."

"But she wants to play one more concert in Vienna."

"That would not be a problem with her marvelous reputation."

"Booking soon enough would. She has terminal cancer."

The humor went out of his words. "How long does she have?"

"She may not see another summer in Vienna."

There came a long, decided pause and then, "Jillian, give me a few days. Let me see what I can do."

What Helmut did took thirty-six hours. What he accomplished was an opportunity for Kerina. He was unusually jovial when he called Jillian a few days later. "I am in concert in Vienna in ten days. There isn't much time for publicity, but my manager is arranging everything." He laughed. "One stipulation."

She held her breath, certain he would want her to run away to Italy with him. "Kerina must play at least three numbers."

Relief poured over her. "Agreed."

"This is the plan then. I am guest soloist that night, and Kerina will be featured as my special guest."

"Which won't hurt your reputation any."

"True. First I will sing 'Valencia.' Then we will do one duet. 'In All My Dreams.'" She heard the subdued crack in his words and knew suddenly that it was not a pat on the back that he wanted. He was helping a friend in the kindest way he could. Without Kerina's support, his dream of success would have died ten years ago. "The orchestra has agreed to play background for Kerina for two numbers. They'll have to know ahead of time which ones."

"Let's settle on the Brahms Lullaby and a Strauss waltz. Oh, Helmut, thank you. How can we ever pay you back?"

416

Helmut told her, laughing, "Decide on Italy someday, *Liebling.*"

Jillian made two more calls. One a surprise for Chandler, the other a trap for Franck Petzold. She gave Ashley the dates for Vienna as quickly as she could. "David and I will be there," Ashley told her. "Could we stay at the Empress Isle again?"

"I'll book rooms for all of us there, but don't tell Chan you're coming. It's a surprise. Right now, he's out walking arm-in-arm with Kerina. I can see them from my window looking the picture of peace and solitude with snowflakes falling on them."

"My son is happy then?"

"It's hard to know whether he's pretending or not."

"No, Chandler is genuine. He has our blessing for whatever happiness he can give Kerina."

Jillian's second long-distance call was to Brooks Rankin at the Coventry Art Theft Registry in London. "It's Jillian Ingram, Brooks. I'm calling from Prague."

She told him about the concert, gave him the place and date. "Can you find a way to let Franck Petzold know about the concert? And will you tell him that Kerina Rudzinski is ill—dying?"

She heard Brooks chewing something and chugging down great gulps of the coffee he kept on his desk. "We'll pass the word along through the art world—through the Black Market if we have to. But I thought you wanted to protect him, Miss Ingram?"

"Only while Kerina is alive."

He voiced his disapproval and then in a wheezy monotone said, "If Petzold steps off Russian soil, he's ours."

"I know. But he has a right to make that decision himself. And you must agree—Kerina is not to witness his arrest."

He accepted the bargain grudgingly. "It's Petzold the Registry and Interpol want. If he goes to Vienna, Miss Ingram, we expect you to call us and let us know he's there.

That will make our job simpler. And salvage what's left of yours. If it weren't for Joel Gramdino, you would have been out the door long ago."

Thanks, she thought. *But even if Franck comes, he won't bring the paintings. So what have you gained? I will give you Franck, but it will mark the end of my career.*

Three hours before the concert, Franck Petzold arrived in Vienna in his friend's private jet. "Are you coming to the concert with me?" he asked Jokhar Gukganov.

"I have business matters to tend to—and I understand the Academy of Fine Arts has another Impressionist collection on display and—I have my caviar and vodka. I won't be lonely."

"Don't take any risks this time."

Jokhar's harsh laughter filled the cabin. "You are the one taking a risk." As they parted, Jokhar said, "You are aware that there are some lovely paintings in the concert hall? Why not make your evening there worthwhile?"

"I have no reason to build my art collection," Franck said. *Before, Kerina was my reason, and she is dying.*

"And no desire to split the profits from stolen masterpieces? Ah! I see by your face you find that distasteful. You have lost interest in life, my friend. What you need is the love of a good woman."

"I've lost the love of a good woman." Franck shook his jacket free of wrinkles and checked his watch. "I plan to take Miss Rudzinski to dinner before I come back."

Jokhar's doleful eyes narrowed. "We have filed a flight plan for one in the morning. If you are not here by then, my friend, we return to Moscow without you." A mirthless smile touched his mouth. "Which wouldn't be a bad thing. You have a number of artifacts and masterpieces in your place that should be mine."

Under his breath Franck muttered, "You have tricked me out of several of them already."

Forty minutes later, Franck swept into the swank, pillared lobby at the Empress Isle Hotel. He hurried past the concierge and the registration desk and avoided the busy elevators. Without even a glance up at the gilded paintings he had coveted on his last visit, he ran up the winding staircase to the second floor. For a moment he stood outside Kerina's suite listening to the sweet sound of laughter inside.

She is happy again, he thought.

She was always happy moments before a concert, drawing from a reserve deep within herself. Other musicians went tense and jittery, demanding the impossible of their managers, screaming and tossing things. But Kerina was the sweetest to him just before she lifted her violin. The brass knob responded to his gentle twist. He opened the door and stepped inside.

"Franck! Franck!" Kerina cried. "Oh, Franck, you did come."

She crossed the room to him slowly, looking thinner but never more lovely in her shantung gown. A young forty-five! Elegant as ever even in illness. Only her eyes convinced him that she was seriously ill. He held out his hands. She took them and he leaned down and brushed her cheek with a kiss.

"Dear, dear Franck, why did you come back?"

"Because you need me," he said confidently. "For almost thirty years I have never missed your concerts. I will be safe. Don't worry about me. Just play well this evening."

"I will. I am ready." She leaned against him. "Everything is complete now. So many of those I love are here."

He slipped his arm around her waist and felt her wince. *The cancer is spreading,* he remembered. *Invading her brittle bones.*

His gaze swept the room and then more leisurely lingered on each face. The McClarens were there, and he recognized Kerina's two childhood friends from Prague. Ashley Reynolds sat in a wing-back chair next to them. Surely the tall, silver-haired man in black tie was her husband. John? David? Something like that. He nodded politely to Kerina's parents sitting side by side on the bed. He had always tolerated the gruff manner of the old man and respected the benevolent smile on Gretchen Rudzinski's face. The handsome young man holding Jillian Ingram's hand had to be Kerina's son, his likeness to Bill VanBurien striking.

The stranger by the dresser said, "Guten Tag, Petzold."

Franck recognized the voice first and then the face as that of Helmut Manchurin, the tenor soloist, one of the many musicians that Kerina had befriended during her long career.

His gaze went back to Kerina. He cupped her cheeks, felt the smooth softness of her skin, looked into those kind, hazel eyes. "My dear Kerina, I missed you. Life is empty without you. But, alas, I have no ticket for this evening's concert."

"I have one for you, Franck," Jillian told him. "The seat next to mine. Fifth row back. Chandler won't be using his— he's going backstage with Kerina."

Franck's place for thirty years. Franck's position.

Jillian crossed the room toward the door. "I'll get the ticket for you. I have things to do anyway. Phone calls to make."

Is she boldly warning me that she will betray me again? he thought. Aloud he asked, "Busy as always before the concert?"

"You know the routine."

His arm tightened around Kerina. "Give me a few hours, Miss Ingram. Just a few hours with Kerina."

Franck stepped aside so Jillian could leave. He wondered what the others in the room would make of his request. Wondered if Kerina understood. They had always understood each other.

She looked up into his face, the woman he had loved from the day he first saw her running across the fields outside of Prague. He knew as he glimpsed the sudden sadness in her eyes that she was aware he would never leave Vienna. He could flee now before Jillian completed her phone call. But, no. He had come back because Kerina needed him. Because he loved her.

That evening Jillian sat in the fifth row of the music hall with Franck Petzold sitting in the aisle seat beside her. She had looked forward to Helmut's concert, yet halfway through the program, she could not recall what songs had been sung. Had she done the right thing sending for Franck? He sat tight-lipped, somber, without joy. Whatever differences they had, she respected him for coming. Whatever he had done in the past had nothing to do with Kerina. She moistened her lips. Had Brooks notified the *polizei* and Interpol? What if they arrived during Kerina's final number? But what she dreaded most was facing Kerina afterwards.

She forced her wandering thoughts back to center stage as Helmut Manchurin belted out the last phrase of "Valencia," his body swaying with the music, his hand to his heart as he sang. The orchestra formed a semicircle behind him, some tapping their feet to the music, others swaying gently. He was backed by the triumphant sound of the horns. The pure tones of the string section. The distinct, sweet notes of the flutes. The reverberating echo of the cymbals. The rhythmic beat of the drums by a female in a chic black dress. The conductor brought them to the final note, and then, when the applause finally subsided to a ripple, Helmut half-turned to the stairs behind him and announced his special guest.

"Please welcome my friend—the lovely Kerina Rudzinski."

The Viennese stood to their feet applauding Kerina as she came down the blue velvet steps on the arm of a handsome young man in a black tuxedo. Exquisitely, courtly, one step at a time. Kerina came with a willowy gracefulness, the audience never guessing that she was weak, ill, in constant pain.

She wore her cranberry-red gown from Paris—low cut, off the shoulder, the flaring skirt revealing her elegant ankles. Ashley and the hotel seamstress had come to the rescue with a needle and thread, taking in a tuck or two so no one could guess how loosely the gown now hung on Kerina. Franck had fastened the bloodstone pendant around her neck. Cosmetics hid the pallid skin and the dark circles under her eyes.

The stage lights highlighted the reddish flecks in her hair as Helmut stepped forward to meet her. Chandler lifted the violin from its case and handed it to Kerina. He exited the stage, leaving her with an accomplished tenor soloist and one of the finest orchestras in the world.

As Kerina raised her bow, Helmut said, "My dreams of singing all over Europe would never have been fulfilled without Kerina Rudzinski. And Miss Rudzinski tells me that all of her dreams have been fulfilled in this city that she loves so much. We join voice and violin to give you 'In All My Dreams.'"

The audience was enchanted, and from some strength deep within her, Kerina followed their duet with two violin solos: Brahms' "Lullaby" and Johann Strauss's "On the Beautiful Blue Danube." And for an encore—because her audience would not let her go—she chose selections from Tchaikovsky's *Swan Lake,* her music filling the vast auditorium, her bow gliding with the same grace as a dazzling white swan on the Danube.

As she played, the *polizei* strolled down the center aisle to where Franck Petzold sat. Jillian's lips went dry as one of them tapped his shoulder. Franck turned to her. "I asked you for a few hours, Jillian. For just a few hours with Kerina."

"I'm sorry. Truly, I am, Franck," she whispered.

He made no effort to bolt but quietly said, "Thank God for the blinding stage lights. Kerina won't see me being led away. Tell her I had a plane to catch. Will you do that for me?"

Nodding, Jillian fought back tears. It was Franck Petzold's final performance. He stood with great dignity, stroked his beard, straightened his back, and shrugged off the manacled grip of the *polizei*. Jill watched him take four steps. Then he glanced back, touched his fingers to his unsmiling lips, and blew a kiss in Kerina Rudzinski's direction, saluting Kerina in his own way as he had always done.

On the last triumphant note, Helmut was the first to applaud Kerina. As he lifted her hand to his lips, the audience rose to their feet. But Kerina, who had thrived on the adoration of her audiences—she who had always blown kisses to them, lifted her Stradivarius, one palm extended, offering praise to the One who had waited long years to receive it.

Kerina's face turned radiant. While the applause still filled the auditorium, she placed her Strad in its case and reached out her hand to Chandler, who had been standing offstage. He stepped to her side and presented her with a bouquet of red roses.

Holding them, she took the microphone from Helmut Manchurin and waited until the audience settled back into their seats. Then she said, "My dear friends, this has been a glorious evening for me. Truly this is the city of my dreams. You have given me so much. You have always welcomed me. Always loved me."

To Jillian she sounded short of breath, but she went on. "This has been such a special day—I wish it could go on forever. You have shared your hearts with me. Now, I would like to share my greatest treasure with you."

She smiled up at Chandler. "This is my son, Chandler Reynolds."

Murmurings swept through the audience. Then, as the Viennese had always done, they stood again to applaud Kerina Rudzinski—and to welcome her son.

Days later, Kerina collapsed in the lobby of the Empress Isle Hotel after spending the day riding through the city she loved, strolling through the park, and walking along the

Danube River. She was coughing as Chandler lifted her in his strong arms, streaks of blood trickling from the corner of her mouth.

"That was silly of me," she said. "I am sorry."

"We did too much, Kerina. You're exhausted."

"Yes, Chandler. But no ambulance. . . . Please."

"All right. We'll use Jillian's car."

Hours later, she was resting in her hospital room when the doctor met with Chandler in the lobby. "Miss Rudzinski is very ill. Are there other family members to notify?"

"We're all here," Chandler said. "But I don't understand what's happening."

He smiled patiently. "Cancer has invaded your mother's body. The lungs. The bones." He shook his head. "There's been a slight hemorrhage, perhaps more blood clots in her lungs."

"Then do something about it."

"We can give her medicine to try and dissolve the clots. Or offer aggressive treatment, more chemotherapy, but she has refused."

Chandler's knees buckled. "So what happens? What are the risks?"

"A severe hemorrhage. A stroke. We have to wait and see."

"Can we take her back to Prague?"

"Don't move her, son," David said, stepping forward.

The doctor nodded. "Mr. Reynolds is right."

Jillian slipped her arm through Chandler's. "This is the city she loves more than any place in the world. The city that welcomed her and loved her. She's just come home again, Chan."

He brushed them aside and walked to the window to look out on the river flowing gently through the city. He braced his hand against the pane, felt the coolness against his palm. "She wanted to ride on the Danube. I promised her we'd do that tomorrow."

Jillian touched his arm. "Chandler, she hates hospitals. Can't we take her back to the Empress Isle and get a room that looks out over the Danube?"

The doctor had walked up behind them. "I don't recommend moving her. We have a wing here at the hospital that gets a view of the river. We can transfer her there. She'll get good medical care here."

Chandler glanced at the doctor through the reflected glass. "How long does she have?"

"Days. Weeks. Don't ask us to be heroic."

Chandler glanced at Karol and Gretchen, agonizing for them, and then he faced the doctor again. "It's happening so fast. Kerina doesn't look that sick. She's strong." And then with his throat tighter than a drum, he faced the bitter truth. "We want the right to be with her, twenty-four hours a day."

The doctor's gaze strayed around the crowded lobby.

"They're all family, sir. Her parents. My parents."

"And distant cousins, I assume." But there was a twinkle in his eyes. "I will write the order for the family, Herr Reynolds."

Five days later Chandler sat by Kerina's bedside as dawn broke. They were waiting for the nurse to come in and restart the IV infusion when she said, "Chandler, I want to watch the mist rise over the river one more time."

"We could push her bed to the window," Jillian suggested.

"I have another idea." He winked at Kerina, pulled back the covers, wrapped her in a fleecy robe, lifted her gently into his arms and carried her to the window. Together they watched the morning mist rise above the Danube, watched the river wind its way slowly through the city they both loved.

"An der schönen blauen Donau," she whispered.

He felt her chest convulse, knew that she was fighting off another coughing spell. "Strauss put the blueness in the water with his song," she said. "History made it a legend. And legend tells us that those who love see the blue in the river."

"Then it is a cobalt blue this morning, Kerina."

The sun formed a burst of colors on the horizon, the spires and domes of Vienna sparkling like glittering diamonds. At last Kerina rested her head on his shoulder. "I'm tired now."

He carried her back to the bed and they made her as comfortable as they could. "My violin is yours now, Chandler."

He nodded. "I'll take it everywhere I go."

She winced from the pain. "Any place in mind?"

"London with Jillian. Bosnia someday. California."

"Good." The word caught in another spasm.

As he fingered her worn copy of T. S. Eliot's poems, she said, "Read to me. *The Waste Land*."

Chandler's voice remained deep and strong as he read, "April is the cruellest month, breeding Lilacs out of the dead land—"

She wrapped her hand over his. "Your father loved to quote those words. I felt that way for years. You were born in April, Chandler, and I lost you then. Each year as your birthday rolled around, I dreaded the coming of memory and desire." Her eyes searched his face. "I am so sorry. I always wanted to spend your birthday with you, and now I won't even be here for the next one."

"We could celebrate early."

"No." She rested and found strength to go on. "April has become special to me now. It was April when I heard from you again. Eliot should have written, April is the happiest of months, but then he did not know you." Again she rested, waiting for more strength. "The lilacs and the dull roots of my life have come together, Chandler. They have come full circle."

Kerina was dying, and she had told Chandler twice that eternal matters were a private affair. She had brushed him off when he talked of God, raising a wall between them. But could he let her go that way?

It was Friday afternoon before he found the courage to say, "God loves you, Kerina."

Her dark eyes settled on him. "How do you know that?"

He felt awkward, foolish. He was clinging to some words from his dad's sermons, hanging on for dear life like a man caught in an ebb tide and being swept out to sea. But it was his birth mother, not Chandler, drowning in her own fluids, slipping beneath the surface, dying. He was desperate to help her.

"How do you know God loves me?" she rasped.

"God sent all the proof we need. He sent his Son into the world to die for us."

"Here in Prague?" she murmured distractedly.

"Anywhere. No city limits." He didn't tell her they were still in Vienna. In the last few hours, her speech had slowed. She had drifted back to the land of her childhood and he let her. He saw no harm in it. He wondered what kind of unprepared sermon his father would call it. But he sensed how David Reynolds felt when he stood behind his pulpit in clerical garb and reached out in love to drowning people. "God gave his only Son, Kerina."

She gasped for air, struggling for each breath. Struggling to reach the surface, to come back to him, to keep her focus on him. "Gave . . . his Son away . . . like I did?"

He eased another pillow behind her back and groped for the right answer. "Gave him up from his place of fellowship. And sent him to earth with all the angels looking on."

Kerina's chest heaved, collapsed, did not rise again.

"Breathe," he begged her. "Breathe."

Beneath her bed linens, her chest rose again. "No flowers, Chandler. . . . No flowery words."

Her despair knocked him down a peg. He kept to the facts this time. No flowers. No flowery words. No angels thrown in.

"God loved you so much, Mother, that he sent Jesus to die for your sins. He cleans the slate if you ask him."

"Will . . . he wipe away the guilt of giving you away?"

Chandler swallowed the rock in his throat as his gaze strayed to Jillian. She was biting her lower lip, listening. His eyes went back to his mother's face. "I forgave you. And God is a whole lot bigger than I am and much better at forgiving." His deep voice wavered. "He loves you just the way you are. Blunders and all. Just believe in him. Trust him."

As she sank back against the pillows, he took her cold, limp hand and held it. The tears balancing on her long dark lashes fell, rolling over her high cheeks and down the pallid skin. This time he was certain that the tears were not for him, but between Kerina's God and herself. He used one corner of the bedsheet to stem the flow. The tears came again. He let them.

At last she quit fighting and allowed her swollen eyelids to close. She looked peaceful, but he watched her breathing grow shallow, saw the dark blotches appear on her thin arms.

"Let her rest, Chandler. Go lie down yourself."

"No, Jillian, I won't leave her."

"Chan, I called Kerina's parents and left a message for them to come back as quickly as they can."

He nodded. "I know they said their good-byes this morning. But they will want to be here. I pray that they make it."

Chandler was still holding Kerina's hand and Jillian on the other side patting her arm, when Kerina's exhausted body finally relaxed in sleep.

She awoke once, her eyes unfocused. "I'm here, Mother," he said. "Right here with you."

A smile touched Kerina's lips. Then she drifted again, this time deeply into unconsciousness. Moments later, Jillian shook her, but she would not awaken again.

"She's gone," Jillian said.

"I know."

He laid Kerina's hand gently to her side and touched her still warm, soft face.

Jillian put her lips against Kerina's cheek and kissed her. "Good-bye, sweet friend."

She slipped around the end of the hospital bed and put her arms around Chandler's neck. He made no attempt to hide his grief. His eyes brimmed with tears, the tears he could not shed while his mother was dying.

"Chandler," Jillian whispered. "Do you think they have violins in heaven?"

He clasped her hand. "Harps. Choirs. I don't know about violins."

"If they do—if she's found one, I'm sure Kerina is already playing it for God's Son."

He nodded, comforted. Jillian pressed her cheek against his, and utter stillness filled the room.

Epilogue

Chandler arrived in London in the middle of June with memories of his childhood replaying themselves in his mind, like dusty but cherished relics. Rocking on the porch in Ashley's arms at the old homestead in Everdale. Being pushed higher and higher on the swing by the gazebo. Climbing the picket gate. His mother swooping him up in her arms and singing, "London bridge is falling down, falling down."

Why those particular memories lingered he did not know. There was little else of those first three years of his life in Everdale that he could recall on his own, except the pungent smell of wood smoke and dead leaves burning, or the spring air scented with honeysuckle and roses. The sound of twigs snapping beneath his feet as he walked in the woods with his father. And the sound of the piano as he sat on the bench with his mother, picking out the tune of "London Bridge," one note at a time.

Jillian Ingram had awakened his longing to see London. And now he was here with that childish rhyme running competition with the sights and sounds of London proper. He stood watching the broad sweep of the Thames, a deep blue this morning as he stood above its embankment, and watched it wind its way toward the Tower Bridge down the river a pace. Across the waters lay the historical landmarks as sturdy and steadfast as the Londoners themselves. The Houses of Parliament bigger than life, flying the Union Jack. Big Ben ticking away in the Clock Tower and booming its hour-bell. The Westminster Abbey with its High Altar and oak coronation chair. Chandler brought it down to his own generation, remembering the cadenced steps of the Welsh

431

Guards that had borne the casket of the Princess of Wales through those massive doors.

If he crossed one of the bridges that spanned the Thames, he would be within walking distance of the Queen's Residence and have a better view of the Royal Standard fluttering from the top of Buckingham Palace. Instead he took note of the rain clouds beginning to form a canopy over the city. Chandler had ordered sunshine for his first day in London, not a cloudburst. He had planned his arrival in London three weeks early to surprise Jillian. He knew now that he had arrived three days late for the trooping of the colors on the Queen's birthday, something that Kerina would have loved. She had been like his father David with his ties to Scottish ancestry. They both liked pomp and ceremony and would have enjoyed the flying past by the R.A.F. and the gun salutes to the Queen.

Almost four months had slipped by since Kerina's death. It had been almost that long since he had seen Jillian. In her letters, Jillian boasted of her perfect view of the heart of London from her windows. He checked the address in his hand and crossed the bridge. If Jillian's flat was anywhere near here, she was right in the middle of a business district.

He checked the numbers again, and perplexed, turned to the constable with a telescopic baton in his hand. The chin strap held the policeman's helmet in place, but it didn't cut off his smile. Chandler remembered that Jillian's only run-in with the law was dating a London Bobby; he sincerely hoped this was not the same man.

"I'm looking for my girl's flat. She's moved just recently."

The Bobby studied the address for a second. "Won't find it on these streets," came the friendly reply. "Believe that's the Art Theft Registry, two blocks on." He pointed with his baton. "If you hurry, you'll be there before the storm hits."

Art Theft Registry? An uneasy discomfiture churned inside, like the low ebb feeling he had after Kerina's funeral when Jillian refused to wear the diamond ring he bought her. She had insisted on time alone to grieve for her friend. He understood. He had gone through it after Randy died in Bosnia. But Chandler called Jillian weekly, sometimes twice a week to tell her how much he loved her.

Jillian was friendly and cheerful, but she still held back. While he despaired over what had gone wrong these last four months, he spotted her hurrying along the street in a stunning, gray business suit, her tawny hair flecked with glimmerings of gold. He ran to catch up to her.

"Jillian," he cried, expecting her to break into a smile and fly into his arms.

She whirled around, looking stunned. "Chandler! What are you doing here?"

"I came over to get married."

Her cheeks turned scarlet. "I was going to send you my home address before you came—but you're here three weeks early."

"I missed you. I wanted to surprise you. Look, is this the kind of greeting you give the guy you're going to marry?"

She gave him a quick hug, brushed his cheek with a kiss.

Uncertain now, he tapped the small case under his arm, "I came in time for the London Symphony. I took in some samples of my work to the *Standard*—a review on the symphony and an article on my friend Kemal Kovic, the cellist in Tuzla."

"And?" she asked softly.

"I was hoping for a hearing—for a chance to prove myself."

She touched his cheek and ran her fingers over his lips. "And you were disappointed?"

"I didn't even get past the receptionist," he admitted. "Kemal wrote a beautiful composition during the shelling of Tuzla. I'm just trying to get it published."

"Let Kemal help himself, Chandler. Let him fly over to London or Vienna. You can't afford to worry about some musician in Bosnia. Worry about establishing yourself as a music critic."

"He's my friend, Jillian."

She wiped the raindrops from his cheek. "Oh, Chandler, you can't carry Bosnia with you forever."

The corner of his mouth twisted. "I can't leave Bosnia behind either. Sweetheart, could we go somewhere and talk? Just the two of us."

Above them the sign to the Coventry Art Theft Registry creaked on its hinges, caught by a sudden breeze from the approaching storm. It was an artistic, gilded sign with what looked like the face of a Mona Lisa engraved on it. The wind whipped around them. Raindrops started to fall.

"Chandler, if you are expecting to get somewhere in the music world, it's who you know that counts. If you weren't so proud, I could help you. We could live on my salary for a while."

"I told you I won't let a wife support me. And you know how I feel. Opportunities should come from honest hard work and because you meet the qualifications. And I do."

"Luckily for you, my father is in town."

"I wasn't expecting to meet your father today."

"Nor he you. But he insists on meeting the man who wants to marry me. Besides, he knows the people who could help you."

She glanced at her watch. "I'm late for a luncheon appointment. No, Chandler, it's not what you think. I work here. It's part of my job to meet with an art collector."

The sign swayed above them, spraying water on them. "You work here?"

"Yes. At the Art Theft Registry."

"I thought you were working as a publicist again."

"I didn't tell you that. So don't give me the third degree."

She brushed her wet hair from her forehead with quick, irritable strokes. Something was wrong. With him? With them? She looked annoyed, petulant.

"Chandler, it's not a new job. I've been working for the Registry for three years."

"But you worked for Kerina."

"Sort of. Partly. Oh, I did both."

He stared at her, trying to put it all together, but melting as he always did when he made eye contact with those sapphires.

"You're into art theft?"

"Into recovering stolen masterpieces. I'm sorry, Chandler. I was going to tell you."

"Like I was going to surprise you. It looks like we were no more ready for surprises than we were for the rainstorm that's pelting us."

He eased her back against the building, but there was no real shelter from the downpour. If they didn't shrink, their good suits would. "You worked for my mother for a year or more. And now you're telling me that this creaking sign above us—"

"That's right. It's my job. Where I do my nine-to-five everyday. Except we do overtime when we're on a case."

"Was Kerina a case?"

"That was part of my job as an art investigator. I was assigned to the team working on the concert thefts. Seven years of them."

"And you thought Kerina was involved?"

"At first. I told you, you didn't really know me." Her eyes filled with tears. "I said you wouldn't like me when you did."

"That doesn't make sense. Of course I know you. Look. I'm going to go back across that street, walk to the middle of the bridge and start over again. You pretend you're expecting me."

She was starting to giggle now and managed to wipe a mixture of tears and rain from her eyes. "I loved you, Chandler. And I loved your mother. At first I really did think she was involved with those thefts."

"You didn't trust her?"

"I wasn't there for long before I believed in her and fought to prove her innocence."

"And Franck? Franck Petzold? What about him?"

"What about him?" she repeated.

"The concert ends and he's gone. That was tough on Kerina. He didn't really go back to Moscow, did he? You lied about that."

"I was just doing my job, Chandler. And I didn't lie. You never asked me about it." She ran her hand distractedly through her limp hair again, pushing it away from her face. "Franck was a thief; don't you understand that, Chan? A common ordinary thief."

"He was my mother's friend."

"Those stolen masterpieces were worth millions. Recovering them was my responsibility—the same way you think that all of Bosnia is dependent on you. I loved Kerina as a friend. Don't forget that, Chandler Reynolds!"

"Did my mother know who you were? What you did?"

"No. I never had to tell her. We were friends. That's all that mattered. But in the beginning we honestly thought she might be working for Franck and transporting those works of art in her luggage. Kerina was well received in Moscow—customs gave her luggage cursory inspections. After all, she was the world-famous violinist. The beloved Kerina Rudzinski."

"She wasn't a thief." He turned and strolled off in a huff.

"I told you! I knew you wouldn't like me once you knew the truth," she called after him. "I was afraid this would happen. That's why I wouldn't take your engagement ring in Vienna."

He stopped in his tracks and turned back. The half-carat diamond was burning a hole in his inside pocket. He had planned to give her the ring on the bank of the Thames and then take her to dinner. He certainly didn't plan on the rain. "You deceived me, Jillian."

"Oh, Chandler, I thought you grew up on forgiveness."

"I did, but I was never good at putting it into practice."

"Go on then. Run away from the truth."

"If I did, I'd be running away from you."

"I don't care—but I do care. I defended Kerina."

He thought about it. The rain was washing his brain clear. Jillian had given Kerina some of the best days of her life. "She never really knew about Franck, did she?"

"I think she knew. But their friendship went back a long way. She protected him. And it took courage for Franck to come back and be with Kerina. Try to forgive him. Try to forgive me."

He felt like a drowned rat, the two of them standing outside shouting at each other like peevish children as the people of London hurried around them. The rain splashed down, water-logging his expensive tweed jacket.

He looked at Jillian and broke into sudden laughter, his anger dissipating with the rain. "You're all wet. But I still want to marry you."

She gave him a grudging smile. "It rains a lot here. I didn't want you to come early. I just moved into a new flat."

"What was wrong with the old one?"

"It wasn't big enough for two. I still have to put up the curtains. All I have now are cartons all over the place."

"I'll help you unpack."

"But I wanted to surprise you," she wailed.

"But you don't like surprises, Jillian."

"I do if I plan them. Do you like walking in the rain?"

He took a step toward her. "Did it a lot in the army."

"But did you like it?"

"It was a muddy mess . . . and you weren't there with me."

He stood facing her now. "I am serious about marrying you. I don't care about the concert thefts. You can explain them to me later. And I don't care whether the boxes are unpacked. We can do it together, but, Jill, I really don't know how I'm going to make a living."

She reached out and tentatively touched his cheek. "It doesn't matter, even if you take that government job."

"Maybe I won't. Maybe I better."

"Doesn't matter. The truth is I can't imagine life without you, Chan. I love you. If the CIA sends you back to Bosnia, I'll get a dog to keep me company. And I'll sleep in the living room so I won't know you're not home."

"You're crazy. You can't coop a dog up in an apartment all day. They were meant to run free."

"So was I. So why do I still want to marry you? Maybe I'll get a house cat to keep me company when you're gone."

"I hate cats, Jillian."

He was close enough to see the tears in her eyes now.

"Santos and I were engaged once," she admitted. "And he changed his mind before the wedding."

"I won't change my mind. Or hurt you like he did. I love you. You have to marry me. Mother likes you. Both of them did."

"What about your dad?"

"You're not marrying him. But he's willing to tie the knot."

"You mean go all the way to California?"

"My folks would like that."

"But *my* dad wouldn't."

"Well, it is a long way to Dad's church."

"Let me call my dad. He lives outside of London. He's a great cook. Steaks mostly. Has a fireplace to dry us out. He wants to give his approval."

"Oh," Chan said. "You told me he checks out the eyes."

"He does, but you'll pass. I told him that your eyes are the color of autumn leaves."

"Bet that went over big."

"You'll pass inspection."

He held out his arms and she went to him. The rain had put a sparkle in her sapphires. He brushed back the tawny wet hair from her cheeks. "You're beautiful even if you are all wet. Would you consider walking along the banks of the Thames with me?"

"Now? In this rainstorm?"

"We're already drenched, Jillian." He wouldn't let her go, ever again. He kept his arms around her. "I had it all planned, Jill. I thought it would be a sunny day, and since we don't have the Danube, I was going to take you to the banks of the Thames, give you a dozen red roses and put a diamond on your finger. . . . Could you pretend that it's a sunny day?"

"Do I have to pretend I'm holding a bouquet of roses?"

"Afraid so. Didn't have time to buy the flowers."

She leaned back her head, the rain washing over her lovely face and smiled as his lips came down on hers urgently, tenderly.

Minutes later the two of them were running, laughing, splashing through the puddles. Dancing along the streets of London, hand-in-hand. Dashing lightheartedly toward the banks of the Thames. Together, outstripping the wind and the rain.

Golden Hills on the Windrush

by Doris Elaine Fell

Prologue

Sydney Barrington ran along the riverbank, her bare feet leaving shallow imprints on the hard-packed sand, the chilly breeze of the early spring morning snapping at her slender legs. She jogged against the wind, her strides strong and even, her face turned to the dusky sun, her chestnut-brown hair wind-tossed and tangled. Across the river, the melted snows of winter had turned into torrents cascading over the mountain cliff, the deluge crashing and thundering against the weather-beaten rocks in the riverbed in a vigorous display of power.

Sydney loved this time of year—the closing of one season, the beginning of another. Even more, she loved these solitary moments by the river with the roaring waterfalls teasing her memory with shadowy images and stirring emotions both happy and sad. She had everything and should be grateful, joyful, but she felt at the moment as though she had nothing.

No one seeing her now would recognize her as the elegant, successful chief executive from Barrington Enterprises—envied by some for her wealth and beauty, feared by others for her drive and high expectations. Not even gallant and charming Randolph Iverson could guess how desperate she felt competing in a global market, pouring her life into expanding Barrington Enterprises for her dead father.

Jogging on in this private world of hers, she felt a part of nature, a solitary figure with a circle of ambitious dreams that had never found fulfillment. Nearing exhaustion, she stopped running and leaned against a gnarled tree to catch her breath. Her face and neck were wet with the morning dew, her sweat top damp from running. Without warning, tears welled in her eyes, eyes that Randolph kept telling her were both kind and cruel at the conference table, pensive and alluring when he was alone with her. She thrust the sleeves of her baggy sweatshirt above her elbows, brushed a twig from her faded cutaway shorts. The river rushed on, swirling, tumbling, winding around the bend in its race toward the sea, toward the open waters.

Rushing on without her.

On the other side of the pond—that vast ocean that separated them—another woman, with stately carriage and shiny, silver-gray hair, plodded slowly down the dank entry hall of Broadshire Manor. Abigail Broderick's flagging heart set the pace, her pulse so irregular she could not count the drumbeat of her own heart.

She had spent her lifetime tucked away in Gloustershire in a small English village rooted in the past, untouched by the passing of time. She knew nothing of fame nor fortune, yet her years of living here had made her wiser, peaceful. But taking the next step, she felt an age-old pain deepen inside her as she thought of Sir James Alastair and the four young refugee children still in her care. The thought of permanently closing the doors of Broadshire Manor filled her with foreboding. *I am ill, but how,* she asked herself, *can I desert the children in my care? I must find someone to take up my work.*

The tower bell in the village church chimed the hour, its sonorous tone slicing into her thoughts. Her chest constricted with pain when she swung back the massive door as she always did at sunset to make certain her children were all in.

The sloping hills of the Cotswolds cast their golden glow in the fading twilight in a sky still lit with a murmur of blue. The spring air was scented with flowering shrubs and the wild English primroses that thrived against her stone wall. It was all there—the peaceful setting of a lifetime spreading out before her. Beyond the gate lay the thatched and tiled roofs of her neighbors, their gardens filled with snowdrops and pink peonies, with anemones and yellow daffodils. Above the emerald fields, fleecy clouds drifted toward eventide, hovering above a village quiet now as one by one the children were called in for the supper hour and bedtime.

A rustle in the bush at the foot of the steps caught her attention. "Gregor?" she called.

The nine-year-old peeked out, grinning. "Yes, Mother Abigail."

"Have you been with Jonas again?"

He nodded. "I helped him take the sheep in."

She could not fault him for this, not when he felt safe with Jonas. But she said, "Jonas should have sent you home sooner."

"But we saw a stranger down by the river."

She allowed her eyes to graze past the thicket of woods east of the manor to the silhouette of the bridge where so many of her children had crossed over, where so few of them ever came back.

"I see no one, Gregor."

"But he is there. Me and Jonas saw him."

443

"Jonas and I," she corrected. "Now you'd best come in and wash up. Your supper is getting cold."

Gregor's hands and face were smudged, his shoes wet from sneaking down by the river with Jonas, but she reached out and squeezed his shoulder as he darted past her and headed for the kitchen. She had salvaged him from the tinderbox in Kosovo, snatched him from the arms of an Albanian guerrilla in a tattered surplus uniform. Gregor was a solemn boy with lustrous black eyes and a fragile smile that had tugged at her heart from the first time she saw him. He was always the last one in.

Abigail lingered in the open doorway, her ear tuned for the sound of Jonas's bagpipes, but she heard only the bubbling gurgle of the winding Windrush as it flowed beneath the old stone bridge. The river was dear and familiar to her like the bleating sheep in the meadows or tea and crumpets with Jonas in the late afternoon; it was as comforting as sitting with Sir James and patting his wrinkled hand while he rambled on about matters aged as the hills around them.

She kept her eyes on the cottage on the edge of the property until the light in Jonas's window flicked on. She loved Jonas as her own son, but she could not ask him to take over the care of the children or Sir James. At thirty-eight, Jonas should be finding a life's companion, settling down to his own happiness. Or going back to the navy career that he loved.

From where she stood—reluctant to close out another day—she stared into the growing darkness, her focus once again on the bridge. This time Abigail saw someone crossing over—a lanky man with a small bundle sheltered in his arms and with another child by his side. They came stealthily now in the shadows of the evening, making their way toward the manor.

"Abigail," the man said as he reached her doorstep. "I was afraid you would shut the door before we could reach you."

She recognized him, a young man who had once lived in her home. A bleak twig of a man now.

"Conon O'Reilly, " she whispered. "You've come back."

"And I brought my children with me."

The boy in his arms was three at most; the little girl clutching at his side not much older. Conon's presence set Abigail's heart to racing erratically. The last she knew, the British were searching for Conon as a suspect in the Omagh bombing. Numbness gripped her as she remembered that broken peace treaty. She had not wanted to believe the rumors about Conon. Now, as she gazed up into his hollow, empty eyes, she knew that a young terrorist, a revolutionary, stared back at her. There was only one reason why he would risk traveling from Belfast to the Cotswolds. Conon needed her. He was still one of her boys, her troubled Irish boy. With hesitant fingers, she touched his ruddy cheek and discovered that a deep scar ran the length of his jaw.

"Am I not welcome, Abigail?" he asked.

Stepping back to let him enter, she felt a jolt of pain in her chest. "This is your home, Conon. Your running away ten years ago hasn't changed that."

He shifted the child in his arms as he crossed the threshold and locked the door behind him. In the light of the hallway, Conon looked older than his twenty-seven years. The boy in his arms was gaunt and appeared feverish. The redheaded girl by his side had Conon's wariness, his intense green eyes. A stubble of beard marred Conon's once handsome face, his wiry red brows unable to hide his haunted gaze.

He was always in trouble as a boy, the outcast of the Broderick household because of his loyalties to the IRA. Conon, the firebrand, the malcontent among the other children, defending Northern Ireland's conflict with Britain. A child constantly at war with himself. A man still at war, bedeviled, tormented. Even his worn tweed jacket and dark corduroys were not nearly warm enough for a man on the run.

Abigail reached out and linked her fingers with the sleeping child in his arms, then asked softly, "Why have you come back, Conon?"

"I want you to take Danny and Keeley and raise them for me. They'll be safe with you."

"No, Conon. I'm too old to take on any more children."

His voice turned bitter. "Then what will I do? My wife is dead, killed in the crossfire at Omagh. My friends—my loyal friends—will no longer shelter us. Please, Abigail. You must help me. I will send money whenever I can."

Conon stiffened when the housekeeper stepped from the shadows, surprise lighting her tired gray eyes when she saw him. "And what do we have here? Not you, Conon O'Reilly?"

"Yes. And my two hungry children. So you remember me, Mrs. Quigley?"

"Couldn't forget the likes of you. So you're finally back? I trust Jonas doesn't know you're here. He has strong feelings about what you've been doing." She reached out her rough-red hand and gently touched Danny's cheek. "He's feverish," she scolded.

As she had done over the years, she took the boy in her arms and smiled down at Keeley. "Will the children be staying with us, Abigail?"

"At least for the night, Griselda."

Strands of wiry gray hair slipped loose as Griselda shook her head. "That's what you always say. Should they sleep on the second floor with the other children?"

Alarmed, she said tersely, "No. Not tonight. After supper, take them to the safety of the west wing."

Doris Elaine Fell followed a multifaceted career as teacher, missionary nurse, and freelance editor and author. Her writing credits include more than fifteen books and numerous articles. She writes from her home in Huntington Beach, California.